CALL ME

WHEN

YOU'RE

DEAD

ALSO BY A. R. TAYLOR

Jenna Takes the Fall
Sex, Rain, and Cold Fusion
Male Novelists and Their Female Voices:
Literary Masquerades

CALL ME WHEN YOU'RE DEAD

A NOVEL

A. R. TAYLOR

SHE WRITES PRESS

Published 2022
Printed in the United States of America
Print ISBN: 978-1-64742-223-3
E-ISBN: 978-1-64742-224-0
Library of Congress Control Number: 2022904388

For information, address:
She Writes Press
1569 Solano Ave #546
Berkeley, CA 94707

She Writes Press is a division of SparkPoint Studio, LLC.

Book design by Stacey Aaronson

For Vanessa Taylor, my hero, my role model,
my beloved daughter.

THE CRASH

P eople made one simple mistake about Sasha Cole—they thought her too beautiful to have trouble in love. Her classmates when she was young, her superiors at work, even her mother—all of them saw her lodged in a private realm of intelligent and heartfelt grace. Especially her high school friend, Eleanor Birch, who sat across from her now in an uptown Manhattan bistro, bewildered at the tale of a romance about which she knew nothing. "'Every frame a Rembrandt,' that's what Jon says about his television commercials," Sasha said grimacing.

"He's in advertising?" Eleanor said.

"He's in it, he's of it, he works twenty-four hours a day. Overworked and overpaid, I call it. After two years, how could he, Ellie?"

"How could he what?"

Sasha went on as if she hadn't heard her, "He was so kind and funny when I first met him, I figured he was gay. He got all my jokes, thank God. Most men can't keep up."

"Sounds wild," Eleanor said, unsure what to make of the man.

She leaned in toward Eleanor, fingering the pearls around her neck as if they were worry beads. "Now that son of a bitch has cut me off, not one word, not a phone call in ages. He hasn't died, has he? He's disappeared into his advertising agency, that's what." She was miserable, as tortured romantically as any lesser mortal.

"Why haven't I heard about him before?"

"It was so on-again, off-again. Besides, I'm superstitious. I don't like to talk about men."

Eleanor gazed at her friend's exquisite face: such animated features, a strong nose, and beautiful dark eyes. Her soft, thick hair, more red than brown, she often wore long, but tonight it was held loosely on top of her head with two diamond clips. "I'm sorry, Sasha. For someone like me, it's hard to believe you could have any romantic problems." At Dudley-Holcomb School for Girls in Connecticut, Sasha had spun mightily at the center of the social world, whereas Eleanor rotated on a lower rung, but they had been close nevertheless, though of late they got together only once or twice a year. She had always admired her friend, not only for the glorious face and shape, but for her brilliant, go-ahead spirit. Now, at just thirty-three years of age, that spirit seemed crushed.

It was a steamy evening in August, and as they leaned in to talk over their tiny table, Sasha's voice rose higher and higher. "He sent me one final email only, announcing 'I'm going crazy.' What the hell does that mean? 'Going crazy'? He inhaled crazy. Promise me something, Ellie," she said, stabbing a beet on her vegetarian *plat du jour*. "If anything ever happens to me, I want you to get him."

"Oh, stop."

"I'm deadly serious."

Eleanor laughed, but her friend had a strangely exhilarated look on her face, so finally she said, "I'm a medical librarian. We are a notoriously peaceful lot."

She had always been flattered that Sasha seemed to like her so much, without really knowing why. Now as she stared at that beautiful, enraged face, she wondered how much she understood her. On other evenings, this rant might have been the single malt scotch talking, since Sasha was a famously wild partier, but tonight she seemed to be on a health kick. How different the two of them were, Eleanor thought, as she stared at herself in the round mirror behind their table. She turned her head slightly, observing her nose, too pronounced by far. Why did her hair flare straight out like a flat sponge dunked in water? Red cheeks, black hair, a strange green dress, especially tired-looking. Upscale homeless, she noted to herself, or desperate peasant. She shifted in her seat, adjusting her bra straps to hide them. There was Sasha, all six feet of her, wearing her sleek black dress as if it were skin.

For someone like Eleanor, Sasha's world appeared exotic, excessive. She never seemed to stay at home in Manhattan. A consultant for startup internet firms, she traveled the country to commune with older executives on how to keep their genius geeks from killing each other, a task she described as "sticking my little finger into a dog fight." Eleanor found it odd though that she drove everywhere, even across country, bragging that she never missed a meeting, and knew that it was a symptom of deeper fears. She hated to fly and had once become sufficiently paralyzed in the Cleveland airport that she finally boarded a train.

As they stumbled into the August night, hot air radiated up from the concrete. Eleanor hugged her old friend. "Don't worry, I'll take care of him," she promised with a dour face, pulling an imaginary gun from her side and clicking the trigger. Sasha laughed and clasped her hand, but after she raced off, Eleanor realized she'd heard only a first name, Jon, and knew nothing else about the man. Still, she was oddly flattered that she'd be assigned to *get* anyone, secreted away as she was in Ithaca, researching diseases like ankylosing spondylitis. Indeed, she preferred the calmer reality of her own restricted sphere, starting with her wooden farmhouse upstate. As she made her way to the Port Authority for the long bus ride home, she could still smell Sasha's perfume.

Over the next few weeks, she called her friend a number of times to leave messages of encouragement. In response, she got only brief emails: "I'm so busy I can't call," or "I've got a new acupuncturist—no time to talk," along with summaries of her problems at work. Nevertheless, Eleanor continued to mutter sympathetic greetings into the phone, hoping that whatever difficult situation prevailed in the summer had vanished by fall.

Almost two months later, while Eleanor was channel flipping from one disaster to the next, she stopped short at pictures of a horrific accident outside South Bend, Indiana. In heavy fog, a bus and a car had plowed into each other at high speed, strewing smoldering piles of wreckage across the road. Patting her cat, Coco, she momentarily looked away but then heard the name of one of her favorite rock bands, Mother's Laundry. Apparently, the tour bus had belonged to them, and one of their members had died, the drummer, along with the driver of the other car. "How awful," she said to the warm kitty beside her, clicking off the tube.

Later that week, she noticed a three-day-old email from Sasha: "I'm off to Chicago to help an alpha dog beat back the younger pooches at Coolclick.com, a hopeless enterprise, but I'm bringing my whip." She sounded fine, her old self, and Eleanor vowed to worry less about her. Instead, she needed to worry over her boyfriend, one Peter Franzen, a chemistry professor in his mid-forties who worked out all the time. Recently he had announced that he was taking a semester off to train for a triathlon. Now all his waking moments would be devoted to physical perfection, and she wasn't sure she wanted to lash herself to that particular obsession. She decided to consult Sasha, despite her friend's recent romantic discontent. "Sasha, call me please. I need love help." Eleanor said this into her landline, her cell phone, and then even tried a text. So far nothing and no more emails.

That night at the gym, Peter treading furiously beside her, walking miles and miles on an upward graded strip of rubber going nowhere, she lazily pulled herself forward on the rowing machine, glancing every so often at the tiny televisions above them. Unable to hear the sound, she saw more pictures of the car wreck, and this time she spotted the twisted front end of a blue Audi A4, a car like Sasha's.

How odd. It couldn't be. South Bend was indeed on the way to Chicago, but what were the chances she had been on that road, at that time, in that car? She tried to think herself out of this idea, finally to laugh herself out of it, since Sasha was an accomplished, if manic, driver, but she couldn't get the picture of the blue Audi's broken front end out of her mind. She left several more messages for her and told herself to stop thinking such crazy thoughts, but even Dr. Gupta, who had her researching pectus excavatum, noticed her distraction. "Poor Miss Eleanor, why so sad and worried?"

She doubted the crash would remain in the news for long, but contrary to this expectation, the pileup became a major item. Every day she stopped at the newspaper box in front of the Schulman Medical Library to see if she could learn anything more, and finally she did. The cover of the *New York Post* had the burned Audi and the bus with an insert picture of the band members. The headline read "Fog, Flame, Rock 'n' Roll."

At the end of the day, she folded up the paper and took it home. Pouring herself a glass of red wine, curling up on the couch with Coco, Eleanor found a long article on the accident. She read that in addition to the drummer, the lead singer of Mother's Laundry had also succumbed to his injuries. Then there it was: "The driver of the second vehicle, Manhattan resident Sasha Louise Cole, was dead on impact." She felt herself go hot and faint.

Haunting the cable news channels, Eleanor took a week off that consisted of television, wine, more wine, and more television. She felt heavy, sick at an unfamiliar world stained with burned-out cars and bloody bodies. On the Sunday after she learned the news, she got out of her pajamas and into regular clothes, cleaned up the house, and sat down with a strong cup of French roast. Her first day back at work, she buried herself in the pectus excavatum problem, compiling a list so long that the young man who was having his sunken chest hacked and screwed back into a normal shape would no doubt be reassured in the reading of it all.

When would she hear more about Sasha? Should she talk to the family? Just before she steeled herself to phone them in Greenwich, Sasha's attorney called with an astonishing piece of news. He had an envelope for her. "For me? I don't understand."

"Miss Cole was an exceptionally organized person for someone so young," he said in a gravelly voice. "May I read this note to you?"

"Please." She could hear the man ripping open a letter.

"It's a check, along with a note, written by hand: 'Fifty thousand dollars for whatever may be required regarding Eleanor Birch's personal obligation to me, plus a bonus when the job is complete.' I can't tell you what the bonus is." The man sounded uncurious about what all this could mean and offered no additional information.

"This is incredible," Eleanor said. "What's the date on the note?"

"August the twentieth of this year, if that provides any further clarification."

Eleanor checked her calendar and realized that it had been written three days after their dinner. She reflected back now on their bizarre conversation. At the time she had given no serious weight to Sasha's remarks, figuring it the usual bad boyfriend chatter, but after the attorney's shocking phone call, the gist of the conversation came back to her in all its intensity. Could Sasha have had a premonition of doom? Turning her dead friend's words over and over in her mind, she was left to contemplate every which way she could interpret the meaning of "get." What did it mean to "get" a man? How does she "get" him? Where was he? In New York advertising. Beyond that, she knew nothing.

The following week, at the end of October, Eleanor found a card in her mailbox announcing a funeral service in Manhattan the very next Monday. She shivered in her robe as she ran back inside. Blood and bones formed a horrid landscape in her mind, and she wanted desperately to find something that would blot out the pictures, but nothing could silence the news announcer's ghastly words, "The victims were burned beyond recognition."

After a tedious bus trip into the city, Eleanor pulled her poncho around her shoulders and pushed herself against the wind blowing down between Park and Madison. Inside the church on Eighty-Ninth Street, she saw sixty or seventy people, not a one of them, she supposed, prepared for the ensuing scene. A coffin rested atop a catafalque in the middle of the aisle, and as she picked up the program for the funeral, she couldn't stop thinking about what was inside. Unwinding her scarf, she surveyed the mourners. Where was the delinquent boyfriend? How would she ever recognize him?

The minister began with the Order for the Burial of the Dead, somber words that comforted, but when he came to the passage, "though this body be destroyed, yet shall I see God: whom I shall see for myself, and mine eyes shall behold, and not as a stranger," Eleanor dissolved into sobs, while others wept beside her. How had whatever was left of Sasha come to rest in this dark, austere little church? Had she been secretly religious and attended services here? Sasha's uncle gave the eulogy, a reflection on the bitter fate that had deprived them of someone so young. Eleanor began to cry again. She could only pull herself together by grasping at her assignment. Yes, it must start right now. Scattered here and there were single males, standing singly anyway. Would the lout even come to the service? Did he know she was dead? Eleanor counted six apparently unattached males and vowed to follow them to the National Arts Club, where tea and cookies awaited.

Only three single men made the journey downtown, and Eleanor found herself watching their movements carefully. Before she could approach any of them, Sasha's mother, a thin woman with tight blond hair, brushed past her whispering, "Ellie, haven't seen you for ages. Dudley-Holcomb graduation, I think. So glad you're here. Sasha loved you." The Coles were a notorious family in Greenwich, rich and eccentric. Sasha's father had died of lung cancer several years before, but Eleanor remembered that at some point her friend had stopped speaking to many of her relatives. "Terrible bunch of drunks," she had called them. Once, years before, she'd recounted the story of her grandfather getting so loaded that he fell out of a third-story window. "He was fine, only he had to be thawed out by the gardener."

Eleanor psyched herself up to mingle, never a good idea for her. Long ago she vowed to stop meeting new people, since she so rarely encountered anyone interesting, but she had to find the errant boyfriend if he was here. Feeling cloddish in the presence of these sleek New Yorkers, she began to sweat, pulling at her black stretchy top and heavy jacket. She first approached a dapper man who was sitting on a banquette. He announced himself as "an old friend of Sasha's, Teddy Bonin. I'm an art dealer. So sad isn't it?" and stuck out a soft, pink hand.

"It's awful. Lovely to meet you," Eleanor said, turning away as quickly as she could. Only two hours until the bus back to Ithaca, and she had to get to everybody. Moving toward the other end of the room, she inched up to a handsome man who looked Italian and was talking intensely to a much younger woman with jagged orange hair. "Yes, but you see the content of the whole thing is what got me. No content, no fucking content." This mysterious pronouncement found Eleanor awkwardly in the middle, apparently becoming the "content," while these two people stared at her.

"I'm Eleanor Birch, one of Sasha's old friends." In a vague feint at friendliness, they both reached out to shake her hand, and then there was a silence. "I'm a medical librarian," she said. If she'd called herself a "sewage systems engineer" there couldn't have been a more contorted look on their faces. "In Ithaca." This didn't help. "How did you know Sasha?" she said, desperate that they not walk away.

"I'm at Saks, the online catalogue business, and she consulted for us," the orange-haired woman said.

The elegant man muttered, "Sasha and I met at her favorite bar, the King Cole bar at the St. Regis—"

The woman interrupted him. "He runs a hedge fund. Perhaps you don't know what that is?" She had an air of big-city nastiness, inexplicable in this setting, and it made Eleanor angry. She wanted to say, "Do you know what ankylosing spondylitis is?" but she wasn't there to make enemies. Smiling sweetly at the pair and saying not a word, she headed straight for a single-looking African-American male who stood munching a cookie. He had a distinguished face, wavy black hair, and wore a finely cut, loose-fitting beige linen suit. Fashionable indeed, but in a good way, to Eleanor's eyes.

He spoke first. "I recognize my old friend, the art dealer Teddy Bonin, but who are these other people?"

"They're residents of the third circle of hell. I'm amazed they even knew Sasha."

"She seems to have picked them up randomly, through her work maybe. I used to wonder why she didn't let any of her friends meet each other. Now I understand."

"They don't seem upset enough somehow, but maybe I'm just talking to the wrong ones. Sorry, I have no social graces. I'm a medical librarian."

"I'm an actor, Tony Lowe. They're in shock. Funerals make people angry, reminds them of their mortality. They're particularly angry now, since she was only thirty-three." Whatever the others felt, this man certainly seemed to bear the full force of death's grip.

"What are you in, or have you been in anything?" Eleanor asked, feeling light-headed, almost unhinged.

"I'm actually in a new Broadway play about advertising."

She lifted herself out of her grief. "Advertising, that must be fun. You're not one of her boyfriends are you?"

He chuckled, "No, I'm one of her gay friends."

"What a relief."

Now he stared. "You're amazing, the things you say."

"Yes, it's too bad. Anyway, do you know who her boyfriend was? He was in advertising. And is he here?"

"No, it's very strange. I expected to see him. I worked for the guy for a week, between jobs you might say, a year and a half ago. I'm sure that helped me get the musical, because I could relate to the whole sick, twisted environment."

"So you know him?" she said, "Jon, he was called Jon something."

"Right, I'm trying to think of his last name. I don't know him at all really. It was just a brief employment gig. He was pitching a new account but said LaGuardia and Knole was going through what he called a soft patch and needed 'employees.' Sasha gave him my number, and he hired me and a bunch of other actors to make it look as if the agency was doing a land-office business. 'Bodies in the shop' he kept calling us. My job was to draw diagrams and bullet points on a whiteboard, all meaningless of course, for the benefit of the head honcho from some big company . . . hmm, what did they do? I can't remember, and we were told not to say specific stuff anyway. Since we didn't know anything, we didn't want to be asked anything either."

"How weird."

"Weird but ingenious."

Eleanor didn't dare tell him of her assignment but questioned him further and got only vague answers. Even though Tony had known Sasha for years, he had never socialized with the two as a couple and still couldn't produce the boyfriend's last name. "I've had a lot of temp jobs, Eleanor." He could only say that he seemed high up in the organization. Delicately she tried to enlist his help in finding the man, but he pleaded rehearsals and finally said, "Do I look like a gumshoe?"

"To be honest, you look more like the king of a Polynesian island in an Armani suit."

"Thank you, I guess." He grinned. "Give me your phone number, and I'll call if anything comes back to me," he said, promising her house seats should the musical keep running. "Why do you want to know?"

"I can't tell you right now," she said. Tony just frowned.

At the end of this miserable day, after avoiding the rain in a filthy old-timey phone booth on Twentieth Street, she searched her cell phone for LaGuardia and Knole's address. Quickly though, Eleanor realized that she was a victim of her own limited thinking. Why had she followed only single men? The disappearing boyfriend could have been married, though Sasha had never added this to his list of offenses. Should she even try to find the advertising agency, apparently in the Meatpacking District? In the wet and the cold, she stared around her. Her mother had accused her once of the habit of retreat. She refused to be guilty of that now, and as she fought her own reluctance, a taxi dumped an elderly man out right in front of her. She leapt into the cab, directing the driver to the address.

Among warehouses and truck garages, Eleanor finally spotted LaGuardia and Knole, its address hammered in steel lettering above the doorway of a squat building, medieval and forbidding, with little turrets on top like a stunted castle. Emerging from the cab, she walked backwards away from the place and then lurked at the end of the block, positioning herself to watch people go in and out. Several employees, muffled in gear, pushed themselves forward against the wind and the rain. They barely noticed the girl with soaking black hair in an enormous poncho.

Eleanor needed a plan, she knew, but was too upset, sickened at being in an area that smelled of rendered fat washing down through the gutters. After all, there must be meat to pack. Had the boyfriend even heard about Sasha's death? She looked down at her watch and realized she had to make the last bus if she wanted to get home that night. As she fruitlessly ran after three or four cabs, she presumed it would be ages before she could get back here, and in a way she was relieved. This was too much of a burden; she carried Sasha's heavy heart on her shoulders, and she had absolutely no idea what to do with it.

two

THE AD

Two weeks later, Tony Lowe called Eleanor. He remembered that the boyfriend, Jonathan Neel, was a copywriter who worked on a fast-food account. "Come on now, why do you want to know about this guy? Just because he wasn't at the funeral?"

"I don't know if I should tell anybody."

"Oh, tell the Tone. Everybody tells me everything. I could make a living selling to *The Enquirer.*"

Eleanor liked this man's voice and had been having difficulty knowing what to do, so she decided to confide in him. "Before she died, Sasha said to me if something ever happened to her, I should *get* her old boyfriend."

"'Get?' Only Sasha would say something like that."

"I'm still trying to figure the whole thing out." She hesitated, then blurted out, "I got a check for fifty thousand dollars from her estate to help me with the assignment."

"Jesus, now that's truly strange. Old Sasha was very careful with money, so she meant what she said." The line went silent for a moment. "Lately she seemed wired about men in a way I hadn't seen before. I couldn't understand what was wrong with her. Maybe it was thirties angst, wanting to settle down, if you know what I mean." Tony cleared his throat.

"I didn't talk to her that often, but when I did, she struck me as completely uninterested in marriage, just glamorous and exotic, living in another sphere," Eleanor said sighing.

"Do you think she was afraid he was going to do something to her, as in, 'If he knocks me off, go after him'?"

"How could that be? She died in a car crash. No, no, she was mad because he hadn't called her in two months."

"So she must have wanted revenge. What's the basic idea? The punishment should fit the crime."

"By that reasoning she won't ever speak to him again; she's totally gone from his life, so even if I don't do anything, he'll suffer."

"That doesn't make any sense—he wasn't talking to her anyway. You've got to formulate a strategy, and I'm going to help you," Tony said. She promised to call him when next she came to the city.

Reluctant to tell him everything of her plans, though, Eleanor had developed an idiosyncratic line of attack. She would locate this Jonathan Neel and inform him how horrifically Sasha's life had been extinguished. In her own peculiar system of thought, that would be punishment enough. He would realize that through his betrayal, metaphorically at least, he had contributed to the death of a loved one.

Ten minutes' research on the web indicated that a Jonathan Neel did indeed work at LaGuardia and Knole on the account of Buffalo Grill, a fast-food restaurant at which Eleanor had eaten at once or twice. She couldn't remember much about their food, but she could certainly recall an eerie, breathy voice from their ads that chanted "Buff-aa-ll-o Grii-ii-ll" over and over again. She made her first phone call armed with this information, but it proved surprisingly difficult to get an appointment with the man. First his assistant wanted to know her company's name, supposing her to be a prospective client, then whether she was a close friend. Finally, on her third try, Eleanor announced, "This matter is personal, and it's urgent. Involving a death." She fought a wave of tears as she said this, realizing that her task had been keeping her from her grief.

The abrupt girl at the other end of the phone said, "A death? Why didn't you say so? Hang on and I'll set something up." She nevertheless sounded skeptical, as if death were merely a ploy to get into their building.

A week later, in the cold and the rain, Eleanor once again braved the New York Port Authority, since she couldn't bear to think of driving her own car into the big city. At the metal door of LaGuardia and Knole, she tried to peer inside the building, but the windows were covered with bars. It was like standing in front of a dungeon. Before she could get herself positioned properly, adjusting her skirt and lifting off her hat at the same time, a woman's voice blared through the PA system. "Are you the messenger?" she said.

"I'm here for Jonathan Neel," Eleanor burbled into the intercom.

The door opened and a sleek young black woman said, "Sorry, I thought you were here for some tapes. Do you have an appointment?" Without waiting for an answer, she asked, "You know Buffalo Grill?"

"The fast-food place?"

"'Casual dining, casual dining,' please. We're right at the start of a new campaign." The young woman grasped her arm and pulled her into the cavernous lobby of a building that really did look like an old slaughterhouse, with metal floors, metal ceilings, and metal furniture. Eleanor was relieved not to see a drain. "You say you don't have an appointment?"

"I do have an appointment for five o'clock. It's personal, confidential." Even to herself she sounded like a stalker. She saw only two or three employees, unsmiling and in black.

"Wait here," the young woman said. With her damp cloak and sopping hat, Eleanor plunged down into the lone velvet chair and proceeded to spread everything around her to dry. She sat for more than forty minutes and had the annoying experience of watching three separate clocks tick away the extent of her vigil in Los Angeles, in Tokyo, and in Paris. Just as she vowed to refuse to leave the building until Mr. Neel saw her, the young woman reappeared. "Sorry. Listen, Jon's at Black Dog, an editing house up at Forty-Second Street. His assistant said for you to go over there, and maybe he'll break away."

Eleanor's quarry, her prey, was at that moment standing behind a couch staring at twin television monitors above the video editor's desk. With one hand, Jon Neel brushed his longish dark hair behind his ear, and with the other he grabbed some M&Ms. He wore a black T-shirt and blue jeans and, except for a grainy complexion and flecks of gray in his curling hair, he might almost have been a college student. At thirty-eight, he had spent at least seventy percent of his adult life in a dark, windowless room watching digitized images slide back and forth on the monitor before him as he, a video editor, and an art director wrestled into perfection the tiny creation before them, a thirty-second speck of time as finely tuned as a concerto: a television commercial.

On this cold evening in November, Jon felt guardedly optimistic. At last he had found a new context for the signature Buffalo Grill tagline, "Buff-aa-ll-o Grii-ii-ll" whined, keened really, as if the restaurant haunted the past or heralded the future. Impossible to find any kind of setting for it that wasn't absurd, but Jon thought he had finally succeeded where his predecessors had egregiously and expensively failed. Buffalo Grill's 86.7-million-dollar annual contribution to the budget of LaGuardia and Knole said that he had better succeed. His latest thirty-second spot was about to air on the evening news, and if a success, a whole new campaign based on the same idea would follow. Though he'd seen the ad hundreds of times, he wanted to watch it as the consumer would, bookended by TV clutter. "Turn up the sound, would you, Jacky?" he said to the editor, as they eyeballed the monitor.

Just then a woman's voice blared out over the speakerphone. "Someone here for you, Jon. She had an appointment earlier and missed you."

"Who is it?"

"An Eleanor Birch. From Ithaca."

"I don't know anyone in Ithaca."

"Says it's important, about a mutual friend."

"Can't talk to her. Tell her to wait."

But Eleanor was already right behind him, desperate now, covered in soggy wool. "I can't wait," she said, staring up at him. In spite of her mission, she was taken aback. His face was very fine, with warm, dark brown eyes. He was taller than she had imagined, imposing in frame and presence. During her August conversation with Sasha, she had pictured a short, anxious man.

Her head began to pound, and she felt her face burn. "Jonathan Neel?" He nodded warily. "I'm Eleanor Birch. I have some news that, uh, it's my understanding, would be important to you. I felt I should come and give you the information myself." Exhausted, she pulled off her hat.

"Yeah? This sounds important." He ran his hands through his hair and examined the girl in front of him, dark eyes looking startled behind her wire-rimmed glasses. Didn't look like any of the hard-bitten media sluts around LaGuardia and Knole. He helped her remove her coat.

"It is."

"I'm not ready for anything important. I have a serial crisis I'm trying to deal with today. What did you say your name was?" At last he smiled at her.

"Eleanor Birch. I'm a medical librarian in Ithaca."

"Wow, fantastic." He said this as if she were a goat from New Zealand. "We need to speed it up, Miss Birch. I've got five minutes. You know Buffalo Grill?"

"I've eaten there a few times." On impulse she mimicked the notorious wheeze, "'Buff-aa-ll-o Grii-ii-ll.'"

"Ha! You do know it. A real agency killer, the Buffalo Whisperer's song, I call it. Many I consider my betters have gone down to defeat in its dust. All my client thinks about is steaks and burgers, burgers and steaks, and they're having a hell of a time because, let's face it, it's a tofu world. I told him to do a tofu steak, and he almost puked on me."

Eleanor smiled but thought immediately of her awful assignment. "I'm a friend of Sasha Cole."

"You are?" He frowned. "Do you have a gun?" he said and laughed.

Annoyed by his joke, she found it awkward to proceed, since he kept looking at his watch and patting the shoulder of the man at the console, who so far had barely turned around. Jon pulled a strand of red licorice out of a candy bowl and stuck it in his mouth, saying, "Whatever it is, it has to wait. We've got to watch the new ad. Turn up the sound a little, would you, Jacky?" he said to the editor. Several assistants drifted into the room and sat on the couch, watching intently. No one bothered with Eleanor.

On the television screen appeared the *CBS Evening News*. The natty reporter talked about a car bomb in Egypt, next came a flood in Tennessee, then a new Alzheimer's drug, and finally a commercial break. In a strange, otherworldly scene, an elderly woman with curly gray hair sat alone on a couch, hands folded neatly. Behind her, floating beyond the window, a Buffalo Grill sign flashed in glittery starlight. A dog's bark sounded in the background, then two young children and a plump Mom ran into the room, followed by the pooch itself. "Where should we go to dinner?" asked the younger woman. They all clasped themselves onto Grandma, who looked out the window at the glowing sign and said, "We should go to a better place." Spooky music and unearthly electronic bleeps rose up around her words. She said it again, slowly. "We should go to a better place." Then a voice out of the void whispered, "Buff-aa-ll-o Grii-ii-ll." A louder voice repeated, "Buffalo Grill."

Everyone in the room clapped, exclaiming over what one young man called "a simple, audacious message, the weird sign in the background, the mother and her apparent clairvoyance at the thought of dinner." "Very post-bomb," another man in black announced. A young woman agreed, "Deconstruction at its best." Despite her mission, Eleanor giggled. Though it didn't seem to make much sense, she liked the commercial's goofy charm.

"It will run one more time on the news, so let's just leave the sound down." Jon took Eleanor's arm, not introducing her to anyone but drawing her toward the small kitchen across the lobby. As he made the two of them cups of espresso, he kept looking out of the corner of his eye at another television monitor perched high above them. "Sasha and I had problems," he said, finally sitting down and taking a sip, but he jumped up again right away. "What the fuck is going on?" he shouted at the TV. Almost immediately the spot had reappeared two more times, the same mother and grandmother, the flashing Buffalo Grill sign, the peculiar slogan, "We should go to a better place." Now he seemed alarmed. "Traffic. Somebody call Traffic," he yelled. Several young men swarmed toward him carrying sheets of paper. Jon glared up at the screen, muttering to Eleanor, "Traffic is in charge of which ads run when, and this one is running too often." Stock market news, then the ad came on again. The man before her with the extraordinary face turned grim. "I have to sit here, Miss Birch," he said, "and check out what may be a problem."

The two of them sat or stood in front of television monitors for a solid hour as the Buffalo Grill commercial ran fifteen times. The offbeat otherworldliness of it now seemed positively sinister, as if an alien church were beaming messages into the tube. People kept running in and out of the editing room, sheaves of papers in their arms, everyone trying to figure out what had happened. After another forty-five minutes, Eleanor lay prostrate on the couch. She'd gone from fiery rage, because she couldn't even get a chance to talk to the man, to a burned-out stupor. For Jonathan Neel's part, every word of the ad squirted itself into his head like a poisonous injection. He swayed from side to side, gradually curling himself into a ball. Suddenly he flung himself forward and began phoning the network. Amid shouted calls and hysterical ranting, it seemed apparent to Eleanor that no one could answer the question as to why the commercial kept reappearing. It was just an all Buffalo Grill evening on CBS. Afraid now to try to talk to him, she didn't feel she could leave. When he sank down at last on the couch next to her, he unaccountably grabbed her hand. "OK, Jacky," he said to the video editor, "What's going on?"

"We've been fucked."

Eleanor jerked her hand away and shoved it into her pocket, but he barely noticed. Dumbly they watched as a hospital drama came on, an annoying shaky cam show in which actors ran up and down the halls jabbering about cancer, IV, stat. Yet again there was another Buffalo Grill at every break. Jon put his hand to his forehead, "Either I'm having an aneurysm, or someone is trying to kill me," he shouted and jumped up to get more espresso. Somewhere, somehow an employee of LaGuardia and Knole had either accidentally—or worse, deliberately—arranged for the same commercial to run thirty times in two hours. He sank back down on the couch, almost sitting right on top of Eleanor. Who was she again? Jon often didn't register people, but his career, that was something he could see vividly. It flashed before his eyes now. His baby, his love, the thing he'd ditched every other thing in his life for, the thing that meant he hadn't called his girlfriend in a month or two, or was it three? That career, starting with an international shipping company in Chicago ("Where Tomorrow Happens Every Day"), on to cars, then fast food, where he'd stayed now for several years, Clios, *AdAge* awards, his picture in *Adweek*—that gold mine to which he dedicated every conscious hour of his life.

The square, ruddy face of James Emerson Goodlaw, founder and CEO of Buffalo Grill, loomed up in front of him like some hideous cartoon villain. This was a man who once threatened to kill him with a shotgun if he didn't put more hairspray on a tomato. He could hear Jimmy now, shouting the words of the commercial—"'We should go to a better place'—You fucking will, buddy." That's how he would put it to Jon. No gratitude, no loyalty for the five years he had devoted to every miserable whim of his client. No care for a man who had ruined his life and his health to present to the world Buffalo Grill's hockey-puck piece of meat, made to look juicy and succulent, surrounded by the most gorgeous potato on earth and vegetables that had never seen a farm.

The third hour of the Buffalo Grill ordeal began as the commercial continued to run. Jonathan Neel curled up on the couch, convinced that God despised him. Everyone but himself, Eleanor, and the video editor had left the building. He turned the sound down so that each time Buffalo Grill came on, he could hear only bits, "We should go—" "Buff-aa—" "Grii-ii—" the dog barking.

Eleanor had memorized all the ad copy, and though she'd never had one before, was convinced she had a migraine. "Are we near a hospital?" she asked, but nobody was listening.

Jonathan Neel was trying to figure out what to do. By the time they'd seen the last Buffalo Grill spot, it had run thirty-five times. Occasionally different ads broke the cycle, and finally public service announcements inserted by a network executive who'd been alerted to the crisis, but other than that, it just kept going. The phone bank flashed lights on every line, but Jon refused to answer a single call. The horror of it, the contorted face of Jimmy Goodlaw—he could picture every subtlety to his particular form of revenge. No mistake about it, there would be reprisals from boss, client, and colleagues alike.

Whether this latest incident was the result of a corporate goof or the work of a rat fink, a lot was at stake. Jon didn't often focus on the dollar amounts involved in his work, but in fact a thirty-second advertisement could cost from two hundred thousand to one million dollars to make. Add to that the cost of buying time on the network, anywhere from five hundred thousand to two million dollars, meant that a single commercial involved serious money. "Pentagon ashtrays may cost five hundred dollars a pop, but the ad industry makes the equivalent of a B-52 every two weeks," he liked to joke to his mother. Martha Neel had laughed at the time but told her son he made more money than was good for him. A failed musician herself, she pushed him to be a cellist, not a copywriter, and had forced lessons upon him for almost ten years. He'd had to lug a cello through his high school and college hallways, thereby preventing anyone from getting close to him, as he often thought of it. Now he sported the title of chief creative officer at LaGuardia and Knole, though his actual job was heading up the Buffalo Grill account. He earned fantastic sums of money for making art, in his own mind, and he applied to it an artist's attention. Radiant lipstick, the bubbling hot steak, the artful drops of sweat on an athlete's leg; it was an alternate reality, if not soulful, at least reaching for the perfected spirit.

This same man, artisan of the spirit world, downed a scotch

neat, having raided the booze stash beneath the espresso bar. "Want a drink anybody?" he yelled toward the editing room, but nobody answered. Jon wandered the floor, drink in hand, sick with pain. He went outside to a small patio. Before him rose the Seagram building and to the south the Empire State building, lit up now in red and green, a gorgeous glittering landscape. It was his domain, and he its god, at least until tonight. Who would want to do him in? Who had the clout to do so? He closed his eyes to stop his pounding heart and began to visualize the power tree of the agency, the one he frequently revised in his head. Two people were above him, the CEO, Claudia Thompson, and another person directly beneath her, the president, who had to be a strong suspect in this debacle: the squinty-eyed, bushy-haired man with the small white scar on his forehead who smiled dreamily all the time and never finished a sentence.

Guy Danziger was one of the few people with the power to derail a commercial that cost a million dollars to make and another six hundred thousand to put on the air. Formerly an art director, with an immaculate sense of design and years of experience, Guy now had authority, in name at least, over every creative project issuing from the agency. Jon and Guy were the two males vying for the top job currently held by the indomitable Claudia, a scary woman of indeterminate age impelled forward by a blend of marketing savvy and new age cure-alls. She had installed a full-time massage therapist in a basement office to keep her workers productive.

Brutal bloody thoughts roiled his brain. Whoever had engineered this caper was marvelously creative. How was he to find the culprit? Prime suspect Guy figured as a formidable opponent. Somehow or other he had just managed to acquire the eighty-million-dollar account of Synergene, a company at work on targeted genetic cures for cancer. This gave him even more power at the agency. Unnerved, Jon wiped his forehead with his shirt, and then instantly decided that yes, he must figure out exactly who had sabotaged him and eviscerate that person, as he himself had been publicly humiliated. He would start with Guy, and since he knew a number of his rival's faults, it would not be difficult to find out what he was up to. Confession was Guy's middle name.

First though, he had to waylay Mr. Buffalo Grill, Jimmy Goodlaw, and head him off at the pass. Just as he finished his drink, the tired young woman, Sasha's friend, peered at him through the door. He waved her outside onto the patio, and there they stood in the freezing night while he poured more scotch for both of them.

During this entire period, Eleanor had probably said fifty words. She'd never seen anything like the kamikaze craziness of this one man, his world, his job, and had no idea whether to point out the folly of his ways or just leave. Nevertheless, she gripped her mission tightly to her heart. "Do you know about the crash?"

"Crash? Who else has crashed besides me?"

She was toting up his sins and here was another one, grotesque self-absorption. "No, the car crash."

He finally focused his eyes on her. "What car crash? No, I don't."

"Prepare yourself."

"What's happened?" He stared at her, alarmed.

"I have some terrible news for you. Sasha Cole was in the automobile crash outside South Bend, Indiana, the one that killed several members of Mother's Laundry. She died too. Three weeks ago there was a funeral service for her at a church on Eighty-Ninth Street. It was all over the TV. They're still trying to figure out what happened." At last she had gotten his attention.

"Are you sure? You're making this up," he said, suddenly angry.

"What's wrong with you? I wouldn't make up something like this." She felt as if she might cry.

He looked at her for a long time, finally sitting down on one of the patio chairs. "My God. I don't watch the news, just get it off the internet when I have time. I never see anything but commercials on TV." He ran his hands through his hair as if combing a lawn, then curled his arms around his head. Normally, Eleanor would have comforted someone in this situation, but she still had the "get" assignment, whatever that might mean, and couldn't think what to do next.

"We hadn't spoken in a while, but I did try to call not long ago. She seemed like the only person who would understand. Do you know about me and Sasha?"

"She mentioned you to me in August. She was angry." Eleanor felt herself sweating, still enraged but embarrassed too, and sat down suddenly in the chair opposite him.

"Things weren't working out, or I wasn't working out in it, something like that." After a moment he said, "I couldn't understand her. She was a mystery to me." His cell phone rang. "Sorry," he said, and this time he answered it. "Yes? Jimmy, great to hear from you. What a surprise. No, no just kidding. You're here? Downstairs? Right. I'll come down." Jon hung up and fixed her with wild, exhausted eyes. "Look, Eleanor, I know that you and I have to talk about this, but right now I will literally be dead myself if I don't talk to the president of Buffalo Grill. To say I'm in the shitcan is putting it mildly. Assassins are looking for me, some of them right in this building."

"They are?"

"I'm joking," he said, regarding her strangely, unused to someone so literal-minded.

Before she could quite figure out what was happening, he pulled her over to the window. Below them on the street gleamed the lights of an enormous black limousine. "See that? That's my client. We've got to go down there, confront the beast."

"I don't have to do anything with you. Isn't this news about Sasha more important?"

"She *is* important, but what can I do about it right this minute?" He grabbed the scotch bottle off the table and pulled Eleanor through the lobby. "Give me your phone number, and I'll call you." He made it sound like a date.

"You don't have to call me! That's not why I'm here," she sputtered, conscious of all she had failed to do in her errand. Together they descended in the elevator, Jon looking over at her every few moments, Eleanor flushed, seething, as if in a hot tunnel. Outside, he hailed her a taxi and without thinking she leapt into it, but not before she heard him yell toward the limousine, "Jesus, Jimmy, is that you in this floating fuck palace? Want a drink?"

three

OLDER MEN

J on pounded on the limousine window that night with no
plan in mind whatsoever. Horrified by the news about
Sasha, crazed by the mysterious deviltry behind his ad snafu, he
was flying on autopilot. Jimmy Goodlaw, a short, heavyset man,
was slumped down in the back seat, watching a small television
and drinking a glass of vodka. The sight of Jon's insanely cheery
grin threw the older man into a rage, and he pounded with his
fist against the glass, at last opening the window an inch. "You
killed me, Neel. If you'd stabbed me it couldn't have been worse.
Think of all the workers, all the people who live off Buffalo
Grill, including me!" His Texas twang rose to a screech.

"I know, I know, I'm sorry. I have no idea what happened."

"Why is it, I can get every restaurant to look the same, I get
my steaks the same size at every single outlet, but somehow or
other, the ads, for which I pay a goddamned fortune, are always
turning into something else, something you fuckers call art. It
looked as if we were advertising a cult!"

Rather than mount any defense, Jon launched into an apology so heartfelt, so abject, that even the owner of a billion-dollar business was momentarily silenced. But not for long. Jimmy dropped his window down all the way and started yelling again. "I would fire your ass, if I could stand dealing with another fucking ad agency. I can't even talk to the creepy sons of bitches in your line of work, all wearing black T-shirts and never smiling to show how serious they are, how hip. And I know you hate my food."

"Now, Jimmy, I do not—" Jon was about to assert how much he loved Buffalo Grill, but like everyone else in fast-food advertising, behind Jimmy's back he called it a "squat and gobble" restaurant. Just sit down and shovel the food in.

"You poor bastards eat tofu and oyster mushrooms, mochi and other beige substances invented to simulate food! How can you even think with that crap floating around in your guts?"

"I don't eat that stuff, and you know it, Jimmy."

The two men ended up not at the trendy restaurant Fressen, which was close by, but at the Hog's Breath Inn, a steamy, sophomoric bar frequented by a mix of college kids and Harley-Davidson bikers. As they swung themselves onto barstools in the shape of motorcycle seats, they had the alarming experience of seeing their commercial air one more time on the Fox Network, where by now the subject had been taken up on the eleven o'clock news. They couldn't hear any of the commentary, though, because the moment the line "We should go to a better place" came on, several guys at the bar started chanting, "We should go to a better place! We should go to a better place!" like coked-up cheerleaders.

Jon pounded his head down on the bar. "Jesus, how the fuck did this happen?"

Jimmy patted him on the back. "Maybe it'll be good for business, ha ha, yeah, that's right. That's the view I'm going to take of it. I'm going to have to take that view with the board of directors, who will want my ass!" This last he shouted into the void, as several Hog's Breathers eyed him suspiciously.

Suddenly the noise level dropped. Jon listened while a white-haired anchorman expounded on "saturation advertising," akin to saturation bombing, the only cogent explanation for this new ploy to get the attention of bored American television viewers.

After double orders of ribs, French fries, salad dripping cheesy dressing, and two slices of apple pie, plus the martinis, they were bloated and bilious, but during this time a change took place. They began to think the catastrophe funny, themselves wholly innocent, and concluded that in this crisis no force could sever their peculiar bond. "A united front," Jon moaned while Jimmy ordered them cognac.

Without warning, a fight broke out at the Hog's Breath, wherein several beefy characters tackled a couple of college kids. The bikers had the advantage, and the younger guys could only roll away from their punches, outweighed and outmanned. After a moment's hesitation, Jon and Jimmy eyeballed each other, "Yeah!" they shouted at once and launched themselves into the fray, wanting to be beaten up by something real.

At this moment, the thought of his whole career going away, *poof*, like a feather waving away a boulder, made Jon giddy. The threatened loss of that totemic activity had a wondrous effect on his immediate emotional tone, and he felt lighter, freer, as if the monkey had jumped off his back. He realized that he had more or less disappeared into an editing suite at the age of twenty-three, emerging for shouting matches with bosses or girlfriends, but only in the service of buying more time to work. In one particularly difficult situation with Sasha, when she called him from a yoga class in tears about some "spiritual opening" she had experienced, he had gotten her off the phone with a joke about how incredibly busy he was, asserting that his own personal mantra was, "I work, therefore I am." Drunk with guilt over her, consumed with fear about his job, he flailed madly at the bikers, only once actually getting hit.

Jimmy shouted at Jon above the fray, "I refuse to let one silly ad break my balls," just before he got squarely punched twice. After they staggered to the men's room, washing their wounds with shared paper towels, they swore eternal loyalty and vowed to maintain a united front in the face of this dangerous, but surely salvageable episode. "Someone is out to destroy our working lives," Jon said.

Jimmy assented grandly, "We will hunt down the miscreant and retaliate."

As they tromped back to the agency on Little West Twelfth Street, Jon glimpsed their reflection in a store window. To his startled eyes, he and Jimmy looked mighty vengeful, mighty self-righteous, like Puritans in black coats and stiff white collars looking for a witch to burn.

Unfortunately, before them stretched a weekend during which friendships could disintegrate and embraces slip apart. Jon ended up sleeping for twelve hours, then going to the gym and striding the treadmill, next straight back to his apartment at Eighty-Seventh and Park, and finally to bed. He got himself into a state so manic that even thinking about Sasha proved impossible; he justified his denial by envisioning a thoroughly destroyed career. Eventually, though, he got out of bed and opened up his photograph drawer, groping through the pile. There were a number of old birthday cards, one from a Deborah, whom he couldn't remember, another from Betsey "Love, love you to bits, Betsey." Finally he found photos of the two of them, one in front of the Christmas tree at Rockefeller Center, one at the Boathouse Café in Central Park, another of Sasha mugging on a ski trip. Way at the bottom of the drawer was a card. On the front a red flower drooped, swaying above a gorgeous green stem. Jon was afraid to open it, but when he did, he recognized her bold black handwriting. "Dear Jon, Besides being crazy, you're the funniest person I know. You take advertising more seriously than anyone else on the planet. Call me soon, and we can discuss burger patty ratios. Your Sasha." It had been written over a year ago.

How had he let so much time pass without calling her? He recalled now that heavy, blocked feeling he had had each day, knowing that he was mistreating someone close. She was too much for him, that was it. Too complicated, with her ever-changing health food regimens, her insomnia, the strange family members calling on her cell phone in the middle of the night, about what, Sasha would never say.

He got up and poured himself a glass of scotch, contemplating Eighty-Sixth Street from the south-facing window in his living room. Pedestrians huddled in their coats against the wind. He glanced over at the pile of unread *New York Post*s on the coffee table. He hadn't read the paper in weeks, but now he unrolled several of the soggy pages, determined to regain some equilibrium. Mostly it was the same old stuff dressed up as news, but then he spotted a month-old headline: "Mother's Laundry Lead Singer Succumbs to Injuries." Jon sank down on the floor, reading a full description of the car crash that had killed Sasha. It had happened around seven thirty in the morning on the interstate just west of South Bend, in heavy fog, both tour bus and car traveling at high rates of speed. According to eyewitnesses, the bus swerved to avoid a car in front of it, then did a 180-degree turn, just in time for Sasha's Audi to smash into its side, further spinning the huge vehicle around, slicing her car in half, at which point both vehicles burst into flames. Jon lay down beneath the piano he never played, the cello he used to play, and cried.

Later that night, in bed and unable to sleep, he went over and over in his mind the two recent calamities visited upon him. Years of vanity and privilege in relationship to women had made him think that by ignoring someone, he could deal with her. So too, absorbed in his own well-being, he had closed his eyes to a potential problem, Guy's envy of him as a younger, fitter rival for Claudia's job. At this moment, he vowed, by way of atonement for Sasha's death, that he would find out if Guy Danziger had indeed tried to ruin him and then go after him any way he could. If not Guy, he would discover the guilty party and slay that particular dragon or dragonette, at whatever cost to himself. An odd penance, he knew, but for someone with a work-imposed moral code, this was the only way he could prove to himself that he was still worthy to be alive.

The target of Jon's outrage, Dysfunctional Guy, as everyone at the agency called him behind his back, had spent a tortured evening of his own at his favorite Soho tavern drinking martinis and contemplating a juicy, expensive steak. A temperamental man, a creative man, for much of his life fifty-two-year-old Guy had mystified and enraged everyone around him, including his wife. He smiled, stared off into space, and let the world finish everything he had to say. He knew that his moods depended on his location in a four-year cycle that inevitably climaxed with several months in rehab. The first year, he was in a state of stony, pained sobriety; in the second, he was delicate, like a wavering flower in the breeze and took a few drinks; in the third, he was tentatively back using substances and balancing them to stay on track; but by the fourth, he was in a glassy-eyed, walking coma, his only real goal getting his dealer, Terry, to call him back. It was a wretched trajectory, he knew, and he never could quite figure out why his wife and colleagues suffered through it with him over and over again. Why did he remain gainfully employed when he should have been lying in a ditch?

Bored and restless after the long dinner, Guy stared at his agitated wife downing her third glass of chardonnay and wondered dreamily what was happening on the television set above the bar. From behind him, way up in a corner, he heard the signature Buffalo Grill whinny. Turning, he listened carefully. Ahh, that whispery voice. How had it managed to sell so many small, unattractive pieces of meat?

Marsia was saying something. "Guy? Guy, how about talking to me tonight." She was a tall, muscular woman with long brown hair and a wide handsome face, the exact duplicate of her Serbian grandmother's. She wore a blue suit with a plunging neckline, and she unbuttoned the top button as she spoke.

"Just a minute. That's one of—" he said pointing to the television.

Marsia squinted, "Yours?"

"Umm," Guy murmured, still looking. "Not mine. Jon Neel. Let's watch this."

Marsia hadn't eaten much food tonight and was staring down at her plate. When she looked up, it was only to shake her head. "I won't watch this stuff anymore. I have to watch every commercial you do. No matter how you try to sell it, Buffalo Grill's food is disgusting."

"This spot is running an awful lot," Guy muttered. Sure enough, before they could go back to their languid dinner conversation, Buffalo Grill came on again. People at the bar strained upward to see it as well, some motioning toward the TV, others laughing.

"Can't we have one night where we don't talk about advertising?" she said as she sipped her wine. Still her husband wouldn't turn around, so she slammed her fist onto the table and yelled, "Guy, listen to me, talk."

"About what?" he said before he realized what was coming out of his mouth. Because of his long years of substance abuse and recurring rehab, Guy Danziger retained a blank innocence about much of his own life. Whole decades had flown by in a cloud of drug and drink, and he liked it that way. He thought of himself as an astronaut circling the earth, happily retaining his youth through the miracle of relativity. Yet here was this very real woman, attractive, smart, known to him for twenty-two years, yelling as she often did on a Friday night, his particular favorite evening of the week. If it was Friday, could a party be far behind?

"You don't seem too broken up. Won't it damage the company?" As she said this, the Buffalo Grill sign flashed once more up on the small screen.

"It puts an eighty-six-million-dollar account in jeopardy," he said and took a sip of his wine. He wasn't supposed to drink the martini, the wine; he wasn't supposed to drink anything, but this was year three, during which he carefully monitored his substances to maintain the right balance with the world. Briefly he focused his baggy, tired eyes on his wife, then stared back at the monitor. His white hair fell forward like a mop, though he kept pushing it back to scratch a small scar on his forehead.

Pained, exhausted, she said, "You look like Geppetto."

"What? Geppetto, the guy in Pinocchio? He was really—"

She finished his sentence for him. "Old. I want a divorce," she snapped and strode out of the restaurant. He stared after her, wanting to follow but unsure whether he could walk, even though their townhouse was only a few blocks away.

four

SECOND THOUGHTS

By the time Eleanor returned to Ithaca from her foray into the New York advertising world, she was in a black rage. What kind of man would hardly register the death of a former girlfriend and race off to talk to his client? He must be hardened, oblivious, sick with self-absorption. Why had Sasha even cared about him in the first place? Any revenge against such a person seemed impossible, especially for someone like her. "Thank God I don't live there," she said the next day to Mrs. Forrey, her assistant at the library.

"Where, dear?" asked the gray-haired woman working next to her.

"New York City. Everyone's crazy there."

"I have a friend whose son works at an advertising agency in the city, in research. They call him a 'planner.' Don't you love that? 'Research' would be too simple."

"It's not LaGuardia and Knole, by any chance, is it? I just met someone there who's a lunatic." Eleanor was compiling a bibliography on exotic brain cancers and filed research papers as she spoke.

"No, I don't think so. Some long name. I'll remember it. Actually I know several young people in Manhattan. It helps to be young there, like you."

"I might have to spend more time in the city," Eleanor said and right then wondered how she could do that. She would lose her job, and she couldn't imagine supporting herself on Sasha's money, even while carrying out her assignment. None of it made any sense, so when she got home that evening, she decided to consult the one person who might have insight into this bizarre proposition, her mother. She hadn't talked to her in a month, and this would be a good excuse to call.

Eleanor had no brothers or sisters, and the whole world of family relations was a bit of a blank. Her mother, christened Victoria but calling herself "Rini," had led a troubled personal life up until her attachment to Michael di Lusco, who became Eleanor's beloved stepfather. Her birth father, Terence Birch, a professional golfer in Fairfield, Connecticut, died of a heart attack at the age of forty-three. Di Lusco was dead now too, and Rini lived with her third husband in Chicago, a man whom Eleanor barely knew. Her mother had just returned from Singapore and was busily recounting all the exotic meals she and Phil had eaten, when Eleanor broke in to tell her about Sasha and the request she had made. There was silence on the other end of the line until Rini burst out, "How can you be so naïve, Ellie? It's not necessary to follow the wishes of that woman. Even as a young girl she was strange. Was she drinking at the time?"

"No, Mother, she wasn't drinking at all. I feel so obligated, and then there's the money."

"It's unreal. She didn't foresee she would be in a crash, did she? I don't know how I can help you. I didn't approve of your friendship with her at Dudley-Holcomb, too sophisticated by half."

"But wouldn't you feel duty-bound if one of your friends asked the same thing of you?"

"No, I wouldn't feel any such thing. You can't take all the world's problems on your back. It prevents you from having a real life of your own. Keep the check and do something fabulous."

"I couldn't do that. It wouldn't be right," Eleanor said, in shock at her mother's callousness. Though she rarely got any real support from her, she never stopped trying.

She had been in Ithaca for eight years now, since she'd finished her master's degree, and for the last two conducting her desultory romance with the chemistry professor. Originally she had had real hope for him. Her girlfriends, one an English composition instructor, the other in hotel management, thought he was hot, but they hadn't tried to talk to him beyond social chitchat. Peter Franzen looked much younger than his age, was rosy-cheeked, frazzled, and perpetually in training. As the school year went by, he demanded that Eleanor spend more and more of her time at the gym. Not only did they not speak while pumping various forms of iron, but the constant image of tougher, thinner women rousting about put her into a funk over her own more substantial charms.

The life of the body was fine, but it should never usurp the life of the mind, and she proved that by reading Thomas Mann's *Magic Mountain* while on the treadmill. Still, Peter would hop over and demand that she "concentrate, focus, Ellie. Soon those buns will be tight, tight, tight." His microscopic interest in her rear end caused anxiety, since she seldom got a good look at it, and when she did was rather pleased. She had a nice shape, even if it was rounder, more comely than that of the women frequenting the juice bar. She suspected Peter's body fixation was not only a product of age panic but also a creepy wish to turn himself into somebody else.

Tonight Peter was rowing away on an imaginary sea, and Eleanor had to shout twice to get his attention. "Peter, there's something I need to ask you."

"Two more reps, babe, and then I'm all yours." She seriously doubted that. When he wasn't working out, he read magazines about working out and was currently addicted to *Men's Health*.

"I have a moral dilemma," she said, and Peter frowned at her.

"Yes?" he replied skeptically. She proceeded to sketch out Sasha's remarks and the subsequent large check while he peered at her, unbelieving. "Incredible, the whole deal. Forgive me, Ellie, but it's such a girl thing, 'getting' somebody. Men just punch people out or haul ass away from a situation, which is better, obviously. You know, I've been thinking of taking a sabbatical in New Zealand, where I can train full time. What do you think?"

Eleanor stared at him. Why had she even gone out with this man? He couldn't concentrate on anything or anyone else for more than two minutes at a time, and then it was back to his bod. He was good in bed, an important consideration, but clearly she would have to wave him off down under and start to look for someone else halfway decent to date, though the guy pool was droplet size in Ithaca. "New Zealand's good. You should go, for sure."

Even he was confused at the swiftness of her assent, rubbing her arm affectionately, and she knew that he'd expected a protest or an offer to go with him. He tried now to answer her question.

"Your friend must have been disturbed, and doing a note up with her lawyer, plus money, that's nuts. Maybe she was stalking the guy, and she wanted him killed?"

"So she hired me? Peter, you can't seriously think of me as a hit man?"

"No," he said laughing. "You can be scary, but not that scary."

For this evening anyway, she could see that Peter was trying to focus on her remarkable problem. "She couldn't have meant 'get' as in death, anyway. It would have to mean something like make him suffer, but he was suffering already when I left him. Maybe that's enough?"

"I don't think so—fifty thousand for that?" He encased her in his buffed-out arms as they emerged into the cold night air, sweaty and overheated. "Really, she's a stalker. You should report her to the police."

"She's already dead, Peter," Eleanor said dryly.

"Right, sorry, I lost track for a minute."

She knew that he wanted to come to her house and make love to her that night, but she pulled away as they walked to her car. If she had to say good-bye, she might as well start now.

At her desk the next day, Eleanor came across a notice from New York Hospital/Weill Cornell Medical Center offering transfer stints between their libraries and her own, some for three or four months. At once it seemed that fate had taken her hand. She could work in New York and use Sasha's money to sublet a place. The minute she thought this, she rose up out of her chair in alarm. Did she really think she could uproot herself to fulfill a dead friend's wish? She thought of talking to Mrs. Forrey about it, but then ruled it out immediately. She'd suggest psychiatric help. Over the next several days, Eleanor became quite miserable. She couldn't sleep and couldn't think whom to confide in; it all seemed too outlandish. How could Sasha have done this to her? Didn't she have other friends more suitable for the job? A bad headache was upon her when she finally decided to call Tony Lowe.

His voicemail announced that he was at rehearsal, and she clicked off. Nervously she formulated a message and called back. "Hi, Tony, it's Eleanor Birch. Do you remember me?" The instant she said this, she almost hung up. How could she be such a clod? She plunged ahead. "I'm thinking of coming to New York again and wondered if we could get together, you know, about Sasha and the whole money thing. Please call me." She left her phone number again, thinking he might have lost it. How many numbers would a man like that collect? Thousands.

He did return her call the next afternoon, and when she heard his deep, smooth voice on the phone, she couldn't even believe she knew someone like him. "Eleanor, you must come. I've been thinking about you."

"You have?"

"Absolutely, in between rehearsals. When are you coming down?"

"Maybe next week."

"Perfect. If it's a Monday night, we can have dinner at the new place, El Dharam, too hip to have a phone number, but of course this guy knows it."

"I might be able to plan a Monday to Wednesday kind of visit."

"Grand. I await you."

At last, one person who took her concern seriously. As she trudged up her icy driveway that night, she was pleased to know the man and felt taller and better looking just because of the conversation. For her solitary dinner, she prepared chicken breasts with sun-dried tomatoes and rice, the cat looking up at her inscrutably all the while. Somewhere between the chopping and the frying, savoring the fine art of the small meal, she realized that the only friend who could truly have appreciated the nature of her dilemma was Sasha.

five

SABOTAGE

That Monday morning after the Buffalo Grill disaster, poisonous air seeped through the walls at LaGuardia and Knole, as if rat sandwiches were rotting under the conference room table. It was the air of sabotage, and Jonathan sniffed it uncomfortably, then eyeballed two of the scarier females in the agency standing by the coffee machine in the front lounge. He waved and turned his back but not before overhearing part of their conversation. "God, what's next?" asked Janey Peet, the creative department operations manager.

"What's next is somebody gets the knife. It's only a question of who and into which body part," Serena Rawlinson said. Chief agency producer, Serena oversaw all the television commercials that issued from LaGuardia and Knole, supervising the production companies and directors responsible for their creation.

Jon wheeled around to face them both. "How are you ladies this morning?" He beamed, adopting an uncharacteristically cheery exterior. Young Janey was hard around the eyes, thin, self-confident, and she sported a sharp bob with black bangs straight across her forehead. Constantly atremble, sensitive to the smallest vibration around her, how she had made it to thirty-two without keeling over, Jon couldn't figure out. He considered her too nervous to try to do him in but vowed to watch her latest doings closely.

"Have a cappuccino," Serena said, smiling at him and handing him a cup. In her late forties, Serena had adopted an urban equestrienne look, complete with turtleneck and short black jacket, her scraggly gray hair in a ponytail. Truly she looked as if she might have recently mucked out the stalls. This woman rigorously clocked the inflow and outflow of millions of dollars to select fiefdoms within the agency; from Buffalo Grill to Synergene to Roundhouse.com to Allegheny Beer, which way would the green tide shift next? Staring at Serena for a moment, Jon contemplated her as a potential saboteur. She knew everyone and everything and wore a small Mexican bracelet around her wrist, dangling with little knitted people. It struck him as a sign of satanic warning: "I've got your body on my bracelet." Rumors told of a husband and two children, but he had trouble believing they even existed. Would she have tried something so detrimental to everyone in the agency? He couldn't tell, but she seemed to derive all her emotional satisfaction out of personal plotting on the job.

"Great coffee," Jon said to her, and as he made his way down the long hallway, he glanced back at the pair of them. They leaned forward, whispering over their mugs, looking ever so much like witches waiting for the cauldron to bubble.

At LaGuardia and Knole, almost every feature or appointment of the interior was metal or concrete, right down to the desks and chairs. It really did look like a meatpacking house.

The only signs of human life were two large portraits of the agency founders, Richard LaGuardia and Piers Knole, long since decamped, beneath which rested the unexploded shell of a World War II torpedo. In such a forbidding environment, Jon had turned his corner office on the eighth floor into an adult PlayStation. He had an elaborate video setup and monitor to watch TV spots, along with a Bang & Olufsen stereo system. A Nerf basketball hoop and a mechanical dog named Snide (if pressed on the nose, the dog said, "You lazy motherfucker") occupied his desk, and from the ceiling dangled a pair of papier mâché breasts. On the floor rested a dismembered toy robot Jon was readying for the office War of the Bots.

As he started up his computer, he noticed that he had almost one hundred emails. Too many to deal with. Instead he punched buttons on his phone to listen to those hateful messages that must have poured in on Friday before he and Jimmy had vowed eternal fealty. Jimmy Goodlaw: "Jon, where the hell are you? Can you fix this?" Head of Traffic, Tyrone Duneau: "This is the list as we got it, bro. What else can I say?" Jimmy Goodlaw again: "What the fuck?" His mother: "Jon darling, I saw your ad quite a few times. Was there something wrong?" Mona Janke, head of planning: "Umm, Jon, I don't, I'm watching and the whole—" Jimmy Goodlaw again: "You'd better pick up that phone, you bastard—"

He got the drift, nothing he didn't already know about, but what happened that unbearable day hit him once again. Then he heard the last message, spoken in the magisterial tones of the CEO of LaGuardia and Knole, Claudia Thompson. "Jon, I'm watching now and, well, we should get together Monday morning. I didn't call you this weekend because I was thinking things over." This probably meant she had hired a team of hit men. A mistress of understatement, a woman who always talked in a low voice, Claudia cultivated scary, and she was scary, at least as far as he could figure her out. Would his lifelong bonds so recently forged with Jimmy Goodlaw survive the weekend and that man's own difficult Monday morning? He wasn't sure and began tossing Nerf balls furiously into the net.

Still no word from Guy Danziger, the possible Wizard behind Jon's particular Oz. Of course, who would be so stupid as to ring up and say, "Hey man, you're getting fucked on TV?" So maybe it wasn't Guy, but Jon vowed to use any contact with the man as an opportunity for surveillance. On the corner table was a pile of New York Posts and one or two copies of the Times, none of which he had read. Already he had replayed Sasha's ferocious, blood-filled automobile accident over and over in his head, and he was afraid to learn still more about it. Because of the involvement of several members of Mother's Laundry, this was no ordinary crash, and its cause and possible remedy in terms of traffic safety had become a media obsession.

Like Jonathan Neel, Guy Danziger was in mental flight from the industrial meat- cutting style that characterized LaGuardia and Knole, cocooning himself in an office that looked more like a gentleman's club, with mahogany bookshelves, leather-bound volumes, and several fat, comfortable chairs. Though only in year three, Guy was in a state of dysfunction perilously close to the four-year mark. He could look out over the edge of his ornate wooden desk and see the fiery pit that loomed below. At this moment, hunkered down in a burgundy Naugahyde chair, he stared intently at a dictionary. His wife hadn't left him, at least not that weekend. In truth, his marital life was full of irresponsible remarks and remarkable silences. Not only could he not finish a sentence, he couldn't finish an interaction. He would walk off, saying he had to "watch a game" or disappear into his office or announce that he had to go back to work, whatever he needed to do to end the confrontation. Like a small creature at the bottom of the sea, he just wanted the big sharks to swim by. His wife loomed as a really big shark, one who could take a significant number of his fish.

Guy stared down at a word in the dictionary, *crisis*. "The turning point, for better or worse, in an acute disease or fever," "a paroxysmal attack of pain, distress, or disordered function," "the period of strain following the culmination of a period of business prosperity when forced liquidation occurs." All of the above, that's what struck him. He was about to experience them all at once. "Jesus," Guy moaned. He was getting scared by a dictionary. The immediate crisis, as opposed to those lurking at the margins, involved his new biotech account, the company now known as Synergene. How in God's name he'd managed to land an eighty-million-dollar account in his current state of health was not only one of the great mysteries around the agency but also to Guy himself. He still didn't understand precisely what the company did, though the earnest doctors who ran the place nattered on about "recombinant DNA" and "targeted genetic cures for cancer" and, best of all, arrived with sample bottles. Guy had managed to palm one of these off the president and took two pills just for fun, even though they were normally used to treat melanoma. He'd felt a slight buzz that lasted an hour.

His one major contribution had been to their renaming. When first asked to pitch them in Boston, the company had been called Dy-Gene, due to the kidney drug Dygenate. "Gee, I hate to mention this but—your name—I don't really—" He couldn't finish the sentence without major prompting. "I don't think you should have the word *die* in it, no matter what the context." Gratitude flowed through the company, and after several arduous pitch sessions in which Guy pronounced the newly named Synergene the greatest purveyor of pharmaceuticals in the galaxy, the rapidly growing biotech company signed on at LaGuardia and Knole. High on his triumph, he felt a giddy pride in his knowledge of drugs and how that had helped him. It was like being drunk and getting the Mothers Against Drunk Driving account.

Unfortunately, he had produced no ads for these people in five months, no newspaper, no TV, no nothing, and he could feel the crushing weight of their money on his weary head. That's why he was reading the dictionary, trolling for ideas. His rival for supremacy, Jonathan Neel, cranked out those impossible Buffalo Grill things like sausage, while he, Guy Danziger, winner of 1998's Most Important Man in Advertising Award, was confronted with a stack of blank pieces of paper. He'd assigned a couple of creative teams to do something, but they never generated anything he actually wanted to use, so he was left to create whole campaigns by himself. As he rose in the corporate hierarchy, he had become intolerant of any idea not his own.

Janey Peet popped her head through the door. "Hi, doll, did you see the Buffalo Grill ad?" she said, waving a cigarette, even though the operations manager certainly wasn't supposed to smoke in the office.

"Who didn't?" Guy grumbled. He was deep into self-pity, and Janey looked ridiculously happy.

"Our esteemed leader is on her way in to talk to you about it." With that she backed out, teetering slightly on her boots as if on a ferryboat.

Before Guy could clean up his desk or comb his hair, Claudia Thompson strode in and planted herself before him on those unbelievably strong legs of hers. They appeared to be made of stone. In her red suit and armband of clinking gold bangles, she looked like a boxy general. The number of bangles indicated her state of mind; the more she wore, the angrier she was. Today she sported a store full. Glaring at him, Claudia said quietly, "Guy, did you see the Buffalo Grill stuff on Friday?"

"I certainly did," he said, eyeing her black turtleneck sweater revealed after she pulled off her jacket. She started in on the Buffalo Grill problem, vast, knotty, much larger than the question of that one ad, and for Guy more torturous than actually watching those TV spots because he could hardly hear what she was saying. He amused himself by staring at the twin round globes of her breasts. They were bigger than he remembered. The finely coiffed blond hair, the mottled skin pulled tight over those bones, so tight he had no idea of her age—somewhere between fifty and seventy—these all looked familiar, but her breasts were getting larger. What kind of stuff did she have pumped into them, mattress ticking?

"Guy, Guy, are you listening?"

"Ummm."

"You may have to step in and help out on the next batch of Buffalo Grill ads, just temporarily, if Jimmy Goodlaw wants Jon out of the way. I'm still trying to find out how it happened."

"Step in? Me? I don't know anything about food." He seemed genuinely alarmed.

"You eat it, don't you? How are you doing on Synergene? They've been calling." He blinked a few times and waved several blank sheets of paper at her.

"Those aren't ads, so far as I can see," she said, looking impatient.

"They're ad-like entities," he said.

"How about turning them into something real?" she said, loudly this time. "Listen, Synergene's Oncreon 1 has already been tested on liver cancer and gotten amazing results. It's a miracle that I plan to make known to the world, and I'm expecting you to help me." Guy stared at her as if she were spewing battery acid. "Jesus Christ!" Claudia yelled past his head, more or less in the direction of the window and strode out.

Jon knew the meeting to discuss the "Big Buffalo Fuck," as it was now being called, would be extremely painful. None of this was his fault, but it had been on his watch, and an unaccustomed feeling of guilt pervaded his body, made worse by his horror over Sasha's death. He vowed to take charge of the chaos, and as regarded Buffalo Grill, to use the meeting to develop a list of suspects. Fortunately, Jimmy Goodlaw had already called twice to reaffirm his faith in their partnership, to insist that of all people in the advertising world, he alone should stay at the helm. Jimmy had promised to reiterate this to Claudia as well. Nevertheless, some form of rebuke was inevitable. Though he was chief creative officer, the number three person in the agency after Claudia and Guy, he fully expected to get bitch-slapped upside the head.

When Jon entered the conference room, Guy was slumped deep in a leather chair, awake or asleep, it was impossible to tell. Janey Peet and Serena Rawlinson were in attendance, along with Tyrone Duneau from Traffic. Together they smiled faintly his way, the decorum of the situation unknown. Once Claudia appeared, flopping her papers and charts on the egg-shaped marble table, clinking her bangles, she stared down everyone in the room. In that menacing voice, she began by detailing the contents of her investigation. From what she could determine, the chain of instructions to the network had been followed to the letter. The numeric codes identifying each commercial and what actually ran matched up; worse, the usual people had signed off on the ad and its placement. Either it was a hitherto unexplained computer problem or some person had arranged for the Buffalo Grill "Better Place" spot to run as many times as it did.

While Claudia was speaking, Jon surveyed those assembled therein. Janey seemed hyper as usual, and she stared at him as if she were about to jump up and sing. He couldn't figure out her demeanor. Seated at the end of the table next to Guy, Serena rifled through papers during most of Claudia's remarks and didn't look up. "Something must have been wrong with the codes or the log, Tyrone," Jon announced angrily. "Who has the final authority? You do, don't you?"

Tyrone could offer no explanation. "Everything looked perfectly normal to me," he said, "absolutely nothing out of the ordinary."

"I couldn't reach our computer guy, Seth Greenblatt, this weekend, but believe me he'd better have some explanation," Claudia said. Jon could see that she wanted this all to be a technical error, since any other cause would indicate a malevolent force in the agency. He immediately put Seth at the top of his list for further investigation. He wasn't going to entrust his whole career to the CEO, and besides, people were so afraid of her they never told her the truth.

Jon glanced over at Guy Danziger, who barely looked up. The older man was drawing on a sheet of white paper, some strange oblong outline. At last he roused himself and said, "I think it might have been quite brilliant, modified of course, a new strategy, 'saturation advertising,' like a bombing campaign." An anchorman on TV had advanced this theory, and now he could. What was he if not master of the stolen thought?

Jon stared across at the man who had uttered these words seriously, as if they had an actual meaning. "We could drive the whole nation insane," he finally said.

"They're insane already," Claudia remarked. "What are you drawing, Guy?"

"A liver," Guy said. "I think a lot about the liver these days."

"I'll bet you do," she said acidly. Even Jon had to laugh. There was something endearing about Guy, notwithstanding that he might have tried to sabotage his entire career. Jon ran his eyes over a number of other people at the table. Tyrone was too low down on the food chain; Janey he doubted; Serena, possibly, with help. Was she in league with Seth Greenblatt? He came back again and again to Dysfunctional Guy, drug-addled Guy, nevertheless a powerful man. The audacity of the fuck-up meant that someone seriously resourceful had been at work, and he knew that, even bombed, their president could summon up formidable abilities.

"You'll have to talk with Janey about your system controls, Jon, since there's a new Buffalo Grill commercial going into production in a couple of weeks." She eyeballed everyone at the table menacingly and announced, "We must beat back the beast of inattention." Jon's gut burned with rage. He loathed being told anything like this, especially by Claudia and in this absurd way.

Guy, shivering with pleasure that he hadn't been asked to do anything new, burst out, "Brilliant stuff anyway, Neel. Don't know how you can get that much out of a steak." He fell back into his chair, exhausted, like an old lion waving a paw.

"Thanks so much," Jon said, feeling the burn move into his throat.

Later, sitting in his office patting Snide's nose over and over again, he reflected back on his association with Guy Danziger. Almost a decade ago, long before the two of them had risen to their current executive positions at LaGuardia and Knole, they had worked together as a creative team, Jon as copywriter, Guy as art director. Their coupling hadn't lasted, and he'd finally asked to partner with someone else, but not before becoming familiar with Mr. Danziger's habits. He got very tired, Jon knew, through the pressure of maintaining the ideal internal substance level, and he told a lot of lies. For a time Jon found this amusing, while he observed the man juggle several mendacity balls at once, marveling at how many he could keep spinning in the air. His wife, his teenage daughter, his boss, his clients—they required tending, and Jon heard all of it on the phone since he had shared an office with the man. Now, though, full balls-out entropy seemed to have taken over, as Guy spun ever downward like a tired top. Knowing what he did, Jon vowed to stay even later than usual at the office to see if he could learn more about his rival's current doings.

Evening at LaGuardia and Knole was like a sweeter, softer

day. A few people were still working, mostly in print production, far away from Jon's office. After dining on a Snickers bar, he found himself, with no difficulty at all, in Guy's office, looking through whatever was on the desktop of his computer. He saw a folder for Synergene, another called "My Thoughts," and a folder called "Confessions." Jon could hardly breathe. Guy was so dysfunctional that he left all his personal stuff hanging out, like an unzipped fly. He clicked open "My Thoughts." Guy's thoughts turned out not to be his at all, but those of some exiled Tibetan thinker—Rule with Your Heart, Lead Through Example—platitudinous junk like that. But "Confessions" yielded more of interest.

Guy claimed that he was sleeping with not one, but two women at the office, the very same Serena Rawlinson and Janey Peet. *Could this all be fantasy?* Jon wondered. But here were lists with descriptions of where they went and what they were planning on doing. Apparently Guy liked Janey to dress up in a short skirt, frilly panties, a little halter-top, and white stockings that ended at the top of her thighs. He called her "Good Morning Little Schoolgirl." Serena was a different story, a drink and drug story. Once or twice a month, after a late lunch on Friday, they apparently went to the Geary Hotel bar, downed several martinis, then took a room, snorted coke, and slept there until Saturday morning. These activities were noted in great detail, including Guy's phone calls to his wife to say he was working late at the office. It made Jon's life seem even more monastic than it was, and perhaps it was the age difference, but he was genuinely shocked. Guy was wrecking his home and his working life all at the same time.

About his obsessions, Guy seemed coldly analytical. "I

need to sleep with younger and younger women to have that experience in my life." Absurd comments like, "This is expensive and career damaging but worth every minute." "Marsia is witty, sexy, a delightful wife, and she believes everything I tell her." Did she? Jon had met her many times and thought her sharply intelligent, formidable. There were also remarks on what a great lover he was and vows to stop drinking, along with meticulous monthly catalogues of his liquor consumption. "October 10th: tonight three scotches, did some coke after dinner, one more scotch, then the rest of the cognac." "October 15th: four vodkas at lunch, three at dinner, bottle of Cab." Lists of substances, with no comment at all, days bunched together, sometimes with brackets around them and the word DRUNK in block letters.

Reading these "Confessions" now, Jon guessed that Guy might well have been behind the Buffalo Grill debacle. Despite the little boy lost look, the "I need you, I need you" smile that haunted Guy's working day face, here was a practiced betrayer of friends, family, and colleagues alike. With just one click, Jonathan Neel could send this folder to everyone at the agency. All employees from top to bottom would read the ugly screed and make their own judgments, and few would be surprised at finding this sort of material emailed to them, since they knew that Guy hadn't enough control to know what he sent out. Only one keystroke away from infamy, Jon contemplated an act as monstrous as sabotaging a million-dollar commercial.

six

THE DYING MAN

For Guy Danziger, November meant two things so far: bitter cold, which he hated, and the accelerating hideousness of his personal life. For a whole week after that awful Monday meeting with Claudia and the others, he had been unable to do any work at all. It was now Friday, the evening of his occasional bout of nasty fun with Serena Rawlinson, but he wasn't in the mood as he wedged his body like a knife through the wind on Eighth Avenue. They had chosen the Geary Hotel for their trysts, given its complete lack of chic and accessibility, but lately the management had gotten into upgrading. First the lobby, painted a strange salmon color, then the carpets, now hunter green. The gaudy liveliness of the place had Guy in a state of panic. What if people, real people, meaning someone he actually knew, came here to stay? Of course they wouldn't, but Guy's mental processes had gone south on him. As Serena greeted him, twirling her long gray hair into two plastic clips on top of her head, he had the odd thought that she looked like a sinister version of the cartoon character Tweety. "You look like Tweety Bird."

"Thanks. I knew you wanted to give me a compliment." She

lifted her eyes in delight, anticipating the next several hours of frolic.

"I feel bad," Guy said, and he did, wretched even. His life had gotten so out of control that he was letting the misery maven seated in front of him rule it. Not misery really, just plots, intrigue, the dramas that Serena liked to craft around others. For fun she would mislead tourists who asked her directions on the street. The only plus, she adored hallucinogenic substances and shared them in a manner that both seduced and fatigued him. Her idea of fun was to sneak out of a big meeting at the agency and cavort around room number 18C, high on cocaine and eager to do anything with her body that he demanded, though lately the only thing he wanted was to pass out. He felt suffocated with guilt, bound like an Egyptian mummy in eternal thrall to this harridan. No one else could stand her. She was married, but had anyone ever met the poor bastard? Guy wondered if she hadn't already buried him in her basement out on Long Island.

Ecstasy, their latest plaything, put him in a novel realm, though. Tonight he had taken a pill just before he arrived at the hotel. It fired up his synapses—he could feel the wiring getting crossed, and he liked that. He could sketch tissues endlessly for Synergene, imagining the most brilliant print ad in the world. He could stay up for a full twenty-four- hour stint of work. He could make love at least twice, though why he kept doing this with Serena was yet another source of bewilderment. Where once she'd resembled a charming waif, she now looked mangy, and her plotting quaint. What charmed in an ingenue mystified in a forty-eight-year-old. Still, she was a relief from his beautiful wife, a woman who understood him far too well.

"I wonder if Buffalo Grill will go into review?" she said,

predictably amused at the possibility that Jon's client would threaten LaGuardia and Knole with termination, meanwhile asking other agencies to compete for the business.

"I hope not. They'll drag me into it. Lately I'm too wasted to have any ideas except where I'll sleep next," he said, conscious that maybe he liked her because he wasn't afraid to tell her the truth. "That commercial, though, may have started a bonfire."

"It's only Buffalo Grill. Jesus, nobody we know ever goes there anyway."

Guy straightened himself in his chair, in the firm mental grasp of a designer drug. "Nobody you know? You mean the point-zero-zero-zero-one percent of the American public we call friends? It's a very popular chain of restaurants. Nothing about this screw-up was harmless, and Jon's an all right guy, a little obsessed possibly, but skilled, competent. Besides, Claudia came to me and said maybe I'd have to take over the next commercial shoot for Buffalo Grill. No fucking way. I know absolutely nothing about the fast-food business." Guy sank back down to gulp his Jack Daniel's.

"Everyone will forget about this very soon. It was probably confusion in Traffic. I don't want to waste a perfectly good evening talking about it," she said dismissively.

"Christ, Serena, LaGuardia and Knole is a real live business that employs a whole lot of people. It would definitely not be good to lose such a huge account," Guy snapped back at her and scratched at his scar.

"You talk as if I had something to do with this." She downed her martini. "You know what, Guy, fuck you! Better yet, go fuck yourself," she shouted, irritating two salesmen drinking in a corner, and then she walked out.

With a washed-up Friday evening on his hands, usually the most delicious day of the week, Guy wondered whether he should go home. Marsia had been fed the story that since he worked so late this particular day, and she wanted to leave for their house in Water Mill, Long Island, early that morning, he should just come out Saturday, when there was no traffic. Presumably, his exact whereabouts were a mystery to her. He ordered another Jack Daniel's and contemplated a rare evening alone. Maybe he should call Janey?

This Friday also represented a personal nadir for Jonathan Neel. Normally a rather temperate man, given the standards of addiction in the advertising business, he was more likely to eat too much pizza and too many M&Ms than get inebriated. Tonight though, he downed margaritas at the King Cole bar at the St. Regis, while a fuzzy-looking blond in red leather tried to get his attention. Unfortunately, the drinks weren't making him forget; they were leading him toward teary despair. He shouldn't have come to this bar, Sasha's favorite. He had loved her quirky mind and deep, warm body, but she wanted to do things, go places, have a life. She had hobbies, like cooking, though usually the dish was part of some bizarre new diet, and she was fascinated with tai chi, Reiki, and various other forms of new age exercise. Her most recent discovery, Gyrotonics, involved a large wooden machine that looked like a cross between a loom and a sixteenth-century torture machine. He had helped her park it in a corner of her bedroom, and she insisted on giving him a demonstration. While she grasped two wide paddles and swung herself forward over them, swaying right, then left in a serpentine motion, he said, "Are you sure it's for exercise? It looks like a machine to make boxer shorts."

"You don't understand anything, Jon," she had replied, and now he believed she wasn't far wrong.

Sasha seemed to suck up time, suck up his life. Maybe that was the problem. Jon's work fed him through an iron umbilical cord, and he couldn't imagine existing without such a connection. Still, how could he have ignored her for so long? Why hadn't she just contacted him? He felt now as if he needed her, when it was too late. His brush with the "send" button on Guy Danziger's computer hit him like an electric shock of a thousand volts. With that very button he could have jeopardized the careers of two women at his firm, thrown Guy's marriage into hell, and seriously damaged the older man with his colleagues. He hadn't done it, of course. Guy was just too pathetic, possibly too weakened even to be involved in the Buffalo Grill fiasco. Yet Jon still burned with rage and obsessively contemplated revenge. He could try to steal Guy's new client, he could get Janey fired, he could send Serena out to Bumblefuck, USA, and never let her see the inside of the New York office again, but he couldn't do any of this without knowing the truth. In the smoky, stale bar air, Jon pulled himself back from these abysmal thoughts. Sasha was the only one he'd ever thought of as good in his world, and by his bad behavior, he'd driven her out of it.

"Hey," the blond woman at the bar said. "I'm just visiting, and I'd like to know some cool restaurants around here."

Trying to concentrate, he said, "Right around here?"

"Yes, I don't want to walk too far." She shoved a shapely leg with a red shoe on the foot at him. "My feet are destroyed already."

"There's Michael's, down about two blocks, right off Fifth

Avenue. There's Jack's up at Fifty-Eighth, across from the Plaza, and there's the Plaza itself, the main room, if you want a huge, juicy steak. Of course, there's always Buffalo Grill, down on Forty-Second and Eighth Avenue, for a somewhat smaller steak, only six ninety-nine." He gave a soggy laugh.

The blond woman immediately lowered her voice and intoned, "'Buff-aa-ll-o Grii-ii-ll. We should go to a better place.'"

Jon looked at her for a moment. "Ha, very funny. You do it perfectly. Ha, ha, ha!" He laughed like a drunken monkey, and positively every person in that bar was looking at him. He didn't care, just patted her on the outstretched leg, slapped his money down, and made a quick getaway.

Because of this incident, Jon decided to walk home, all the way up to Eighty-Seventh and Park. It was frigid and windy, but Madison Avenue wasn't too bad, and normally he loved its Friday night feel, on display the most beautiful luxury goods in the world. He peered into the Scully shop, eyeing travel bags, but suddenly a cab slammed to a stop in front of him. Car sounds, brakes squealing, Sasha's death, he couldn't escape his own morbid thoughts, and thus it was hard going. Everyone else was out walking too, maybe to buy more scarves and hats for the coming winter. Even though it was eight thirty at night, he felt curiously unhungry. At Eightieth Street he peered into a French bakery, thinking to get a piece of chocolate. At Eighty-Fifth Street, he crossed over to Lexington, imagining that he would pick up a sandwich at the Korean market, but he didn't do that either. Overheated and sweaty, he felt his heavy cashmere coat stick to him as his face froze. At Eighty-Sixth and Lexington, walking north and passing the entrance to the subway station, he picked up a *New York Times*.

Despite the noisy passersby, he heard a strange sound and turned to look into the subway landing. A man, possibly in his thirties, wearing dirty trousers but naked from the waist up, tried to wrap himself in a filthy blanket and a sleeping bag. He filled the entire entrance. Normally, Jon avoided eye contact with the homeless, but now he looked the man full in the face and saw a skinny, red-faced person, mouth open in a silent howl. Turning, twisting, he was pulling his meager garments around him as best he could, while people stepped over him. To Jon he appeared to be in his death throes. He would certainly freeze. Should he stop and help him? He was afraid to touch him. Instead, he walked quickly around the corner to his own building on Eighty-Seventh Street.

"Carlos," he said, greeting his very young doorman. "We need to call the police and get some help for a man in the subway entrance."

"*Qué dice*, Señor Neel?"

"A man, in the subway. He's freezing."

Carlos sighed, then motioned him up the palatial stairs that led to the lobby. Danny, at the front desk, wasn't much more help. "It's precinct nineteen, Mr. Neel, but I don't think they come."

Jon used the house phone to call anyway and told the sergeant the location and the appearance of the man. "I know who he is. We've tried many times to take the guy to a shelter, but he just won't go," the cop barked.

"Something has to be done. I think he's actually dying. He had almost no clothes on, and it must be thirty-two degrees. You've got to send help over there. People are just walking around him, bumping up against him even."

"I'll see if anyone's available. I told you, we've tried to deal with this person before."

"You've got to send somebody," Jon yelled into the phone.

"I told you we would." Jon didn't believe him and resolved to go out later and see if the man was still there.

His apartment was on the twenty-ninth floor of a new building, with fifteen-foot ceilings, hardwood floors, and gorgeous, seemingly endless white walls. Furnished sparsely, a cello and piano prominent, he had decorated the living room with his younger brother Walter's funny and touching drawings of little green people hiding under purple mushrooms and strange fruits and vegetables all in blue and gold. Walter worked countless hours on these cartoon sagas that spanned centuries, and the pictures were enchanting, but they were the product of a broken mind. Somewhere in the birth canal, his brain had been momentarily starved for oxygen, and that moment defined the rest of his life.

Jon spent that long dismal evening sipping Diet Coke, staring out his living room window at Eighty-Sixth Street, watching the families struggle down the street, trying to imagine who they were and whether they were happy. A stray dog seemed happy in contrast to his own eccentric household in upstate New York. He didn't blame his parents for what they had become, aging hippies obsessively tending their vineyards near Lake Erie, two hours west of Buffalo. What with the rain, the wine, the lake, and their disabled son, they were miserable. On the long winter nights of his childhood, amid frozen fields and bleak expanses of gray water, music had saved them all from suicide, he knew, even though the instrument his mother chose for him was mournful and unwieldy. Nobody sings to a cello. After years of study and dreams of greatness, at a retreat for budding musicians in the Berkshires, he'd heard Buddy Raymondson play, and at that moment knew he could never take seriously his future as a musician, but he had trouble explaining this to mother, who just ranted that he had abandoned his calling.

At college in Syracuse, a writing teacher had adopted him and steered him toward advertising. It turned out he had a gift for the instant, metaphoric compression that is the tagline, plus the discipline of an artist. Jon considered his field a haven for creative people who, beyond wanting to eat, actually wanted to get rich. Did it matter though that at thirty-eight, he made more money than a foreign currency trader, he had accumulated more frequent flyer miles than anyone of his generation, or that he owned a very nice New York apartment? As he thought about his life, he seemed nothing other than the man who had abandoned his girlfriend to a fiery death.

Wandering over to his computer, Jon logged on to all the business sites related to fast food. What should he see at buffalo-grill.com but a chat room full of people announcing that they had "gone to a better place!" At least sixty posted messages. Usually the site traffic consisted of infuriated customers complaining about the chemicals in the salad bar. He could only figure they were all insane; they had no lives. People were so vacant they relied on fast-food restaurants for personal fulfillment, and now they had adopted his demented slogan as a mantra. He assumed it would be temporary.

seven

THE HAIRCUT

E leanor finally got up the courage to bank the fifty-thou-sand-dollar check from Sasha's estate and once again braved the big city to consult with Tony Lowe. At seven thirty on a Saturday evening she stood nervously outside El Dharam restaurant in the West Village. Freezing despite her heavy clothes, she awaited the actor while aggressive patrons swarmed the door, shoving her relentlessly backward. Finally, she pushed through the crowd into a startling interior of red-flocked wall-paper, low pillows, and velvet settees. After shouting Tony's name through the din to the hostess, she was ushered to a booth on the east wall, close to the center of the action. Ordering a glass of chardonnay, hoping to quell her uneasiness, she pon-dered her mission, revenge, though El Dharam seemed an un-likely venue. Indian waiters in white shirts swirled around her, and a woman in a sari moved from table to table giving tarot readings. Feeling terribly out of place, she registered that her clothes were all wrong, too brightly colored, too big on the top, too tight on the bottom. Why could she never look turned out the way New Yorkers did? A good-looking waiter brought her the wine; it tasted dry and fruity on her lips, the glass cold. She stared down at the menu. Rather than vengeance, she contemplated "Items From Our Hot Tandoor Grill."

Suddenly Tony Lowe loomed above her. "Hi, you're here. I thought you might not be able to find it." He hung his coat up on the rack behind the table, sliding into the seat across from her. Heads turned their direction; such was the effect of the actor's remarkable physiognomy.

Eleanor had to catch her breath before she spoke. "I couldn't get a cab, so I had to take the subway, which was a little scary," she said self-consciously. They ordered an appetizer of duck samosas and a long list of Indian delicacies while, for a time, their conversation rambled. Tony was obsessed over a piece of dialogue from the play, wondering whether it suited his character. Eleanor couldn't understand who his character was, so she offered no help. After another glass of wine, though, she described what had happened with Jonathan Neel, how she had left him shattered and grieving on the sidewalk of the Meatpacking District.

"So he's in trouble with his job, and it made him miserable, quite apart from Sasha?" Tony said, sipping on a glass of Indian beer.

"Definitely. It sounded as if he truly might have a problem." Eleanor found herself perplexed by the angst and chaos of Jonathan's world, so she wasn't sure. "He always worried about his job, at least from what Sasha said. She told me he'd suck her into commiserating on some disaster; then he'd get a promotion."

Just as she said this, a teenager sidled up to the table, holding a menu. "I'm sorry to bother you, Mr. Lowe, but could I have your autograph? Just sign it from Dr. Nolasco."

Tony smiled and said "sure," then wrote out his signature with a flourish. Eleanor regarded him quizzically. "Dr. Nolasco. From *The Shadow of Our Dreams*, remember?" She shook her head. "A soap opera I was on two years ago. Everyone loved the good doctor, even though he regularly injected himself with a testosterone-Viagra cocktail and cut off the wrong leg of a patient. Jesus, am I glad I'm off that."

"You're famous though. That must be good."

"A small fame, very small, Ellie. May I call you that? I'm working to make it bigger. Now back to your problem."

"I'm hoping to make it yours too. I need help."

He frowned. "I don't have time for direct intervention, but I will advise."

"So, was that enough? That he's got trouble at his job? I know I didn't 'get' him myself, but just being 'gotten' might be what Sasha had in mind." Eleanor spoke while she struggled to slide a lamb kebab off its stick without shooting it across the table.

"Why do you think she chose you?" Tony said. "You don't seem terribly bloodthirsty to me."

"I have no idea. We were close in high school, but I never fit in with her crowd. She singled me out, though I couldn't figure out why. To me she was so sophisticated and grown-up, maybe too grown-up."

"What do you mean?"

"I've never told anyone about this," Eleanor said, looking around as if to see who could hear. "No one in the world," she said, lowering her voice even further.

"I sense an important confidence coming. If it's about a Connecticut prep school, we have good reason to whisper."

"Dudley-Holcomb in Fairfield. Anyway, I saw her writing a letter one day in study hall—she never studied—and asked her about it. She told me, 'I'm writing to an older man.'" Eleanor leaned forward, her eyes wide. "If you can believe this, Sasha was briefly involved with the father of one of the other students at school, when she was, like, seventeen years old. I mean to us, to everyone else, he was ridiculously old, in his forties probably. When she told me they'd made love during lunch hour at the man's house, I couldn't believe it. It was incredible."

"Jesus, you scared me. For a minute I thought you were going to say she screwed cats."

"She told me later it was just an infatuation but pretty pathetic for a guy that age. She said she led him on for fun. If anyone had found out, it would have set the school on fire. I kept her secret, though."

"Aha, she chose the right person then. I'm not surprised by the story. The first time I met her at one of those downtown parties, she was escaping some investment banker and just threw her arms around my waist from behind. 'Save me, hide me from that dullard,' she said, and that's how we became friends. Men were always after her."

"True. They were," Eleanor sighed. "I'm flattered she trusted me, but a number of the people at the funeral definitely seemed more cut out for revenge."

"No kidding," he laughed. "You seem more cut out for good works or something public-spirited. These ravenous New Yorkers could parboil you, especially the people in advertising."

"Is it my looks? Or the way I dress, that I don't fit in?" Eleanor suddenly resisted the notion that she wasn't tough enough to help Sasha.

"No, no, I didn't mean that, but ad people eat their young. They're not normal. Of course, I'm not normal, and I doubt that you are, but believe me, these guys are way off the normal page. What would hurt you or me won't hurt them. They take a thousand cuts a day."

"It all seems very daunting," she said, shaking her head.

"Look, I've got an idea. Let's get a tarot reading, not on you or me, but on revenge. The tarot of revenge, something like that," Tony said.

"I don't know if I like fortune-tellers."

"Agents of the devil, are they?" He leaned forward, leering.

"Possibly," she said, smiling. He waved in the direction of the dark-haired woman with the cards, and she floated toward their table.

"You wish to know the future?" she said, squeezing herself in beside Eleanor.

"Not exactly. We have a problem and want your advice," Tony said.

Without a word, the woman spread the cards face down, asking each of them to draw five, which she then arranged in a cross with two sidebars—the Celtic Cross. Eleanor watched her long red fingernails in fascination. "The question, I take it, would mainly involve you?" the woman said, looking at Eleanor.

"Yes, I'm afraid so. But he said he would help." She was feeling those two glasses of wine.

"He will help," the woman said and began turning each card face up.

"We want to know whether a man has suffered enough, or should we take further revenge against him for something awful he did?" Eleanor was embarrassed that she was even asking.

"The cards can never be used for ill or evil, but I will consider your question in a more positive light. 'Has the karma of revenge done its will on the man this woman seeks?'" She began turning the cards face up. "In the central place, skill. You have the skill to harm this man. Burdens, several wand cards, all reflecting burdens. It is a burden to you, no?"

"Definitely. I don't want to do it."

"The Eight of Swords. Fear, fear, and more fear, but here is the King of Cups, a heart-centered leader. That is good, possibly this man." She pointed at Tony. "Here the Empress, abundance and fertility, the mother figure. I think that is you." She looked at Eleanor, then grabbed a roll out of the basket, split it in two and started eating. "But it could also be a friend."

"Sasha," Eleanor said, suddenly close to tears.

The woman lined up four cards on the right-hand side of the table. "The outcome," she said, between bites of roll. Dabbing at her eyes with a napkin, Eleanor stared across at Tony. She was becoming less and less sure they should be doing this. "The World, meaning attainment, self-actualization, final triumph as the karmic lesson is complete."

"I hope it's Neel's karmic lesson and not ours," Tony grimaced.

"Yes, this lesson belongs to the man. But here," she turned over the last three cards, the Devil, the Tower, the Hanged Man. They certainly looked formidable, at least to Eleanor. "The Devil, he is chained to something, addictions, yes?" She looked at the young woman for confirmation.

"To work, or maybe to something we don't know."

"The Tower means a fall from grace or banishment from the

Garden of Eden. He is cast out!" The woman said this loudly enough for the people at the next table to look over. "The Hanged Man, now this is one of the most important cards in the deck. He means spiritual growth. There is a white light around his head. The man finally attains insight and beyond." She eyeballed her two customers expectantly.

Eleanor finally said, "So? Do we get him or not?"

"'Get'? I don't like that." The woman frowned. "There is no doubt that the two of you play a role in his karmic uplifting. It's forty dollars, thank you."

Into the night Tony and Eleanor sat at the table and mused over the cards, scrutinizing a diagram the woman had sketched for them. The actor had a cognac and she drank two more glasses of wine—they were floating in alcohol by the end of the evening, and she could feel her heavy sweater sticking to her chest. "What do we do next?" she asked.

"What do you mean 'we,' white man?" He was tipsy.

"Come on, Tony. Advise me." Behind him, she could see teams of well-dressed men and women circulating near the bar, where loud Indian music played.

"Advice? I've never been too good at it, Ellie, and I make a practice of never taking it."

"But you said you would."

"I will. I'm resolved. Besides, he hasn't suffered nearly enough," he said. "Sasha was extraordinary, too amazing ever to be forgotten. That he did shows he's lost, a heartless man. I want to see him suffer, and we have to make sure we don't back down. You'll be the agent, but I'll be the manager." Tony looked down at his plate, then rubbed his hand across his forehead in distress. She'd not seen real grief in the man before now and reached over to clasp his hand. He gripped hers back. "Yes," he said, "yes, for sure."

She excused herself and went to the ladies' room, and when she returned attempted to cheer him up with the general problem of trying to slap her hair into submission or smash it under a hat in the New York winter. "Sometimes I feel completely lost in my clothes. I mean, I can't figure out how the people in this restaurant manage to look so good. In Ithaca it all seems to work, but here I'm the poster child for wool and fuzz."

"You have such beautiful white skin. The rest though, the hair and everything, that's easy to fix. You know, you should stay in the city if you can, acclimatize yourself to New York, really get into it. You've got the money to do it, and how else can we make any kind of plan?"

"I know, but I'm guilt-ridden. If I'm not actively pursuing the guy with a gun, shouldn't I give the money back or give it to charity or something?"

"Oh, my God, what the hell are you talking about? Sasha obviously wanted you to have it, for your quest, so to speak. Just think of everything you do here as relevant, and I mean everything."

"Does that include the Brontë manuscripts I saw this afternoon at the Morgan Library?"

"Hmm. What did they look like?"

"Tiny little books with minuscule writing. Heathcliff plotted revenge for two decades."

"We don't have that much time. You know, I've got a friend, Jamiesen French, magnificent hair cutter. Famous. I was just thinking—"

Eleanor giggled. "You want us to cut Jonathan Neel's hair?"

"No, no, of course we could get into a Samson thing, but that'll be later. Your hair really is fantastic, Ellie. Maybe you could get a bit of a trim and it would, I don't know, get you more into the swing of things?"

"I know, it's major frumpy. I went to a barber for a while," she said, patting her mane self-consciously. She used it to hide her face as often as not. "I don't see how my hair is related to any plans." She felt sensitive about her looks. Her glamorous mother often criticized her for not "doing more" with herself.

"You're so rational, Eleanor. I'm just trying to help the little girl from Ithaca get jazzed about taking on the big bad wolf."

"When you put it like that—" She laughed and for the first time got a glimmer of the changes that might come to her from the journey Sasha had laid out before her. "You know, my library in Ithaca has an exchange program with Weill Cornell Hospital. I could look into it."

"Brilliant. I have friends who are always traveling for work and want to sublet for short terms, like two or three months. You need a change of venue if you're going to do anything."

She pulled out a pen and wrote "Plans" on the backside of the tarot diagram. "Hair" was first then—what? "I'm very good at research—"

"You could stake out his apartment."

"Why?"

"I don't know. That's what they do in detective stories."

"Research of some kind, we'll figure out what later," she said, writing it down.

"Research is good, but revenge, you've got to think big, the way Sasha would: 'Come, the croaking raven doth bellow for revenge.' That's Hamlet. Or how about Macbeth? 'Murder most foul, help me, ho I am murdered.' 'Blood will have blood.' 'Let every man be master of his time,' that sort of thing. I played Macbeth in the Public Theatre production last year—of course you can't learn anything from him, a complete whack job, obviously bipolar."

Outside of the restaurant, while waiting for a cab, Eleanor contemplated the hair problem as a way to keep her mind off the bigger steps this whole business would entail. "Could you get me an appointment with your friend?" she said.

"Of course."

Two days later, they met up at French and Partners on Madison Avenue. While Eleanor squirmed in the chair, Jamiesen himself, at Tony's request, surveyed her abundant curly locks and pronounced them "too big, too long." He proceeded to trim, shear, and slice while the hair fell in clumps around her. When he was finished, Eleanor had a perky bob that stopped just above her shoulders. He'd added some highlights in thin strips near her temples and then pulled her hair through a brush to wind its over-eager curls into a smooth shell that was more sophisticated. As she stared at herself, she barely recognized her own face, framed now with controlled shapeliness. Her oblong brown eyes suddenly seemed exotic and enticing rather than scared. Her nose, with the very slightest curve in the middle, settled back somehow in her face, and the proportions worked better. She looked younger and infinitely lighter.

She stared at herself. "I do like it, I do," she said, protesting to the famous haircutter, who was preening, he was so proud.

"Yes, it's perfect. Your face now emerges. Please stop hiding it."

Outside, on an icy November day, Eleanor felt frightened

and energized at the same time. Tony had to rush off to the theatre but kissed her on the cheek and promised to call that night.
She wandered into a café at Sixty-First and Madison, sat by the
window, and ordered an espresso, surveying the well-dressed
passersby. Her head felt completely different. She seemed to
have lost a pile of something that had made her stoop and bow,
and now she could sit up straight and look people in the eye. She
felt like one of the handsome people racing along in front of her.
What to do about Mr. Neel? On a small napkin she drew little
circles, then squares, pentacles like those on the tarot cards, finally wheels with a star in the center. Fifty thousand dollars—so
far she'd used about five hundred. Research was the only thing
she really enjoyed, and she knew so well the leathery-smelling,
book-lined caverns and hidden places in a library. There was
something comforting about books, the feel of old knowledge as
it bled through the stacks. In the medical library where she
worked, new knowledge supplanted old very quickly, and she
had the proud sense that much of what she learned immediately
translated into a better life for some unknown patient.

*Who was this Jonathan Neel person? What was his history, and
what did he care about?* she wondered as she nibbled on a chocolate biscotti. Perhaps she really should stake him out, but how?
Her mother had once announced that "detectives know everything. They can find out anything in an hour's worth of research.
It's all on the public record." Was that true? She tried to work her
cell phone, but it was dead.

"Do you have a pay telephone?" she asked a handsome Italian waiter.

"In the back," he pointed.

There she found the yellow pages chained to a metal shelf

and had to juggle the tattered book in her arms as she surveyed the half-page ad for the Herscholt–Zeiss detective agency at Park Avenue and Twentieth Street. On impulse, she flew out of the café and hailed a cab. Why not? She had the money, another two hours before the bus, and she needed a leg up on this Jonathan Neel. Alighting fifteen minutes later in front of a handsomely remodeled building, she was reassured to find an attractive receptionist and walls covered in what appeared to be original oil paintings. They must have had some success. Mr. Zeiss, a youngish, red-haired man, identified himself as the rightful heir to the legacy of Henry Herscholt, the most information for the least amount of cash: discretion, competence, and completion. "Everything you want to know, Miss Birch, and more!"

eight

THE SLIP

G uy Danziger employed a perfectly beautiful Wednesday to drink gallons of water and concentrate on his computer. If the last several weeks had shown him anything, it was that he must stop the downward slide and take his life into his own two hands. He felt that if he cleaned up his computer files, more complex elements in the mix would also clean themselves. Unfortunately, his relationship with this machine was as checkered as all of the others in his life. He'd finally learned how to write on the thing, but he wasn't really comfortable with moving files or emailing or any of the work that was routine at the agency. When he first sat down at his office desk in the morning, he would gingerly slide the keyboard toward him, then tap the power button. Amazingly, it would make noise and come alive. A voice invariably said, "Hello, Guy," and he loved that. It was heaven to be wanted.

The morning hum of activity vibrated outside his door. Even though he had an excellent view of the Hudson River, he rarely looked at it, since he was afraid of heights. Now as he tapped the keys to open certain files, the immensity of the vista impressed itself upon him in a happier way, even more so the amount of writing evident on the machine. "Jesus, I can do something," he said out loud. At that moment his phone buzzed. His assistant wanted him for a meeting. "Just a minute. I'm cleaning stuff up." He sat before the repository of all of his work for the last three months like an eager schoolboy collecting his notebooks. Every time he clicked on a new file, he lined it up next to the previous ones. When he came to the folder marked "Confessions," he paused and tapped the mouse. He knew this file well, since he added to it frequently. Just then he thought of reading his emails for the day, so he logged on to the interoffice mail system. The list was incredibly long, filled with important memos mixed in with dogs for rescue or potluck dinners to attend or "Elena is taking a sick day today." He leaned forward to stare at the icons on Microsoft Outlook—he had never really understood them. One looked like a small hammer, another like a twisted wrench. What could they mean?

Though it made him feel important to have so many letters awaiting him, he wondered if anyone else had access to them. The office computer guy, Seth Greenblatt, often warned that the system was "permeable," and therefore not secure. What if Serena decided to extend her plotting to him? Did she know about Janey, who always wanted him to get rid of his wife, and then they could play "Good Morning, Little Schoolgirl" all they wanted? He found it endearing, romantic, and hopeless, obviously, but he viewed himself as protecting her from the knowledge of his deep corruption, which would send her flying.

What about Jonathan Neel? Could he break into his computer and read his files? To be helpful, Janey had already printed out a sheaf of ideas from Buffalo Grill, "borrowed" from Jon's machine. They lay on Guy's desk now. Surely Jon could do the same to him. A flame of fear rose up his spine. Panic dripped acid onto his bones, as he slid farther down in his chair, so that his wide, heavy feet rested straight in front of him. He began to sweat and wiped his forehead, picking at his scar. Revelation, revelation, now there was something his world didn't need. The phone rang, and as he turned toward it, the "Confessions" file and the email files still open on the desktop, he closed both, feeling momentarily in control.

Jon Neel had been taking these last couple of days to adjust to Sasha's death, going in to work but doing very little. In the months preceding the breakdown of their relationship, she had been sad and angry. He'd chalked it up to annoyance at him and their failing romance, but he had never really asked her about her feelings. What with his career, his troubled brother, and then Sasha, he couldn't handle all that emotion. Now, as he sat at his desk trying to work, he stared at the nerf hoop, then at his mechanical dog Snide, as he randomly doodled on a notepad and went over every single minute he could remember from their romance. He'd met her at a party for an internet company, Fishnet Media, in the East Village. She stood out for her height, of course, and for her classically modeled face, but also for the luxuriant dark hair and the lilting voice that was alive with energy and joy. She seemed very much a grown-up woman, not like the stringy, paranoid females who haunted advertising at every tier. They'd started going out, though he didn't make love to her for almost five months. "Are you gay or something?" she'd finally been driven to ask. Later, of course, they wouldn't get out of bed for an entire weekend, would eat there too. She loved to drink and talk dirty and watch old movies. At first, the only negative had been a puppy she took in, half German shepherd, half black lab. The damn thing would take a flying leap and land in the middle of her bed. Sasha just laughed, but it struck Jon as obnoxious. The canine needed more discipline. "If you had a dog, it would be locked in a closet," she accused him.

As their affair progressed—and it was an up-and-down matter since they both traveled so much—Jon came to see her as a serious impediment to his work. Into his thirties, as his ambitions increased, his focus narrowed. Every minute away from the office was a problem. Sasha wanted to see all the latest art openings, she wanted to scour the boroughs for good Colombian food, was infinitely curious about all sorts of performance art, especially dance, and often she coerced him into sitting through atrocious concerts with people in black leotards who hurled vegetables and chanted Sanskrit. Jon had put up with it all because he knew she needed an expanding universe and wouldn't want to eat Chinese take-out forever. Still, he began to see the raging fullness of her life as a sign of desperation, as if silence frightened her. Normally exhausted from work, he began to pull away when it seemed that his already hectic life would merge with another one fully as explosive.

But why had he let so much time go by without even calling her? It wasn't as if he had other women. Over the years he had had three or four serious girlfriends, but when they became too proprietary, he withdrew, as if his quota of loving had been expended on his brother. Suddenly Jon felt the emptiness that would come with no Sasha, ever. She had cared about him. She used to curl her body around him at night and kiss him on the back. That was love, and what had he given back? Nothing. He had abandoned her, and then she'd died a horrible death. There could be no worse punishment for him than his own bad opinion, and it seemed beyond redemption.

At his computer, he began going through the usual endless emails until he chanced upon a most intriguing subject bar —"Confessions." It couldn't actually be Guy's incredible file? Jon began to sweat. He knew he hadn't sent it out, or had he? He opened the missive, and there it was in all its revelatory ugliness, every word the same. With a title like this, it would become an instant must-read, and according to the time stamp on it, the thing had been floating around in cyberspace for hours. Serena Rawlinson would have seen it, and certainly Janey Peet, two of the principal actors in the sexual playlet on Guy's particular stage. He knew that Serena was down in Florida on a shoot, or by now Guy's head would have been dancing on her bracelet. Not possible that Jon had sent it out inadvertently, Jesus, no. He'd spent his whole life working with computers and was careful enough not to do that. He had to believe so. Otherwise, he'd collapse, given recent events. Had their mighty leader, Claudia Thompson, read it yet? Suddenly Jon had the unnerving thought that someone at the agency other than himself hated Guy so much that he or she had stabbed him in the heart. Had that same person tried to do him in as well with Buffalo Grill?

Guy, of course, was wholly unaware that his "Confessions" were spreading themselves across every desktop at LaGuardia and Knole. At this moment he was sunk in his chair, sketching ideas for Synergene, glancing all the while at some of Jon's storyboards for Buffalo Grill. Maybe he could have a strange voice whispering "Syn—er—gene," but even he dismissed that thought. Jon had one idea for stampeding buffalo that he thought promising. Couldn't those big hairy animals just go straight toward the errant cancer cells? He was sketching some possible scenarios when he heard footsteps running down the hall. From outside his office, he heard the screeching tones of Janey Peet. "Guy, open that door. I know you're in there!" His instinct was to hide, but then he wondered why, after all?

Guy opened the door to the enraged young woman, hair flying all over, carrying a Big Brown Bag from Bloomingdale's. "How could you? You bastard, I'll get you for this!" She flung herself across the room and started randomly grabbing books off the shelf, throwing them onto the floor.

"What's wrong with you?" Guy backed himself up against his desk.

"I read your so-called 'Confessions,' you miserable son of a bitch. I wasn't exactly alone, now was I?" She kept pacing and swearing, hardly looking at Guy, who began to tremble.

"What do you mean, you read them?"

She pitched her hand out and swept his leather pen and pencil set off the desk. "I read them on my goddamn email. Serena Rawlinson? She's my friend."

"Jesus." Guy sank down in his chair. His "Confessions" file out there somehow. "How did that happen?"

"How do I know how the file got out, you miserable piece of shit? It's not secure, you baboon, the whole network is totally insecure. You need to watch what you're doing!" Her voice had now risen to a shriek.

"I didn't send it out. Are you crazy?"

Janey didn't listen to him. Instead, she reached into her paper bag and began flinging its contents about, the girlish halter-top, the short skirt, the lacy panties, the white stockings, and the ribbons she tied her hair with. All over his office, these items hung, limp, accusatory. Then she stalked out.

This little performance sent him straight back to his computer. "Hello, Guy" sounded in his ears now as a threat. He logged on to his email but couldn't figure out what had been sent out and what hadn't. He called the office computer center. "Could you get Seth up here?" At least he had the presence of mind to determine immediately what to do—unsend the hateful missive.

Seth Greenblatt, a lumbering, ungainly fellow in a Patagonia jacket, already knew of the crisis. He'd been alerted by one of the secretaries, who had had the happy thought of taking care of Guy's problem for him. But it wasn't so easy. Seth fiddled and played with the machine like a concert pianist, oblivious to the little girls' underwear scattered about. "Just get it off there. Unsend the fucking thing. Get it back." Guy wanted like crazy to have a drink but restrained himself. He stared out his big glass window and wondered if he could open it and jump.

"It's not that easy." Seth didn't ask the president of the company whether he actually wrote the thing. "I can tell you who's read it though."

"Don't. I don't want to know." Guy held his head and swizzled his thick hair upwards like a top. He opened a drawer in the cabinet near the window and grabbed a bottle of vodka. He didn't care if the little pischer saw him. "Want a drink, Seth? This calls for serious alcohol."

"No thanks." Seth worked on, announcing periodically the names of the people who had seen the email, despite Guy's request. So far nobody important except Janey and Serena. Then he mentioned Jon.

"Oh no, oh no, oh no, now I'm done for." Guy started to moan like an abandoned puppy. "What about Claudia? Please tell me she hasn't read it."

"From what I can see, no."

"Thank God. Now just delete it or whatever it is you do."

"I can't without crashing the whole system."

"Crash it, kill it, burn down the wires, do anything you can. Pull the plug."

"I feel there might be an ethical problem with that, sir. I mean, people depend on this to get their work done."

"Oh, don't give me that horseshit. They play solitaire, they watch porn, they check their stocks. It's just a toy."

"Not everyone does that."

Despite his reluctance, Seth finally agreed to shut off the entire interoffice communication system, along all the important platforms, and to post a message saying, "Down for repairs. Log on in the morning." This was unheard of, of course, and ineffective, since out of the fifteen or so people who'd read the email, five or six had already printed it out, to savor, to reread, to show their friends.

Later that evening, Claudia Thompson stopped by the office after a charity "do" to see what was going on. Nothing. The place was deserted, though a light came from under Guy's door. She knocked, got no sound, and entered to see scattered all around the room the little schoolgirl clothes. The lacy panties perched on Guy's computer, the halter-top on the desk, and the white stockings curled around themselves on the floor. She sank down into a chair, but instantly jumped up again and started going through his drawers. After finding his vodka bottle, she un-screwed the top and took a swig. For at least twenty minutes she sat there drinking, getting quite tipsy, staring at the underwear. Finally she took a small yellow Post-it from his desk, wrote on it, "Love you, Claudia. Call me," and stuck it to the panties.

nine

THE WRITTEN WORD

E leanor Birch was firmly ensconced at her desk at Schulman Library in Ithaca when she checked her messages at home and learned that Herscholt–Zeiss planned to FedEx their report to her at work. She shivered. What she had done was way past the bounds of propriety. She didn't even know if she wanted the information anymore, but here it was. In the meantime, she worked diligently on a bibliography about bariatric surgery. One of her favorite doctors had a young male patient who weighed three hundred and twenty pounds and had finally decided on a stomach stapling operation that would shorten his intestines by ninety percent. "Amazing isn't it, how the written word can make you feel better," she muttered to Mrs. Forrey as she piled up a series of research reports for the doctor.

"Yes, it is, Ellie. I always think people are the poorer for not being cathected to the written word." Eleanor started. That was it. Cathected, as in Freud, married to it, wanting its reassurance. If it was written, she believed it, even in the national tabloids. "Here are some more words for you." Mrs. Forrey handed her the FedEx package, which turned out to have been there for several hours. Eleanor tucked it into her backpack, resolving to read it later.

That evening she stood with Coco at her big living room window and watched the snow fall. It floated down silently onto the hills and the wide expanse of lawn that stretched out to the road. The evening was so peaceful, as if God himself were lying down to rest. A wave of grief washed over her. Poor Sasha, she would never see the snow again. At that instant, Eleanor caught her breath and felt the sting of something like the extreme consciousness of life.

With a renewed feeling of responsibility, she turned to her task. From what she could see of the detective agency's investigation—credit reports, auto rental receipts, notes about his purchase of a co-op at East Eighty Seventh Street, anything on the public record about Jonathan Neel—he seemed unremarkable. Occasionally he was late paying his bills; that appeared to be his only crime. A high amount of cash showed in his checking account, though. Then other, smaller bits of information came to light. His high school transcripts—he was an excellent student but got bad marks for citizenship, many A-5s, meaning the worst possible conduct. In addition to his records from Syracuse University, first a music major, in which he received Cs, then English and As, she also had photocopies of teachers' reports. One struck her in particular. His cello instructor wrote almost an essay on the shortcomings of Jonathan's playing and concluded it by saying, "For a cellist, this young man would make a very good car salesman." What a cruel thing to say. And yet here he was, making six figures now, selling steaks.

Eleanor loved the cello and was surprised that the man she had met could study that soulful instrument for such a long time. She thumbed through the pages, and a picture emerged of one very bright student, rebellious, difficult, but popular with his teachers. While she was reading, Mr. Zeiss called to ask if she was satisfied or wanted more information. She'd only spent five hundred dollars on this preliminary report, and it seemed a waste. "We could get more juicy stuff if you'd let us follow him, photograph him to check on his associates, look for fraud."

"No, no, absolutely not. What you've sent is fine." She felt guilty enough already.

As she continued to read, there was, however, one entry in his college records of interest. He'd skipped an entire semester to go home to deal with "family problems," then a note from the Dean saying, "Student has mentally disabled brother in need of care." Now that really struck her. She wandered back over to the window, observing the snow again, falling in thick, white flakes. A wild turkey planted each foot as it made its way toward the woods.

Ever since Sasha's death, Eleanor had been sorrowful and confused, but in the last few days she had begun to feel a new kind of disturbance, as if her own landscape had shifted. While this charge or assignment from her friend had at first seemed like a burden, it was beginning to fill her mind with possibilities. She had left off thinking of revenge as a murderous act, since obviously she couldn't do anything like that. No, the mission presented itself to her as an opportunity. Sasha had once said to her, somewhat cryptically, "You're like a child, Ellie. You love being a romantic, but it's dangerous. Look at the world straight on, and then you'll be ready to receive it." Perhaps she was beginning to understand what her late friend meant.

Happily, she realized her good fortune in finding an ally like

Tony Lowe. Vowing to relay to him all pertinent information, she would ask him what to do next, which she did in a very long phone message. Over coffee at the library, however, Mrs. Forrey passed on to her another piece of news. "I talked to my friend, and her son was at a different advertising agency in research, but now he works at the one you mentioned, I think, LaGuardia and Knole, as a computer expert, Seth Greenblatt. According to his mother, he loves New York. Maybe next time you go, you could get together with him, and with several other young people I know of."

"Oh, wonderful, thank you, that would be great." Eleanor knew that Mrs. Forrey meant her remarks in the matchmaking vein, but she was thinking of this guy as a source of information, maybe even as a spy.

When she got home later that night, she had two excited communiqués on her phone from Tony. "Hey, girl. I've got the perfect revenge. I'm not kidding. It came to me in a flash, but I refuse to tell you over the phone. You have to come to the city, soon, but definitely for opening night next week." The next message: "Ellie, I've gotten you a house seat for the opening. It'll be fantastic or a huge fucking disaster. Either way, it'll be great. I love life-and-death situations. But then everything does die in winter anyway, doesn't it?" He was yelling into the phone. Eleanor grabbed up Coco and started petting her furiously. The next morning she arranged an interview at Weill Cornell and for the first time in her life couldn't wait to get into the city.

On the same evening that Eleanor had received Tony's messages, Jonathan Neel was having dinner with Jimmy Goodlaw at the

Buffalo Grill on Twentieth Street and Second Avenue. This particular restaurant hadn't been doing too well, but tonight seemed packed. "It's a falafel and tabbouleh crowd," Jimmy opined, sipping the house wine, a fruity, sweetish blend that Jon was drinking as well. Red or white at Buffalo Grill, that was it. The decor, standard in every franchise, featured sepia prints of Western heroes like Billy the Kid, Jesse James, Emiliano Zapata, and yes, the Buffalo Soldiers, hence its name. The color scheme ran to brown, orange, and green. In each corner were jukeboxes and quaint penny slot machines from the early 1920s, which Jimmy had collected over the years. Employees wore brown Western-style shirts and bolo ties. The simple menu, hardly even necessary, included drawings of steak and broccoli, steak and baked potato, steak and fries.

Tonight Jon enjoyed his food more than usual, probably because he hadn't been eating much lately. Coffee, Twizzlers, peanut butter, carrot sticks—remarkably short of an actual meal. Here he'd gone for the full deal, all sides included, and was digging into a butter-covered potato when Jimmy shoved a flattened piece of chicken his way. "What? You've gone to a better place! The chicken place. Or is this tofu?" Jon practically shouted at the man.

"Don't be an idiot. No, it's actual real live chicken. My son told me to suck it up and just put some white meat on the goddamn menu, so that's what I've done. It's selling very well."

"Not bad," Jon said between mouthfuls smothered in barbeque sauce. The preceding quarter's revenues had been down, so the unexpected crowd tonight really enlivened Jon's client, who ordered a second glass of whatever they were drinking. "You know, chat room activity is up, Jimmy," he said.

"I don't read any of that crap. Bunch of insane masturbators, if you ask me."

Jon got momentarily stuck at the confluence of food and masturbation, but he knew Jimmy and wasn't surprised at anything that came out of his mouth. "They've really taken to the slogan, 'We should go to a better place.'"

"They don't know what it means. Probably got it mixed up with a UFO site," Jimmy said, his face getting even redder than it normally was.

"Maybe, but customers really do seem to like it." Sipping his glass of wine, Jon realized it would be madness to try to sell his client on this tagline one more time. Even Jimmy wouldn't buy a second ticket for the Titanic.

"What you been doing lately, Jon? Hanging out with your friends?" he said, in a tone more appropriate for his college-age son.

"Friends?" Jon functioned with coworkers and girlfriends, and that was it. The concept "friends" didn't really exist.

"Buddies, you know. Are you into sports?"

"I used to play soccer in college, but now I just pick up a game in the park when I get the time." Jon looked into the smiling face of Zapata in the picture across from their table. "I did have a friend, a woman. She died in that automobile accident in South Bend, Indiana, the one that killed those rock stars."

"Oh, Jon, oh no, I'm so sorry. Why didn't you tell me sooner? That happened ages ago, and here I've been berating you about a couple of steaks—not a couple—millions, but still."

"I didn't know about it for quite a while. She and I hadn't been talking, but her girlfriend told me."

"That's awful, just terrible. You must be heartbroken." Jimmy moved from crazed businessman into a real human being, right before Jon's eyes. "Friends of mine went down in Vietnam, but considering how much I fly on corporate jets, those are the only people I've lost. You should take a vacation or something. Try to grieve."

Though these words sounded like a phrase from a ladies' magazine, suddenly, unaccountably, Jon found himself in tears. He hadn't talked to anyone but Sasha's strange little friend, and now he found himself overcome. He wiped his face and straightened up, humiliated to have broken down in front of a client. "Never show fear," that was his watchword. The tense relationship between ad man and client was one he understood very well. "Thank you, Jimmy. I'll have to deal with it somehow." This moment, even more than their debauch at the Hog's Breath Inn, cemented a bond that surpassed most of Jon's relationships in New York. He still hadn't talked to his mother and father about all this, since they were dealing with yet another family crisis, this time over Walter's decision to move out and get his own apartment. "He's thirty-five, Jon. He needs a life." That was how his father put it to him on the phone, but his mother wouldn't hear of it.

Jimmy shoved his own glass of wine at Jon. "Drink up. You'll feel better." He waved his hand at the waitress, who had no idea that she was serving the head buffalo. "Maybe you should show me one of these chat rooms. I don't know how to go in them myself. This 'better place' business might be a winner."

This determination led them back to LaGuardia and Knole, but as Jon and Jimmy trekked down the immense front hall, a young female assistant came flying toward them, breathless. "Umm, could I speak to you a moment, sir?" She tugged on Jon's arm.

"It'll have to wait. This is James Goodlaw, president of Buffalo Grill. We'll be in my office." He tried to back away, but she seemed on the verge of some revelation.

"I need to speak to you—"

"Not now." Jon was amazed at her behavior. At LaGuardia and Knole, the client was king and should never be dragged into internal troubles.

Inside his office, he and Jimmy were leaning in over the computer, scrolling through every chat room message. The whole "Go to a better place" idea was indeed taking hold. Riffs on the theme had developed: "How do we get there?" and "Who's actually at the better place?" and people claiming to be there already. Worse, they were scheduling meetings at Buffalo Grill. "This is bad. It's like a witches' coven," Jimmy said.

"I don't know. If they eat the food, who cares?"

Jimmy's voice rose to a screech. "I don't want a bunch of crazed lunatics hanging out in my restaurants, scaring off families from Nutley. Also, they sound significantly younger than the normal Buffalo Griller. A head of household will drag at least two-point-six children to the restaurant, and that's important. These guys probably have no relatives willing to be seen in public with them." Jimmy wiped his sweating forehead. "Got any booze?"

Jon provided him with some single malt scotch he had stashed in a drawer, and they sat silently surveying the crowd of steak eaters who wanted to chat. Despite the late hour—it was now after nine—there was a knock on the door. Seth Greenblatt almost shoved himself into the room. "This is James Goodlaw,

Seth, CEO of Buffalo Grill. He and I were checking chat room activity for the restaurants," Jon said.

The announcement of a civilian in their midst did nothing to deter the man. "I have to talk to you about the office computer system."

"Now?" Jon piloted Seth outside the door. "What are you doing? I'm working here with one of our biggest clients."

"I just wanted to let you know that the office email system will be down for the next twelve hours, so, in case you—"

"If it's overnight, that's no problem." Jon made as if to go back in the room, but Seth pulled on his arm.

"I wanted to let you know that, um, I see that you read—"

"Spit it out!"

"Guy Danziger's 'Confessions' file somehow was sent out over the whole network, and he asked me to shut it down for a while so I can delete it. But I noticed that you had actually read it." Seth seemed out of breath and embarrassed.

"Watch what you say next, Seth. I might have to kill you."

Seth didn't blink. "Don't worry. Soon I'll know everything."

"I did read it on his desktop file, but I sure as shit didn't send it over the email system." Jon was almost certain he hadn't and wanted to reassure himself.

"I'm still looking into the matter, sir."

"Jesus Christ."

"Yeah, that's what I thought."

"Look, I have to get back in there, but, well, you've shut the system down?"

"Right, and I've deleted it now from everyone's email, but frankly it's too late."

ten

LOST MINDS

I n his gleaming white kitchen the next morning, Jon stood drinking a cup of coffee, chewing on a dried-out bagel, and trying to read the *New York Times* when Claudia called and demanded a report on everything he knew about Guy's "Confessions," which despite Seth's best efforts, had shown up on her computer late the preceding evening. "Who sent the file out, Jon? Someone really wanted to screw him. Who would hate him that much?" He paused a moment in silence, perplexed. She sounded like a real human being, and he wanted to help her but wasn't sure how. Almost certain he hadn't sent the file out himself, he didn't want to finger anyone else, not until he learned the real culprit from Seth, though he might not talk even then. *Never tell anyone all that you know*—another one of the stealth moves in his secret playbook. "Jon, are you there?"

He heard himself say, "There's just no way to figure out what happened, not at the moment. I thought Seth Greenblatt had shut everything down to prevent the thing getting around."

"Jesus Christ. I can't believe it. Anyway, the system is up and running now, but I still had the 'Confessions' file on my machine."

"Those pesky little data bits are remarkably hard to get rid of, aren't they?" Jon said. Claudia sighed in agreement, seemingly defeated, an unusual posture. He himself was angry at the ad land hell that LaGuardia and Knole had become. If all guilty parties were immobilized by scandal and ineptitude, work would come to a standstill. "I'll try to sort things out," he said and shoved his makeshift breakfast into the garbage can.

When he arrived at work, LaGuardia and Knole was curiously silent, the usual jaunty laughter, sounds of commercials being played backwards and forwards, beepers bleeping on and off, cell phones ringing—all vaporized in the bleak air of betrayal. Fear stalked the halls. Unfortunately, no one in authority had suited up to meet it or dissipate it, and even Claudia was still at home. So far, the consensus of those few actually at the agency was that Serena Rawlinson must have broken into Guy's computer and sent out the file in an attempt to blow Janey out of his life, thinking that she herself was above any harm to her career. Who else would do something so evil? Viewpoints coalesced on this subject, as scattered employees huddled around the espresso maker. Jon determined to drag out of them whatever they knew.

"Janey's not here," Tyrone Duneau, the head of Traffic said and looked over at Jon meaningfully when questioned on her whereabouts.

"Do you know where she is?"

"I heard she went to see a lawyer, her cousin Jerry from Queens. Wants to sue Guy for libel," Tyrone said.

"What about Serena, any sightings?"

A young woman whose name Jon couldn't remember said, "She was in Sarasota, Florida, on a shoot, but I hear she's flying back, more or less as we speak."

Tyrone chimed in, "Yeah, her assistant told me she kept screaming 'What the fuck? What the fuck?' over and over again on the phone."

The young woman interrupted, "She called Janey Peet a scrawny little bitch."

Tyrone stuck his hand out and drew circles in the air. "Serena's mind was racing like a rat on a wheel. I can just see it," he said with a laugh.

"Great," Jon said, "This is simply terrific. Thanks for the info. I needed to know how bad it was going to get."

Ever since he learned about it, Guy's solution to the "Confessions" problem had been to disappear, terrified but also consumed with trying to learn who had sent out the file. For the last twenty-four hours he had locked himself away in his study at the townhouse in Soho, smoking, drinking vodka, eating a pastrami sandwich, then back to more vodka, refusing to go into the office. He made lists of suspects; he made lists of lists of suspects by department, though he knew junior people only by their first names. Searching all the LaGuardia and Knole phone books he had at home, he got lost trying to figure out which employees still worked at the firm, since he interacted closely with no more than ten. Hiding from his wife, he had fallen asleep that night on the fold-out couch.

"Guy, Guy, what's wrong? It can't be all that bad," Marsia yelled into the room in the morning, sounding frightened. He was so ashamed and by now so loaded he couldn't even respond. He just wanted to set himself on fire. The thrill, the wonder, the passion of all those secrets was that they had been secrets—no-

body knew. Now everybody knew. Guy was not one for self-re-
flection, but he did value the view that others had of him, even
knowing it was entirely fictional. He had crafted that fiction,
sort of a warm, friendly, fuzzy kind of man, out of it sometimes,
yes, but lovable. His "Confessions" were not lovable, and he
knew it. Worse than all of this, what if Marsia should find out
what was in them?

Endlessly his wife kept exhorting him to come out, almost
on the hour, but mentally Guy had dropped into military jargon
to rationalize his current behavior; he was hardening his position. He would remain in his study for as long as necessary,
where he had a refrigerator and wet bar to keep himself going,
and he hoped that Marsia would repair to their Long Island
house in frustration. She had done so in past crises, but this time
around he could hear her moving through the house. Of course,
there was his daughter, a junior at a private school in the city.
What with sports and after-school activities, even during normal
times, Rory merely passed her father in the hallway. In the midst
of Guy's terror, familial activities seemed to be still flowing on
around him.

The phone rang all day, and by now it was almost three thirty
in the afternoon. He hadn't picked it up, not once, petrified that
it would be one of the players in his own little Kabuki theatre,
Serena or Janey, or maybe Claudia, worse yet, Jon. It had to be
Jon who sent out his "Confessions," probably because he figured
Guy as the one who'd engineered the Buffalo Grill disaster. Several people had hinted to him that he was the prime suspect, and
he had done nothing to deny it. It enhanced his mystique and
struck fear into people if they thought him capable of such a
deed; indeed vengeance had a long and noble history in his

mind. Whatever anyone else did to him, it inflamed him to formulate countermoves.

Two days before the "Confessions" catastrophe, in hopes of
saving his career, Guy had gotten his assistant to email off the
proposal he'd devised for Synergene—galloping buffalo herds
stampeding over cancer cells. The CEO of that company, Dr.
Leslie de Santis, awaited him at this very moment in the La-
Guardia and Knole lobby. Despite numerous calls and pages, she
hadn't been able to raise the man responsible for bringing notice
of Synergene to the world, and so, on impulse, had taken the
morning shuttle down from Boston and dropped by at the
agency, unannounced, to discuss his ideas and, if workable, put
them into motion. Her company's eighty million dollars ensured
that she could arrive any old time she wanted, and there she was,
a substantial woman in a navy suit with a fake red flower on her
shoulder. It was four o'clock on a Thursday afternoon, but the
receptionist was so stumped at the current disappearance of
everyone in authority that she lied to the woman and told her
Guy would show up any minute. With one hand, Dr. de Santis
tapped on the antique bomb that was the main floor's most no-
table decoration and with the other thumbed through the *Jour-
nal of the American Medical Association.*

Still at home, Guy could hear his wife continuing to harangue
him through the door. "Guy, what's wrong? You should come out
and have something to eat," Marsia yelled.

"I'm sick. I really am. I just need to be alone." He could hear
her impatience and figured that shortly she would call the para-
medics.

"Serena Rawlinson called you very early this morning, from the location in Florida. I didn't know what to tell her."

Guy rolled onto the floor from the couch. "She's just a producer. It's probably nothing. She's hysterical all the time." He was preparing the groundwork of slander against her, though previously he had fed Marsia a number of other stories to make Serena seem indispensable to his life and really a terrific little person. His lies were beginning to jostle up against one another.

"She seems very anxious to talk to you."

You betcha, Guy thought but yelled back through the door, "Ignore her. She's meaningless."

"As soon as her plane lands, she's coming straight over from the airport to bring you some papers. She'll be here pretty soon."

"What?" He scratched his head feverishly, then clasped his hands together over his head.

On the other side of the locked door, Marsia began to pound. "Come out now, Guy. This is ridiculous. You're hiding from me in our own house."

Hearing the front doorbell ring and his wife's footsteps trailing away from him, Guy flung himself down one more time on the couch. Who, who had done this? He would get that person. Could he kill? Could he harm another human being? He'd end up in prison. Maybe that wouldn't be so bad? As an ad executive, he'd merely get life. They'd feed him anyway, though he doubted there'd be booze. What was happening downstairs? He tiptoed to the door and listened. Marsia was speaking in a low, intense voice. He could understand nothing. Slipping back onto the couch, he furiously sketched stampeding buffalo—they would get those cancer cells no matter what. In extremis, Guy clung to his work like Ishmael to Queequeg's coffin. Suddenly he heard footsteps coming up the stairs. He lurched over to the door and listened.

"Guy, you've got to come out. Serena Rawlinson is here, and she needs to talk some business." He sensed that they were close, very close outside the door now.

The phone rang and, for the first time that day, he picked it up. He would talk to anyone, positively anyone, rather than the two women standing outside his door. "Yes, it's Guy here," he said.

"It's Leslie de Santis from Synergene. I'm at your office and wondered when you were coming in. We need to talk about this idea you sent me."

"I'm so glad you called. I'll be there in fifteen minutes." Such was Guy's status at LaGuardia and Knole that his own personal driver, ensconced in a Lincoln Town Car, awaited him at the corner coffee shop, a good distance from his house so he wouldn't have to stare at the imposing vehicle from his bedroom window and feel guilty about not going into work. Now this appeared to be the perfect escape route. He would nail down the buffalo shoot with Leslie and get out of the house. Looking into the mirror, he ran a small paring knife through his thick white hair to straighten it out. He pulled up his collar and threw on a rumpled jacket nearby, then opened the door like a gladiator entering the arena. He tried to point his eyes straight ahead and barrel past the women, shouting, "I've got work to do, ladies," but he couldn't avoid seeing them. There stood his spouse, glaring at him like a pit viper, and there too was Serena Rawlinson, little knitted people shaking crazily on her wrist, hair in two topknots, red-faced, like a mad cowgirl. Guy shoved past them both and took the stairs two at a time. A busy man, a lavishly paid man, he sure as hell didn't have to talk to crazed females out to get him, even if one of them was his wife.

eleven

THE OFFICE

G uy slid down the street toward the corner, banging on the window of the awaiting Town Car, so grateful for his escape that he vowed to drink water for the rest of his life. In the service of this, he grabbed a bottle of Evian from the bag of goodies that always hung behind the passenger seat, while his driver, Jorge, looked back at this new water-swilling Guy in amazement. In his briefcase he had the buffalo drawings on tissue paper, and he was making up in his head how to show the actual attack of Oncreon 1 as something concrete, like an animal assault. Tigers were always being used to depict cars. Why not buffalo as targeted cancer killers? With the cunning of an addict, he fleshed out an entire campaign in the twelve minutes it took to arrive at LaGuardia and Knole. He splashed water on his jacket and rubbed it with a handkerchief; then he pulled up the collar on his blue shirt, enough to make himself presentable, if tired looking, the bags under his eyes significantly puffed out. Still, those bags made people think he was working hard.

As he exited the car, he wondered how his cohorts would react to his presence, after he had, in an epistolary fashion, mooned them. For Guy, who'd experienced more or less every disgrace in life except falling into the gutter, this was not an insurmountable problem. Attitude was all. He blew past the amazed receptionist and strode down the hallway. He knew that Leslie would be waiting in the fat leather chairs outside his door, and there she was, formidable legs crossed, sipping a coffee. "Leslie! Wonderful to see you. Come into my office."

The big woman appeared momentarily unnerved by the ladies' underwear strewn around, and so was Guy, who had forgotten his instructions to the janitorial staff, "Never move any object or piece of paper that belongs to me." He instantly recouped by grabbing up the little skirt, the halter-top, the stockings and shoving them into a filing cabinet, all the while muttering about "Some new clients, in the lingerie business. We were batting around ideas." Belatedly he spotted the panties and yanked them up too, but in that moment had time to glance down and see Claudia's note, in which she apparently professed her love. Petrified, he stashed them into another cabinet. His brain roared. She was in love with him? Inhaling deeply, he lowered himself into control mode. "Leslie, we've been a little slow in getting ads to you, I know." He looked at the forceful woman with short gray hair who stared at him intently. Had he zipped his fly? He was afraid to look down. He knew that a hug was out, since he hadn't even showered. "Anything to drink?" He motioned toward the glass table, adorned every day with mineral water and fresh cut limes in a porcelain dish.

"We really do need to get some ads out there. This is a very big discovery, and we're ready to tell the world."

"I know, and you should be." Guy proceeded to dazzle one

very smart woman, a doctor of medicine, the founder of a large biotech firm. After he had finished describing those stampeding buffalo, she was ready to ride one herself. The whole spiel was typical of his brilliance when he pointed his boozy brain in the direction of a goal. These wouldn't be irrelevant tigers roaring by a car. Guy's animals, formerly Jon's, would represent a perfection beyond nature, create a feeling of possibility, even triumph over disease, all from the mighty hand of Synergene.

"Thank you, Guy. This is wonderful. I'm so relieved. I knew that you'd do something brilliant for us." She grasped his hand as he steered her toward the door.

Leslie de Santis signed off on the campaign, authorizing the expenditure of almost a million dollars for their company's first television advertisement ever, meant to stamp their brand onto the American hide.

After she'd gone, Guy sank down in his chair, sweating, conscious that he really did smell. He took a napkin, poured out some Evian, and began wiping it over his face and up around his neck. One down, two, three, or was it four to go? Next up, Jonathan Neel. Guy had stolen his pitch, basically his storyboards for Buffalo Grill. Maybe he could steal something else off his computer? But he was afraid to go out into the hall. He searched his file cabinet until he found the panties and snatched off the note from Claudia. Reading it again, he shivered. Then he realized it must have something to do with the underwear. Was she into underwear?

Jon's office was only steps from Guy's, and he figured he could somehow sneak in. But where was Jon? He went to his own computer, author of his woe, enemy, villain, and started punching at the keys randomly. He didn't have the courage to see what had happened to the email system. He hoped it had exploded. Were people talking about him on it? He went to his office door again and peeked out. Nobody was around. He opened the door slightly, and who should come loping down the hall but Seth. Guy made as if to slam it, but the computer expert strode toward him, determined. In a sudden about-face, he yanked on Seth's shirtsleeve and pulled him into his office. "You bastard, you son of a bitch, you've ruined me. I should kill you now, here, at the foot of this fucking machine."

Frightened, Seth pulled back. "Why are you yelling at me?"

"You sent that thing out, you little pischer, you measly-assed computer hacker. That's what you did. You read it and thought, let's have a little fun with someone," Guy was screaming now, "who is the president of a major corporation!" He strode over to his desk and grabbed an enormous pair of scissors.

Seth Greenblatt, for all his paunch and retiring nature, could drop Guy Danziger any day of the week. He straightened himself up, ready to slug it out with a man who could not only fire him, but also cause him to be permanently unemployed. "You sent it out yourself, sir."

"Shut up, you criminal."

"You sent out the 'Confessions' file yourself."

"Are you insane? Why would I do that?"

Seth chose this moment to take a flight of fancy and drift off into poetry. "Ours is not to reason why. Ours is but to . . ." Guy advanced on him, still clutching the scissors. "Look, you must have been reading it or adding to it while the office mail system was up and then—zap. Microsoft Outlook can be dangerous. I'll give you the date and time."

"My God, my God," Guy moaned and sank down into one of

his fat chairs, still gripping the scissors. "I'm going to kill myself."

Sympathetically, Seth muttered, "Maybe you could get some kind of help."

"Help is all I get, and it's killing me."

"People will forget about it anyway. Nothing's real on the web."

"Somehow I don't think my wife is going to take that view."

"She didn't see it though, did she?"

"No, but one of the several adwomen cannibals in my life is probably telling her everything right this second." There was a knock on the door.

"Go away!" Guy shouted.

"I should take off. Just let me know if there's anything else you need." Seth was better with computer cables and software than with suicidal art directors, and he wanted to get away from the man.

Guy grabbed him by the shirtsleeve. "Don't you ever tell anyone that I sent out the file myself, or I'll kill you, I swear to God I will. No one must know."

"Fine, fine. It'll be our little secret."

Guy yanked him as if he were a dog on a leash. "Swear!"

"I swear. Jesus—"

"Guy, I need to talk to you." It was Claudia's distinctive voice from outside his door.

"Go!" Guy yelled and shoved Seth through it.

Decked out in a black dress, black stockings, and black shoes, Claudia looked like a powerful Sicilian matriarch, even with the blond hair. She wore an armful of silver bangles, an indicator of heavy irritation, and came around to the front of Guy's chair, squatting down in front of him. Good God, was this some prelude to seduction? Closing his eyes, he said, "I'm having a stroke. Call the ambulance."

"Guy, you're not having a stroke." Her voice was really low now. He could hardly hear her. "I want you to go home and get some sleep, and we'll talk about all this tomorrow."

"I can't go home." He opened his eyes. She still squatted before him. He was afraid she was frozen there, and he would have to pull her up, too much physical contact for him right now.

Her voice lowering even further, she said, "All right. Stay here. In ten minutes I'll take you out for an early dinner, and we can talk over recent events." She stood, all on her own.

"OK," he moaned. Was she going to declare herself? Oh God, why did so many women love him?

Between the time he talked to Claudia and headed out to Fressen, he put on the clean shirt that always hung in his closet—in case of an all-nighter—brushed his teeth and combed his hair. Eyeballing himself in the mirror, he said out loud, "I look like a troll," then realized that very shortly he would have to contend with both his wife and Serena Rawlinson. He'd have to kill that mangy producer, that was the only solution.

At the restaurant, Claudia welcomed him with a black-gloved arm, and he ordered a martini dirty with olives, defiant against the rule that he never drink in front of anyone of importance in his firm. "Guy, Guy, what am I going to do with you?" She stared at him now through her tight skin and carefully arranged hair. "Why are you such a bad boy?"

"I don't know what you mean, Claudia?" He gulped his drink.

"I can only do so much for you."

Unfortunately, Guy processed every remark of hers as some

offshoot of the putative love note he'd received. He didn't know whether to go for flirtatious or coy, worse yet, he'd lost track of whether or not she'd read firsthand his own mini-memoir or someone had merely summarized it for her. Looking at her obliquely, he decided she wasn't too bad, when the lights were dim. Might be fun, with the legs.

"Guy—"

"Claudia, I got your note."

"Yes, I wanted to talk to you about that. I'm sorry to say, I'd been drinking."

To confess this to him was like kissing the ring of the pope. "Well, I don't know what to say—" Guy drifted toward the flirt.

Claudia's voice dropped even lower and in the restaurant din, he had to lean in even closer to hear. "I was bombed, Guy, hammered. I did it as a joke, probably because I was drinking straight out of the vodka bottle in your desk."

"Thank God. I thought yet another woman was in love with me."

"I've read your 'Confessions.' I don't think so."

He wanted to take the high road of moral outrage here, accuse her of invading his privacy, complain about the disloyalty of various so-called employees, but he didn't have the heart to do so, especially given the recently revealed intel that he'd sent the email out himself. Claudia slapped him on the arm. "Your activities have destabilized our entire operation, and you've involved two pivotal players, Serena and Janey." He certainly didn't want to talk about this, didn't even want to react to any of it. Instead, he chose this moment to break the news that he'd finally succeeded in creating an ad for Synergene which, as of this very day, Leslie de Santis had committed money to. He described the spot in detail, trying to underscore its vast importance to the agency. "We seem to have a preponderance of buffalo in our ads these days," Claudia noted, "but if Leslie has signed off on it, it's a go. Jon Neel has something like this in the works. Maybe we can double up on the shoot. You can go out to Arizona together." Did she know that he had filched the idea? He vowed to stonewall if she should ask.

Claudia ordered another apple martini. "I thought you were a cross dresser when I saw all that underwear." Guy started to laugh. He hadn't laughed in weeks. They amused themselves on into the evening over fried calamari, baked swordfish, and two bottles of a crisp, rich Merlot, and when they finally staggered out into the street, Claudia said, "We'll take you home."

With a start he realized that he couldn't go home, and as he slid across the pungent leather of the back seat of her sedan, he said, "You can leave me off at Dean and DeLuca's. I need to walk, maybe get another coffee."

"Are you sure? It's starting to snow." Nevertheless, that's what Guy did, getting out several blocks from his house. Even that had him in a panic. The moment Claudia's car swung out of view, he hailed a cab and made his slow way up to the Lowell, an elegant European-style hotel directly off Madison. With nothing but the clothes on his back, Guy Danziger spent the night in a junior suite, going out only to get a toothbrush and a comb. He felt curiously free, as light as the snowflakes that came down softly in the deep night. He couldn't sleep though. His problem: he rehearsed over and over in his mind the inevitable events that would occur in the next few days. He knew every word that the fight with his wife would entail. He could hear its beginning but could not foresee its end. A furious storm of wrath would erupt from Serena, something he would have to contain, how he did not know. As for his work, each step in the laborious process of getting a commercial on the air was engraved onto his brain and had been for years. It involved the ability to focus on details, especially in the editing room, where he earned his huge salary with a meticulous sense of art and image. All these scenarios collided in his psyche, torturing him with fear. He climbed out of bed and grabbed one of the small vodka bottles from the minibar, twisting off the top. As he drank, he watched the snow fall. It was beginning to stick.

twelve

THE PLAY

E vents moved so swiftly after Eleanor called Weill Cornell that she began to think the fates actually wanted her to move to New York. The exchange officer was thrilled she might be available, and almost as soon as she faxed in her resume, called to suggest two medical teams she could join. Tony emailed her the name of one of his buddies, a dancer who was headed off to Europe for three months and wanted to sublet his Gramercy Park apartment for a ridiculously low sum of money. After a brief conversation with the man, she made an appointment to meet him there on the same day as her interview. Even Mrs. Forrey helped out, suggesting the name of a student to stay in Eleanor's Ithaca house and watch Coco. The older woman also slipped Seth Greenblatt's phone number, along with those of several other promising young men, whose parents she knew, into her purse when she wasn't looking. As for opening night, Eleanor did have one black evening dress, rather low cut though. She'd worn it only twice, and now the thought of it, and of her new haircut, seemed intensely appealing. She burned to know what Tony meant about the "perfect plot" in his phone message.

By now her assignment loomed as a sacred trust, and she believed that Sasha had spoken true words in the heat of passionate intent. Thus, for what she came to regard as her first important venture into the city, Eleanor felt no guilt at all when she splurged and took American Airlines. She brought a huge suitcase because she wasn't quite sure what each event would demand in terms of dress and had, in her usual fashion, piled in the sweaters. Still, her hair was intact. She had spent several hours with the brush and blow dryer making sure she'd mastered Jamiesen's instructions and now considered herself a pro. Regarding the interview, scheduled for two hours after her arrival, she'd decided on a green wool suit with a black turtleneck underneath. The outfit was classic, vaguely intellectual, with a hint of that color Sasha once decreed essential to the true New Yorker: "Black, Ellie, at once impeccable and threatening."

The New York Hospital/Weill Cornell meeting went so well that the young man questioning her suggested she come right away. He wanted her to join a neurological team involved in treating epilepsy and other brain lesions, and the assignment sounded much more demanding than her work in Ithaca. "When do you think you can be here, Eleanor?"

"Let's see, I don't know, two weeks maybe. How would that be?"

"Great. Remember, though, the group is already working, and they need all their research documented as soon as possible."

She had to race to get a cab for Gramercy Park, at rush hour with her suitcase, but even the snow and icy cold didn't dull her excitement. Tony's dancer friend was in his fifties, sporting a dark brown toupee, frantic to get someone to take care of his pet bird, an orange-and-yellow sun conure who sat demurely on his perch in an antique cage. "His name is Harry, don't ask why. He often takes to someone, but then again he squawked so much at the cleaning lady, she quit." Eleanor moved her hand into the cage slowly, while Harry shook his head from side to side, fluffed up his feathers, then hopped right onto her finger. "He likes you!" Tony's friend beamed, and it was a done deal. The studio apartment was in a historic building just off the park and consisted of a cavernous living room with a sink and hot plate hidden away from the big room by a blue velvet screen. On the walls were oil paintings, mostly still lifes. It had an old-world feel, slightly decayed chic. She thought it was grand.

Meanwhile, Eleanor's intended victim had succumbed to his own sense of obligation and gone to the family residence in Westfield, New York, to talk to his brother about the question of moving out, even though he knew he could stay only overnight. Stupidly, Jon had promised to attend the opening of a new musical that someone named Tony Lowe was starring in back in the city. Because of the scrawled note on the envelope saying, "I know our friend Sasha would have wanted you to see this," guilt had made him accept the invitation. Due to weather, the flight to Buffalo had been the usual painful comedy of delays on the ground and delays in the air, so three solid hours after the scheduled arrival time, he rented a car at the airport and headed west. This year he found the perilous two-hour journey through whiteout conditions comforting.

His boyhood home, a cabin-like structure built from an architectural kit by his father, occupied a bluff overlooking Lake Erie. Jon left the red Toyota in the driveway and was trying to wrest his bag from the trunk when Buster, their golden retriever, bounded out through the snow to welcome him. Nothing had changed in the wide, capacious lawn, from the vegetable garden that occupied the far edge of the property to the brothers' childhood wooden swing. It seemed quiet and peaceful, though he registered uneasily that a Neel family scene would be anything but.

Dinner that night was typical, Walter interrupting every minute, holding onto a conversation in his head while the others tried to keep the talk superficial. "Jon, tell them I want to go, I have to go," his heavyset, anxious younger brother muttered obsessively into his ear.

"I will definitely talk to them. Don't worry," Jon whispered back.

Martha Neel, a tall woman with braided gray hair, dressed in an embroidered caftan that she had made herself, gave her younger son a look, while the boys' father, Ron, gulped at his red wine and picked the meat off a chicken leg. Always at family dinners the conversation swirled around Walter, then occasionally dipped down to include the older son, suddenly veering off again. Perhaps this was why Jon could follow even the most bizarre conversational gambits among ad types in New York. He worked well with the convoluted. "We don't have to discuss the idea of an apartment now, Walter. Your brother is here for such a short time, and I think we should find out how his business is going," she said. Though as a copywriter, Jon was a practicing member of one branch of the arts, his mother never deigned to recognize anything but his "business," especially now that he'd become an executive.

"Saw that Buffalo Grill thing. Boy, thought I was going out

of my mind." Ron Neel, twenty years older than his wife, had only a dim sense of where Jon fit in the advertising world, though he'd been told fifty times.

"Believe me, we didn't do it on purpose. I'm still trying to find out who's actually responsible."

"You mean you don't know?" his mother said sharply.

"I liked it," Walter said. "I always wait for Buffalo Grill, but sometimes I don't understand. This time I did because they kept saying it so much. Like my cartoon stories, they kept on going and going. Maybe you got the idea from me?"

"I'm glad somebody liked it," Jon said and patted his brother on the back.

Walter was tugging on his sleeve, "Come see my new drawings upstairs, Jon."

"Walter, could you wait just a moment until we finish dinner?" Martha Neel said. "What do you mean, you don't know who made the commercial run so many times?"

"I mean, Mother, that it was either a genuine mistake by the Traffic Department or somebody has it in for me. Certain people in corporate America will do anything to damage another person who appears to be gaining on them or outdistancing them." Somehow, if he spoke sternly to her, she might, for one moment, realize that what he did was important, though of course he knew he was just reinforcing his mother's sour notions of commerce.

"Insane, that's what I call it. Unbelievable. They're just jackals. I don't see how someone with your temperament, your sensitivity, can put up with it." She broke apart a thick slice of bread and nibbled on it.

"I'm not that sensitive, Mom. In fact, some people would say

I'm just as hard and cruel as they are. My girlfriend who died—"

She jumped on him. "Died? First off, who knew you even had a girlfriend? And now you say she died?"

"Sasha, remember her?"

Walter chimed in, "I remember her."

"How could you remember her? Did you ever meet her?" his father said.

"I have her photograph, one that Jon gave me. She's beautiful. She's *Leptra* in my series, *The Moon Beyond.*"

"Wait, how come you know about her and I don't?" Martha Neel asked.

"I know people," Walter said proudly.

"Of course you do," his father said, glaring at his wife. This looked to be the age-old family interaction that Jon genuinely loathed, the reason he almost never came home, except to visit his brother. He so pitied this scruffy younger version of himself for being stuck in a house with two people who appeared to dislike their children that he determined to do everything possible to get him out of there.

"Sasha Cole, a woman I saw off and on for a couple of years, died in that terrible car accident outside Chicago, you know, that involved the rock singers, two months ago."

"My God," Martha said.

"That's terrible, Jon," his father murmured.

"She died? She died?" Only now Walter realized what had been said about the pretty lady in the picture. He began to wail and rocked his chair back and forth, "I don't like people in my pictures to die. What could happen then? What's going to happen?" Jon took hold of Walter's arm and led him off into the living room.

The elder brother deflected the younger's concern by asking him about his latest cartoon cycle, a series of froglike creatures that swam in pink fountains of soda pop. There were twenty-five drawings at least, and, fortunately, Walter couldn't stay sad for long, as he flipped through the pictures he kept in a large leather portfolio. He too had a girlfriend, a wholesome-looking woman with short brown hair, photographed at the mental health center where Walter worked. "I want to have sex with her. I've already done it, and now I want to keep on doing it. But they don't want me to."

Jon put his arm around his brother's shoulder. "Take heart, buddy. They don't want anyone to have sex. "

"Nobody?"

"Show me your images of *Leptra*, Walter." In among more drawings and small paintings, his brother searched out several sketches of a tall redhead wound in black leather off conquering tiny twig-like creatures on the moon. The face looked remarkably like Sasha's. Jon felt his vision blur. "Can I have one of these?" he asked carefully.

"Sure, take all you want."

"No, just the one that looks most like Sasha."

"Sasha, Sasha!" Walter started wailing again.

"Where do you want to move?" It was always easy for Jon to distract his brother.

"To an apartment in Jamestown. I already have it—Susan and I put down money. I'm leaving here no matter what, I swear."

"I know you are." Since Jon sent Walter a thousand dollars a month, and he made another thousand at his job, with no real expenses, his younger brother had saved a lot.

Trying to sleep in his old room, soccer trophies still up on the wall, Jon worked on plotting how to get Walter out of the house the next day. He needn't have worried, as his brother had a plan. Later that night the younger man sat on the edge of the bed, fingering an ancient slinky toy, to explain. "I've got my bags all packed. At breakfast something will happen, and we can race out."

"What will happen?" Jon asked him.

"Wait and see."

The next morning, at a tense, silent meal, Walter took a bite of toast and suddenly reeled backwards in his chair, falling down with a great clatter. "What's wrong, darling?" his mother cried, while Jon sprang up and tried to pull him from the floor. Ron Neel just kept on reading the paper.

"Walter, can you breathe, can you stand?" Jon knelt beside him. Walter opened his eyes and mouthed the words, "Outside, outside."

"I'll take him outside," Jon said while the younger man hung onto his older brother's arm, tongue lolling out of his mouth, something he never did. Once in the front hall, Walter straightened up, grabbed their jackets off the hook and dragged Jon out the front door. They raced around the back of the house to the car, tripping and stumbling the whole way. Jon felt like a comic book hero himself. Only when the Toyota squealed out of the driveway did Ron and Martha Neel apprehend what had happened.

It took almost all day to get Walter ensconced in his new place, a furnished one-bedroom over the local hardware store in nearby Jamestown. It was simple and clean, and Walter kept bouncing on the bed. The one problem—his paints. They seemed to fill half of the living room. "I'll set them up. You'll see," Jon said.

Unaccountably, Walter now became anxious that his brother should leave before Susan arrived. "She'll see you and then she won't want me."

"Don't be silly."

"No, she will. You get everybody. You always did." Jon really did want to meet the girl, but his brother was becoming frantic, increasingly upset too about what the parents were doing right at this minute. "Will they call the police?"

"You're thirty-five years old. It's ridiculous. You can live on your own."

"With Susan."

Jon left his brother beaming in the door of his first apartment. There would be no smiling at the family manse, such as it was, but he had to go back and explain or at least protect his brother, a role he had played his whole life. At heart, he was embarrassed by his own good fortune; he chose to ignore it, consumed by the ever-present problem of keeping Walter happy and placating his mother over his abandoned musical career. Whenever a radio performance came on or a televised symphony, Martha Neel would insist, when Jon was there, on turning it off. She refused to let the wound heal. Finally he told her, "Look, I just didn't want to play in the Toledo Symphony. I wasn't good enough for anyplace else."

"You're wrong, totally wrong. Besides, what's so bad about Toledo? You never know what you can do when you start out with a talent like yours."

"I had no talent, Mom. I had a little learning and a lot of practice," he said, but it was a dead conversation. Martha had stopped listening the day he abandoned his music major; she sold his expensive French cello a week later. The one he had in his New York apartment was a new German thing, as young as a sapling.

Jon girded himself for a scene at home. When he opened the front door, he stepped into deep silence. His bags, which had been in his bedroom, now stood in the hall. His father was nowhere to be found, but he could hear his mother upstairs. She folded laundry in Walter's old bedroom and still didn't look up when he went into the room. He sat down on the side of the bed, but she refused to make eye contact. "It had to happen, Mom, you know it. You couldn't keep him here forever. And he's fine, the apartment is pleasant."

"I know he's got a girl." She said this softly. At least she was rational.

"It's a good thing. She seemed very presentable in the picture, but he didn't want me to meet her."

His mother finally looked at him. "Of course he didn't," she said angrily.

"Mom," Jon said and reached out to touch her on the arm.

Flushing red, Martha Neel cried, "Get out. Just get out. I can't stand the sight of either one of you."

Inside the rental car, Jon felt oddly relieved. At last his mother had uttered a true sentence. He knew that she resented her two sons, hated them even, and that she'd never been suited to being a mother. She would have loved to play in the Toledo Symphony.

After traveling hours appropriate for an arctic journey, he really just wanted to settle into the safety of his apartment, but Jon had to prepare himself for an evening out. If it was Sasha's friend, he had to go, even though he didn't recognize the name "Tony Lowe," even though he was uneasy about his brother and troubled over his job. He still hadn't identified whatever big dog snapped at his heels. He sank down, scotch in hand, pondering the forces of doom vectoring in upon his very self. The invitation from Tony lay on the coffee table, *Blowing Smoke*, opening that evening at eight.

In the meantime, Eleanor had upgraded herself from a tiny hotel on Lexington and was staying at the Hotel Wales on Ninety-Second and Madison. Breakfast came with the room, and there was tea in the afternoon on the second floor, along with piano performances, so civilized, she thought. In preparation for the big theatre opening, she'd gone back to the same hairstylist for a trim. "Why don't you let Marla try some of our new makeup on you?" Jamie suggested after he'd finished, and his assistant proceeded almost to remake the lines of Eleanor's face. Now, staring at herself in the hotel bathroom mirror, she looked truly different, more exotic, the white in her skin and the color in her cheeks somehow more outstanding. The black dress swept over her shoulders and cupped her full breasts most beautifully. It draped down to her ankles, and on her feet she wore delicate black satin shoes with minute bows. Over her shoulders she carried a burgundy velvet duster, Edwardian in feel, that she'd had for ages but never had the courage to wear. Surely this alluring costume would suit for *Blowing Smoke*, a musical starring someone she actually knew.

The front desk buzzed. Her livery car awaited. Tony had adopted the point of view that, for tonight anyway, Eleanor's feet should never touch pavement, and so her inadequate wrap would work, despite the cold. As she made her way toward the revolving door, she was conscious that several people in the lobby of the Wales had turned to gape. Maybe one of her nipples showed. She looked down quickly. She was so nervous in the back of the sedan that she kept trying to get a glimpse of herself in the mirror, even though it meant occasionally catching the eye of the driver, who looked back at her and smiled.

At the theatre, she tried to open the door herself, but the driver ran around to help her out, pointing out exactly where he would wait after the performance. What incredible luxury, she thought, and everyone looked so beautiful. A confluence of the handsome and well-dressed had converged on this very spot. She possessed one of two house seats allotted to Tony Lowe, and slowly she moved to the seventh row center. The orchestra rose up into full chorus as the house lights dimmed. Just as they did, Jonathan Neel came striding down the aisle and sat down right next to Eleanor. She looked over with a start, but he seemed even more upset than she was. She smiled weakly and prepared to spend two hours looking at her handsome friend up on the stage.

Blowing Smoke involved the life and times of an advertising executive, played by Tony Lowe. It detailed his upward movement through the ranks and sported revolving sets and scores of dancing minions dressed as production assistants. Tony's songs contained raunchy lyrics about success and failure, and he proved to be an agile dancer and a witty interpreter of singspiel, which offset the dour story line—a man who advertises cigarettes nearly dies of lung cancer. Enchanted to see someone she knew dominating the stage of a Broadway play, Eleanor could almost forget the man who sat next to her.

He certainly couldn't forget her. The way Jon was posi-

tioned, he looked straight down into the décolletage of her lus-
cious black dress. He was acutely aware of her beautiful shoulders as she relaxed against the back of the chair. Besides her hair
and her costume, though, something else was different about
her. He hadn't seen anything of her body before, hidden as it had
been beneath all those ponchos and heavy sweaters. She
breathed beside him now, face uplifted toward the stage, with
bright dark eyes, and he startled himself with the sexual nature
of his own reflections. Here was a woman, lively, intense, and she
hated him.

During intermission Eleanor stood awkwardly and finally
wedged herself out of the row past Jonathan Neel. Just as she
snagged a glass of wine from the tiny bar in the lobby, Jon approached. "I'm sorry. This is probably very unpleasant for you,
that we'd be sitting next to each other," he said.

"I am surprised. Tony Lowe didn't tell me you were coming,"
she said, glancing in his direction. Despite her harsh feelings
against him, she had to admit he was an imposing figure.

"Tony Lowe? The lead? Do I know him? I must. I really can't
place how I know him. I meet a lot of people. Half of them I
don't actually know, if that makes any sense to you."

"No, it doesn't make much sense." Her new hair and clothes
made her feel much bolder. "Are you going to the party after the
play?"

"I'm invited. But maybe you'd prefer it if I didn't go."

"Of course not. You should go. Tony must have wanted you
to." She spent the second act in painful anticipation of what more
her Machiavellian actor friend might have in mind for them.

thirteen

THE PARTY

After the curtain fell on a rousingly well-received play, Eleanor felt she must offer Jon a ride in her car, since they were both going all the way downtown to Perestroika, a nightclub off Spring Street. As they sat awkwardly in the back seat, she could think of nothing to say, no topic without difficulties. Finally, Jon asked her what she thought of *Blowing Smoke*. "I loved it, and Tony was so wonderful. It's amazing to know someone as a real person and then see him as a character up on the stage."

"The material was pretty thin, though. Our business is always the subject of dumbed-down ridicule."

"You mean it's not funny on its own?" Eleanor remarked.

He looked at her sharply and said, "How does a medical librarian know Tony Lowe?"

"Why are you asking? You don't even know how you know him."

"True. But you should."

"I met him at Sasha's funeral."

"Hmm." That finished him for a moment. He stared out the window at the thick, soft snowflakes.

Perestroika, which one entered by walking down from the street into a cave-like structure, was filled with principals from the play and a host of other alarmingly trendy people, and as Eleanor looked at them, she shrank back. She hated moving into crowds alone. She backed right into Jon, who grasped her by the arm and shoved her forward. "Let's go see how well I know Tony Lowe." Suddenly the waves parted as the two headed for a table somewhere in the darkness. Exuberant, the actor glowed in the happiness of his success, as everyone clamored around him, but when he spotted Eleanor, he jumped up and leaned way across the tiny round table, embracing her. "Ellie, you look incredible."

"You were wonderful, Tony, magnificent."

"It's just a goofy comedy, *mit* songs." He threw his arms out and everyone laughed, then he beamed at her and said, "Have a Monopol. It's two kinds of vodka, one from St. Petersburg, the other from Siberia somewhere." Everyone turned to look at Tony's favorite woman. Jon stuck out his hand and introduced himself, and the actor replied, "I worked for you, for like a week or two, pretending to be an employee."

The man next to Tony snickered. "What could that mean?" he said.

"You did? Yes, I think I remember you."

"Who could forget Tony?" a fawning young woman remarked.

"We were on a slight downturn," Jon said.

"This man actually hired people to fill the office so the big clients wouldn't think they were going under. Brilliant, in an ad-biz kind of way." Tony was already slightly drunk and declaiming to his pals at the table.

"Weird goof," somebody muttered.

"We try a lot of creative ploys in advertising, most of which you didn't show in the play tonight."

"Sounds more like fraud to me," Eleanor muttered.

"That will be *Blowing Smoke Two*," Tony said and sank back into his chair.

Because they didn't know anyone, Jon and Eleanor were perforce joined together, especially in the consumption of Monopols. After two each, served up in oversized martini glasses, Eleanor was having trouble remembering her own name, though the drinks tasted pleasantly dry and woody. She wanted to speak to Tony about his idea for the perfect revenge, but she didn't see how she could face him again in the midst of his entourage. Instead, she excused herself to go to the ladies' room, and when she returned, felt as if she was floating in a sea of unknown faces. She scanned the crowd, but finally Jon waved her over. "I should go speak to Tony," she said to him, convinced she absolutely must achieve something with the evening, instead of just drinking quarts of vodka. As she pushed herself through the rowdy partiers, she could see the actor muscling his way toward her.

"I want to talk to you," Tony said.

"Yes, definitely. What did you mean in that phone message? You've got an idea?" All of this she yelled above the clamor surrounding them.

"I've got it," he shouted back and then pulled her into an alcove by the front entrance, where they could at least hear each other speak. "Listen, seduce and abandon. That's it. You do to him what he did to Sasha. Isn't it delicious?"

"I am so drunk, Tony."

"So am I. Who cares?" He backed her farther into the corner, trying to whisper above the noise. "This is war, Ellie. You've got to think like a general. And wouldn't Sasha just love that. In fact, she probably had it in mind all the time."

"How could I? I'm not Sasha."

"You're beautiful. Look at you. You've transformed yourself into a player. Seriously, I've had four Monopols, and I'm going directly to Bellevue after this and check in, but you should get cracking on this plan. I'll help. There's nothing so bracing as seduction."

Eleanor's head was starting to pound. "I don't think I can bring the verve to the project that you could."

"I'm not going after him. What would my boyfriend say?"

"Boyfriend? Boyfriend?"

"He's a veterinarian in Arizona, Logan Piersall, wonderful guy, totally unlike all these New York weirdoes. I see him every couple of months. That's plenty. I don't do well with domesticity, or cows." Since every eye in the room was upon them, Eleanor felt her face flush and go red. Bad enough to be among his groupies, but to be the focus of their attention, now that was frightening.

"I've got to go back to the hotel, but I'll—"

Tony put his arm around her and kissed her on the cheek. "I'll call you as soon as I sober up and read the reviews. Just don't leave town."

Eleanor's heart sank when she realized she'd probably have to take Jon to his apartment, but he saved her by announcing that he wanted to stay for a while and "enjoy the party." As far as she was concerned, he should be weeping and wailing and putting his head in a sack, but none of that appeared to be happening. No subtle signs of sorrow, though perhaps there was something behind the eyes.

"Yeah, party down," she said and made her way through the drinking, smoking crowd, out into the frigid night and her awaiting car.

Two days later, having postponed her departure for Ithaca several times to accommodate his schedule, she met up again with Tony at the Metropolitan Museum's Temple of Dendur. "My favorite place," the actor announced. The reviews had been good, for him at least, though they were critical and dismissive of what they called "an advertising musical that turns grim at the end." Tony had been described as "dazzling, charming, with a strong voice"; he was relaying this to Eleanor at breakneck speed as they sat throwing pennies into the moat surrounding the marble statues that flanked the temple. Above them soared a pyramid of glass, covered now with snow.

"I know. I read the reviews myself. It's fantastic."

"A little less than that, but still, it means the play will run for some time. And they'll sell some spinoff merchandise. Whenever I get depressed about my career, I tell myself it's better than working at Dunkin' Donuts in Albany, my first job if you can believe that."

Eleanor laughed, but she was beginning to get anxious. "I couldn't sleep all night because of your idea. And I feel guilty that I'm enjoying New York so much on Sasha's money."

"Honey, Sasha knew what she was doing when she put you on the case, so forget about it. I repeat my proposal, seduce and abandon."

"I'm not his type, I don't think, for starters, and he appears to work twenty-four hours a day."

"Hmm, maybe you should get a job at the agency. Guilt him into hiring you. You can have the apartment, at least that's what my friend said. Harry the conure has approved you."

"The thing I was thinking, actually I've sort of worked it out already, an exchange between the Schulman Library and Weill Cornell Hospital Library. That way I could spend three months here."

"Brilliant. Once you're in town, everything falls into place. You can ask him out, work your wiles."

"I don't have any wiles."

"We must conjure some up." As they wandered through the Egyptian sarcophagi, Tony seemed enchanted with the remnants of death and kept crossing his hands over his chest, intoning, "Revenge, a dish best served cold."

Despite his intriguing suggestion, Eleanor found the prospect unnerving. "It was just a failed romance, after all. We don't have to make him dead. It isn't his fault that her car crashed."

"Romance never fails, it's abandoned. Hmm, brilliant, I wonder what that means. I should be a writer. Anyway, how would you feel if you turned your back on Sasha's request?"

Eleanor shivered. "I would dream about her and hear her voice telling me to 'get' him."

"We want her to rest quietly, in peace, if you know what I mean—" Tony's voice broke as he turned away a moment.

"Don't say that, it's too sad." She clutched his arm. In front of Egyptian temples and dead pharaohs these thoughts and plots somehow made sense, but Eleanor knew that deceitful action, the kind contemplated here, was utterly foreign to her nature. Her face bespoke her heart. The realm of duplicity was one she only wanted to read about.

fourteen

THE BOARDS

F or Guy Danziger, duplicity in the form of plots, subplots, customary deceit, and unaccustomed retribution were the very lifeblood of a troubled existence. Two days without calling his wife, it was some kind of record, but he was too frightened to risk it. The thought of Serena Rawlinson in conversation with Marsia was unbearable, and even thinking about it blew out his brain circuits. He spent the whole of this miserable time at the Lowell, consuming all the liquor in the minibar, several bags of nuts, and one container of chocolate candy. For what he'd paid, he could have eaten at Le Cirque. Furthermore, his clothes had been so inadequate upon his departure from the family home that he'd gone to Barneys and dropped three thousand dollars on a leather jacket, four shirts, and a cashmere sweater, plowing through the snow in all of them.

Guy emerged from the hotel onto deserted streets piled two feet high with blackened slush. Feeling quite lost without his car and driver, he realized that public transport would be the only way to get to work. After a crowded subway ride that gave him plenty of time to reflect upon his entrance at LaGuardia and

Knole, he made his way into the building quickly, scooting to his office and slamming the door. He listened and noted the pleasant hum of voices. They were still in business. His office looked the same, but there was a note on his desk requesting his presence at an eleven-thirty meeting, signed by Serena. Would Jon be there? Surely yes, and would he instantly see that Guy had stolen his storyboards for the Synergene commercial? Rooting around inside his desk for a vodka bottle, he figured the only way to cope would be to lace his coffee. Already ten thirty, he had some time to plan, but he didn't, instead falling asleep on the couch.

He awoke to Janey Peet pounding on his office door, announcing that they needed him right away in the conference room for the meeting on the combined shoots of Synergene and Buffalo Grill. Guy groped around for a sweater, splashed some cold water on his face from the carafe, and loped down the hall, terrified at what he might encounter. "We'll shoot in Tucson. It's rocky, deserty, and picturesque. The only potential ding—we'll have to truck the buffalo in from southern Montana. I'll hire a vet who'll take charge. The date—second week in January," Serena intoned, barely glancing his way as he entered the room. Guy began a slow doodle on the pad of paper before him, not looking up. Like a blind man, he could recognize the participants by voice. "I do have an important piece of news. I've hired Juan Angel Peña as the director," Serena announced.

Guy focused on her seriously for the first time. "Why Juan Angel?" he said slowly. Peña was an imposing Argentinean whom everyone feared, not only everyone in the room, but vast numbers of workers throughout advertising.

"He knows animals, does all those amazing Ferrari commercials. He can make something out of nothing, which seems to apply in this case." She smiled toothily. Guy looked down again and continued drawing circles around each other. He felt as if he was sitting there stark naked with his penis glued to the top of his head.

"He's such a son-of-a-bitch. He'll kill us or we'll kill him," Jon said.

Hearing his rival's voice, Guy reared up suddenly, in time to see the younger man studying the Synergene storyboards, full of raging buffalo charging down a hill to cure cancer. "He's a real cocksucker, he fights with all the actors, and his daily rate is something like fifty thousand dollars," Guy muttered, frightened to throw himself into the fray but hoping to deflect any other missiles lobbed at him, whether by Jon or worse yet Janey. His little schoolgirl had been staring across the table at him as if he were Vlad the Impaler.

Serena now turned the full force of her producer-hood onto Guy's quaking frame. "I don't think you're in a position to bounce him off the team unless you want to find someone else at this late date yourself." She spit these words like a termite squirting poisoned juice, and he finally got the courage to look up at her.

"Maybe it'll be fun to be out in Bumblefuck, USA, with a ravaging Argentinean who makes it seem as if everyone really needs a Ferrari," Guy growled. He was beginning to think Sing Sing would be fun.

At last Jonathan Neel spoke up. "Nothing about this will be fun. I'm amazed at these buffalo, Guy. How did you think of them?"

The room fell silent. Guy sniffled slightly into his spiked coffee. "They came to me in a dream," he said, and Janey Peet began to laugh.

"Guy, could I see you privately, please?" Serena said, standing abruptly. Guy didn't want to see her, didn't want to know her ever again. He wanted her to die like a flame before his very eyes. Nevertheless, he had to get out of that room, so he stood and followed her. As they entered his office, he turned, thinking somehow to embrace the reedy harridan and stop the flow of awfulness coming his way. Just as his face swiveled toward her, she leaned in as if for a kiss, then threw a right upper cut straight to his jaw. Down he fell, like a tree.

Caught between outrage and perplexity at Guy's raging buffalo, Jon decided to compare the two sets of storyboards and determine how large the theft. In Buffalo Grill's early days, scores of the hairy critters had galloped across the plains, dying to be steak, but that had all ended in the early 1980s, and the client hadn't used any image of the real animals since. First off, the connection between running haunches and an actual piece of meat seemed altogether too bloody. Secondly, whoever dreamed up "Buff-aa-ll-o Grii-ii-ll" as a whistled cadence strained the imaginations of succeeding copywriters to fit this paranormal bleat into any real-life setting. This time, finally, Jon had managed to merge all elements into a Western tableau that made some sense, with the slogan as a disappearing cry over the mountains, away from the animals themselves, and off into the Native American past of nobility and courage.

Guy seemed to have stolen the whole look and feel of Jon's commercial, but of course not any of the copy and obviously not the tagline. He had set his little vignette in a rocky desert valley that suddenly, horrifically, became suffused with digital blood.

Pounding hooves would thunder along in the background, and then a herd of buffalo would stampede forward, blowing the blood away as if Moses himself had appeared to part the Red Sea. Music was to be classical and bombastic, a paean to the forces of charging drugs, and who better to know their power, Jon thought? The perfect match of subject and man.

He fingered the boards and looked out his window at the snow that continued to fall. Confronted with the outright theft of an idea, he was momentarily stumped, stuck in the torpor that Sasha's death had created and unable to feel he deserved anything better than what he was getting. Karmic forces were now pushing him toward revenge, though, and if it was Guy or Guy and one of his minions, a singular piece of good fortune had come his way. He already knew how to deal with their director, Juan Angel Peña, a notorious figure who had a gift for spotting weakness and would, if he wished, press someone until the knuckle went all the way through to the bone. Out of his filing cabinet Jon pulled old storyboards for a Japanese sports car to relive his former experiences with the director. They'd done a standard automobile shot of the car driving fast on wet pavement over curving coastal roads, but the haunting lyrics of a suicidal seventies musician underlay the striking images. It was magical, having won Jon several awards, and Juan Angel had played a serious role in its creation.

Suddenly he decided that this Arizona jaunt was quite promising, since if all else failed, he could manipulate their perennially loaded president into inflaming the director, with who knew what nasty results. The man who could steal his storyboards could also be the Buffalo Grill mastermind, but he had to have concrete proof of Guy's guilt, and for that he needed the services of the redoubtable Seth. The computer expert wasn't saying much, though, and reiterated this as he stood before Jon, shifting from one foot to the other, sipping a cup of coffee. "I can't believe you went through all the Traffic logs. How long did it take you?" Seth asked.

"Hours. I lost track." In his one serious attempt to detect the criminal, Jon had indeed spent a mind-numbing amount of time inspecting the logs, to no avail. Now he motioned for Seth to sit down on one of his couches. "The network said the spot ran as per our direction, so someone high up—and I'm beginning to think it was Guy Danziger—must have created an alternate log and sent it over to CBS, one that we don't have here."

"That's a pretty complicated thing to do with the system, and I've got to tell you, Guy doesn't know bupkis about it. He could never have done that."

"Maybe someone helped him," Jon said, suddenly realizing that this young man might have been involved in the whole evil caper.

Seth sipped his coffee and finally said, "Some strange stuff has been happening on the system."

"What do you mean?"

"I've been sworn to secrecy, but frankly, I'm getting a little tired of all this cloak-and-dagger stuff. Why don't people just do their work?"

"Why indeed? Come on, Seth, spill it. What is it you want to tell me? You can confess, you know."

"Hey, I had absolutely nothing to do with the Buffalo Grill foul-up."

"I didn't say you did, but you might have helped someone, perhaps inadvertently."

"No, no way, I would never do anything to jeopardize the agency like that, but remember the 'Confessions' file? I know who sent it out and basically how it happened." Jon just looked at the man, praying that he himself wasn't the guilty party. "Guy sent it out all on his own by mistake! He got confused while working with the file on his desktop and office email. They were both open at the same time, and he must have clicked on 'send' or 'enter.' But he told me not to tell anyone. In fact, I think he threatened to kill me."

"Thank God."

"What?"

"No, I just mean, thank God it wasn't me. I couldn't really be sure."

"I'm sure. But you can't tell him I told you."

"I won't. Thank you, Seth. I want you to look into this Buffalo Grill thing and try to figure it out. Who would have had the expertise? That person could have helped Guy." Seth promised that he would in his spare time.

The firm thwacking rendered to Guy Danziger's head had had a bracing effect. Without pursuing Serena down the hall, he vowed that finally, absolutely, he must go home. Whatever Serena had told his wife, it would be better to hear it from her than from an aging Tweety Bird. After all, Marsia did love him, he was sure of it. And he loved her, if only because she made the world safe for him. She was the mother of his child, a young woman who showed every sign of being a far better person than her father, and surely his wife was responsible for this. Besides, the holiday season was upon them, which Marsia took seriously. She loved

Christmas festivities, planning huge spreads and lavish parties, while Guy just liked to hide in offices and editing suites. Knowing this about her made him feel ashamed, vulnerable. He packed up his newly acquired Barneys clothing and set off for Soho.

No sign of Marsia, only a note on the front hall table. With trembling hands he opened it. Rory had scrawled that she was going skiing for three weeks over Christmas, thus thoughtfully taking herself out of the domestic mix. The house was clean, nothing out of place. "No sign of foul play," Guy said out loud. At one point, he'd had the mad thought that Serena had actually knocked off his wife so they could march down the aisle. Then he remembered there'd be a bunch of them marching, namely Serena's husband and her two children. He peeked into a few of Marsia's drawers, everything neat as usual, the beautiful silks seemingly color-coded. She must have gone to Long Island.

Grabbing his weekend bag from the closet, Guy determined to travel to their house in Water Mill that very night, though it was the middle of the week. He reclined in his big Lincoln Town Car, sipping vodka, pondering what his story should be. He would have such an advantage if he just knew what Serena had said, but could he call her? He certainly had never phoned her at home, in fear of the mythical family members. She had a cell phone, which seemed to be implanted in her skull. That was risky too. His own cell was always on, his one concession to the wired world; it helped create the illusion that he worked. The thing started chirping. Should he answer? He poked the button and held it up to his ear, saying nothing.

"Hello?" a woman's voice said. He waited for the caller to reveal herself. "Hello, Guy, is that you?" As if being vectored in by his thoughts, it was Serena.

"Yes?"

"Where are you? We have to talk."

"The last time that happened, you hit me."

"You deserved much worse than that."

"I don't know what I deserve anymore, Serena. I just need to rest. I'm going out to the island to find my wife."

"Your wife?"

"What did you tell her?"

"You'd seriously like to know that, wouldn't you?"

"Yes, I most definitely would," he said, aware however that any direct request would inflame her perverse soul.

"I'm just going to let you find that out all by your little old self!" As the line went dead, Guy held the silent phone out in front of him. It was a defining moment. He had to get rid of her. No matter what happened with Marsia, he had to offload Serena Rawlinson from his life. She would threaten him, that he knew, and with something big, if she hadn't already done it in speaking to his wife.

As the black sedan came to a stop in front of his modified farmhouse, so expensively repaired, Guy spotted a light upstairs. Standing out in the cold, he surveyed the soft, snowy landscape. Marsia's rose garden lay buried, but he could see the pedestal of the birdbath and the upraised arm of a cherub. Trying to figure out what was going on inside the house, he stood for a moment before the front door but could hear nothing. He pushed on the door; it was open. He stepped over the threshold of what he took to be the second half of his life.

His heavy steps on the wooden stairs groaned through the house. Whoever was upstairs certainly had fair warning. A light came from under the bathroom door, but it was closed.

He could hear splashing. He planted himself in front of the door, then tapped slightly. No answer. He tapped again harder, and the door swung open before him. Marsia extended herself full out in the immense tub, her right leg arched slightly, her dark hair piled up on top of her head. She looked like the strong, strange goddess that she was. Turning her face toward her husband, she grimaced, then picked up the glass of red wine that rested on the stonework around the tub. She cupped the goblet in her hand.

Unable to breathe, Guy sat down on the stool. His wife said nothing but stood up, still holding the glass, bubbles from the bath dripping down her naked body. He had no choice but to stare straight at her torso. For a woman in her late forties, Marsia had a magnificent shape, flat belly, small round breasts, strong legs and thighs. He watched as she swirled herself in a towel and walked out the door into their bedroom. He stumbled after her. "Marsia, I'm sorry that I didn't call." She had her back to him, that back he loved to curve around at night. She dressed herself in a green velvet robe, fanning out her wet hair with her hand. "What is it? What did I do?" Of course he knew in shrieking, horrific detail what he'd done, had written about it and told everyone. "What did Serena tell you? She's lying, you know that. She's a fucking psycho, a maniac. People are afraid of her at work. Look at those tiny people dangling from her wrist. They're trophy heads of her enemies. She's like a headhunter from New Guinea." He felt himself babbling.

Marsia turned to stare at him. She looked tired and pulled some strands of hair away from her wet face. In a quiet voice, his wife finally spoke, "She didn't tell me anything, Guy. She was there to see you, to give you production sheets for a commercial shoot in Arizona." He wanted to embrace her out of sheer relief, but she left the room.

She wandered out to the screened-in porch on the second floor, from which she stared out at Mecox Bay. Guy followed and drew himself up behind her, putting his hands on her shoulders. "You know I love you, babe, despite all the bad things I do."

"It's a terrible thing to be loved by you," she said, in a soft voice, and patted his hand.

fifteen

MUSIC

Days after his encounter with Eleanor Birch at Tony Lowe's play, Jonathan Neel still couldn't get her out of his mind. She seemed changed. What was it about her? She looked better for one thing, dramatic, whereas before she'd seemed dowdy and weird. She was intense too and had listened to that musical with almost no moment of inattention. He assumed that he would see her again shortly, as he'd gotten another invitation from the actor, this time for an evening of opera at his Chelsea loft, on a Monday night when his play would be dark.

Succumbing to an old urge, he pulled his cello up from beneath the piano and grabbed the dusty bow along with it. A spot of Gabriel Fauré might cheer him up, *Après un Rêve*. But as he began the strange slow piece, his bow dragged and shagged over missed notes. He'd always been too impatient for music anyway, too anxious to make it perfect without practicing. He began again, more slowly. Mournfully the notes rose up around him. Even in this, its most mediocre representation, the genius of it filled his soul. Only fill a space in a beautiful way, hadn't Georgia

O'Keeffe written that? "How beautiful my Buffalo Grill?" he said out loud. The phone rang.

"It's me, Jon." Walter's anxious tones were instantly recognizable. "Could you send me two hundred dollars?"

"Sure, but Mom says you just use it to drink and play the lotto."

Walter started screeching. "Don't listen to her. She hates me, she hates Susan."

"She doesn't hate you. She hates me and my failed cello." These thoughts presented themselves as too complex for Walter.

"Your cello. I like your cello. You have the best cello."

"Forget her," Jon said carelessly.

"She's my mother," he yelled again.

"Calm down, buddy. Listen, I'll send you an extra thousand for this month, right away. How's that? And I don't care what you do with it."

"Thank you. I love you, Jon, you know that? I have a new picture for you of the beautiful lady."

"I love you too, Walter. Can't wait to see your new painting." Pain surged through his throat. He'd never told Sasha he loved her.

He found himself going through old photographs of the two of them. She always looked as if she was having a wonderful time, while Jon seemed perplexed. What had he been thinking at the time? Probably work. Below another batch of photographs, he found a small white satin bag enclosed with a gold ring. Was it something of Sasha's? He slipped off the ring and out fell a necklace, blue enamel and marcasite, with a tiny watch as a pendant. Antique, so Sasha, definitely hers, and he remembered that she'd worn it often. He slipped it back into the bag and put it in his pocket. Should he keep it or give it to Sasha's friend?

* * *

Eleanor arrived in town for Tony's musical event early, in part to finalize her sublet, in part to talk to New York Hospital/Weill Cornell about further arrangements. All of this made her feel more self-confident about the city, but when she stood in the doorway of Tony's apartment, she felt as if she wanted to run home. With its high ceilings and massive windows that looked out over Twenty-Fifth Street, his living room was splendid, and the party was already going full blast. Well-dressed guests hovered near the kitchen, grabbing food off the hors d'oeuvre plates, while Tony helped the caterers, but when he spotted Eleanor, he rushed over. What a blessing. Without him she might have been tempted to wriggle out of her assignment. She would have rationalized Sasha's comments as idle ranting, the result of overwork and disappointment. "There's no proof of sincerity like fifty-thou, Ellie," he kept saying to encourage her. Eyeballing her carefully contrived outfit of a filmy black top over a purple camisole and a black leather skirt, he exclaimed, "You look incredible, sexy dominatrix mode."

"I was afraid it was too much."

"It's wonderful."

"I've never known anyone to have real live opera at his very own house before. Is this more plotting to get me and Jon in the same place?"

"Of course not. I've had jazz bands, a violinist, and there are lots of other people you might like to meet, though not many potential dates." He laughed. "But seriously, we do have to talk about seduction before Jonathan Neel gets here."

"I don't know if I'm up to all this, Tony," she moaned.

"You're ready. I can see it in your eyes," and as he said this, a man in a tuxedo sat down at the piano. "We'll have to wait. They're starting."

An imposing young woman appeared from a side door, dressed in layers of shimmering brown velvet. She arranged herself in front of the unruly group, and Eleanor thought she recognized some famous faces pitched in among the crowd, but she couldn't spot Jonathan Neel. Finding no place else to sit, she sank down on an embroidered footstool. The young woman started slowly with an aria Eleanor recognized, the haunting melody from Catalani's *La Wally*, "Ebben? Ne andrò lontana." She felt overwhelmed by tears, and just at that moment, Jon appeared beside her.

He knelt down, whispering "Hello. You're the only person I know here, except Tony." Someone behind them muttered "Shh." She turned to see his extraordinary face looking distressed, tired, annoyed. His thick scarf fell for a moment on Eleanor's leg before he pulled it away. A second verse filled the room. Eleanor had to hold back her sobs and found herself poking in her purse for a handkerchief, until finally Jon handed her a Kleenex. She was annoyed at his attention and realized right then that she couldn't even think of seducing the man. She detested him, and surely that feeling would show on her face. Not that she'd actually ever seduced anyone. She'd have to give Sasha's money to charity.

Later, after much Mozart and a fair amount of Richard Strauss, circulating as best she could, Eleanor gazed at Jon from across the room. Laughing, enjoying himself, she was sure of it. And why shouldn't he be? What could he do for her dead friend, become a monk? She noticed that he spoke animatedly to a sleek, too thin blond woman in her twenties, and her contempt rose even higher. She was a certain New York type, the stringy, wild-eyed girl who seemed to have something wrong with her, really wrong. Eleanor had observed such women before and always wondered how men couldn't see that with this one they might end up on the losing side of a lawsuit, or with the girl in the hospital, or themselves lashed to a stake. That a man who had known Sasha would flirt with such a girl was a mark of his failed spirit. Eyeing their prey also, Tony came up beside her. "It would be so much easier if he were gay," the actor said. "Then I would know what to suggest."

"I'm losing heart. I can't do it."

"I see what you mean. He's distracted all the time. It'll be difficult to get him to focus."

"He appears to be focusing now," Eleanor said acidly.

"On Tawny Spahn? She's in the chorus of our show. He must be stupid with drink. I'll go over and break it up."

"No. My stepfather used to say, 'Let men show you who they really are, Ellie, before you get involved.'"

"What a concept. If I knew who all my dates were, I'd hang myself. But we do need a plan. Wiles—I said that, didn't I? For instance, 'Keep them in the dark.'"

"I need something more specific."

"Scarcity, that's always worked for me." As they talked, partygoers swirled around them.

"I don't think he knows or cares about me. How can I be any scarcer than that?"

As if reading their thoughts, Jonathan Neel made his way toward them. Over the din, he said to both, "Fantastic music. My mother used to sing it."

"Oh really?" Tony said. "She was a professional singer?"

"Not at all. She loved the piano, though, and would play and sing before dinner. I struggled away at the cello for years." At last he had said something of interest, and Eleanor tried to draw him out on the subject, but he seemed distracted by noise and the approach of the blond girl. However, he turned his back on her as she moved their way. Tony had drifted elsewhere, and Eleanor now smiled for the first time in his presence. "You liked the music?" he said.

"It was beautiful, and so magical to hear it in a private home like this. I loved the Catalani."

"Oh, that one. It's an old shoe in the repertoire, used on movie soundtracks all the time." Eleanor couldn't believe what she heard. He was criticizing the music. A flame rose into her cheeks, and she turned away. "I found something that might interest you, a piece of jewelry Sasha left at my house." He stumbled a bit at the mention of her name.

"She left it at your house?"

"She left things periodically, that is, sometimes she did," and here he stopped, not wanting to catalogue all that had been left. He pulled the worn satin bag out of his pocket and held it toward Eleanor.

Slipping the gold ring off the top, she pulled out the blue watch fob, which fell before her, twisting and dangling on its little chain. Softly she said, "I've seen it many times. Her grandmother gave it to her for high school graduation." On impulse, she undid the clasp and put it around her own neck.

"It fits you perfectly," Jon said, taking a sip of his wine, and then awkwardly he announced, "You take it. It looks just right for the outfit. I think she would want you to have it."

Eleanor stared at him a moment, unbelieving. She struggled

with the tiny clasp and shoved it back into his unwilling hand. "It belongs to the family. You should return it to her mother."

"I just thought—"

"Why did she leave it with you in the first place? You don't wear this sort of thing, I take it?" Annoyed and offended, Eleanor had become quite queenly.

"I don't remember when she left it. It was a long time ago." His voice rose as he too began to get angry, tired of acting like a whipped dog around this woman.

"What else is there just lying around waiting for you to find? I'll bet you lose a lot of things, working as you do night and day to sell people little fast-food steaks." Even in the clamor of the party, her loud voice caused people to look her way.

"I'm sorry," Jon almost yelled right back at her. He put the offending satin bag into his pocket. "Please forgive me if I was trying to give you something, a memento of Sasha's."

"You had a little trouble remembering her, didn't you? She just drifted out of your consciousness, like a piece of jewelry left in a bag."

Tony Lowe chose this moment to intervene, putting his hand on Eleanor's arm and pulling her away. "My dear, you are becoming positively exercised. Let me fan you." He began waving a napkin in front of her face.

"Stop that," she snapped.

"Now, now, you need to channel this anger into something more productive, I told you. You need to get him out of the 'hate' mode and into the 'I'm interested in you' mode."

"That just won't be possible, Tony. Look at him. He's a bum. He tried to give me a piece of jewelry from Sasha—he just found it in a drawer, he says. Right, just lying around waiting for him to give it away, an heirloom. Naturally, he didn't bother to return it to her family." She watched as Jon moved toward a row of over-coats in the hall.

"But if you let him give it to you, then you can have the fun of giving it back."

"I have no idea what you're talking about."

Suddenly Jon was upon them again, reaching for Tony's hand. "Good-bye. Thank you so much for the wonderful evening." He didn't even look at Eleanor.

Watching him retreat, Tony folded his hands in front of him. "He's definitely a hard sell, that's for sure. I wonder how Sasha made it as long as she did with him."

"You know what? I should just forget this whole thing. She was overwrought, she didn't know what she was saying."

"Sasha always knew what she was saying."

"She didn't know she was going to die. How could she?"

"She was fatalistic, she worried a lot, always carried talis-mans, a Saint Christopher medal and Muslim worry beads. For someone so excited about life, she often seemed afraid of it. I used to tell her she was like a little old person."

"I never saw her afraid of anything except flying."

"Probably she showed us different sides of herself." Tony shook his head, overcome. "Ah, she was wonderful, but strange."

"Maybe you should try to 'get' Jon?" Eleanor groaned.

"Don't you see? She knew you'd have a hard time fulfilling her request, and that's why she asked you."

sixteen

THE PAYOFF

After Guy and his wife had returned from Long Island, life settled into an edgy calm. Marsia went about her daily routine, leaving him more alone than usual but still greeting him with kisses, if restrained, and hugging him at night as they slept. He spent much of the week working at home, as a man in his position was allowed to do, and in this instance even encouraged to do by Claudia. He sat now in his study, shrouded in cigarette smoke, pondering the three people on his list who had to be dealt with: Jon, Serena, Janey. Might as well start with the easiest one, the person least likely to strike back at him with a knife, and that was clearly Janey. In her case, no matter how much fun the little schoolgirl routine was, it had to go. She had to go, and preferably away from LaGuardia and Knole. Could he have her fired? Not a good plan, because their relationship was already known, and he would thus be ripe for a lawsuit. Could he get her another job? He was powerful enough to do that, but he wanted the entire association to end, and such help might inflame her to want more.

He looked out of the window onto Wooster Street, a narrow,

cobblestone road redolent of old New York. What did Janey really need? Money probably, and he had plenty of that. He would buy her off, pay her for a year of work. What could her salary be? Probably about a hundred thousand dollars. Surely he had that much money lying around. For years he'd been getting long documents with red wax seals from the French conglomerate that owned LaGuardia and Knole, indicating vast numbers of stock options available for his use five, ten, even fifteen years hence. Since Guy always figured he'd be dead by the end of any given year, these pieces of paper moldered in his files, then got handed over to his accountant, who parlayed them into actual stock or cash. He did occasionally see his stock portfolio and was amazed at the number of shares, but Marsia handled all financial transactions for the household. He only knew the name of their bank because he took five hundred dollars out of the ATM machine every two days.

Guy sipped his scotch and realized, with a hiccup, that for years Marsia must have been monitoring his vast use of their mutual cash. His drug dealer occupied the role of counselor, nag, friend, often giving him birthday special discounts, but this cheery little felon had a serious appetite for the green stuff. Nevertheless, Marsia had never once questioned him about the extraordinary outflow. He knew they kept a very high balance, how high he only realized when he braved the hermetically sealed door to Citibank five blocks from his house. He had improvised a speech about needing to pony up for some real estate in Florida and was anticipating a certain amount of opposition.

Inside the small office of the bank manager, Guy prepared for the business by taking his ATM card out of his wallet. The manager, a reedy, gray-haired man, looked at him expectantly.

"I'm buying a condominium and would like to take the money for the down payment out of my account. One hundred and twenty-five thousand dollars to be exact." Guy tried to sound like a rational man. He had decided to add twenty-five thousand dollars to Janey's putative salary as a tip.

"You want a hundred and twenty-five thousand off your ATM card?" The bank manager said, astounded.

"Out of any one of our accounts. I know that we have several."

"Do you have a blank check with you?"

"My wife handles most of the money, but this is my transaction, Mr. Twining," Guy said, eyeing the brass nameplate on the man's desk.

While Guy spoke the manager punched several keys on his computer, then shoved a small keypad forward and said, "Put in your PIN number please." These numbers were engraved on Guy's skull, and he tapped them out rapidly. The bank manager raised his eyebrows at the balance he saw before him and swiveled the computer monitor toward his customer. In a regular checking account resided one hundred eighty-three thousand dollars and forty-eight cents. He brought up another screen. The Danziger time deposit account contained two hundred and thirty-nine thousand dollars. "I don't know, we might have to file a suspicious activity report," and here the little gray man laughed, "because it's such a large cash withdrawal. In case you're a major drug dealer."

Guy laughed along with the man, too loudly, and proceeded to describe an entirely fictional condo on the inland waterway in Ft. Lauderdale, a place where he could get away from it all, just his own little piece of Florida swamp. He was talking too much, he knew, and expected the ancient security guard to flash his sidearm at any minute. "Fortunately for you," Mr. Twining said, "You have a dual signature card on file, which means that you can do this transaction entirely by yourself, without the missus' signature. Of course, she could do the same." Guy could feel the bank manager getting a distinct sex vibe out of this conversation. They were dirty old men talking together and doing bad things.

"It's really a surprise for my wife," Guy said, growing more comfortable with the fiction he was creating. "She will be so thrilled. This is something she's always wanted."

"Right," Twining said, winking. "I think a cashier's check should do fine."

"Oh no, I want the money in actual cash. I'm meeting with the sellers today. That's what they expect."

"You're not seriously saying that you're going to put a hundred twenty-five thousand dollars into your own pocket and take it out of here?"

"Yes, actually, that was the plan."

"I wouldn't advise that, Mr. Danziger. New York is a lot safer than it used to be, but there are still muggers out there, you know." He frowned. "How will you get it home safely?" Guy hadn't thought of any of this. He'd been obsessing over how to present this bribe to Janey without getting punched or throttled, and the brilliance of drowning her in a wad of money required bundles of real green. Mr. Twining had a point, though. In a determined effort to hide his tracks, he'd taken a cab here instead of the ubiquitous livery car, but now he had no safe way home. Still, only he would know about the treasure in his pocket, or . . . where would he put it?

"And where will you put all of it, anyway?" Mr. Twining said, echoing Guy's own thoughts. "This will be a fat package."

"Maybe you could wrap it up for me."

Thus Guy Danziger departed the bank carrying a large bundle in brown paper that looked like a cross between dry-cleaning and a down pillow, stuffed with one hundred and twenty-five thousand dollars in hundred-dollar bills. Such was his state of mind that he didn't really care if someone shot him. He clutched the package to his side, thinking perhaps that he should stop at a Hallmark store for wrapping paper. It didn't look very fetching, after all, and since Guy had the eye of an accomplished art director, he knew that this little giftie required a certain amount of graphic design to glam it up and sweeten the painful, not to say illegal, message that it conveyed. He slipped into a tiny stationery store, squeezing himself between the overstuffed racks. What would be appropriate? Not little gold stars in a blue sky, not fat red Santas, not bears holding up yellow balloons. Hush money wrapping, that's what he needed. Finally, he found a glossy roll striped in lighter and darker shades of green.

As Guy walked the streets, frozen in his leather jacket, clutching his bundle, he felt a sudden rush of joy at all the money he had. There were more accounts, he knew—brokerage accounts, CDs, bonds, stocks—a mountain of safety underneath his feet. Quietly he snuck into his house by the back entrance. It was eleven in the morning, and he knew Marsia was out at her regular charity gig at a thrift store uptown. Nevertheless, he took the steps two at a time and raced up to his study, slamming the door behind him. Sitting cross-legged on the floor, he encased the package in the green paper with perfectly square corners and transparent tape, turning it over several times, satisfied that it looked like a major gift. Should he attach a card? He recalled that he hadn't even talked to Janey at all since the underwear throwing incident, had seen her only once, at the meeting on the Arizona shoot. He was sure she was consulting a lawyer or worse yet, a hit man. Though she was a gentler person than Serena Rawlinson, she hadn't worked in advertising for nothing. She knew where the bodies were buried, and she could make them rise up like Banquo's ghost.

When he called her at the office, he was patched over to Serena, a fact he realized before he could hang up. "Janey's right here, looking at the Arizona shoot schedule," Serena said. "We're going to Old Town in Tucson. Won't that be fun? A nice mix of man, maniac, and buffalo." She positively cackled.

"Peachy," Guy announced.

"I told Juan Angel we'd be combining the shoots, so he'll have storyboards for each. Day one for prep, day two will be Synergene, day three, Buffalo Grill. Animal trainers, vet, though I haven't talked to him yet, ancillary personnel will be at each. We're saving big money on the animal people and the location."

"Sounds fabulous," Guy said, about to pretend they were being cut off.

"Did you want to talk to Janey?"

"Not really," he said.

Serena exclaimed, "Oh, yes you do. And don't forget, Juan Angel comes to New York next Monday to meet everybody."

"Hello, Guy," he heard Janey say, uncharacteristically subdued. "I'll put you on hold for a minute."

From her own office, Janey started in on yet another tirade against her errant lover, but he stopped her with an invitation. "I want you to meet me at Le Cirque for drinks after work. I have a surprise for you." He was feeling flirtatious and giddy and knew that his tone prepared her for an altogether different kind of rendezvous at a place so public, so potentially crowded with people they knew that she might indeed expect some sort of proposal. He couldn't help that. He just had to get her there.

The bar at Le Cirque seemed a friendly place to Guy's drug-clouded brain, as he ordered the Happy Hour specialty, a Caribbean gimlet. He watched the bartender mash sugar and mint at the bottom of the big goblet, squeeze some lime juice into the glass, then pour the syrupy Absolut. Seating himself at a table near the bar, he hid the green package under his chair with his foot resting upon it. Isn't that what his wife always recommended? In a restaurant, keep your foot on your purse at all times. Guy had done himself up for this tryst in a dark turtleneck and a sumptuous beige overcoat, conscious that he must charm and cajole, not to say grovel and crawl on the floor, should it be required. If someone he knew saw him here, he would say he was giving a gift to a departing employee.

"Hello, Guy," Janey said, standing before him in a flowing purple wool dress. Her blunt cut black hair seemed even more stylish than usual, and as she placed herself assertively on the chair in front of him, she waved to the waiter. "What are you having?"

"A Caribbean gimlet—it's wonderful."

"I'll have the same." She glowed in front of him with all the hopeful, wistful promise of someone who should have been going out with a man her own age. Guy wondered how in God's name he could actually do what he was about to do. He had a strategy, which was to stay away from emotional conversation, to try not to rile her up; he couldn't face the inevitable bitterness.

"I have a gift for you, Janey, and I hope it means as much to you as it does to me."

She smiled with delight. "A gift? This sounds promising."

"Yes, and I've given this a lot of thought." He motioned to the waiter and ordered another gimlet, along with some fresh vegetables and dipping sauce. Janey sat patiently, while they made small talk about the agency. Finally Guy bent down and pulled the heavy package up to his lap. "This signifies something important. It's meant to help you in your career. It's meant to give you the time and space to consider what your future should be." He handed her the bundle.

Janey apparently awaited a declaration of love, and this seemed curiously not of that order. "Are you trying to get rid of me?"

Guy pulled out a cigarette. He fixed her squarely in the eyes and said, "We can't go on as we were, Janey."

"I know," she said eagerly. "We should go on in a different way, a more committed way. I love you. I always have." She held the package unopened.

"Janey, I'm a married man."

"But you're unhappy. You're not suited to each other. Look at what you said in your 'Confessions.'"

"Don't remind me."

"But you have to stop sleeping with Serena, right now. It's incredible, unspeakable. How could you have betrayed me that way?"

The convolutions of Guy's sexual life were certainly not made for drink time conversation. Sordid, that was how they struck the man himself, and he was terrified of hearing the particulars out loud. "Janey, I appreciate that we had some good times—"

"You love me, I know you do."

Sadly, he had to lie, he knew, to get out of all this. "I do love you, but in a unique way. I need to straighten out my life. Open the package, but don't let anybody else see what's inside."

Janey fiddled with the green paper and then had to tear at the heavy bank wrapping underneath. When she glimpsed the first hundred-dollar bill, she was stunned. She flipped through several more bills, only to see packets and packets of them. "What is this?"

"It's one hundred and twenty-five thousand dollars, your salary plus a bonus. It's my gift to you. Take the year off, find yourself. Maybe you should leave advertising and do something more rewarding. Go save the rain forest." This little speech, so foreign to Guy, so pointed, its meaning utterly clear, might have been spoken by another person altogether.

Janey sat speechless before him. She took a big gulp of her gimlet. "What does this mean?"

"It means the end," he said and hauled himself up out of the chair, flopping three twenty-dollar bills down for the drinks. Outside, it had begun to snow, fat flakes that hit the pavement and melted away. Guy stuck out his arm and watched as his palm filled with white diamonds of water. He wiped his hands together, rubbed them over his face, and hailed a cab.

seventeen

BRAIN MAPPING

Ensconced in her amazing Gramercy Park sublet, Eleanor found herself afraid to go outside. For several days, the noise, the sirens late at night, the screeching on the sidewalk had her up and awake, looking out her one huge window and wondering what would happen next. She felt safe where she was, but the minute she stepped out her front door, she joined the life just beyond her apartment, and that life was immense. Nevertheless, four days after her move to the city, she walked all the way from Twentieth Street up to the Weill Cornell Medical Center to begin work on her new job. Assigned to a project in the neurosciences department, she joined a team dedicated to brain mapping, the study of specific parts of the brain that appeared to be causing seizures in people with epilepsy or other disorders. Doctors were attempting to stop the seizures without affecting any nearby speech centers, but those centers had to be found, "mapped," in a procedure much like an electrocardiogram, while the patient was awake, skull open. The team consisted of a psycholinguist, neurologist, surgeon, anesthesiologist, and Eleanor, who was responsible for all research, documentation of the findings resulting from the operations, and collection of notes the doctors wanted saved. The idea was to create an informational archive at the hospital for an entirely new center on the subject.

As she wandered the wood-lined halls of the old medical library on First Avenue, in contrast to her feelings about the rest of the city, she felt completely at home in its dark homey interior, almost august in its dedication and seriousness. What a relief from the bizarre goings on at LaGuardia and Knole. Ever since the opera party, she had been completely stumped as to which direction to take. How was she to seduce such a man as Jonathan Neel? In him she found everything intimidating about a male, his looks, his height, his easy existence in a high-speed world. His values were a mystery. He invested advertising with the earth-shattering importance that she was only willing to give to, say, brain surgery. Where was the common ground? She vowed, however, to take a proactive stance, to think of him as a citadel to be stormed, a town to be sacked.

In service of this goal, Eleanor had noticed a Buffalo Grill several blocks from the hospital, where she determined to start her campaign by lunching at the very center of Jon's existence. The place was almost full, and she had to wait a moment at the door, wet and freezing in the snow. Inside, she noted the nouveau cowboy theme, the huge salad bar, and picture after picture of some variation on steak and potatoes that hung above the grilling stations. Even more noteworthy was an enormous banner with orange lettering and a cowboy sitting on a rearing horse waving his hat. The banner read, "You Have Come to a Better Place." As she yelled her order to the harried cook behind the counter, she had to laugh at the fact that the nightmare ad had become a marketing tool. Did Jonathan Neel know that they were now celebrating his line? Squeezed between two other tables, she dug into her steak and potato, accompanied by two huge stalks of broccoli smothered in butter, all of it brought to her by a waitress. Not bad, she thought, though not what she usually ate. She looked around her. The clientele consisted mostly of medical workers, some families too, and elderly people probably visiting at the hospital.

Cutting into her piece of apple pie, she remembered the look on Jon's face when she'd refused his gift of the necklace. Hurt, angry, appalled, that was the word, appalled. Had anyone ever refused him anything? Suddenly though, she remembered that Sasha herself had tried to give her expensive things. On one memorable occasion, she had spread five or six cocktail dresses out on the floor of her dormitory room and told her to choose a gown or two as thanks for tutoring her in French. "Just take whatever ones you want, Ellie. They're perfect for you." She had held up a blue velvet princess cut creation that looked vastly too old for either of them and forced her to try it on. "Twirl, Ellie." Twirling wasn't easy, as the dress was way too long for her. Nevertheless, Sasha had insisted on demonstrating to Eleanor the proper way to enter a room. "Realize that you are about to win the Nobel Prize, a fact unknown to the assembled guests. They've called you from Sweden that very day, and it's in an exotic branch of physics only you understand. These dudes at the party wouldn't know a gopher from a galaxy. They think string theory involves a kind of cheese. Carry this knowledge in your heart, and it will open your soul."

Opening her soul, now there was something to think about, as she finished off her pie. Several girls in school uniforms had entered the place, pulling at each other, talking loudly, falling off the chairs. No such behavior would have been tolerated at Dudley-Holcomb School for Girls in the wilds of Fairfield. There the students stood every time a teacher entered the room. An invisible hand, or possibly that of their very athletic head-mistress, Miss Julia Odom, watched over their every move. She often responded to bad behavior with a yellow Post-it Note that contained a frowny face, with no accompanying message, as if a cosmic schoolmarm were spying on them from above.

Sasha was one of the social leaders at the school, and in a prom dress she could pass for twenty at a time when the other girls looked like scarecrows, but she often ignored her school-work. A well-meaning French teacher had chosen Eleanor to help her, and that's when they became friends. She found Sasha smart, though easily bored and uninterested in memorizing much. When she'd learned enough to pass the test, she stopped studying and brought their ancient spinster teacher some flow-ers that she'd picked herself and arranged in a basket she'd stolen from the cafeteria. Now, as Eleanor looked at the teenagers hav-ing a high old time at Buffalo Grill, she couldn't imagine an older man having any interest in them, or for that matter, in the awk-ward, neurotic loonies at her own school. And yet there had been Sasha's affair.

The man had encountered Sasha at a school drama club meeting since, apparently, he'd given money for a new theatre. All the girls had noticed that this particular father was much handsomer than the dreary businessmen dads of their other friends, and somewhat raffish in his trade—he owned a slot machine manufacturing company and had a second office in Las Vegas. A year later, the man and his family, including his daughter, moved west, probably, she figured, because of his sexual indiscretions. Poor Eleanor was lucky if she had any date, ever. "You're too serious for them, Ellie," Sasha would say. "You have that look behind your eyes that says, 'I take you in, I understand you.' They don't want to be understood, not in that way. And whatever you do, don't tell them everything you know."

These reflections occupied Eleanor as she sat staring at the scrambling populace, happy to be inside the door and even happier to get food, while outside the snow and the sleet were raging. She stared down at her plate. She'd eaten every single thing in record time. Not altogether unpleasant, nothing like the standard burger joint. She pulled her heavy coat around her shoulders, stuffed her red velvet scarf close to her neck, preparing to step out into the cold.

As she shoved herself through the revolving door, she ran smack into a tall figure in a black coat and, looking up, was stunned to see Mr. Neel himself. He peered down at her. "Hello, I . . . uh, what are you doing here?" he said, as he backed up to let her pass.

"I just had lunch," she said, feeling guilty and embarrassed somehow, as if she'd been spying on him at his place of business. "Why are you here?"

"Usually I eat at every Buffalo Grill in the city, but I haven't been doing that lately, not since the big ad disaster," he said, as the wind buffeted them against the side of the building.

"You're in for a surprise."

"Oh no, it had better not be like the last one."

"A little bit."

"Want to show me?"

"Sure."

Inside the noisy restaurant, Jon surveyed the usual fast-food landscape. Nothing out of the ordinary so far, but then his eyes caught the big brown and orange banner. "You have come to a better place," he said, mimicking that strange voice in the commercial.

Eleanor laughed. "I guess you won after all. Your line is famous."

"They changed it a bit. My client, Jimmy Goodlaw, obviously had his in-house people do this. He never said anything to me about it, a real no-no in advertising, if you know what I mean."

She didn't understand what he was talking about but said, "Oh, yes."

"Would you like some coffee? Their coffee actually isn't too bad."

"I'd like to but, unfortunately, I have to get back to work." Eleanor was thinking of Tony's suggestion—scarcity, don't make yourself too available.

"I thought you worked in Ithaca."

"I did, but I got an assignment here."

"What kind of assignment?"

"I'm working on the brain-mapping team at New York Hospital."

Jon looked horrified. "You're not a brain surgeon, are you?"

Eleanor felt her face flush with anger. Clearly he hadn't registered much about her at all, and she said rather sharply, "Of course not. I'm compiling an archive for the project."

"Oh. Fascinating. What is brain mapping?" As she sketched out the complicated procedure, all Jon could think was that perhaps Walter could benefit from such research, but he didn't tell her anything about his brother.

"I must go," she said looking down at her watch.

"Does this mean you're here permanently?" he asked.

"It's just a three-month assignment, but who knows?" This had been one of Tony's other instructions. "Always keep them guessing about your own schedule." She turned away from Jon and plunged out of the restaurant, this time for good.

In her cozy, slightly weird apartment, decorated as it was with a quantity of antique ballet prints, she phoned Tony later to relate developments. "Very good. You did right to just leave him there," he said.

"It seemed rude, but then I thought, who cares if I seem rude? He's rude all the time."

"Rude is good, rude is kick-ass. Maybe you should go to a dominatrix store and get some clothes that will make you feel terminally rude."

"Oh please. It's the holiday season, Tony."

"Even better."

"Listen, we need an alternative plan of attack, because seduction is out. He's just too weird, and besides this is the kind of man who would never even call me."

"What kind of other plan?"

"I have absolutely no idea, but I got a call on voicemail from another guy who works at LaGuardia and Knole. Yuck, a blind date. Anyway, he wants me to have dinner with him. He's the son of a coworker of mine up in Ithaca. I was going to say no, but maybe I can get information out of him, something that would give us a new strategy against Mr. Neel."

"Brilliant. You could pick up some dirt on him; better yet get info on his current romantic status, if he's seeing someone now because that could be important to our plans."

An awful thought, this, and Eleanor wasn't so sure she even wanted to know if that was true. She put off calling Seth Greenblatt back.

eighteen

JUAN ANGEL

"Too much goddamn weather here, folks," Juan Angel Peña barked, glowering through the window at the falling snow. "I'm only staying today, then right back to Los Angeles, thank God. Don't know how you can stand it. Where's that drug addict, Danziger?" He turned to face the assembled advertising victims, his splendid, chiseled features screwed into a grin.

"I'm sure he'll be in here soon," Serena said, trying to regain control of the meeting. "The shoot is in Tucson." She sat at the head of the conference table.

"The Spaniards called the local Indians there the Sin Aguas. You see, no water, but they figured out a way to bring the animals there. To breed." He turned his back on all in attendance, fiddling with his shoulder-length black hair. He wore blue jeans and sported a silver bolo tie.

Jon eyeballed Serena, who had apparently gotten herself up with special care for this confab, in tight beige jodhpurs and a red turtleneck, perhaps plotting a little tryst with Juan Angel. Unfortunately, the director wasn't responding to Serena's charms, even when she chimed in assertively, "We can make Tucson look like a place with water," directly to his back.

The director snorted in her direction, and Jon watched this scene with trepidation. Juan Angel had many lady friends, in addition to a sleek Iranian ex-wife and three sons, and was excessive in every conceivable way, regularly ordering two-thousand-dollar bottles of wine at the most expensive restaurant in town, where he liked to sup in the manner of Henry the Eighth. He was just as likely to lop off a head. On a shoot he had once threatened the young man in charge of computers with a baseball bat when the poor guy couldn't make anything work. Jon had stepped in to stop him because he understood that the big bull inside the Argentinean could be quieted with a strong riposte or a soccer game. Juan Angel loved to play *fútbol* and hired his crew based on their abilities in certain positions.

"See you're still doing that Buffalo Grill crap, Neel. When are you going to get out of fast-food hell? Saw your ad the other night. I'm not going to ask what happened, right? Somebody fuck with you, *esta puta vida, todas esas mierdas,*" the director ranted and threw his hands up toward the ceiling.

"Some *mal carne* there for sure, way bad meat." Juan Angel appeared taken aback by Jon's swift Spanish reply.

"Where'd you learn that, gringo white boy?"

"Same place you did." Jon just blurted this out, having no idea what he meant. The only thing he understood about what the director called "this fucking life," and "all this crap," was that you had to give it back to him full in the face. Juan Angel registered the response and seemed about to ratchet himself up to increased rage when the door opened, and Guy Danziger, covered in Patagonia snow gear, struggled through the door. The director shouted out a greeting to the terminally trembly Guy.

"There he is, the man, thought you got caught in a snow-bank, you geezer. Aren't you too old to still be in advertising? I expected you to die before I ever got a chance to work with you."

This astounding greeting threw Guy into consternation, but it lasted only a moment. Despite his short stature and ambiguous emotional state, he could be imposing in his own right, and he straightened up, expanding his chest as he emerged from the heavy jacket. He hadn't won fourteen Clio awards for nothing. Then he spotted Serena, looking remarkably done up, and sat down as fast as he could without saying a word. Because of his substance situation, Guy was an insomniac, and the night before he'd stayed up to watch an Arts & Entertainment channel investigative program on bribery and extortion, crimes it appeared that he had just committed. Would he be put in jail? He obsessed over this subject even as he stared at the imposing Latin American declaiming before him.

Serena Rawlinson fixed Guy with a look as she tried to hand the agency's work to the man who would direct the commercials. "Here are the storyboards. We should go over these before we get out to Arizona."

Juan Angel brushed them away. "I've seen them already. Are you guys collaborators now? How did you happen upon these charging bulls or whatever the hell we got here? I see the Buffalo Grill connection but Synergene, *cabrón*. I repeat, there are no indigenous buffalo out there, whatever you two have hatched here."

"How about beefalo?" Guy said in a quiet voice.

"What the hell are those?" Juan Angel said.

"A cow and a buffalo," Guy managed, as he chewed on one of the sandwiches supplied by the caterer. This bit of information stopped conversation dead. Jon guffawed, and Serena glared at her errant lover. The two junior members of the team had been instantly frightened into submission by the irascible director and were like children who hoped not to be called upon. They looked down and scribbled on their notepads.

"I don't care if it's a rat-bastard Chihuahua." Juan Angel was enjoying himself.

Serena tried to take charge and announced, "We will arrange for the animals to be brought in by truck, and a vet will be with them. We only need fifteen or twenty. We can fake the thundering hordes."

"Nothing with animals is easy. Fifteen or twenty you say, but each one weighs twenty-five hundred pounds. They're stupid and mean. They have to be driven very hard even to get them to move. If they turn on you, they can kill," Juan Angel said.

"We can handle them," Serena announced.

The rest of the meeting consisted of schedules, crew arrangements, all of the business that belonged strictly to Serena, but Juan Angel grew impatient to leave and rocked back and forth on the heels of his cowboy boots. "One thing I didn't mention. It would be better for me if we went earlier, end of next week actually. I have a Boeing shoot that conflicts. Had to bump you. Didn't my assistant pass along the word? *Lo siento,* as we say." Serena glared, speechless. This change would back the Tucson trip right up to Christmas, making the participants even more unhappy, if possible, but there was nothing anybody could do. They were his hostages and, short of firing him, they had to conform to whatever schedule he dictated.

Guy paid little attention. He and Serena had had no conversation since their last hasty cell phone discussion, and he needed desperately to ensure that she wouldn't talk to his wife ever again. How to do this weighed on his mind. He couldn't possibly buy her off the way he had Janey. Now he knew that he would be traveling with her or at least occupying the same patch of dirt, and this presented opportunities. Should he still sleep with her? Would she want to? What possible inducement could there be for her to keep her mouth shut? Only if she wanted to continue the frolic, that's how he thought of it. But Juan Angel's last remark might signify a happy development. It meant that Guy was leaving town immediately, and that could only improve his situation.

"By the way, you need to redo these storyboards, get something that I can film, and do it before we get out there. I know for you guys it's a big deal to leave this frozen dump and sit around in Arizona. For me, it's work and not as simpatico as Los Angeles. After all, Tucson is not really where I want to eat my last meal." He threw his suede jacket over his shoulders and made as if to leave. No one else would ever wear such a thing in this weather.

"Last meal? So far as I know, no one's trying to kill you—yet," Jon said and waited for the silence around him to expand.

Juan Angel glared at him, but then he broke into a laugh. "They always want me dead, but when? That is what I ask myself. I tell you, I am prepared," he said and pulled a keychain shaped like a revolver out of his pocket, "To remind myself, *la muerte, siempre la muerte.*"

The moment Peña strode out the door, the room felt sucked dry. Jon was tempted to laugh, but the others just looked deflated.

Finally Guy said, "Fuck him. His gun's too small." The junior people giggled.

After a moment Jon asked, "What's the date of this fun-fest as it's currently configured?"

"December twenty-first through the twenty-third," Serena said, thumbing through sheets of paper.

"Merry Christmas everyone," Guy muttered and stood as if to go.

"Let me tell you what we are about to experience," Jon said. "It has a five percent chance of being a decent shoot with no screw-ups or problems. It has a ninety-five percent chance of being the single most excruciating experience we've ever had, and I'm not kidding. I've worked with this guy. Why did you choose him, Serena, out of all the hundreds of talented directors? I don't get it."

This speech shocked Guy like a hot glue gun to the brain. He glared at her, grasping the nature of the situation before him. "May I see you, Serena, in my office?" he said, having no plan whatsoever but wanting to get the upper hand, to remind her that he was indeed an officer of the company, the man who approved her annual bonus.

"I'm sorry. Can we do it later today?" She said this on her way out, leaving Guy behind with Jon.

"Looks as if she flew the coop, old buddy," Jon said, barely able to keep a straight face. Guy's "Confessions" had been oh so clear as to the nature of their attachment, and once in a while it darted into Jon's consciousness, as in not-terribly attractive pictures of the two with their limbs entwined, Serena shouting, "Yeah, yeah, give it to me, baby, give it to me!"

Guy couldn't speak, confused, guilt-stricken. So now everyone knew he had stolen Jon's buffalo idea. He decided to plunge right to the center of his fear and fight back. "Too bad about that ad running so many times, Jon. That's the kind of thing, over time, it becomes immortal, like a legend, something you can never get away from. Jimmy Goodlaw's probably talking with other agencies as we speak."

"The funny thing is that 'You have come to a better place' is now a banner at Buffalo Grill. Old Jimmy took to the idea, and so did all the computer nerds who actually eat there."

Guy reared back like a frightened horse. Could this be true? He fully expected everyone to lie to him now, just as he was doing to them; thus he wasn't sure. If so, the wheel was turning, and it was turning him on his head.

The late afternoon meeting between Guy and Serena did not go well. He suggested several times that they hit the bar at the Geary Hotel, but she would have none of it. "Let's keep it professional from now on," she said to his unbelieving ears. Whatever else she'd made clear to him over the years, it was that she would never let him go, even if *go* were a relative term, given their marital status.

"What are you talking about?"

"It's too dangerous. We both have too much at stake." Here was a perilous turn, and Guy was so deep into his own paranoia that he didn't even want to explore it.

"Why did you hire Juan Angel Peña? After all these years, we have a stable of directors who do a good job, Serena. I just don't understand the necessity for that foul fiend from Argentina."

"Don't be silly. He's the best. We're lucky to get him. Think what fun it will be to be in Tucson, all warm—well warmer than here—all Western, all buffalo-y." These strange remarks hit

Guy's ear like a gong. She had a plan afoot, otherwise she wouldn't be voicing these insane sentiments. Nothing fun arose in his own mind except a hoof-filled disaster. "I think you should rework the storyboards though. Otherwise, you know, he's notorious for demanding rewrites on the set, and we can't afford that. If we go over a day, it could cost a hundred thousand dollars, all told."

She made as if to leave, but Guy grabbed the sleeve of her sweater. "What are you trying to do to me?"

"The same thing that you're doing to me."

nineteen

CHANCE MEETINGS

S cheduled to meet Seth at a new Ecuadorian restaurant in Midtown, Eleanor vowed to get more information about Jonathan Neel. She feared asking her blind date for romantic gossip directly but figured that somehow or other, since he'd been so chatty on the phone, she'd get the young man talking and lead him on from there. Standing back now from the mirror on the closet door, she surveyed her outfit—a dark green knit dress with a deep V-cut in the front. It looked fine, sexy librarian chic, though her hair was full of electricity. Since New York had grown frigid in the last twenty-four hours, she would have to wear a hat and a heavy coat to the restaurant. As she fingered the velvet on her coat collar, suddenly it came to her that it was not so much Jon Neel's new girlfriend she needed to check up on, but a woman concurrent with Sasha. Men usually blew up relationships when they had someone else. Yes, that must be the answer, though she had no idea how to learn whether or not it was true.

Seth had announced that he was tall, "burly," he said, and would be wearing a black leather jacket and a blue shirt. She recognized him immediately, though the noisy restaurant was packed with Friday night drinkers availing themselves of a dazzling display of appetizers laid out on the bar. Instead of crushed, her hair popped out of her hat more electric than ever, and she patted it aggressively as she sat down before him, trying to smile. He was a shy but eager sort of person, and he and Eleanor began talking right away about various computer problems they'd each been experiencing at work. "The whole system at LaGuardia and Knole is teetering on the brink. It's completely overloaded, and no one really knows quite how to get around its limitations. Memory overload especially, what with layouts and pictures, videos and every other damn thing, I'm constantly upgrading, but that involves explaining to everyone, and believe me, with some of those people, it's hopeless." Seth grinned self-consciously as he drank an Ecuadorian beer.

Smiling at his description of the ad people athwart their own machines, she sipped a cocktail consisting of rum, tequila, and lime juice, called an Esquisito. From what she'd seen already, she was surprised they ever recovered enough from their attention deficit disorder to sit down and type. She told him of her job in Ithaca, her new work in Manhattan, and of an actual brain-mapping operation she had watched earlier in the day. "The patient has been epileptic since she had a cancerous tumor removed years before, and now they're trying to treat her recurrent seizures. Apparently the childhood operation left scar tissue that was causing all the trouble, and in this next surgery the doctors wanted to remove that scarring without damaging the speech area in her brain. It was incredible. I stood off to the side and stared straight into the face of a girl whose head was wide open while her brain was being stimulated by electrical currents. The psycholinguist asked her to identify 'a vegetable, long and orange.' I kept thinking, I don't even know what it is, but finally the girl muttered, 'Carrot,' and then, 'When will this be over?'"

"Fantastic, now that is really important work. I just try to figure out who screwed stuff up, and believe me, they all lie about what they did. I've started lying too, in self-defense."

Unfortunately, when Eleanor encouraged him to talk more about his bosses, he brushed that aside, saying it was "dull, very dull" compared with what she did. After another beer, though, he warmed to the subject of the office War of the BattleBots scheduled to take place in the spring. He had constructed a re-mote-controlled robot called Death Rattler II, which had a long, heavy claw that would simply bang to death any opponents. "I suspect my only serious rival will be the chief creative officer of the company, Jon Neel, who told me he was going to make one himself. Everybody else will buy something off the Web and slap together a machine destined to croak after one good hit."

Eleanor started at the mention of Jon's name and immedi-ately attempted to draw Seth out. "Why Death Rattler II, I mean, if this is the first contest?"

"Just to make them fear whoever Death Rattler I was, some-one they'll never see."

"How clever," Eleanor said. "Is it surprising that a chief cre-ative officer in the company works on these games?"

"Games are important there. Besides, it's a very democratic place. Everybody does everything." Since she'd seen several Bat-tleBot episodes on Comedy Central, she proceeded to pump him on the subject until nothing would do but that, after their choco-late flan, he took her back to LaGuardia and Knole to get a good look at his amazing machine.

While attempting to tame her hair in the ladies' room, she fretted, though, as to whether this visit was really a good idea. Would Jonathan Neel be there? While she wanted more information, she didn't actually want to run into him. On the plus side, Seth had already told her people left early on Fridays, so someone as high up as Jon probably did too. Deciding that she should chance it, she figured she might learn something substantive about his love life, past or present, perhaps from his calendar or daybook. Could she possibly get a look at either of those?

It was ten o'clock in the evening when they made their way to the Meatpacking District. Inside LaGuardia and Knole it was silent, something Seth noted as he muttered in her ear, "They've finally gone home, thank God. A few of them seem to live here."

Eleanor laughed but was seriously creeped out once again by the metal decor and the hard, concrete floors. It felt like a prison, worse yet a morgue. Seth's office was on the eighth floor, "Where the big guys are," he announced, and as they ascended in the industrial-style elevator, she worried a second time whether she had done the right thing in coming, especially since she probably wouldn't even be able to get away from her date. Almost obsessed, he burbled on about Death Rattler II, muttering into her ear, "He's a killer, or he will be when I get his big claw to move." Before them stretched the long hallway she remembered from her first visit. Seth took her arm, and she noted with relief that when they passed by Jon's office it was dark, but then, as they turned the corner, a light gleamed in the distance.

"I thought no one would be working," Eleanor said.

"There's always some poor bozo stuck here, usually not on Friday though." They kept walking, but shortly thereafter he pulled her up short. "This is weird," he said. "Someone's in my office."

"Did you lock it?"

"No. I never do. We have a security guard, and the building is like a vault, so nobody ever locks up. It's a so-called open office." Tiptoeing, the two drew closer. The metal door was closed, and as they both leaned forward, they could hear nothing. Finally Seth said loudly, "Hey in there, what's going on?" and shoved himself into the room, Eleanor right behind him.

None other than a startled and embarrassed Jonathan Neel occupied Seth's chair. He stood quickly and brushed back his hair. There was a moment of silence before the two men both started talking at once. "Hey, Seth," Jon managed.

"Jon, what's up?"

"Oh, gosh, I was looking for—" but then Jon registered the presence of Eleanor. "What are you doing here?"

Horrified, Eleanor clutched her purse to her chest and finally managed to say, "Seth and I had dinner, and he asked me back to meet the Death Rattler." She might as well have been standing there buck naked as she spoke, such was her mental state, but even in this crisis had the presence of mind to remember Tony's advice—"It's good when they think you're dating other people."

"Here he is," Jon said and pointed to a mass of metal and robot parts strewn across Seth's desk. He ran his hand through his hair again and added, "I was looking for one of those micro-screwdrivers you have, to work on my own BattleBot, at the moment nameless." He seemed out of breath when he finished talking. "Sorry I just let myself into your office, but I wanted to work on it right now." Seth cut him off by opening his desk drawer and pulling out the smallest screwdriver Eleanor had ever seen, handing it to him.

"Thanks very much. I'll see you, Ellie," Jon said and stepped in front of them, clambering over several computer monitors and keyboards piled up on the floor as he headed out.

"Do you know him?" Seth said. "I can't believe it, you actually know him."

"Not really. He's a friend of a friend," Eleanor stammered, flushed with guilt and discomfort.

"He's a very major deal here at the agency. He sure seemed to know you."

"No, he doesn't. It's just this person we both knew who's dead," she said.

"Oh, my gosh, I'm sorry."

"Yes, it's dreadful, the whole business," Eleanor said, shaking her head. She'd better do something fast or she would start screaming or crying, she didn't know which. Finally she said, "Isn't it peculiar that he was in here?"

"Not that strange. Doors are open all the time, people go in and out and borrow stuff off desks. It's always been like that, though maybe that's why everything's so nuts lately." They spent the next several minutes inspecting Death Rattler II, especially his claw, and Eleanor got a dim sense of how he would look finished, though she felt so anxious she kept straightening the shoulders on her dress and wrung her hands several times before she finally just clenched them together. Wholly absorbed in his creation and his explanation of its projected killing abilities, her date didn't seem to notice.

* * *

Back in his own office, Jon grabbed a paper cup full of cold coffee and gulped it down. He was a wreck, caught red-handed in Seth's office, and by Eleanor too. What the hell was going on? He'd actually been in there to check up on the guy. Whoever sabotaged his commercial would have needed Seth's help, and he figured there'd be some evidence of that on his computer. He'd only been in there a minute or two, legitimately looking for the screwdriver as well, but long enough to eyeball the desktop display. He'd seen something critical, a file called "Alternate Log." Unfortunately, he hadn't had time to open it and so was left to ponder its meaning.

Rather than leave the office after getting caught *in flagrante*, Jon actually did use the handy little screwdriver to get his robot's front wheels rolling, relieved that he could make some of his lies real. Did Eleanor guess he was spying? She obviously disliked him already, and this chance meeting would confirm her opinion. He refused to worry about that now, not with other pending crises. After about ten minutes, though, having gotten one of the wheels properly connected and deciding on the name "Torquemundo," a terrible sound reached Jon's ears. Out of the depths of the building, he heard loud, hysterical crying. He stepped into the hall, and the wailing got louder. He began to run toward the sounds, and as he turned the corner, saw Serena Rawlinson's office door open. From within he heard more painful screeching, then the words "He'll pay, that son of a bitch will pay!"

In the darkness, Jon almost collided with Seth, who was headed in the same direction. "Go get security, will you? I might need help," Jon said. He didn't think he actually would need assistance but wanted no witnesses to what was bound to be a grisly scene.

Outside Serena's office Jon could hear Janey Peet's voice, "I hate him. I'll kill him." He knew the two inamoratas had been close friends before the "Confessions" episode but assumed some sort of later breach. He could hear a soothing tone in Serena's voice, though he couldn't hear the words. Just as Seth loped away down the hall, Serena leaned her head out and said, "What are you doing here?" She surveyed him, then pulled him inside. There sat Janey, in sweatshirt and jeans, hunched over the mangled-looking green package from Guy. She continued to sob, grabbing Kleenexes off Serena's desk.

"Oh no," she screamed when she saw him. "Now he'll know everything too."

Jon thought he knew what she meant, about the "Confessions," and while patting her gently on the back remarked, "Everyone knows everything around here, Janey." She bawled even louder.

"You're a big help," Serena said, frowning.

"I'm sorry. I thought someone was being knifed."

"Not quite. Show him," Serena said.

"I don't want to. My life is ruined, and now it'll be even more ruined," Janey moaned.

"Show him," Serena commanded and motioned toward the package. Janey pulled apart the much-abused tape on the underside of the brightly wrapped gift, and within appeared bundles of hundred-dollar bills. Jon was not an easily shockable man and fancied that, what with his family and his business, he'd seen everything on God's earth at a relatively young age, but even for him this was too much. He backed up against a shelf of videotapes. Were employees of LaGuardia and Knole taking kickbacks? He had heard of such things, bribes to agency people for steering business the way of some deserving production company.

"Where did you get that?" he asked.

"Should I tell him?" Janey said, looking up at Serena. From rivals for Guy's affections, they seemed to have segued back to friends.

"Tell him," Serena commanded.

"Guy gave it to me, one hundred and twenty-five thousand dollars."

"Jesus, what for?" Jon asked.

Serena stood with her arms folded across her chest like an angry schoolteacher. "Guy told Janey that she should quit, and he would pay her a year's salary plus bonus if she would just disappear from LaGuardia and Knole. You see what's come of your meddling," she said.

"My meddling?" Jon said, mystified. "What the hell are you talking about?"

"You were the one who sent out Guy's 'Confessions,' weren't you?"

At that moment, the office air turned a poisonous orange. "Are you nuts? I'd never do anything like that. I run an eighty-seven-million-dollar account, Serena. I don't have time to sabotage other people. I don't need to. They do it so well themselves."

"Guy told me you sent it out," Serena announced.

Janey stood now, clasping the tattered bundle, "It was you?" she screeched.

"OK, everybody, take ten deep breaths. I didn't send it out. Guy somehow managed to send it out himself while he was doing his emails. You owe these revelations to that man, not to me.

I suggest you take these quarrels and maybe even your stash there, Janey, to the place where they belong—possibly the Monkey Bar." He left the two women looking even more outraged and went off to find Seth and the security guard to deflect them from the scene.

Left alone with a half-finished robot, Eleanor had quickly gone from panic to a sense of opportunity. Seth had called her on his cell phone. "Jon asked me to stay in the lobby for a few minutes while he deals with a personnel issue. I guess that's all the screaming was. He said he had the situation under control, so don't worry." Did she have time? Probably. She knew where he worked but wondered if she could get into his office. Tiptoeing down the hallway, still hearing loud voices coming from the other direction, she glided into the big playpen he had created for himself. On his desk sat his cyber dog, pieces of robot parts, and beneath these his daybook, wide open. She assumed Seth would reappear shortly, and she guessed Jon would return in a few minutes, just enough time for her to flip through the book looking for another woman's name. Starting with January, she turned the pages slowly, pained to see Sasha's name circled in red magic marker many times, but then in May, fewer times, and finally in June, no mention of her at all. Running her finger swiftly down each column, she couldn't find another woman's name written with that same dramatic flourish until she saw the words "opera" and "Eleanor B" circled in red, then several more times "Eleanor B—drinks? Dinner?" Suddenly she heard footsteps. Rushing to arrange the book in its original position, she inadvertently knocked the dog, who cried out twice, "You lazy motherfucker."

She jumped away from the desk, giving a little shriek. Afraid to run, afraid to hide in the room, she stood immobilized.

At that moment, Jonathan Neel opened the door and walked in. He looked at her hard, then smiled, saying, "That's Snide. Forgive him. He's a dog."

Eleanor had stopped breathing; she just stared at him and patted furiously at her hair. "Oh, uh, Seth wanted to get the screwdriver back, and I decided to help since there seemed to be some sort of problem." She moved away from the desk as if to leave, but Jon put his hand on her arm.

"Did you find it?" he said.

"What?" Eleanor was flustered.

"The screwdriver." He looked down at her empty hands.

"No, actually, I didn't really have a chance to look, just found your office a moment ago, and I was still trying to get my bearings." She babbled all this at high speed.

Jon moved the daybook aside, and under a file folder located the tiny tool, handing it to her. "Tell him thanks," he said wearily. "I'm really surprised to see you here. How do you know Seth?"

"He's just a friend of a friend. Anyway, I'm surprised too, I mean, to see you."

"Well," he laughed, "I do work here, at least for a while, until someone tries to sabotage me again."

"Did you find out who ruined your commercial?"

"No, but I'm working on it. It's complicated, as is mostly everything."

"True," she said, breathing at last, edging toward the door. "Goodnight. I have to go find my date." She fled down the hall-way.

twenty

REFLECTIONS

S tunned by the oddity of this encounter but not suspicious, Jon sat in his darkened office later that night, watching the gleaming screen of his computer, looking but not seeing. He was even more perplexed by Serena's news that Guy had fingered him as the evil emailer. He wasn't sure he believed that his rival would say such a thing but thought it possible that Serena wanted him to think so. The woman was capable of anything. At a conference in Italy, she once misdirected a group of agency people to the incorrect bus so that they wouldn't be able to find the A-list party. That was the kind of prankster she was, throwing hostile jests out into the universe, and she might well have had something to do with the Buffalo Grill disaster. Perhaps time had rubbed off her fear of him or she'd gotten bored with her regular crop of victims. It was discomfiting to picture himself out in the desert with Serena, Guy, Juan Angel Peña, and his jittery client, an unappetizing mix in any season, but in this, his season of need—the commercial absolutely had to be a home run—it felt vaguely apocalyptic.

As he sat sipping a scotch, he recognized in Guy's attempt to bribe Janey a further gauge of his rival's slippage. Only a madman or a megalomaniac would try to buy off a woman with whom he was having an affair, and one that everyone knew about. Perhaps if Guy actually owned the company he could get away with it, but LaGuardia and Knole was part of an international conglomerate. It was illegal, it was actionable, and it would open up their considerable coffers to whatever sum of money Janey desired. That she had revealed the payoff to Jon and Serena meant that two people intimately acquainted with the concept "leverage" had been handed a valuable secret. Serena certainly didn't need any more power than she had already. If she had actually blown up his commercial, then she had enough command to jeopardize the Buffalo Grill account altogether, a stunning prospect. Truth to tell, he loved the old son of a bitch Jimmy, who, in terms of supporting the agency, had been a real stand-up guy, not only lately but for as long as they had had the account.

Jon's immediate problem was Seth, whom he had ratted out to Serena and Janey. Now he would have to placate him, since he definitely had to find out what "Alternate Log" meant. He went down the hall to the computer expert's office, but it was dark and locked. After waiting in the lobby with the security guard, as he had instructed him, Seth must have taken Eleanor home. Normally Jon would have sent him an email, but he was hyperconscious of the current dangers of that form of communication; still, he would have to promise to protect him from Guy's wrath. Worn out, disheartened, he gathered up his storyboards for the Arizona shoot and walked slowly down the hall, listening for muffled cries or perhaps the counting of money. Lights still shown from Serena's office, but he could hear nothing and so went out into the cold December evening with the sad knowledge of a real pile-up of people who couldn't stand him. It was getting to critical mass.

He got out of his cab at Seventy-Second Street and walked up Lexington Avenue, though it was late. Snow had built up around the corners, and he had to jump his way across the streets. It was a crisp, clean-smelling night. He passed the pet store and stood for a moment with several other people as a corgi pup and a poodle tumbled through the shredded newspapers, biting each other's hind legs. A small boy clutched his father's hand and squeezed himself right up against the glass. He remembered back to when his family first brought home their golden retriever Buster. He and Walter had filled a big cardboard box with shredded paper just like this and sat playing with the dog for hours. While the puppy slept, the two kept on watching.

After Eleanor fled Jon's office, she was determined to leave that hateful building forever. Waiting for her in the lobby, Seth sounded even more perplexed as to the evening's developments and was as anxious as she to flee. Outside, in the frigid night, they walked fast, all the while struggling to find a cab. "My God," Seth said, "What the hell was that all about?"

"What?" Eleanor couldn't think which disaster he referred to.

"The whole scene?"

"I have no idea."

Finally, after walking five uptown blocks, they found a taxi, and Eleanor jumped in out of the cold. She didn't want to speak, she didn't want to think, only to crawl under her coat and hide for the rest of her life. How could she have been so foolish as to enter Jon's office? What must he think of her? That she was the agent of one of those crazy colleagues of his? That she was a thief? She couldn't even fathom how it had all looked, since in her mind, *liar* flashed from her face in neon. Furthermore, she couldn't figure out how to escape this date without saying another single word, but fortunately for her, Seth too was dumbstruck, muttering only that he'd never learned who it was that was screaming. When she spotted Twentieth Street, her heart flooded with joy, and she practically leapt out of the cab in front of her apartment. "Thank you so much," she said, "It was wild." At least that part had been honest. He appeared to want to escort her to the door, but she added, "Oh please, stay in the taxi and keep warm."

When she got inside, she threw off her hat and coat and ran into the bathroom, splashing handfuls of warm water against her freezing face. She looked like a witch, like a crazy person, not like a young woman out on a date at all. Had she looked that way all evening? The wretchedness of the night came over her in all its implications. She would not, could not go on. The whole business was ridiculous. Besides, she wasn't really fulfilling a deathbed request, not by any definition.

Almost twelve thirty, just about the time Tony usually got home from the show, she called him, filling him in on the whole sordid story. Unfortunately, he thought the encounter funny. "It's too much, Ellie. I can just see you there, and with computer nerd Seth. It must have had poor J. Neel wondering and wondering, really in the dark."

"Wondering? He thinks I'm insane, some sort of snooper."

"He was snooping too, wasn't he?"

"I don't know, I couldn't tell, there was so much screaming."

"Say what?"

"I don't know what it was, a woman screaming, that's all I know."

"They probably scream there all the time. Did you find out anything?"

"Sasha's name was circled dramatically in his daybook, I guess every time they had a date. Then there were blanks when they weren't seeing each other. Next he had a notation about me and your opera night, then other times my name and 'drinks' and 'dinner' circled in red the same way, but with a question mark. No other names were so vividly blocked out. I didn't get much information."

"Aha, but you did," Tony said, with a drawl.

"What do you mean 'aha' like that?"

"You're the only two names, much significance there."

"Stop it, Tony, there's no meaning—probably he doesn't have time to write much in there anyway, too busy with his War of the Bots and other office hysteria."

"It's safe to assume that there was no other girlfriend while he was seeing Sasha and hasn't been one since, except you. A guy like that, if it isn't in his daybook, it doesn't exist."

"That doesn't mean he's interested in me, though."

"Look, I'm guessing that the 'seduce and abandon' thing sounds a little overwhelming for you at the moment, right?"

"You said it."

"In acting, when it's tough to get into the head of a character, someone you couldn't possibly know or understand, you start slowly. Forget the goal, that's too far ahead. Just think about an action directly in front of you, like finding a hat the character would wear, or finding the right pair of shoes, something that will engage you with the person. Your action has to be asking him for that necklace. Get cracking."

"Won't it seem ridiculous after I made a big fuss about giving it back? Besides, where will that get us?" Eleanor said.

"We don't know, but it will probably strike him as captivating, especially since you rejected it once, and now he's seen you with another man."

"I don't have time for all these games, Tony. I just want to do my work."

"Sasha made this your work."

Indeed she had, and Eleanor was beginning to feel more and more resentful that she was living out someone else's life plan. Look where it had gotten her, in trouble already. On Sunday afternoon, nevertheless, as she was watching a cooking show on TV and going through the paperwork she'd brought from Ithaca, bills and tax forms, she found several scarves at the bottom of the box, one green silk, one black and brown, and another, burgundy velvet on one side, robin's egg blue on the other. This last one was recognizably not her own, obviously that of her dazzling friend Sasha. She must have forgotten it at some dinner long ago, and Eleanor had never returned it. Though seriously rumpled, she threw it around her neck and wore it the rest of the day, only occasionally gazing outside her window at the snow.

That night she dialed Jonathan Neel's home phone number. "Hello, is that Jon?" she said when she heard his deep voice. He sounded surprised to hear from her, but she plunged ahead. "I'd like to invite you to dinner next Tuesday night." She waited nervously.

"Sure, thank you. That would be nice," he replied. "Where did you have in mind?"

Pressing open a restaurant guide with her left hand and holding the phone with her right, she said, "How about Drago, on the East Side at seven?"

"I love Drago. That would be great."

"And could you bring the necklace? I've decided that I want it."

There was a moment of silence, and then he said, "Of course."

twenty-one

BUFFALO

The following Monday further troubles dogged LaGuardia and Knole, as evidenced by the three pounds of gold bangles knocking against each other on Claudia Thompson's wrist. Leslie de Santis had phoned to say that she was "not sure about those buffalo. I mean, what do they really have to do with a cure for cancer?" It was eleven thirty, and still Claudia couldn't find Guy to warn him about their very big client's second thoughts and her imminent arrival to discuss the problem. There was no time for any thoughts at all, let alone second ones. Soon they would all decamp to Arizona.

Not yet at the office, Guy had taken some extra hours off this morning to soothe his wife, who sat at the breakfast table drinking coffee and staring out the window. "I envy you going to Arizona at this time of year. It'll be warm," she said. She looked weary and absently fingered her coffee cup.

Trying to stave off any attempt of Marsia's to join him—what kind of hell would that be?—Guy inhaled deeply on his cigarette and pointed out, at length, how boring a commercial shoot was and the fact that Tucson might actually be cold. "Juan Angel is a real wild ass. I don't think you'd want to be in the same state. I'm not sure I want to be." He thought too of the other players, especially Serena, and vowed that he would station himself on the tarmac if need be, to prevent his wife from going.

"Still, it's beautiful country down there."

"There will be buffalo, lots of them. I think they're just big and hairy and smelly." He said this as he rose to go to work.

"What do buffalo have to do with a cancer drug?"

"I'll tell you tonight," he said and got out of the house as fast as he could, only to be besieged with beeping from his cell phone. They were hysterical to have him at the office, and he had to beg his driver to floor it through the slush and snow and the hordes of shoppers.

Leslie de Santis sat in the conference room staring at the storyboards one more time. Claudia made a somewhat lame attempt to explain the concept, but she was floundering, as was Serena. Moments later Guy rushed into the room, giving Leslie a big kiss on the cheek. Despite his haggard appearance and slapdash apparel, he proceeded to sketch with great eloquence the metaphoric significance of the legendary animals and the fact that they were meant to call up beauty and strength, the kind the pioneers had. Leslie said doubtfully, "My concern is that they'll be, I hate to use the word *hokey*, animals running around or being put next to a bottle of pills, the way tigers roar on cereal boxes, though their presence makes no sense."

Guy reassured her. "It will be magnificent but subtle. I promise. If it doesn't bring tears to your eyes, you can fire me."

He saw Claudia glaring at him, no doubt alarmed at the word *fire*, which he knew should never pass the lips of any employee at LaGuardia and Knole, but he soldiered on. "Besides, Juan Angel Peña, one of the best directors in the world, wouldn't consent to shoot anything hokey. He's a perfectionist demon," Guy said, but as he was talking, the assembled conferees became distracted by the sound of running feet headed their direction, then a knock on the conference room door and shortly thereafter a pounding.

Claudia reached for it, but before she could grab the knob, Janey Peet flung herself into the room, shouting, "I'm going to sue that fucking asshole for every dime." She opened her mouth to say more but got yanked back outside from behind. Her savior was none other than Jonathan Neel, who had heard the ruckus in time to pull her down the hall.

Claudia turned completely white, struggling to catch her breath, while Serena sat smirking. Leslie gasped, "Oh, my goodness, oh dear, is there some sort of problem?"

Claudia clinked her bracelets for a moment, not looking at Guy. Suddenly she said in her very low voice, "I'm so sorry, Leslie. It's a mental health issue, sad to say. There's dementia in the girl's family. We've tried so hard to keep her on staff, but—I don't know. Something like Tourette's."

Serena chimed in, "It's sad, really, such a talented girl, brought so low." She glared at Guy as she spoke.

Amazingly, after this stupefying interruption, Guy regained the high ground and went on to sell Leslie completely on the buffalo idea. He was passionate in describing the poetic "home on the range" that could be saved only by these powerful beasts, who swarmed out and overcame every single toxic interloper on the plains. Leslie announced, however, a further concern. "You make it sound like hordes of buffalo," she said, "but I thought you'd contracted for only fifteen."

"Don't worry, Juan Angel can make fifteen look like twenty thousand," though as he said this he realized that certain of his storyboards could never work, no matter how talented the director was.

"It'll be interesting to see how that's done," Leslie said, and of course Guy suddenly remembered that she would be there, a fact he had never focused on seriously before. The client always had a representative, and she was it. At that moment Arizona loomed up before him as a more concentrated, more difficult version of his New York reality, complicated by the presence of two unknowns, Juan Angel and Leslie de Santis, and fifteen utter mysteries in the form of buffalo. He felt the need for something a little stronger than his vodka.

When Leslie finally left, reassured as to the great importance of Synergene to LaGuardia and Knole, Guy slunk back to his own office to refill his coffee mug and do something, anything to get his mind off the odious vortex of events engulfing him. Finally he picked up the dictionary, always a comfort, and had made his way to the word *pile* when Claudia knocked on his door. "I get my best ideas from this book," he said, hoping to ward her off.

"That's heartening. What the hell was that little scene?"

Though he knew each and every one of his depredations by heart, he never spoke about any of this out loud. Even in his head there was a silence. "She's got mental problems," he muttered, sipping his vodka-laced coffee, "Just as you said. I'm amazed that she's still got a job."

Claudia sat down in one of the heavy chairs. "You know,

you're astonishing, Guy. You have more nerve than anyone I've ever met. You just stole my idea, right in front of me. It's a gift."

Guy didn't like the word *steal* any more than he liked *pile*. "What are you talking about, Claudia? I'm focused on my client, and you should be too."

Looking defeated, she said, "Janey's not going on the shoot, so at least we don't have to worry about that. I'd fire her, but we can't afford any downtime now. What do you think?"

"We need her for the time being, but maybe after that?" he said, working up what was for him a long-range plan. Surely she would not survive the kind of pressure he knew he could exert to make her leave the firm once the shoot was over.

"Guy," Claudia said, standing, "You need to clean yourself up. We are beginning to have a disgraceful situation here, one that at some point can't be remedied. Can you do that?"

"I don't know what you're talking about," he said. In all the years he had worked for her, she'd never demanded anything of him except that, no matter how loaded, no matter how addled, he had to perform superbly at his job.

"Oh, come on. We're past that little performance, aren't we? What's in your coffee mug?" she said and tried to grab it away from him, but he clutched onto it like a dying man.

"What's wrong with you, Claudia? Have you been drinking?"

Despite herself Claudia Thompson burst out laughing. "Oh, Guy, I love you, but don't worry, not that way. I truly love you. Think of me as your mother, though of course I'm not old enough."

* * *

As the recent rescuer of Janey Peet, who was now stuffed into a chair in his office, Jon pushed the top of his electronic dog to cheer her up. "You lazy motherfucker," Snide announced, but she didn't laugh.

"I . . . I'm sorry, I just think I'm losing my mind, I don't know," she snuffled and sobbed into a tattered Kleenex.

Jon patted her on the back, handing her a glass of water. "You need to get a grip. I say take the money as a kind of gift and just keep on working here, no matter what Guy says. Think of it as a little retirement fund and also something that, should he make any more trouble, you can just blackmail him with, not that I would ever suggest that. He could fire you, but I don't think he wants the potential legal difficulty. It's as if he handed you a tiny time bomb that you can just stick under his desk any old time you feel like it. Hang on to that bomb!"

"But won't Claudia fire me? I think there was a client in there."

"Yes, Leslie de Santis from Synergene." Janey started wailing again. "Do what I say, and all will be well," Jon murmured, then instructed her to take the day off, actually ushering her out of the building. Talk about a loose cannon, she was it. He had his own problems, Seth Greenblatt being one, the Buffalo Grill account the second, his brother the third, and Eleanor Birch figured somewhere too on the list. Yes, she loomed as a definite problem, though he wasn't sure of what kind. He'd given much thought to their upcoming dinner, and though she had offered, he'd had his assistant make the reservation at the agreed upon Drago, a dark, quiet Italian place he'd been to once before. Curious about her and her work, which seemed to indicate a moral seriousness profoundly lacking in his own world, when with her it was as if he experienced a sort of helpful ballast and was even able to relax.

As he reflected, looking out his window at the falling snow, he heard the cheery tones of Jimmy Goodlaw greeting people in the hall. Jon's door swung open. "Here you are. I haven't seen you in ages, just want to know how the Buffalo Grill campaign is going. Are we ready for the shoot?" He carried a mug of coffee, which almost spilled over, and he looked red-faced and wet.

"We're as ready as can be, Jimmy," Jon said but shuddered inwardly at the blatant lie.

"I'm taking you to lunch at the York Avenue place. I want to see their banner for myself."

"We're supposed to do all your collateral materials," Jon said, something he had wanted to point out to the man earlier but because of their recent cock-up, hadn't pushed the infraction. LaGuardia and Knole normally wielded iron control over every brochure, every billboard, every piece of print, as well as television, that ever appeared in connection with their clients.

"I succumbed, Jon, what can I say? The chat room idiots conquered my marketing department, and they said we should just put up banners quickly, because it gets kind of a tune going in the heads of people as they wait for dinner. I should have called LaGuardia and Knole but had no time." Ushered into Jimmy's limousine by the driver, Jon didn't feel he could press the matter and instead stared out the window as the heavy vehicle crawled through the streets. When they passed New York Hospital, he wondered if he could drop in on Eleanor but immediately dismissed the idea.

The Buffalo Grill employees at the Sixty-Fifth Street restaurant knew who Jimmy was and were waiting for him. They greeted the two men effusively at the door, though the founder of the company refused to be put ahead of regular customers. Instead, they both stood looking at the banner. "Do you like the line now?" Jon asked.

"It's growing on me. Marketing says it's really taken off. They say we're becoming the Star Trek of the casual dining world, whatever the hell that means. Don't congratulate yourself too much, Jon. It's a fluke obviously and will disappear soon." How soon was a question though, as young people thronged past the salad bar and impatiently waited in line at the grilling station. The tide seemed to have turned for Buffalo Grill, and Jon had been pivotal to its turning—which fact both men grasped. His wacky tagline made him indispensable, at least for a time, and "for a time" was as long as there was in advertising.

Their lunch was short, though Jimmy appeared still concerned about what he called Jon's "recent loss." "I was so bad to her in life, Jimmy. I don't even deserve to call it my loss."

"We always look back and regret the things we did. It's normal."

"There's nothing normal about me and my life, Jimmy. Probably eating lunch here is the most normal thing I do," Jon said, digging into his baked potato.

"I've noticed a kind of vanity, peculiar to people in various branches of the arts, that allows them to claim they're abnormal. Talk to some of my fry cooks and chefs and dishwashers at Buffalo Grill; now there's abnormal. We all share human weaknesses. Some people choose to explore them, if you know what I mean."

Sitting there staring at the "You Have Come to a Better Place," banner, Jon felt a weird disconnect between Jimmy's words and their current location, but he could see that the man really meant it. This sudden intimacy with someone they all made fun of at the agency was disconcerting. Once, after a particularly moronic meeting, the art directors had drawn a cardboard effigy of Jimmy, then shot at it with air guns, filling it full of holes. His rages were legendary, his total confusion every time they presented him with a new idea, notorious. Even to fast food he brought a startling philistinism, and yet here he was, consoling Jon with what appeared to be actual wisdom. "Thank you, Jimmy, I appreciate it. We're not used to kind words from any client at LaGuardia and Knole, no matter how good a job we do."

"You think we're boobs."

"Boobs with money." Fortunately, Jimmy laughed. It was never a good idea to reveal professional secrets to anyone at the top end of the power curve.

The general manager of this particular Buffalo Grill, wearing the characteristic Western getup, chose this moment to greet Jimmy. One of the first topics of conversation was all the new customers who seemed to be coming in. "Has to be the internet, Mr. Goodlaw. And the new slogan. I thought it was pretty weird, but look at them. They're young." And they were. Lots of teenagers from the private schools nearby, even some Hunter College types, along with hospital people. Young was different. At LaGuardia and Knole, they habitually labeled Buffalo Grill customers PODS, meaning "poor old dumb shits."

Jon resisted a triumphant feeling about this latest, unanticipated uptick in his fortunes. He had learned too often that the minute he felt fat, dumb, and happy, something dire lurked on the horizon. The two men walked north up York Avenue, working off the heavy meal, though neither said so. Jimmy's limo followed them slowly. As they passed by Weill Cornell Hospital, Jon said, "I know someone who works here."

"I've had my heart operated on at this hospital, triple bypass surgery. I should kneel down and kiss the ground."

Jon turned to look at Jimmy, who was muffled up to his ears in wool. "I didn't know that."

"I decided not to mention it around the agency. It's not good business to think the CEO might drop dead."

If he only knew, Jon thought. They walked on, past the main entrance. "I feel lousy about my old girlfriend. I can't imagine getting involved with another woman." He glanced into the startled eyes of Jimmy Goodlaw, a man who obviously wasn't expecting romantic confidences. "A friend of Sasha's is on leave from a hospital upstate. She's interesting, but I think she hates me."

"What do women know? If they knew anything, they'd be men," Jimmy said, turning sardonic.

"That sounds like something an advertising person would say."

"I know. Ignore me. Call her, talk to her. That's what my son says, and I've got the phone bills to prove it. Just be there, persist. Of course, I don't know anyone on earth who'd take romantic advice from me. My wife hates me too, at least this week."

Finally climbing into Jimmy's car, the two men made their way back to LaGuardia and Knole in order to look at the revised storyboards. Jon was somewhat anxious about another client braving what had lately been the scene of a nervous breakdown, so he hustled the man into his office, where they agreed that yes, the buffalo would work, and Juan Angel Peña would make them work. After they finished, he and Jimmy got into the building's renovated warehouse elevator, but just before the heavy metal door clanged shut, Guy Danziger, looking as if he had rolled in dirt and hadn't combed his hair for a week, entered as well. He nodded at Jon, didn't even glance at Jimmy, then wound his heavy scarf around his face like an Arab camel driver. He punched the "lobby" button even though it was already lit.

Instead of going straight to the main floor, however, the elevator stopped at every succeeding floor, all seven of them, as they went down. At each stop, one or more people got on, at whose entrance Guy became increasingly annoyed. At floor number seven, he muttered something under his breath that Jon couldn't understand. At number six, he spoke a little louder, and it sounded to his ears like "bastard." Jon glanced at him in alarm. At number five he spoke out loud, "bastard," and several people looked around but then pretended it hadn't happened. Fortunately they didn't appear to recognize the speaker. Jimmy caught Jon's eye and frowned, while the younger man was moved to pull on Guy's sleeve. The president of LaGuardia and Knole just glared and shrugged him off.

Thus at floors four, three, and two, every time a person got in the elevator, "bastard" came out of Guy's mouth, loudly. By now, as all New Yorkers would, the elevator riders stared straight ahead, hunkered down in the presence of a crazy person. Getting stuck next to one was always a possibility, and the standard reaction was no reaction at all, just steely indifference. Jon maneuvered himself directly in front of Guy to keep Jimmy from really seeing his face. If the president of their agency kept this up, he'd be in the hospital, and they wouldn't have any clients. Blissfully, happily, when the doors opened, Guy rushed out first, trailed by a number of relieved, if mystified, employees. They didn't appear to recognize the offender.

Neither Jimmy nor Jon said anything as they marched toward the waiting car, but finally the older man turned to him, "Doesn't that man work at LaGuardia and Knole?"

"He does, but I don't think it will be for long."

twenty-two

LA CENA GRANDE

First thing Tuesday morning, Jon determined to find Seth and confront him about his "Alternate Log" file, trying to fashion an artful way of saying he'd seen it without admitting to spying, but Claudia Thompson collared him first. She made him coffee in her palatial office, and as he sipped the strong brew, he wondered if his boss had heard about Guy's little elevator outburst the day before. She seemed distracted and anxious. "Thank God for Buffalo Grill and Synergene. Without them we'd be in trouble. Jesus, we'd have to look for a new client," she said.

"Considering our mental health situation, a pitch seems out of the question," Jon said.

The phone buzzed, and Claudia picked up. After telling her assistant she would take the call, she propped her chin on her hand and raised her eyebrows. "Yes, of course we'd love that. I appreciate the invitation. He invited Mrs. Danziger? Wonderful, haven't seen her in ages."

"What news?" Jon said.

"Juan Angel Peña wants us at dinner tonight at El Sueño de Oro, over on Fifty-Second and Third Avenue, all of us, and that includes Guy and his wife and Serena and any junior members of the team brave enough to show up. At seven thirty. Maybe we could send Guy to the hospital or something to get him out of the way? Of course, that wouldn't look good to a director who's about to work with him—along with fifteen stampeding buffalo."

"Guy has a way of shaping up when absolutely necessary," Jon said, but then realized with a start that he would have to postpone his dinner date with Eleanor.

"Please help me with him, would you? He may seriously be going down this time, and he can't now, he simply can't. Synergene is crucial to this company. They've found important cures for certain types of cancer, and this agency is going to help them tell the world. It's our civic duty, it's what we were put here to do."

"I'll give it a shot," he said, but didn't really want to have anything to do with his rival's resuscitation. As soon as he knew definitively whether or not Guy was responsible for the Buffalo Grill calamity, he might want him dead.

"For me, for the good of the company, for those with cancer. Think of them."

"Come on, Claudia. People with cancer have already connected with Synergene through their doctors. They don't need thirty-second ads telling them to do so." In spite of his work obsession, he was in touch with the fact that advertising alone did not rule the world.

"Yes, but the drugs are incredibly expensive, and insurance won't pay for them yet. We need to publicize this, so that everyone will make such a noise the price comes down, and doctors will scream for it. That's how cures get made. Haven't you ever seen an Act Up demonstration?" In contrast to her normal, tiny-voiced self, Claudia was almost yelling.

Back in his own office, Jon felt strangled by the twin problems of Guy and Eleanor. With the latter, he would have to change their plans, gracefully somehow, though he knew he would be irritating her further. When he heard her soft voice on her answering machine announcing that she was out, he said, "Ellie, I'm really sorry to do this, but a crucial business dinner came up tonight. I think I could meet you afterward, probably around ten o'clock, if that isn't too late. How about the King Cole bar at the St. Regis?" The minute he hung up he wanted to take back the whole message. Ten was too late to ask someone for a drink, and the Juan Angel dinner would drag on, impossible for him to leave. Why did he always try to smash so many events into one day? He thought of calling her again to make another change of plan, but then couldn't figure out when to see her before the Arizona jaunt. He would have to improvise.

The reason for Guy Danziger's elevator outburst the preceding afternoon had been a phone call from his lawyer, who had, in turn, received a message from Janey Peet's attorney. Jerry from Queens now possessed the story of the money in the bag. Even a young man two years out of law school could smell more moolah where that came from, and he informed Guy's lawyer that an action against him was about to be filed for sexual harassment and libel. Usually Guy subjected himself to soporifics, at least during the day: Quaaludes, liquor, anything to keep the fires damped down, fires unevenly fueled by amphetamines, which he used to keep himself functioning way into the night. The previous afternoon's news had sent him off into a rage, though, that he couldn't control with anything. Ungrateful bitch, horrible little lying shit-monger—that was how his wrath played itself out inside his head. He felt justified at yelling in the elevator. People were getting on just to slow his own progress home. He had jumped into his ever-present car and then sat and sat and sat, as the snow piled up in the clogged streets.

By the time he reached the townhouse, he had done more cocaine than he should and was in a blue blazes, hell-raising temper tantrum. Luckily, Marsia was nowhere to be seen. He stomped into his study and poured himself a vodka, resolved to calm down. He switched on the television and watched a true crime show about a woman who hired a hit man for five thousand dollars and root canal work on his teeth. Jesus, five thousand dollars. He could do that. He could get Janey killed, disappeared. She would be like Jimmy Hoffa and rot under a football field in Jersey. Before any of these thoughts could mushroom in his sodden brain, he passed out.

When he saw the blizzard the next morning, he knew that this was the perfect excuse not to go into LaGuardia and Knole. At ten thirty, Claudia called him and said, "Guy, are you coming in to work today?"

"Hi Claudia, yes, I thought maybe, well—later, I don't know. Perhaps at home—"

"By all means stay home. But Juan Angel Peña wants us for a seven-thirty dinner tonight at El Sueño de Oro. It's a wonderful Spanish restaurant. He invited Marsia as well." There was silence on the line.

"Marsia? What on earth for?"

"I guess he just wants to meet her. It will round out the party, give him someone to talk with about subjects other than advertising, you know, fresh blood." Guy instantly had a vision of Juan

Angel sucking away at Marsia's neck while everyone else slid slowly under the table. "If Juan, for whatever reason, decides not to do the shoot, we'll be stuck with no director at holiday time, so we have to please him. Anyway, do bring her, Guy. She's delightful and will be a real addition to the party." Even though he agreed for the moment, he really hadn't seen his wife lately. She might have moved.

Marsia hadn't moved. She'd been dealing with Rory's school activities, her basketball games, her driver's ed out on Long Island, all the things a mother—and a father—do. Guy knew this very well and was acutely aware too that he hadn't included his wife in any of the usual office parties or anything connected to LaGuardia and Knole this holiday season. When he emerged from his study to tell her about the dinner, she seemed pleasantly surprised and accepted the invitation immediately.

Converging on the restaurant was no easy task in a blizzard. Jon lingered in traffic over a half an hour and finally just jumped out of his livery car and walked. When he arrived, he found Claudia already sipping an aperitif in the Spanish style taverna. A small fire in the grate lit up the room, and the handsome goblets and green glazed plates made for a cheerful warmth. It was an entirely non-New York atmosphere, and Jon was prepared to enjoy it, though he kept worrying about his ten o'clock date with Eleanor, wondering how on earth he could speed the party along. "*Buenas noches*," Juan Angel called out to them and promptly flew back into the kitchen to talk to the chef.

"Oh, I don't know how *bueno* it's going to be," Claudia said, almost wailing.

Jon grimaced and said, "Perhaps we should make a plan."

"There's no possible plan. I'm only trying to ward off disaster." Claudia dabbed at her eyes with a cocktail napkin and sniffled.

Never had Jon seen this formidable woman so close to tears. He put his arm around her shoulders and leaned in to whisper, "Don't worry. I'll try to help," but before they had time to converse further, Serena Rawlinson appeared, looking perky and relaxed, despite the weather. Perky was really the most she could achieve, Jon thought grimly, as he eyeballed the Mexican bracelet with the little dangling people. She had dressed in her usual equestrienne garb, now with a black velvet shirt and a wide rhinestone belt. "Very cowboy nouveau," Jon said, "It suits you."

"Thank you. I'm getting ready for Arizona," she said and boldly looked him in the eye, fired with intention, though Jon couldn't imagine what it was.

"I am so glad you are ready, my dear," Juan Angel said, looming behind Serena. A waiter close by poured from a magnum of champagne into the director's glass, and he offered some all around. "*Nuestra Señora De Las Nieves*, our lady of the snows. I can't leave this stupid town. I'm forced to entertain you poor bastards, who have to put up with this every year. Come to Los Angeles, where there's no weather."

Serena blossomed a moment with his attention, but Juan Angel turned away. Several junior people arrived, struggling with their snow gear, grasping at the offer of alcohol. Just as the guests were beginning to feel their second drink, Guy and Marsia appeared. His usual disheveled self, Guy seemed to have located a suit, even if severely rumpled. Marsia, however, was a revelation to all. Though several of those present had met her previously, many others had expected some benighted little woman reeling under Guy's depredations. But no. She entered the room like the Amazon she was. Her loose dark hair flowed around her shoulders, and she wore a shapely dress of thin blue wool. In fact, she presented an almost alarming picture of health in contrast to that of her husband. Serena looked mortified. Certainly Jon had assumed that someone would rat out Guy to his wife, or that all his shenanigans would float through the ether and be absorbed into the woman's skin. If Marsia had learned anything, though, she showed no signs of it.

Resigned to the inevitable length of the dinner and impossible quantities of alcohol, Jon ate and drank with abandon, filling himself up with green and purple olives, asparagus in a walnut vinaigrette dusted with shavings of sheep's milk cheese, roasted mushrooms with hazelnuts, and tiny carrots in brine. These tapas were only the first course, but he didn't even bother to pace himself. Uneasily he registered Juan Angel's fascination with Marsia, whom he had seated next to himself. For the better part of an hour, the director talked only to her, dramatically excluding everyone else. Once in a while, Marsia would turn to the assembled group and try to include other people, but then Juan Angel monopolized her again. Serena sat directly across from this newly conjoined couple and appeared to be drinking herself into a stupor. Choosing to sit next to Claudia, Jon felt grateful for his boss's lack of small talk and her very low voice. He couldn't hear much, though once he thought he heard her mutter "pig fucker." He turned in alarm, only to see her nonchalantly taking a sip of wine, smiling at him strangely. Twice he left the table to phone Eleanor and leave messages saying he'd be late, but he never actually spoke to her.

Stuck at the far end of the table with junior creative people, Guy talked to no one as if the dinner was a potentially life-threatening event.

Juan Angel finally focused his attention on someone other than Marsia, specifically Jon, just as the waiters brought in the most extraordinary steaks. "You don't get this at Buffalo Grill, Jonathan. Do you think it's moral to sell people such food? I've never done a McDonald's ad or Burger King or any of that shit. I suppose one must sell out at some point, though," he said and laughed. The notion of Juan Angel selling out was so vast and complex that Jon couldn't think of a word to say. Along with his vacation retreat in Sedona, the director kept an apartment in Buenos Aires, another one in London, and it was reported that he occupied a "compound" somewhere in the higher reaches of Beverly Hills. Recently he had acquired a Richard Diebenkorn painting for his art collection—which purchase had been written up in the *New York Times*.

Jon just laughed when accosted this way because he'd had way too much champagne. "Buffalo Grill is good, solid American food, probably why all their customers are in the hospital getting heart bypass surgery as we speak. Buttery, big, a fair price, a real restaurant experience. I love it. Not as good as this, though."

For the first time in an hour and a half, Guy Danziger laughed. "I'd like to go to Arizona right now," he said, startling everyone at the table.

Juan Angel fixed him with a stare. "What will you do out there, old man? Frolic with the buffalo?" After this slight joke, he swiveled toward Marsia, seeking to include her in it. She didn't smile but gazed over at her husband for a moment.

"I'm going to commune with nature," Guy announced, and several people giggled.

"We should actually discuss the upcoming shoot, I think, despite there being someone here who won't understand," Serena Rawlinson said, glancing across at Marsia dismissively. She was clearly loaded, and Jon winced.

Ignoring Serena, pouring Guy's wife yet another glass of wine, Juan Angel barked, "I never discuss work at dinner and certainly not with a PA." She wasn't a production assistant and Juan Angel knew it, but this was one of his tricks, to insult someone by demeaning her status.

Silence descended until Marsia kindly nudged the conversation forward and drew out the director about his latest art purchase. "I love Diebenkorn. All that sensual color, barely contained in those grids and squares." He looked upon her with a more than friendly eye and in the candlelight, with the fire glowing behind him, he did indeed look noble, at least to Jon's eye, like an ancient Aztec king. Juan Angel reminded them of this in his plea for dessert. They all had to eat something chocolate because Montezuma had drunk twenty cups of hot chocolate a day.

Jon leaned into Claudia, whispering, "Look what happened to him! Can't we move this along?" He was in agony over making Eleanor wait at the St. Regis and just wanted to get out of there. He touched his hand to his jacket pocket, checking that he had Sasha's watch in its little satin bag.

"What did happen to him?" Claudia muttered, her eyes glazed with fear and drink. "Did someone stab him?" She fingered her butter knife.

Pulling his black hair behind his neck with a large hand, Juan Angel launched a missile onto the table. "Perhaps Marsia should come out to Tucson with us? At least I'd have a human in the group instead of all you ad types. You're like pod people from a movie."

Claudia awoke out of her snooze and said, "They'll be a lot of you there already, Juan. I think she'd be bored."

"That's very kind of you. I'd actually love to go," Marsia said and looked around for approval, of which she found none, especially not from Guy, who had an agonized expression on his face.

Serena got up and left the table, "For a smoke," she said.

"Why did you buy a Diebenkorn at all? Isn't he somewhat 'over,' as my daughter calls it?" Guy said, exploding into outrage at this big sex-commercial-art machine who was fondling his wife right in front of him.

"*Over*, a term you know about, Mr. Danziger. *Antiguo, viejo, muy fuera de moda.*"

Jonathan Neel knew that the director was capable of launching into a fit of insult so lacerating that none would leave the table alive, and the shoot would be off. Thus, he felt the need for a diversion. Just as the wine steward refilled Jon's glass with a 1982 Chateau Petrus, a three-thousand-dollar vintage, he sliced his hand flat across it and sent it scooting into a mound of frozen chocolate bon bons, and thence onto the floor, where it shattered. A stricken silence blanketed the room until Jon gestured apologetically, then laughed. "Sorry. I owe you money," he said to Juan Angel, who glared at him.

After a long, stunned moment, the director laughed too. He explained that he merely joked with people, and they never understood, but he saw that Jon did indeed understand. "Thank you, gringo," Juan Angel said. "Yes, beautiful Marsia, please come with us. We need a friend in the desert."

twenty-three

WIRED BUT UNPLUGGED

Eleanor too was running late. She hadn't been able to go home to change into her carefully planned outfit, she couldn't really deal with her hair, and, since she was so nervous about the evening, had accepted an invitation from her coworkers to dine at an Indian restaurant at seven thirty. As she whizzed past the mirror in the ladies' room at the hospital, she thought she looked vaguely like a panhandler. Maybe she could stop somewhere on her way to the restaurant on Park Avenue and buy something new to wear.

But she couldn't get a cab. She walked all the way west from York to Madison Avenue where the fashion quotient was high, but she had no time. It was almost seven. Holiday shoppers crowded the street, trudging through the snow with their heavy parcels, bumping up against her. Eleanor looked into each store window anxiously, not finding anything until at Etro on Sixty-Third and Madison, she spotted an extraordinary outfit, a long blue teal skirt with a tight blue camisole top, all made of shimmery material that looked like a mixture of wool and crepe. Over the mannequin's shoulder draped a black scarf with small turquoise beads at the corners. Could she carry something like that off? She flew into the store and raced over to a bored-looking clerk. "I'd like to try on the dress in the window, please. I'm sorry, I'm in a terrible hurry." Eleanor began to sweat under her heavy coat.

"Of course you can. What size?"

"Eight, I think." The clerk disappeared into a back room, while Eleanor kept looking at her watch. She hated to be late.

"There's no eight in the back. I'll check the one in the window." The mannequin was indeed wearing her size, so she had to wait still longer as the woman dismantled various limbs to extract the skirt and top. In the dressing room, the clerk insisted on helping her into the outfit. Suddenly Eleanor's body extended in an elegant line from the shoulders on down. The black scarf, thin but of sumptuous material, curved up toward her neck and accented her rich, dark hair.

"A sophisticated look, miss, very good on you. Do you mind?" The woman brushed her wild locks back behind her ears, the new haircut reasserted itself, and thus she was forced to divest herself of eight hundred of Sasha's dollars. As she stepped out onto Madison, a taxi magically deposited a fur-draped woman in front of her, and Eleanor darted in almost before the woman could pay, as she had seen seasoned New Yorkers do.

The restaurant turned out to be a vegetarian place smelling of incense and curry at Park and Ninety-Fourth. When she unveiled herself in her new attire, the effect on her coworkers was amazing. Even Bernie, the lab technician, appeared impressed. She felt strange emphasizing her breasts as this outfit did, but then remembered Tony's admonition on the phone, "Shadowed, hidden delights, Ellie, just remember. He will want to rip asunder the veil."

"Did you say that in a play somewhere, Tony, because that's the way it sounds?"

"Probably. I'm remarkably without words of my own."

After what seemed like endless variations on cooked lentils, Eleanor realized she'd better check to make sure that Jon was going to show up, attempting with her cell phone to access messages at her new apartment, but a cyber voice kept saying, "Voicemail cannot match your password with your phone number." Fortunately the St. Regis wasn't all that far away, and she didn't mind the walk, but upon setting off at nine forty-five, she realized the streets had become hazardous trenches of ice. When she saw an old woman trying to maneuver across Madison and Sixty-Ninth, awkwardly sliding toward a snowbank, Eleanor reached out her hand and just kept her from a tumble.

"Thank you, young woman," the old lady said, struggling up, still clasping her hand. "I always think I'll fall in the snow, nobody will help me out, and I'll just die."

"I'm afraid of that too," Eleanor said and marched doggedly toward the glittering lights of Fifth Avenue.

The King Cole bar looked festive on this snowy evening, filled with businessmen and clumps of audacious-looking females, somehow still sleek and coiffed despite the woolen hats they must have had to wear. The dress code was black or black-on-black, and there stood Eleanor, defiantly blue. Trying to spot Jon, she waited uncertainly, remembering how at college she'd been too shy to walk alone into the student union. Surely things had changed for the better, and this outfit demanded that she stand up tall. She maneuvered carefully between fashionable-looking couples, seating herself at an empty barstool, plopping her heavy coat on the floor, and noticed that peopled turned to look at her. She ran her fingers through her hair and shook herself a bit. "Do you have a drink that will really warm me up?" she asked the bartender.

The smiling young man said, "How about a hot buttered rum?"

"Perfect," she said, and watched as he swirled the ingredients into a goblet. She took a sip of the warm liquid. How inviting, but with that thought tears came to her eyes. Sasha, poor Sasha. She would never be warm again, and then with a sudden thrill of pain remembered that a man at the funeral had first met Sasha here; this was one of her favorite places. Was that why her very, very bad boyfriend had suggested it?

She looked at her watch, ten fifteen, the exact time she had planned, so that Jon would have to wait. But he was late, and, she realized now, why wouldn't he be? Hadn't Sasha always said that he liked to control other people's time? At ten thirty, after a second hot buttered rum, she braved the intimidatingly ornate lobby and asked to use a phone, since her cellular one seemed to have died. He wasn't home, but she left a terse message. This time, as she walked carefully over the marble floors back to the King Cole, several men eyed her, and one actually seemed to be following her. She turned away as he approached. Her mother had always warned, "Never sit in a bar alone," but here she was.

The place began to fill up and, despite the huge meal she had just had, Eleanor decided to order something to eat, as she was getting tipsy. Before her now sat four Chinese dumplings with an incredible hot sauce. Maybe it wasn't so bad to sit at a bar alone after all. At ten forty-five Eleanor decided that she should leave, but just as she was about to gather up her things, a handsome, fresh-faced man in his thirties sat down next to her and offered to buy her a drink. "Yes, thank you," was out of her mouth before she could think. Never in her life had she been picked up this way.

"I'm in town for several meetings," the young man said, "Ed Scarpino." He stuck out his hand.

She shook it, and it was warm and strong. "Eleanor Birch." She looked into his friendly eyes.

"My company puts me up here once a year. It's incredible. Are you staying at the hotel?" He didn't wait for an answer but went right on about the private butler assigned to his room, the enormous silk duvet covering his bed, and the bathroom bigger than his apartment in Philadelphia.

"I'm just waiting for a *friend*," Eleanor said, emphasizing the word as if her *friend* were as big as an elephant, and therefore he'd better not try anything. "I live down in Gramercy Park." She felt deliciously sophisticated saying that she inhabited such a fashionable neighborhood.

"I'm impressed," he said, and finally Eleanor relaxed enough to smile. Someone was hitting on her at one of the most glamorous places in the city. It was too much. Of course, she didn't want to tell him that she'd been stood up by another man.

"I work on the brain-mapping group at Weill Cornell."

"My God," he said, clearly stunned. "I don't believe it. You're a brain surgeon?"

She laughed, "No, no, just the team librarian and archivist for the project."

"Whew, I thought you might have to open my head right here." He said this as if he meant something else entirely.

Eleanor looked down at her watch. Jonathan Neel wasn't

going to show, and this man was getting awfully familiar. She pulled her coat up around her.

"You're not leaving?"

"Sorry, big operation tomorrow. They might have to go into the amygdala," she said, as if shooing away a dog. She tried to get all her gear without looking at him again, but he began helping her, piling her coat into her arms.

"I'll get you a cab," he said.

"That's not necessary," she said and remembered that if someone acted too friendly, he might be a rapist. She struggled with her clothes as Mr. Scarpino trailed behind her while she marched through the lobby. Somehow he managed to get in front of her and, once outside, gave the bellman a five-dollar bill and helped him hail a cab. She lurched into its dirty interior, thinking she could kick the guy if he tried to follow.

At just this moment, Jon Neel stepped from his own car at the corner and was striding toward the St. Regis. He slid on a patch of ice and, as he did, glimpsed someone he thought looked like Eleanor being helped into a cab by a man. He turned around, not wanting to be recognized. When he turned back, the taxi was gone. Had they gone off together? Had she actually been waiting all this time? He was a little more than an hour late, which for him wasn't too bad.

At the King Cole, he asked the bartender about a young woman with thick black hair, and the man instantly remembered her. "She just left."

Jon sat down on a barstool. "Great, now I'm in trouble. What do you have on draft?"

"Heineken," the bartender said and poured him a beer. "She went out with another guy," the young man added.

"Thanks. That's helpful," Jon said. For a girl from Ithaca, Eleanor was doing pretty well in the dating department, he thought, what with Seth Greenblatt also in tow. He decided that he would sit there half an hour, then call her, though it was way beyond a decent time to phone. What an evening, what a god-awful evening. The only delightful moment had come when Juan Angel flirted aggressively with Marsia and invited her out to Arizona. He wondered what Guy would do with that little suggestion. Or Serena? Probably take out a contract on the poor woman's life. After about twenty minutes, Jon realized he couldn't call Eleanor at this hour, especially after his egregious behavior. Still, it wasn't really his fault. Circumstances had intervened, it was unfair, and if only he had someone in his family to talk to, he would have told that person that the whole universe was conspiring to make him look like a bad man to this one particular woman.

Guy and Marsia had ridden home in silence after the extraordinary dinner. Even by their standards, the meal and the drink were excessive, and Marsia, in particular, kept rubbing her hand over her forehead. For Guy, of course, it was a publicly sanctioned booze fest, oh so rare these days, since people only drank cranberry juice and Perrier or other such rot. *Where had all the partiers gone?* he wondered as he stared out of the Lincoln Town Car's window at the snow.

"What a wonderful man," Marsia said, and patted Guy on the arm. "He seems so creative and interesting."

"Yeah, he and Hitler should tango."

"You don't like him?"

Guy sucked on his cigarette. "Like? I don't think you can like Juan. You can experience him in all his megalomania and genius and hatefulness and everything all at once. He's *sui generis*, like his own continent." These were the most coherent words he'd uttered in weeks.

"Have you ever worked with him before?" she asked.

"Never, but the stories about him are legion. Remember the famous Yoshida Easy Camera spot? The one with the beautiful woman trying to work the zoom? There's a reason the girl's eyes bug out of her head in such surprise. Seems the actress couldn't get the facial expression or the words straight so Juan shoved a fire extinguisher up her skirt, then blasted away."

"You haven't talked to me this much in weeks. You must have enjoyed the dinner."

"I just wanted to come in out of the cold," he said, and considered for a moment trying to explain something of his recent behavior but immediately thought better of it. The car stopped in front of their townhouse. As they struggled up the front walk, Marsia put her arm around his shoulders. "It's not really a good idea for you to go on the shoot, Marsia. You know that, don't you?" Guy said, as he hung up their coats inside the warmth of their home.

"Arizona would be a nice change. I could get a Kachina doll," Marsia said laughing. He growled something and headed for his study. He needed a vodka. Hunkered down in his big brown leather chair, smoking a cigar, enjoying the woody taste of the liquor, he wondered what the hell Juan Angel was up to with his wife.

* * *

After one message from Eleanor on Jon's answering machine, the "Where are you?" message, there was nothing. He knew she was furious and that a phone call from him would be a bad way to encourage that wrath. The next day, he decided to surprise her at work and take her for a wonderful lunch, assuming however, that she hadn't fallen for some guest at the St. Regis hotel, about which he would have to inquire. Usually he wolfed down a sandwich from the basket the girl always brought around, as meals weren't on his priority list, but he'd better make it a priority this time. "Do you hate me too?" he said to Snide, who responded, "You lazy motherfucker."

At Fifty-Fourth and York Avenue though, he began having second thoughts and considered making the cab turn around. Maybe she didn't like spontaneity the way he did. Maybe he'd walk in on a patient with his skull open trying to get mapped. "I'm experiencing resistance," he said out loud.

"What, buddy?" the cab driver said.

"Nothing. Stop here please."

The Brain Mapping Center was clearly labeled in the directory, the fourth floor, and Jon found himself winding through a maze of corridors and small offices until he found its homey-looking waiting room. "I'm looking for Eleanor Birch. I think she works here," he said to the nurse behind the admitting desk.

The gray-haired, unfriendly woman stared. "Are you a patient?"

"No, no, just a friend. I wanted to surprise her." There was a blizzard outside, little children in New Jersey were staying home to watch *Sesame Street* and eat Fruit Loops, but Jon had decided to stop by a major research hospital. It sounded stupid even to his ears. "I have something I was supposed to give her last night and, um, I didn't get the chance."

The nurse suddenly beamed. "She's over at the other library, but she'll be back in a few minutes. Why don't you wait? This sounds important—only today, eh?" She giggled.

Jon sat down in one of the chintz chairs, grabbing a magazine. He didn't really want to wait. It was a schlep up here from the Meatpacking District, and his time frame was tight; but then he thought, *no, this takes precedence.* He thumbed through several magazines, a dreary lot that included *Modern Parenting, Prevention,* and *National Geographic.* Still no Eleanor. He stole a glance at people he presumed were patients. One young woman had on a baseball cap over stubby hair, another older man wore a black homburg. He grabbed his cell phone and punched in Walter's number. Whenever he wanted to feel better about himself, he called his younger brother. He, at least, loved him. "Walter?"

"Hi, it's you, Jon. Why don't you call me?"

"I am calling you," Jon said, speaking louder than normal, as he always did with his brother.

"Where are you?"

"I'm at the hospital." This announcement set off moaning. "No, no I'm fine. I'm just meeting a girl, a friend."

"She's not sick is she?"

"No, she works with sick people."

"I'm not sick." Walter said this firmly.

"I know you aren't, buddy. You're great, and how's the painting?" He wanted to get Walter off any uncomfortable questions.

"It's good. Susan says it's good. Want to talk to her?"

"Ah, sure."

He waited a moment then heard a soft voice say "Jon?"

"Yes, it's me. I'm sorry we haven't met yet, Susan."

"We will. Walter loves you so much."

"Thank you. That's good to hear. Everyone hates me in New York."

"They do?"

"No, they don't. I probably just hate myself."

"I'm confused," she said, and Jon reassured her. He shouldn't be pouring out his self-loathing to a young woman in her situation.

"Listen, Susan, can I talk to Walter again?" He tried to tell his younger brother that he was going on a shoot in Arizona in two days and that he'd be back right before Christmas, so not to worry if he had more trouble than usual reaching him. Walter seemed fine with all this, only wanting to tell Jon about a new painting of Susan that he was doing. As he hung up, he spotted Eleanor in a white lab coat carrying a pile of file folders. She saw him too and scowled, then walked behind a partition. Apparently the nurse spoke to her in a way that demanded her attention, so she came back out into the waiting room.

"What do you want, Mr. Neel?" she said.

"I wanted to apologize for last night and see if I couldn't make it up to you by taking you out to lunch."

"Make it up to me? There's nothing you can do for me," she said and hurried back behind a door.

Jon didn't know what to do. The helpful nurse was looking at him. Finally she got up and vanished behind the door herself, then returned and gave him a smile, as Eleanor reappeared. He leaned in over the counter. "There's a beautiful restaurant right near here, and I have something for you."

"It took you long enough to get it to me," she said and glared at him. "You know, I really should have expected what happened last night. Sasha told me you always mess with other people's time. It's a sick habit." Nevertheless, she handed the file folders to the nurse, hung her lab coat over a chair, and retreated for a moment to get her winter gear.

Outside, the blizzard had ground much of Manhattan to a halt. It was a frozen, snowbound world. A cab had gotten stuck in the middle of the street, and there it still sat, like an exhibit at a museum. As they tried to walk, they kept sliding forward until finally Jonathan took her arm, but she shook it away. "Where are we going?" she said.

"Le Perigord," Jonathan said. "It's one of my favorites." They trudged on, but suddenly out of nowhere the York Avenue bus seemed to pitch itself right toward them. They'd both been looking down, trying to get their footing, when Jon heard the noise and grabbed Eleanor, shoving her backwards, almost knocking her to the ground.

"Stop that," she gasped, just in time to look up and see the bus bearing down on them. She clung to his arm, and they both fell now, at least out of the bus's path. It glided on the ice, then cantilevered itself sideways, finally coming to rest not five feet away from them. Eleanor tried to struggle out of the snow but couldn't get up until Jon finally pulled her up. Cheeks red and glistening, she took off her glove, wiping the snow off her face. "I met a woman who said she dreaded going out in this weather because she thought she'd die in a snowbank. We almost did," Eleanor said, out of breath.

"Nah, it wasn't even close. I was here," he said.

"Right, I'm so thankful," she sighed.

"I like to risk my life for lunch," he said, momentarily cheery at the idea of rescuing Eleanor. "I do it once a week at Buffalo Grill."

"Ah yes," she said. "It's so difficult being you, isn't it?"

They were alone in the restaurant, as very few others would brave the weather. The French maître d' welcomed them heartily and explained that their menu was somewhat smaller than usual, as half the provisions hadn't arrived. Once they ordered, Jon tried to explain his lapse of the preceding night. He elaborated on the wine, the food, the endless courses. "It was a true *festín*, as Juan Angel called it. I had to stay at that dinner. It was a matter of life and death."

Eleanor frowned at the incomprehensible seriousness with which this man took his work in advertising. Twenty minutes before, she'd been sitting in a room with people who'd had their heads split open. She could feel no sympathy for his plight and certainly didn't wish to commiserate, which seemed to be his goal in the conversation. Also, he clearly regarded the dinner as a punishment or problem of some kind, whereas most people would have been thrilled at such an opportunity, such food, such luxury. "The sacrifices you make," she said.

"I know it sounds ridiculous, but it was a sacrifice of sorts. The man is a ghoul, and we'll be out in the desert with him, not alone exactly. They'll be fifteen hairy beasts and several others who claim to be human, but the jury's still out on them. Alas, I'm a monk for advertising." This speech was meant to get a laugh, but Eleanor was in no mood.

"An odd sort of monkhood, I would think. The monkhood of excess."

"You think it's excessive in ad land?"

"Don't you? Probably not, but then maybe you've 'come to a better place.'"

"Undoubtedly. Look, I called you, and I kept calling you. Besides, didn't you go home with somebody else? It didn't look like Seth Greenblatt either."

"I most certainly did not go home with anyone else. A young man got me a cab, that's all, and Seth's just a friend," but the minute she said this, Eleanor started. Tony had emphasized over and over that the more men Jon thought were after her, the better off she'd be.

"Anyway, you need to be totally available electronically in this city."

"Why should I be available to you?" she said without thinking, then saw the man flush and turn away. "That very bar was Sasha's favorite. Why of all places, did you invite me there?"

"I don't know, I'd forgotten about that, I guess, though I remembered later."

"Do you have the necklace?" she said, wanting now to get away and stop this hateful conversation.

Jon pulled the small satin bag out of his jacket pocket and handed it to her over a plate of prosciutto and melon. She pulled the blue enamel and marcasite piece out, slipping it over her head. It dangled right at the V of her sweater. She looked down at the watch, but not before Jon reached over and turned the small knob on the side to set it. Awkwardly she sat, as he fumbled perilously close to her breasts. Even the maître d' watched with interest. Finally she pulled back and said, "I'll do it," in time to look into his eyes.

Jon took a sip of Evian and squeezed a lime into it. "Why

don't you have a cell phone or some way of getting hold of you? There was just no way to get in touch."

"I have a cell, but it doesn't always seem to work here. The company told me there's so much fraud in this city, they'll cut off your phone before they even tell you."

"Yeah, it's a real fraud-fest, drug dealers on every block, some of them very close to our building. We try to work with them though."

"It's a funny business you're in, anything for a laugh, eh?" she said but suddenly felt anxious that they discuss nothing more in that vein or he might grill her on what she had really been doing on her nighttime visit to the agency.

"It may not always be fun, but it's always funny, that's what a friend used to say. Of course, he's dead."

Eleanor was getting seriously annoyed with his jokes. "I have to get back."

"Have you made any progress in brain mapping?" he said, not wanting their lunch to end on quite this note.

"I don't make progress, the doctors do. But it's a fascinating study, yes." She suddenly smiled up at him the way Tony had taught her to, with warm eyes that lingered, in a contrived attempt at seductiveness. "The brain seems to be made up of hundreds of team players, each with a very specific position, any number of whom can take over for a downed player in an emergency and then learn to do the new job even better." Eleanor ran her hand through her hair. She felt ridiculous talking about science while concentrating on the tilt of her head.

"You actually watch operations?"

"I've watched one, and the woman was awake for part of it."

"It sounds like very advanced research."

"Amazingly enough, they do it all over the country now."

"I ask because my brother has some problems mentally, and I wonder if somehow this could help him."

Eleanor remembered the brother from the Herscholt–Zeiss detective report. "Does he have seizures?"

"No. His brain was deprived of oxygen at birth and so he's slow, he's different, all emotion."

"How sad," she said, and she meant it. Despite his air of pre-occupation and superiority, Jonathan Neel had a soulful quality, and she could feel it now.

"He's fine, moved in with his girlfriend, actually, though my parents are furious with him. They've been his caretakers for so long. You know how that is."

"Were you his caretaker?"

He looked at her in surprise. "I was, in a way, but I always pretended he was normal. I don't know if that was the right thing to do. He's a very good artist. I have some of his work in my apartment," but here Jon stopped himself.

"I absolutely must go back to work."

"Wait a minute. I'll walk you," he said.

"No, now that the bus has been immobilized, I have nothing to fear." She left the restaurant without looking back. Outside, in the white emptiness of a city in a snowbank, she breathed hard with relief. He had drawn her so physically close at several moments that she'd almost had to touch him herself, if only to push him away. She felt overheated, so hot that she opened her coat to a blast of cold air that left her, unaccountably, smiling. In the space of twenty-four hours, someone had found her attractive enough to pick up, here in the big city, where beautiful women swarmed in every bar. Eleanor glowed with an unaccustomed feeling of power and then closed her hand around Sasha's watch fob. Yes, she knew now she could "get" Jonathan Neel, but she would have to become more aggressive in her strategy.

twenty-four

IMPORTANT CALLS

Eleanor finally managed to listen to her calls from the previous evening on her voicemail. The first from Jon was garbled, as if from a cell phone. In the second, he was frantic and embarrassed, no jokes whatsoever. He made the dinner sound much more gruesome than he'd portrayed it at lunch, and she figured this embroidery of effort was typical. Even more interesting were three more calls, two from Tony Lowe, the other from Sasha's attorney.

Tony sounded almost hysterical. "Ellie, you're never going to believe this. It's karma, it's kismet, it's an act of God. I'm not going to tell you now. You have to call me. I'll be up late after the show. Just call any time." According to the machine, he had called ten minutes later even more excited. "I'm wired, Ellie. You've got to phone me, girl."

Sasha's attorney was more subdued. "Miss Birch, I'm finishing up the loose ends around the estate of Sasha Cole and wanted to check with you on this bonus matter. Could you call me on my cell? Thanks."

It was almost eight o'clock, and she still hadn't had any dinner. Why would she need it after that huge lunch? She opened her fridge and found some goat cheese, a few crispy crackers, and some olives. Watching the snow out her window, she sat down on the big velvet couch and ate. She didn't want to wait up until eleven thirty, when Tony got home from his show, so she left him a message telling him to call her at work the next day. About the attorney, she felt guilt-stricken. So far her records showed that she had spent only five thousand of the fifty thousand dollars. This was paltry indeed. The man obviously didn't know of her assignment; that is, she was pretty sure he didn't, but then she began to wonder. Perhaps he did and would be angry at how slowly she was going? The phone rang, and it was Tony. "What are you doing home?" she said.

"The show was cancelled. Nobody could get in from Bayonne. Very unusual. Anyway, listen, this is so incredible. Are you sitting down?"

"Not only that. I'm drinking a glass of wine."

"Perfect. None other than my boyfriend, Logan Piersall, veterinarian extraordinaire, has been hired by LaGuardia and Knole to oversee the buffalo being used in the Arizona shoot. Can you believe that?"

"Amazing."

"That's what I said when he told me. I confided in him about Sasha's little assignment, and he's totally up to speed."

"You told him? Can he be trusted not to tell Jon about it?"

"Of course. He'll do anything we want."

"That's wonderful, Tony, but what can we ask him to do? I mean, we're not going to try to kill this guy with a buffalo."

"I wouldn't totally rule it out! Anyway, Logan can be our mole, our informer, our man in Tucson. We've got to think how he can help us. Come meet me on Friday for a late lunch, and we'll figure something out."

Eleanor stared out at the snow, feeling queasy. This was getting all too real. Jon and his colleagues would be together in Arizona and here she was, engineering some crisis for him. Surely true revenge would harm her more than it would hurt him. Did anyone bad ever really get punished in the modern world? Most people got slapped down and jumped right back up again. Publicly humiliated, they went to jail, they lost all their money, shortly thereafter they were back in the newspapers, driving a Rolls.

Eleanor called Sasha's attorney the next day and left a message, but didn't hear from him until Friday, just as she was on her way out to meet Tony. The man's intimidating voice made her nervous, and she took the call in one of the back rooms of the library. "As I said in my message, I'm tying up loose ends on the Cole estate. It all went very quickly because Sasha made so many plans in advance."

At that moment, Eleanor felt sure he must know more than he was saying. "Isn't that odd for such a young woman?" she said. "I know very few thirty-three-year-olds who even have a will."

"It is a little odd, but she earned a great deal of money. Of course, her family's quite wealthy too. They may have guided her in the principles of financial management."

"Still, it's downright spooky, don't you think?"

There was a silence on the other end of the line. "Speaking of which," the attorney cleared his throat, "how are you doing on your assignment?"

"I'm making progress. It's a difficult matter, very personal. You must understand, since you're her lawyer."

"I don't know what it was that she asked you to do, only that it was important enough to give you a considerable sum of money, with a bonus. When I talked to Miss Cole, she said you would know when the job was finished. 'Tell her to keep the extra money, Harold,' she said, 'and do something worthwhile with it. I would trust Eleanor with my life.' Those were her exact words. 'You can give her the bonus when she tells you to.' You see, she had faith in you," the lawyer said. "Unusual in the modern age, don't you think?"

"It certainly is."

"I've got the bonus right here. It's contained in a letter. How should we leave this? I must say, this is one of the stranger requests I've had from a client."

"Yes, how are you to know I've done it?" she said, wondering how she was to know herself.

"Remember, she trusted you. That's all we can ask when we respect the wishes of the dead."

Eleanor shivered. She didn't like to think of Sasha as dead, even though she could picture her gravestone and knew exactly where she was buried on Long Island. "Please hang on to the letter until I call and tell you that the job is done. How's that?"

"Satisfactory," he said and hung up.

As Eleanor made her way down to the Buffalo Grill at Forty-Second and Eighth Avenue, where Tony had insisted they eat, she marveled at the trust her friend had had in her. It was heartwarming and must have come from the fact that during Sasha's outrageous love affair, conducted practically on the grounds of Dudley-Holcomb, where a girl could get expelled for smoking, Eleanor had told no one what she knew. Gossip was better than gold in that environment, and yet she had never even been tempted to reveal her friend's secret. Perhaps too all the years of quiet friendship, interest, and concern in what she was doing, the small attentions that Eleanor paid her had meant more to Sasha than she had ever told her.

At lunch she recounted to Tony the story of the lawyer's call. "How strange this whole business is," the actor said. "It's very Sasha though. She was fatalistic. But how could she foresee her own death? When did she write this will, right before the car crash?" He said this as he looked doubtfully down at his plate, which contained that day's Cowpoke Special, a double-sized steak, a baked potato covered in melted cheddar cheese, and three of the largest stalks of broccoli ever seen. "Four pounds, this is going to add four pounds to my body." Already several Buffalo Grillers were looking over at Tony. They weren't sure who he was, but they knew he was "somebody."

"I don't know when she wrote the will, but she arranged the money for me late in August, three days after she and I had dinner. Whenever I speak to her lawyer, he seems to be weighing what he says against 'attorney-client privilege,' holding back somehow. Why do you say she was fatalistic?"

Tony frowned. "Before she stopped flying, she took more and more drugs to get over her nerves, Xanax, Ambien, Halcion. I actually got worried about the stuff she was ingesting and gave her a lecture. 'Don't worry about me,' she used to say, 'It's all in the numbers, Tony. It's a statistical thing, how long you're going to make it in life.' Then she stopped flying altogether and would drive half the night to get to a meeting on time, in that tiny car and way too fast. Poor Sasha. I miss her." The actor wiped his eyes with the big orange Buffalo Grill napkin, and Eleanor laid her hand on his for a moment. "Anyway, as to your assignment,

Dr. Piersall is at our command out in the wilds of Arizona. It's too much, don't you think?"

"What should we tell him to do?"

"At the very least, he can report back on what's going on."

"Jon has it in for his rival, a man named Guy Danziger. Remember the eternally running Buffalo Grill ad? He thinks Guy might have set the whole thing up. Jon might have some scheme for them in the desert, though he hasn't said what it is. He seems like a pretty ad hoc guy. To show up is a plan in itself, if you know what I mean."

"I know the type."

"Maybe what we need from your boyfriend is an objective assessment of Jon's character. How does he behave to subordinates? Beyond our peering eyes, is he a bum or a good guy, at least to someone who doesn't know him?"

"That's doable and a very good idea. It'll allow us to gauge the severity of the punishment he deserves." Tony scooped up more sour cream and mashed it into the cheddar on his potato. "This food is like chow on steroids. I'll be ready for the World Wrestling Federation Smackdown when we're done," he said.

"It's grease fried over and over again," she said and noticed there was yet another banner announcing, "You Have Come to a Better Place," Jon's words immortalized.

"Is he in love with you yet?"

"Of course not, and he never will be. No one's ever been in love with me except for my mother, and that was brief." Eleanor shocked even herself when she said this. Truly, she had had few serious boyfriends, and in the last year and a half, the errant chemistry professor/athlete, working on his deltoids down under, had sent her only two cards.

"Ellie, you look better than half the women in the chorus of the show, better hair, better boobs, if you'll pardon the expression. Where does this burst of self-loathing come from?"

"I've always felt this way, though with my new haircut I do feel a little perkier." She smiled at him and tilted her head, puckishly, just as he'd taught her.

He laughed. "I don't have time to render emergency psychological therapy right here, not at Buffalo Grill, but let me just say that you look great. Any self-respecting heterosexual male would love to canoodle with you, don't you love that word, I say canoodle in no uncertain terms."

"Thank you. Jon actually does seem interested in a way I can't quite put my finger on. Let's see, when he pauses from his attention deficit disorder, he looks into my eyes and seems to see me for real. I often feel he's on the verge of saying something important, but then he doesn't."

"He gave you the necklace. You should wear it every time you see him to make him feel bad."

"I should probably give it back to Mrs. Cole."

"Don't do that. She has way too many jewels already. You have to get more aggressive, maybe even go out to Arizona."

"That's too nuts, Tony," Eleanor said, but knew that if she didn't get a little nuts about this, nothing would happen.

"Oh well, Logan will tell us everything anyway. Our secret agent!"

"Perfect."

During these same days Jonathan Neel was involved in several important, not to say hysterical phone calls himself. Holidays were always the very busiest season for him, and this year he'd be in Arizona right up until Christmas itself. Walter wanted him to come straight to his apartment on December 25th and was uncomprehending when he said he probably couldn't. "But we can cook, really we can. Susan has a book, and we've been making things. We made chocolate chip cookies with Corn Flakes."

"If I come to you without seeing Mom and Dad, you know something terrible will happen. They'll get out the shotgun."

This thoughtless remark threw Walter into a frenzy. "They'll shoot us? Susan, Susan, come and talk to Jon about the guns," he shouted into the distance.

"I didn't mean that, Walter. Please, look, I'll arrange to visit you right after my Arizona shoot, but it might slip over into Christmas, so I may not be there on the day itself." These words inflamed Walter into more worry, and they had an unsatisfactory conversation. He left his younger brother with a cell phone contact, two landline numbers, even a pager he used for shoots and finally, inexplicably, with Eleanor's phone number, though he didn't know whether or not she would even be in town. She seemed so responsible, and then there was her medical connection. He should inform her about this, but he didn't know quite how.

He phoned her at work and for once was actually able to reach her. She sounded surprised at his greeting. "I'm sorry just to call like this. It's my brother. I have to leave town tomorrow, and though he has all my numbers, I wondered if it would be all right if I gave him yours, in case of an emergency. I'm sure there won't be one anyway. He's thirty-five years old and lives with a girl named Susan."

Eleanor didn't know what to make of this call. She agreed,

of course, but was startled. Her victim was now asking her to
help him. He was walking himself into the jaws of fate, all on his
own two feet. "That's fine, Jon. I plan to stay here in any case,
except for maybe some time back in Ithaca to see my cat, but I'll
let you know if I leave town." She hung up the phone in consternation. What could he mean by it? Maybe he was confused and
still took her for a doctor. That must be it. He could focus so little
on who and what she was that he thought she was someone else.

Several days after the grand *festín* with Juan Angel, the
Danziger household was preparing for Arizona as well, though
Guy still hadn't figured out how to derail any possibility of
Marsia's going. Lately she'd been saying that she should get a
pair of cowboy boots. She obviously had done so, and he
looked down now at a pair of the round-toed black things in
her closet, professional looking, not "dude" stuff at all. Jesus
Christ, this was getting serious. That bastard Juan Angel had
planted a bad idea, and he would now have to unplant it.
Whatever Marsia knew of his personal exploits, he could tell
she had her radar up and was scanning the screen for bogeys.
There were some pretty big ones that he might have to shoot
down before she got them in her sights. The phone rang. Lately
he'd been avoiding that object as if it were his sworn enemy.
Whether Claudia, Janey, or Jerry, the lawyer from Queens, or
worse, Serena, they were all out to get him, and he refused to
talk to any of them. His phone list consisted solely of Leslie de
Santis. It rang again, and he heard Marsia's loud, cheery "hello"
downstairs. Suddenly worried about who might be trying to get
in touch with him, he picked it up and listened.

"Marsia, it's Juan Angel Peña."

"Juan Angel, what a surprise. Are you basking in the sun out in California?"

"*Qué lástima*, yes. It's seventy-five degrees. Please come with us to Arizona, lovely lady. We will be bored out of our wits out there. I will be bored. Those advertising people are dull as dirt and mean as shit. They frighten me, though I've known them for twenty-five years. You and I can visit Canyon de Chelly."

"Won't you be working?"

"It takes them hours to set up and then hours more to wrangle those damn animals. All the while, you and I will dig for artifacts." Guy snorted at this, and there was a pause on the line. He hung up gently.

Guy poured himself a glass of vodka, though he already had had two. He put in a slice of lemon, for a vegetable, he thought. That son of a bitch was trying to séduce his wife. As if he didn't have troubles enough, the giant Argentinean was trying to wreck his marriage or whatever was left of it. He sank down into a chair and watched the snow fall. He should kill himself. But how? Everyone would come to his funeral, and they would feel bad. Or would they feel good? He was so afraid of death. Oblivion was a wonderful thing, a mellow thing in the middle of life, but death, Jesus, it might last too long. He heard Marsia's footsteps on the stairs. She came into his study without knocking. "Why were you listening in on my phone call?" she said.

"I thought it was for—uh—" Guy's sentences were once again beginning to lapse. "I'm a very busy man, Marsia, in case you haven't noticed."

His wife gave a small yelp of derision. "I know you're busy, Guy, I just don't know what at."

"Yeah, well what's with the Argentine seducer? Why is he calling you? Have you been calling him? You're interfering in my business, aren't you? Flirting with the director of a potentially life-saving shoot."

"Life saving?"

"For people with cancer."

"Guy, you're amazing. I couldn't make you up as a character. He was just being polite, after that dinner."

"He's not polite, he's not nice, he's the fucking Antichrist, and believe me, I know. I know a lot of Antichrists, and he's the worst. You want to sleep with him, I can see it in your eyes."

Marsia gathered her chiffon robe around her, watching her husband as he railed, his shirt hanging over the top of his boxer shorts, gripping a large glass of vodka. "Guy, is it possible to reach you at all? Is there any shred of a person left inside?"

Clasping his wife's hand, he pulled her to him. "You can't go on the shoot, Marsia. It would be too much pressure for me. It's, I don't know—hard." He appeared close to tears.

She pulled away from him. "At least you want something, Guy. You haven't seemed to want anything from me in a long time."

twenty-five

FAREWELLS

LaGuardia and Knole labored forward, even if several of the principals had gone AWOL. Jon hadn't been able to locate Seth Greenblatt in days and was anxious to talk to him before he left town to ascertain the meaning of the "Alternate Log" file on that man's computer. He was so nervous about this that he diverted himself by lobbing nerf balls into the basketball net at the end of his desk. What should he do when he learned the truth? Impulsively he went down to Seth's office and, without knocking, shoved open the door. Before he could say anything, Seth burst out angrily, "Hey, man, you promised not to tell anyone that Guy had sent out the 'Confessions' himself. Serena told me you told her, and now everyone will know. He can fire me."

"He's not going to fire you over that, believe me. He's got bigger problems. I'm sorry about it, though. I had to straighten out the record. Serena was telling people that Guy told her I'd sent it out." Even Jon could barely keep clear on office machinations, as he said this, and having returned to the scene of his late-night snooping, he felt acutely embarrassed. Such was his position at the agency that he too could get rid of Seth, so the contest was unfair, and they both knew it. Still, the computer expert informed him that he considered it a real violation. "I'm really sorry. There was no other way to get out of a very messy situation."

"I don't know what's going on around here anymore," Seth said.

"That makes two of us. Listen, any progress on the Buffalo Grill thing?" Jon hoped that he wouldn't have to admit to peeking at Seth's desktop files.

"I've been searching old logs and emails related to the codes sent to the network. So far nothing."

"What about that "Alternate Log" file there?" Jon bent down and touched the screen where he saw the tiny folder.

"That's just where I keep all the info on my search. It wouldn't interest you."

Jon wanted to see that file and would do so by force even if he had to steal the computer and drag it down the hall. "Listen, how about I give you my BattleBot for the office contest? I call him 'Torquemundo' and he can kill even as he's being drilled from the right and the left." Here was heavy bribery, and Seth looked at him in amazed delight.

"Along with your help in fixing the Death Rattler?"

"Absolutely. Now show me that file." It was exactly as he had described it, lists of log entries with numeric codes, but it didn't contain an alternate log in its entirety, and that's what Jon had been looking for. "Fine so far, Seth, but keep working on this. CBS would have another copy of the log, right? Could we get it?"

"Networks never show us anything about their internal workings. You'd have to know someone there, and even then I can't see it. They regard us as the enemy."

"I can't imagine why," Jon said dryly. They were lucky that

the whole office hadn't been assassinated en masse, since Buffalo Grill was an embarrassment to CBS and must have been remarkably effective in driving away viewers. "Keep working on this. I'm counting on you," he said, and Seth nodded, once again pounding the computer keys. Jon liked the man and didn't really believe that he had had anything to do with knifing him, especially since he was a friend of Eleanor's, a woman who surely wouldn't go out with anyone that ghoulish. "How do you know Eleanor Birch, by the way?" Jon asked.

"My mother knows her assistant at a library up in Ithaca. Cool woman, that Miss Birch," Seth said. "I think she was freaked out by what was going on in the office."

"Any normal person would be," Jon said, not wanting to talk about or relive that gaudily awful night. "Do you see her regularly?"

"No, unfortunately. She seems quite busy."

Relieved that Seth didn't linger in any enemy camp, including Eleanor's, Jon went back to his office and decided to phone the war zone that was his family. "I'm sorry not to have called in so long, Mom, but I've been overwhelmed with work. I'll miss being with you at Christmas this year too," he said, grimacing at his lie.

Martha Neel had heard the work excuse so many times she barely reacted. "We know that, Jon. We're glad to hear from you at all."

"I'm on my way to Arizona shortly and just wanted to update you on Walter, if you don't already know."

"Don't mention that boy's name."

"He's not a boy. Anyway, I'll email you all my phone numbers in case of an emergency."

"He's got his girlfriend now. He doesn't need any of us."

"I don't know why you're acting this way, Mom. He's a grown man. He has to have a life."

"Please don't lecture me on what my son needs. Have fun on your shoot."

"It's not fun, it's business. I actually work eighteen hours a day when I do one of these." Whenever he tried to convey the nature of advertising, his mother tuned him out, certain he had wasted his life and his talent.

After this unsatisfactory conversation, Jon decided to stop by to talk to Claudia, assuming she would have a list of instructions for him before he left town. He found her confusedly punching buttons on her phone. First one line buzzed, then another. "Oh, Jon, sorry, my assistant's at lunch," she muttered. "Remember, I'm counting on you to get Guy through this shoot. I don't want him drunk or dead out there under a saguaro tree or whatever the hell they call it. Don't let a prairie dog eat him, though he'd probably be grateful."

"I'll try to keep him upright," he said but was getting tired of this request. Why the hell should he be Guy's little enabler?

She rattled the twelve hammered silver bangles on her arm and responded to yet another buzz. Picking up the phone and listening a moment, she mouthed the word *what?* at Jon and frowned. She held the earpiece away from her head, staring at it, then brought it close again, listening. Her voice became even lower, as she almost whispered into it, "You do, oh, you do?" She listened again. "We'll see, honey, we'll see." She hung up.

"Should I leave?" Jon said, and he meant that in every sense of the word. If Claudia too was having an affair, he'd just have to quit.

The CEO of LaGuardia and Knole stood up from her chair, then sat back down, apparently floored. She reached for a glass of water. "You will never, uh, oh my God." She pulled a handkerchief from the desk drawer and wiped her eyes. "I believe I was talking to Juan Angel Peña, though he obviously thought I was someone else. He was trying to get me to go on the shoot, muttering things in Spanish, sweet nothings I would imagine. Incredible, he had no idea who he was talking to."

"The digital age is remarkably imperfect. If someone's on your speed dial, things can get pretty weird."

Claudia looked at Jon and said, "He thought I was Marsia Danziger."

"Jesus, you know, it seems like a madhouse around here."

"A madhouse that sits on top of a billion dollars," Claudia said, then announced an immediate visit to the acupuncturist on the fourth floor, to "clear my medians."

When Jon got back to his office, he called Eleanor, hoping to confirm all the information he'd given to her on his contact numbers now that he was actually leaving town. At the hospital, they couldn't find her, and at her apartment he could reach only her machine. "I'm off to Arizona tomorrow, but, um, you've got my numbers, so I'm off."

Eleanor retrieved his messages after a long day at work, and she immediately called Tony. "This is such a big responsibility. The brother is really damaged, I think, and I've never even met the man."

"He trusts you, that's for sure. I don't know if that means you've succeeded or failed."

"Don't say 'failed.' I can't think I've failed. I'll just have to feel my way toward what's right." She had called Jon back at a time when she was sure she'd get his voicemail, to say that she indeed possessed all the information.

"I've got the Tucson info myself, so we're doubly informed," Tony said. "Here's hoping the hairy old beasts don't lie down and die. I worked with lions once in a commercial, and they absolutely wouldn't do anything. You have to give those cats amphetamines, otherwise they just sleep. I think our guy used a cattle prod. Anyway, we will get daily reports from Logan, who says he's making more money than he could in a whole month for only four days' work."

"Does he understand exactly what we want to know about Jon?"

"I hope so."

For his part, Guy determined to finalize his Arizona preparations with a night out on the town with Marsia. He had bought her an expensive gift, which he planned to lay upon her after copious liquors and foods at a renowned Midtown seafood restaurant. She wouldn't be able to resist and would surely never, ever see the state of Arizona, at least not this December. As he fingered the black velvet box with his hand, he watched the waiter debone a filet of salmon. His wife looked beautiful, glowing in a red dress and a black-and-red shawl. Her brown hair curved around her ears, and she had on a pair of diamond earrings, the product of yet another crisis, Guy thought grimly. This was all getting quite expensive. Marsia sipped a glass of Sancerre and gazed at her husband, who stared back at her, trying to strike the right note. "I've got a present for you," he said. He pulled the box out of his pocket and shoved it toward her.

Inside was a diamond necklace of graduated stones that went from a quarter of a carat to three carats at the center. Truly magnificent, it outshone any jewelry he had given her in their long association. She gasped and struggled with the clasp. Nevertheless, Marsia knew his tricks well, and this time she seemed aware of the direct purpose of the gift. "Guy, why don't you want me to go to Arizona? It's such a little thing, such a small trip, only two or three days. I've never seen you so anxious."

"I'm not anxious," he said, clasping a large glass of vodka. His eyes were bloodshot, and his shirt rumpled beneath a scruffy black jacket. He glanced down at several small paper cuts on his fingers.

"It can't be Juan Angel. You don't seriously believe that he has any interest in me?"

"What about you? Are you interested in him?"

In any marriage of long duration, there come moments when a few lethal remarks can destroy the relationship. Guy had been waiting to hear these for a long, long time, and he wondered if he would hear them now. "I'm interested in him only as a fascinating friend, not anything else, Guy. We are still married, after all." She said this last as if it would be big news to him.

It was always news to him, not that he was married, but that she would stay. She should have jumped ship decades ago, if she had had any sense. He gave less and less credence to what she said the longer she continued to live with him, especially because she periodically threatened divorce but never followed through. "I told you, he's the spawn of Satan."

Through the candlelight, in the plush interior of the restaurant, with the waiters murmuring, pouring water, bringing plates piled high with food, Marsia drew her wine glass to her lips and said, "I'll give some thought to Arizona, not going that is. I want you to do something for me in return."

"Name it," he said, smiling boyishly. Maybe she wouldn't take the necklace at all, and he could give it to Serena as a bribe.

"You must go into rehab for as long as it takes." She fixed him with her dark eyes. "You have to sober up, or I won't go on. I know I've said this before, but I'm serious now."

Guy flung his napkin down in front of him and paused. Pulling his coat up around his shoulders, he stood surveying the restaurant, then walked out. In the snow-covered street below, he backed himself up against a store window and pulled out a cigarette, waiting for her to follow him. After ten minutes and no Marsia, he signaled to his driver to open the car door and left her there to find her own way home.

In truth, he really liked his current state of loadedness and believed that it had something to do with his creativity, though he hadn't created anything lately. Should he agree to Marsia's terms? He looked out at the snowbound world of Soho's brick houses and shops. "Stop here, Jorge," he said to the driver. Clambering out, he tromped through the snow for several blocks. It was beginning to get ugly, blackened by soot, yellowed by dogs, and his beautiful shoes were soaked. What was the world really like when looked at sober? He didn't want to know. Again, Guy thought about killing himself. Somewhere in his battered mind and body he knew that he couldn't last long the way he was going. Why not hasten it all?

It had to be short and painless. He wobbled into the street. Only a few taxis were out, but surely he could get hit by one of them. They were always hitting people, even those poor souls who actually looked both ways as they stepped off a curb. The snow had frozen into hillocks, and he tried to find the middle of the road, where he would just stand. For what seemed like a long time, that's what he did. Several pedestrians passed by, eyeing him strangely. As he got colder, despite his heavy coat, he lifted first one foot, then the other, in an attempt to warm himself. Where were all the cabs? Suddenly behind him he heard the rattling tin of a New York taxi and the characteristic crunch of its tires in the snow. Afraid to look around, afraid to look his killer in the eye as the sound approached, he knew he couldn't get himself out of the way. Finally though, he turned in time to see a big yellow blur swerve expertly around him. All Guy felt was the swoosh of snow and wind.

In an instant, this suicide plan didn't seem so terrific, first off because he could picture his bloody limbs splattered all over the road, and second because his feet were numbing up on him, and that momentary perception of cold bolted through him like the shock of eternity. Guy didn't want to be cold forever, and death had to be like that. As he tried to hobble toward the side of the road, he spotted another cab hurtling down the street. Slipping on the dirty ice, he flung out a hand to keep from falling face down into it but tumbled anyway and got a mouthful of bitter snow. Panicking, he looked straight at the onrushing vehicle and uttered an agonized scream. Before his terrified eyes, the second taxi slammed on its brakes and rolled to within two feet of him. Through the open window the driver yelled, "Get out of the road, moron," before shimmying away at full speed.

twenty-six

BEASTS OF BURDEN

Loitering near the departure gate at JFK for the evening flight to Tucson, Jon was in an unaccustomed state of panic. He chomped on a Twix bar and jiggled anxiously up and down on his feet as he saw Guy Danziger approach. He'd had a stomachache for two days over what was about to happen. He would have to introduce him to Jimmy Goodlaw. Honestly, he believed that Jimmy hadn't gotten a good look at the elevator offender, since he, along with everyone else, had stared straight ahead when the crazy person began cursing. Still, he couldn't be sure. Guy had never worked on his account before now, but Jimmy must have met him somewhere along the way, either at a business conference or more likely an agency social event. Happily Guy had gone completely Western for this little junket, rigged out in blue jeans and a leather jacket, a getup markedly different from his elevator garb. Maybe that would help. Jon could feel his gut seize up. Was there any way to hustle Guy onto the plane before Jimmy? Alas, no, as a ridiculously happy CEO of Buffalo Grill strode toward them, suede overnight bag in tow. He stuck out his hand, shaking Guy's heartily, even while peering at him a little strangely. "Good to meet you. I hear that we're sharing buf-falo."

"That's the rumor. I just hope they show up," Guy said.

"They'll show up, don't worry. We have a good wrangler in charge of the happy beasts," Jon said, beginning to breathe again, relieved at his client's apparent obliviousness.

"Buffalo Grill's two million dollars says they'd better show up," Jimmy muttered.

Despite his recent suicidal leanings, Guy felt almost jaunty tonight, mainly because his wife wasn't accompanying him. Up until six thirty the previous evening, just before he was to leave for the airport, she'd kept her husband in doubt about her plans. She'd even had her suitcase open, but when he heaved his own travel bag over his shoulder, she pulled back and said, "I won't come, Guy, at least not on this flight. Maybe in a day or so. You enjoy yourself or work or whatever." Giddy with relief that he was still alive and his wife hadn't left him as she had threatened, he was prepared to like everyone, if just for this evening.

While the three men waited near the gate, Serena Rawlin-son, also in jeans and a leather jacket, strode up to them, hair screwed into twin knots at the top of her head. "Hello, bucka-roos. Are you ready for our Western adventure?"

"The usual suspects," Guy muttered and uneasily registered the producer's gaiety.

On the plane, as he reclined into his seat, he surreptitiously ladled two Xanax tablets into his hand. In the old days, the ladling had been done together, and he could feel Serena watch-ing him. Maybe she'd try to seduce him in the bathroom? How

long a trip was it, four or five hours? He vowed not to take a whiz
at all, no matter how desperate he got. By the time they took off,
twenty minutes after getting seated, the Xanax had kicked in,
and Guy felt relaxed, even hungry. When the dinner appeared,
he wolfed down the steak and the potato, while he noticed that,
across the aisle, the CEO of Buffalo Grill did the same.

"An odd fellow," Jimmy muttered to Jon, glancing over at
Guy.

"Hmm," said Jon. "He's brilliant at what he does." He didn't
want to call undue attention to the man and his problems, since
Jimmy might have a recovered memory epiphany about the elevator scene.

"I know him from somewhere, or maybe I've seen him at a
charity do."

"He's got that kind of face, everybody thinks they know
him. He's a very knowable kind of guy." Jon clamped his mouth
shut. This burbling could only make things worse. However,
Jimmy seemed satisfied, leaning back in his seat, asleep before
the flight attendants even served coffee.

The Tucson hotel Serena had chosen nestled back into the
mountains on the northern side of the city. The sprawling property sported streams, cactus gardens, and two golf courses, and
the hotel itself was built out of gray stone carved from the Santa
Catalina Mountains that rose up behind it. At breakfast the next
morning, when the principals converged on a Mexican buffet set
up on a patio by the pool, Jon wondered what had happened to
Juan Angel. "Wasn't he supposed to be here already?" he said, as
he sat down with a heaping plate of eggs, chiles, and muffins.

"He certainly was," Serena said grimly.

Just then that same man appeared at the hostess's podium,

surveying the patio outside. When he spotted the advertising people, he barely nodded, got a plate of food, and sat alone at another table nearer the pool. Several minutes later one of his minions joined him. "That bastard," Jon said, before he realized he would have to explain himself to Jimmy.

"Who is he? He looks like some kind of Indian or a Kachina doll carver," Jimmy laughed.

"That's our director," Jon said, regrouping.

"He's very good, famous even," Serena said.

"Infamous," Guy added. "He's after my wife." Jimmy guffawed, and Serena shot her former lover the look of an adder about to strike.

Guy acted as if he had suddenly discovered food, probably because of the joint he had just smoked, and was plowing through a vegetable and cheese omelet as if he had never tasted an egg, all the while trying to avoid Juan Angel's gaze, which was straight at their table. Authoritatively, Serena reminded everyone that this was a professional adventure, and she embarked on a discussion of what they were expected to do this first day, which was prep, and then what would happen the second and third days of the shoot. The animals were to arrive in two trucks later that morning, along with the man who was both wrangler and veterinarian, Dr. Logan Piersall. "I hope we can pet them," Guy said to a mystified audience.

"They're wild herd animals, Guy," Jon said. "They won't want to get near you."

Juan Angel chose this moment to approach their table. "Good morning, advertising people," he said, "But I see one stranger in our midst." He thrust his big brown hand out toward Jimmy.

Jimmy stood to address the vastly taller man. "Jimmy Good-law, from Buffalo Grill."

"I've never eaten your food, I'm proud to say, though my sons have. Can't keep them out of the place."

"If you ever ate there, you'd know we serve a good, clean American meal, one of the finest available in the world of casual dining, especially for the price."

"Is price ever an object when it comes to food?" Juan Angel smiled down at the table in his fearsomely charismatic way.

"It is for the vast majority of Americans, those who cannot be gainfully employed in a money-gusher like advertising," Jimmy snorted.

Jon rose now to defuse this small bomb, but he was too late. Juan Angel leaned in over Guy, who had been assiduously ignoring him. "Where is your wife?"

Guy lifted his head and said, "She's back home where she belongs."

"But it would have been so charming to have her here. I don't want to talk to any of you advertising assholes."

"Fortunately, you don't have to talk to us at all, Juan. All you have to do is shoot two commercials," Jon said.

"You kept her away from me, didn't you?" Juan Angel still looked at Guy.

"My wife does what she wants. She's an American," Guy said, as if the man before him had just crossed the border illegally in a truck.

Juan Angel reared back on the heels of his boots and glared. "Yes, of course she does. *Qué lástima*, though we can amuse ourselves at *fútbol*. Do you play it, Guy?"

Guy truly detested sports of all kinds. Once, when he was

forced to attend the Olympics, he had stayed in his hotel room and watched everything on television, then regaled his clients with how wonderful it all was at dinner, never having seen a single live event. "Football? Sure, I'm a defensive end."

"Soccer to you, gringo."

"I don't believe in sports. I might hurt my drawing hand. I have it insured," Guy said.

Serena dissolved into giggles, while Juan Angel glowered down at her. "I hope you have a lot of insurance," he said and strode off.

Leslie de Santis chose this moment to descend upon the group. She looked remarkably chipper, and Jon took a moment to pity her innocence. She was a doctor, a discoverer of new drugs, an actual person in the world like Eleanor. Getting strung up with these ghouls, and he included himself, was bound to be unpleasant.

Out in Sabino Canyon, northeast of Tucson, Jon watched as the trucks carrying the buffalo wheeled into view. At this hour of the morning, the hills glowed with soft yellow light, and their location site, an outcropping high at the edge of one of the canyon's most spectacular waterfalls, was covered in saguaro cactus. A tent had been set up nearby where the crew worked to prepare for the next two days' events, while the buffalo clattered down ramps out of the trucks, supervised by several cowboys who looked like the real thing, and another man who must have been the veterinarian. Logan Piersall finally came over and introduced himself. "How are the critters doing?" asked Jon.

"They survived the trip well, though one may have injured his leg when he kicked the side of his stall." Logan was an athletic man in his late forties with brown hair and a beard. He wore khaki shorts, sported a pith helmet, and seemed to Jon seriously focused on making sure that people behaved properly around the animals. "I'd like to see the final storyboards. We need to protect the buffalo, and from what you've sent me so far, it looks as if there may be some danger."

Guy approached the two men, listening, "You mean when they, uh, thunder—thunder—"

"Thunder down the canyon?" Jon said.

"That's it."

"Yes. I don't quite see how you're going to get the illusion of thousands of buffalo," Logan said.

"Juan's a genius, and if you get lucky, he'll tell you about that at length." Jon hoped he was right about what their director could do.

"I've been warned," Logan said. "I have friends in New York, and I've worked on several commercials, though never for this guy."

Serena had scheduled the Synergene shoot first. That meant that Guy and Serena and Juan Angel, with Leslie looking on, sat around a small table in the tent going over and over the preparations. As they had storyboarded it, the buffalo would come racing down the canyon five times. Juan Angel would have to shoot each sequence at a different camera angle, making it appear as if there were thundering hordes, and he wanted the order of the animals switched for every sequence. That meant fifteen buffalo would have to be tagged and carefully lined up for each shot. "Buffalo don't really like to be lined up at all. They move more in clumps," Logan suggested, as he entered the tent.

"This is art. Anything can be done," Juan Angel said. Despite the large group present, the director focused his attention solely on Guy.

A man who was holding up not at all well under the heat and dust of an Arizona noon, Guy experienced the grisly interest Juan Angel extended toward himself as if he were under klieg lights at the police station. The director's constant questions— "What about this, Guy?" "What about that?"—had him in agony. He didn't want to make decisions, he didn't like to, and for years he had worked with people who simply took his ideas and ran with them. "Should we have them come down from the left or the right?" "Let's see, the order. Do you have pictures of each buffalo? What about the color arrangement of the animals? We don't want four brown bunched up and then five blacker or whatever."

Guy finally asserted himself. "How many fucking shades of brown can there be, Juan? It's *marrón*. Just let the bastards run down the hill five times, and we can go home."

Juan Angel drew himself up and fixed Guy with those black eyes of his. "Are you trying to speak Spanish, fucker?"

"They're all over brown, that's what I'm trying to say. The idea that some butthead sitting at home on his couch will be color-coding the buffalo in his mind is just insane. He'll be out getting a beer, anyway." Leslie and Serena sat frozen and silent. Guy stood, wobbling a bit. He looked half electrocuted, his thick, white hair sticking up from the top of his head, the small white scar vibrating. "And you just eat me, you big Argentinean fuck," he announced, walking out of the tent, heading for a chair near where the buffalo were being groomed.

Juan Angel also left the tent and retaliated by calling his crew to come play soccer. Jon heard the shouting from a distance and watched as precious time and money were consumed by their enraged director, who was dramatizing to both client and agency alike the full effects of his power. Every hour he didn't work cost them thousands of dollars, but what could they do? They were out in Bumblefuck, USA, his hostages.

Jon declined to play because for one, he thought he might be tempted to ram him, and killing the director was never a good idea; furthermore he didn't want Jimmy to know that he had been frolicking. His client had shown up early that morning, then gone back to the hotel, but still he would hear about it. "I'm going to pace myself," is how he put it to Jon.

Logan busily supervised the grooming and tagging of the animals. Their hair was matted and dank, and great clumps of it came out when the groomers, using currycombs for horses, would try to pull through it. The sun grew more intense, though the temperature was only in the mid-seventies. Jon grabbed the hat he had stashed in the crew truck and stood watching the proceedings, calmed somewhat by the sight of the big animals. They barely moved, occasionally lowering their heads to feed on whatever poor scrub they could find, their great brown eyes watchful and serene, though he knew they could get mean if teased in the wrong way. Logan had already told him they be-haved best when actively prodded, which on the day of the shoot he would do from a horse. Relieved to feel a moment of peace, Jon moved away from them and sat on a high, flat rock, surveying the landscape.

The soccer game finally ended, Juan Angel dripping with per-spiration as he jogged over to where Guy sat under the tent and insisted that they check out the buffalo together. This show of friendliness momentarily stumped LaGuardia and Knole's president, but he agreed, hiking out with the director to a steep hill near the wash where the animals grazed. Exhausted, without thinking, Guy stumbled down among them, patting them on their rumps, slicking back their thick hair. "See if you can get them to move," Juan Angel said, stepping back. "They look asleep."

"Why would I do that?" Guy said, anxious not to show weakness in front of him.

"To get them ready for the shoot," the director suggested.

Guy pulled off his leather jacket and began flicking it in front of the eyes of one of the larger animals as if he were swatting a fly. Juan Angel laughed, egging him on. Across the wash sounded the voice of Logan Piersall: "Watch it, Guy. The big bull is getting annoyed."

"Oh, let's annoy the big bull," Juan Angel said and handed Guy his own jacket. The Argentinean backed slowly down the hill away from the grazing animals, while the hapless advertising executive stood his ground, feeling momentarily heroic.

Guy turned Logan's way, waving the two jackets above his head. He was giddy, loaded, feeling as if he were somehow in a movie and please God let it be over soon. Logan started toward him at the same time that the bull planted his forelegs, going straight for Guy. The bull lunged. Guy flew up over his horns, onto his back, and down the other side. By the time Jon and the vet got to him, he was out cold. They couldn't tell if he'd been kicked or gored or had just passed out in fear, but when Logan examined him, he could find no specific injury. "Probably just had the wind knocked out of him," he said.

Jon started for Juan Angel, yelling, "You son of a bitch," but the defiant director simply tipped his hat and laughed. A crew member had already called 911, and shortly thereafter, an ambulance came roaring through the Arizona desert. Jon stood by the poor man, as they lifted him up. "Guy, are you all right? Can you hear me?" He twitched and moved a bit but appeared unconscious. "Come on, wake up, buddy." Slowly one of his eyelids flickered upward. Jon grasped his arm and held on to it.

Guy opened his mouth, "Dogs have always liked me," he said and passed out. While the crew gathered round, Jon tried to get into the ambulance with him, but a paramedic told him there was no room and slammed the door, so he grabbed one of the drivers and demanded to borrow his car. He couldn't let Guy just disappear into the emergency room; no self-respecting member of the medical profession would ever let him out.

At the hospital, Jon waited in the lobby for two hours while the doctors ministered to the fallen ad man. He had his cell phone on all the while and had already received frantic calls from Serena, Leslie, and Claudia. "I am watching over him, Claudia, but he's hard to keep track of. Juan Angel encouraged him to dance with a buffalo." She wasn't amused and let Jon know it. His mission was clear—save Guy from himself and anyone else who was trying to kill him. As Jon sat there leafing through *Tucson Living*, he wondered, once again, how he'd gotten himself into the impossible situation of babysitting a person whom he himself had fantasized killing off, professionally speaking, through Juan Angel. He truly wanted to run LaGuardia and Knole. He knew he could do it better than anyone else; he had been training for the job for the last ten years, yet he found himself scheming against this poor, benighted dipsomaniac, a man who could be decapitated by a feather, let alone by a buffalo.

Hooked up to a saline drip, Guy lay covered in sheets, attached as well to a heart monitor. He looked fine, if a little puffy, and his eyes were closed. Jon was on the point of leaving the hospital room when a young doctor appeared, flipping through pages on a chart. "How is he, Doctor?"

"He may have a concussion. We're going to give him an MRI later. Other than that he's fine, except well, he's loaded on a drug cocktail of something we can't quite figure out. You might ask him. We've asked several times, and he denies it."

"He would."

"It's important that we know, in case further treatment is necessary."

Jon sat down next to Guy, who opened one eye the minute the doctor was gone. "Guy, have you been taking any medications that the doctors should know about?"

Now the sick man's eyes widened. His pharmacopoeia was so extensive that he knew pills only by their colors. "Of course not," he mumbled.

"They really have to know what you've been taking, in case they have to release pressure in the brain or something."

Guy stared at Jon in horror. "Get me out of here," he said and ripped out the IV line. "Nobody's fooling with my brain." He raised himself up in the bed, flailing at the sheets. Jon tried to push him back down, but he was amazingly strong.

"They probably won't do anything, just an MRI, but they need to know."

"I haven't taken anything. I'm clean as a whistle, and if you get me out of here, I'll never forget it."

"You might be injured or something if you leave," Jon said.

Guy clawed at his hospital gown and began to wail. "Get me out, get me out, please!" he cried, struggling off the bed. Since the man clearly would flee on whatever steam he had left, Jon helped him into his jacket, then put his arm around his shoulder to usher him down the hall. Nurses and doctors stared, and the young doctor in particular legged it down the corridor after them, but they had too much of a head start.

Out in the parking lot, Guy clasped Jon's arm, "Thank you, I'll never forget this."

"Just get in the car. I think they'll come after us."

"Those motherfuckers, they can't." But two nurses and the doctor now stood at the emergency room door gesticulating and yelling at them. Before Jon could stop him, Guy lowered the car window, leaned out, and shouted, "I'm needed in New York. If you follow me, I'll shoot you with a gun."

Their drive back to the hotel took place in silence, though Jon desperately wanted to listen to the five messages recorded on his cell phone. He had to calm the troops, no matter on which coast they lived. As they pulled up the driveway into the hotel, Guy leaned over to him and said, "I have a confession."

"You do? Whatever could that be? I've exhausted myself trying to figure out what you might have done to me."

"You saved my life, after all." Fed up with the shenanigans of the day, nevertheless Jon was struck by the moment; at last he would learn how Guy Danziger had sabotaged a million-dollar commercial. "I told everyone that it was you who sent out my 'Confessions' file, when it was really me, by accident. I'm sorry, Jon. You didn't deserve it. I was humiliated—I don't know— wretched."

"Is that all?"

"Of course that's all, what do you think?" Jon thought a lot, none of which he said.

Guy staggered off toward his room, and by now it was late afternoon. Jon should have gone back to the shoot location, but he was too tired and figured he had done his bit for LaGuardia and Knole on this particular day. Staring at the cactus garden visible out the giant picture window in the bar, he punched his security code into the phone and listened to the messages on the cell. One was from Claudia again begging him to help Guy, but the remaining four were from Walter, each progressively more hysterical. First from the bus station—"Where are you, Jon?"— then from out on the street and finally from a hospital waiting room. "They're taking me somewhere; I can't find Susan." Walter was so incoherent that he hadn't given him any information on his actual whereabouts. When Jon retrieved his messages from his home answering machine, he learned from Susan that his brother was in Bellevue.

twenty-seven

THE RED EYE

S itting at the hotel bar, Jon swung into action immediately, first by calling Bellevue, but right away a difficulty presented itself. The hospital had one of those endless voice messages indicating four or five choices, none of which applied to a lost relative. Finally he reached a human being, but that person had no record of Walter. When he tried to say his brother would be in a waiting room, the operator pointed out that he was thus not officially admitted. Jon next called his parents, who weren't home. He left them a message telling them what he knew so far and asking them to contact him. Finally he called Eleanor, who also didn't respond, talked to her answering machine, then called her at work. "Is this that nice Jon person?" the nurse said, remembering their brief encounter. "She isn't here, wait, I think there's a note. No, I can't find it or maybe someone threw it out."

"Don't you know when she'll be back?"

"It's the holidays, dear. A lot of people take off extra time."

Jon called Bellevue again and after ten minutes on hold learned no more than he had known a half an hour earlier. He decided to make some contingency plans. "What time are you coming back to the hotel?" he yelled at Serena above the static on his cell phone.

"We'll be back in an hour, but you don't have to scream at me. The person you should really be mad at is Guy."

"What are you talking about?" Jon asked, only to be cut off. Was she trying to finger Guy as the prime mover in his Buffalo Grill disaster?

He called Bellevue again, asking to speak to the intake supervisor, and this time he got more information. Once the woman was convinced that he was a bona fide relative, she told him that Walter Neel was being evaluated at that very moment and would have to spend at least two nights, possibly more, in the hospital. "Evaluated for what?"

"He started causing problems at the Port Authority. Fortunately, someone from social services was there and had him brought here."

"Why is that fortunate? You've incarcerated him. There's nothing wrong. He's a little slow, that's all. Wasn't his girlfriend with him? Susan?"

"I see that there was someone, but she, let's see, I don't know what happened to her."

"You've actually lost a person?" By now he was shouting.

"Being rude to me isn't going to fix anything, sir. I don't see her right at this moment, and your brother does need an evaluation. He was quite belligerent by the time he got here."

"That's because he doesn't want to be there," Jon yelled, slamming his phone down onto the bar. Where was everybody? Had Walter gone to New York without telling his parents? Of course he had. Where was Eleanor? Would she leave town without letting him know that she was unavailable to help? Probably.

There was nothing for it. He would have to go back to New York and get his brother out of stir, then return to Arizona, all in the space of twenty-four hours. His shoot wasn't until the day after tomorrow anyway, and he'd certainly done faster turnarounds in the past. Of course, that left Guy on his own, but it also left Jimmy, who would regard this as a major dereliction of duty. Could he abandon Walter to Bellevue for three solid days? That seemed a betrayal that the poor guy would never get over. "Give me another beer," he said and stared at a round, fuzzy cactus. He broke into a sweat.

What would happen if something else came up, and he couldn't get Walter out in time to get back here for his shoot? He knew that once you were in the hands of social service authorities in New York, you might languish there for goddamn ever. He could picture Walter's incoherent rage, picture him acting crazier and crazier the minute the doctors asked him if he was crazy. He called Southwest Airlines and got himself on the red eye, then booked his return for the next afternoon, which would bring him back to Tucson in the evening. It would work fine, if he could just straighten out his brother's situation. Jon had never been to Bellevue but pictured it the way everyone else in the city did who read the *New York Post*, patients tied to beds, helpless screaming people in straitjackets, a whole host of tortures culminating in electroshock therapy. He had to get Walter out, no matter how dangerous it was for his career.

If for some reason he couldn't get back in time, he would have to ask someone to oversee the Buffalo Grill shoot. Who could do it? Nobody junior, as he or she wouldn't be able to cope with the director, certainly not Serena, and nobody on Juan Angel's crew; that would be a major breach of etiquette. No, it had to be someone from the agency, and there was only one such person with the requisite authority—Guy Danziger. What a concept. The man was one step away from the local Bellevue himself, but maybe a real task would energize him. "Give me a tequila shooter," Jon said. He rang the older man's room. Someone picked up and didn't say anything. "Guy, Guy, are you there?"

"Who is this?"

"It's Jon. Listen, I have to talk to you. I need you to do something for me."

"You need me?"

"I have a family emergency. I have to go back to New York for one night. I should definitely be back in time for the shoot, by tomorrow evening for sure, but in case something unexpected happens, could you oversee at least a half-day of Buffalo Grill?"

"You have a family?"

"It's my brother. He's in the hospital." There was silence on the line. "I'm coming up," Jon said.

Guy's room was in a state of chaos appropriate to that of a fifteen-year-old boy: clothes strewn everywhere, half-opened Cheetos bags lying about, thick coffee baked to the bottom of a little pot, and the man himself sitting in a chair in his pajamas. He hadn't wanted to let Jon in, of course, but he'd pounded on the door so hard that Guy had to. Jon sat himself down on the floor next to him and put his hands on the older man's arm. "Guy, I know you've been messing with my career."

"I have not. What the hell are you talking about?" His state was such that he would have denied his name was Guy. He had a policy, just deny everything and then call a lawyer.

"I need your help now, the agency needs your help, and I don't want you to fuck me up. I'll be gone for a very short time, but you have to appear coherent enough to indicate that you and I have talked and that you can handle everything. You won't have to handle anything. I'll be back by tomorrow night, in time for the Buffalo Grill shoot the next day. But just in case I don't return in time, I have to know that you can and will supervise the shoot."

Guy wiped his face with his hand. "Jon, I—"

"I have to leave for the airport in twenty-five minutes. You can't think about this."

"I'm so sick," Guy wiped his face again.

"Just lie down and sleep it off, and tomorrow you'll do fine. I'll be back. Should I get Serena to wake you up and keep you in line?"

"No," he screeched. "She wants to kill me, the way Juan Angel almost did today." The man was wailing.

"Guy, I have the gift of second sight, and you are not going to die on this shoot. You are going to survive and triumph." Jon made this up out of whole cloth, but then what was his life but a number of startling fictions?

"You do?" Guy clasped his arm. "Thank you, thank you. I don't deserve your help. I should confess—"

"I don't have time for any more confessions today. Just hang on, and I'll be back tomorrow evening, God willing. You can confess to me then." Would the man really admit to the Buffalo Grill plot? At least this gave Jon something to look forward to.

Jimmy Goodlaw's reaction to these events was bound to be even worse than Guy's, but he had to do it, especially since Walter had finally managed to place a call to Jon on his cell phone. "Come get me, come get me. I can't get out."

"Why were you at the Port Authority?"

"I came to see you. Susan and I want to get married. I thought it would be good to do it over the holidays."

"But I told you I'd be out of town."

"You did? Maybe I lost the paper you wrote it on. I have to go, they're making me go now. They're taking my phone," he cried. Jon felt terrible, appalled at not doing something to prevent these troubles. With his sudden entrance into a regular, independent life, Walter didn't understand certain boundaries and was obviously about to get hurt.

He called Jimmy and insisted he come down immediately to the bar for a drink, though the man was slow getting there. Alarmingly cheery, as if on vacation, the president of Buffalo Grill said, "Great part of the country, Jon. How did you do with the big critters? The vet looks good, but what the fuck is wrong with that Argentinean guy? Jesus, I wouldn't want to meet him in a dark alley."

"He's the best director there is, so we put up with his outrageous behavior. I think he tried to kill Guy Danziger after you left."

"What?"

"He got him to play toro with a buffalo, and then *blam!*"

"Bastard. Nobody in my company would ever get away with such bullshit, except me, that is," Jimmy said with a laugh. "That Danziger, I know he's the president of the agency, but since he doesn't work on my account, I haven't had much chance to talk to him. I'm still trying to figure out where I've seen him, though. He's probably on the party circuit."

"Undoubtedly," Jon said dryly, but then looked over at Jimmy in alarm. Best to deflect him, so he added, "As far as Juan

Angel goes, I'd hire Satan himself to get the commercials perfect, as perfect as they can be. I certainly try."

"I know you do. Where others see burgers, you see thirty seconds of art. I appreciate it. You're the Wayne Thiebaud of Buffalo Grill. That's why I've taken so much crap from you guys."

"I'm afraid you're going to have to put up with a little more. There's a family emergency in New York, and I have to fly there tonight on the red eye, in a few minutes actually. My brother's in the hospital." Jimmy rose up off his barstool in horror. "I'll return tomorrow evening, I promise, maybe even before."

"What the fuck are you talking about? You want to leave?" Jimmy screeched.

"I told you. It's just for a short time. I'll be right back."

Jimmy wasn't buying it. "It's an emergency here. It's a potential disaster. Look what happened with the last commercial. My board practically hung me by my nose hairs. Fuck, Jon, you're talking about a big account, you know that. I won't bail you out again."

"I swear on my life, I'll be back tomorrow night if I have to charter a jet and pay for it myself."

"If you're not here, you can kiss it all good-bye. There's only so much I can do to save your job." Jimmy slammed down his drink glass, enraged.

"What would you do if it were one of your family members in Bellevue?"

Jimmy stared at him, shaking his head. "Jesus, all right. At least you care about somebody. Most of the poor bastards I've met in advertising care for nothing and no one. They don't even have time for pets!"

Jon barely made the plane, but when he heard the engines roar, he felt such immense relief that he sank back in a swoon. Two hours later, over America's prairies, he swiped his credit card through the phone at his seat and listened to his answering machine, only to hear Eleanor's soft voice on the line, "I tried to reach you, Jon. I'm down here at Bellevue now. Don't worry about your brother, though it is confusing." He almost cried, whether for his career or his brother or his life, he didn't know which. He stared out of the window at the snow-covered ground, just visible in the clear night. Maybe he should turn around at the airport, get right back on another plane, let her handle the whole thing, but then that seemed wrong, since she probably didn't have the moxie to accomplish anything. He would go to Bellevue, solve the problem, and book an even earlier return flight to Tucson.

Eleanor indeed had never dealt with a situation like the one facing her. At Bellevue, of which she too had nightmare visions, it had taken her almost an hour just to penetrate the intake lobby. Walter had moaned into her answering machine the name "Susan" over and over again, so Eleanor was actually looking for two people she'd never met. She sank down into a chair in a waiting area, stumped, her task apparently hopeless because she wasn't actually a family member, until she thought of calling one of the neurologists she worked with at Weill. He gave her firm instructions and told her to use his name. At least then she could find out Walter's condition and locate the girlfriend, who had to be in the hospital somewhere. By now it was getting on toward six in the morning, and Eleanor had lost track of how many hours she'd been there. "You have to page her, that's the only thing I can think of," she said, throwing herself on the mercy of a friendly-looking black woman with spiky blond hair. "Please, she's a little slow, and I don't know what she looks like. They're keeping her boyfriend in here."

"Honey, I'm not supposed to be doing things like this. The pager is for doctors."

"You can speak with Dr. Woolf at Weill Cornell. He'll give his permission." She had to call the doctor a second time, and he finally convinced the receptionist to page the missing young woman.

"Susan Dietz, Susan Dietz, please come to the reception desk in the main lobby."

Eleanor stood waiting, anxious and resentful. How could she be doing this painful errand for Jonathan Neel? Wasn't she supposed to be Sasha's angel of vengeance, even getting paid for the job? She surveyed the few people in the waiting room. They looked bedraggled, smothered in layers of clothing, and she couldn't really tell families from prospective patients. Out of nowhere a young woman dragging a coat and a shopping bag appeared from down a corridor. "I'm Susan Dietz," she cried and raced toward the receptionist. "Are you calling me?"

"This young lady wants to speak to you," the woman said and motioned toward Eleanor, who had little idea what to say. She didn't have to say anything. Susan rushed into her arms and began to sob. As she related the story, she and Walter had decided to get married right away. Trying to call Jon with no success, Walter insisted they go into the city to find him. This had involved a long bus trip, during which he got agitated. "He doesn't like to take his pills," Susan said. "Then he forgets."

Eleanor clasped her hand and said, "I'm here now. I'll track him down and get him out," though she had no idea how to accomplish this. To her eyes, Susan seemed a fairly well set-up young woman, if slightly blank around the eyes, and she spoke more slowly than normal.

Eleanor left her to sit in the waiting room, eating a box of cheese crackers and sipping a Diet Coke, while she set off to try to find Jon's brother. She had little success. At every turn the problem was her lack of familial connection to the patient. "Look, this is an emergency. His girlfriend is here, I'm here. What else can we do? All you have to tell us is what ward Walter Neel is on," she said to a beady-eyed nurse on the fourth floor, where Eleanor had gone when she followed blue arrows pointing toward "New Patient Registration."

"That's confidential, as you can imagine, Miss Birch. We don't give this information out to just anyone."

"I'm not just anyone. His brother asked me to look after Walter while he was away." Eleanor's voice rose, and she thought she might start yelling. "What's wrong with you people? Don't you care at all about human beings? Why would I be assaulting your hospital in order to find an inmate?"

"Keep your voice down, miss. People are trying to sleep."

"You are not being helpful," she almost shouted. "And I'll wake up everybody in this hospital if I can't find Walter Neel." But she quieted down quickly when she realized they might think *she* was crazy. They could incarcerate anyone, right? Distraught, she grabbed a cookie out of the basket on the nurse's desk.

"We solicit donations for that, you know," the woman said and continued writing on a patient's chart. Eleanor reached into her bag and found her wallet, plucking out a dollar bill, even while she noticed her Weill Cornell identification badge. She stuck the badge in her jacket pocket.

"Thanks anyway, thank you so much for your help," she said, though she hadn't gotten any. She fingered the hidden badge and walked quietly down the hallway toward the elevator but then sped around the corner when the nurse wasn't looking, figuring that prospective patients lurked somewhere nearby. There was a line of locked rooms with narrow windows at the top, and Eleanor had just begun to peer into the first one when a male orderly came into view at the other end of the hall, pushing a breakfast cart.

"May I help you?" he said and approached her, frowning. Panicked, she pulled the badge out of her pocket, trying to dream up a story that involved observing people in the hospital for her own research. At the very least, she could somehow get out of the place without being arrested, and in her nervousness practically stuck the card in his hand, but he barely glanced at it, only saying, "Oh, that's fine, Doctor. Sorry to bother you." He went back down the hall in the other direction, leaving her alone.

She decided to scope out every holding room. Maybe Walter was there, and she could recognize him somehow or make contact. In the first room she spotted an older man hunched over on his bed, in the second, a young woman asleep; the third room was empty, but in the fourth, she spotted a youngish man with a vague resemblance to Jon, heavyset, tall, in street clothes, sitting on the floor sketching furiously. This had to be Walter. He didn't look hurt or abused, just focused. Hardly able to breathe, Eleanor turned back around. What could she do? How could she get him out? The doctor ploy obviously wouldn't work for very long. She examined her card closely again; it had her picture, her name, and the start date of her employment. Anxiously she noted his room number, then headed back down the hall toward the elevator, planning to sit with Susan and formulate a strategy. As she whirled around another corner, however, she ran smack into Jonathan Neel. "Oh, my God, here you are," she gasped.

"Yes, here I am. I couldn't get hold of you and didn't listen to your message until I was on the plane." Jonathan grimaced and took her arm. "I still haven't found Walter."

"I just did, I think. He's in room 484. I don't know what to do now, though. The orderly thought I was a doctor, and that's how I found him." Eleanor was beside herself.

Jon interrupted her. "Look, I left an incredibly important shoot, and I have to get back on a plane as early as possible this afternoon, so we need to get him out right away." He sounded harsh and angry. "I had no idea that he would try to come to town. I told him five times I wouldn't be here."

"They decided they wanted to get married immediately, and I think things just went from there," she said, suddenly close to tears and outraged at his condescending tone.

"You told them you were a doctor? You lied?"

"I didn't lie, I just showed them my New York Hospital identification badge, and they assumed the rest. I kind of became part of someone else's personal fiction."

Jon smiled. "Good move. It's because you have such an honest face." At that moment a man who walked with the unmistakable authority of a real doctor came their way, looking none too pleased. "Maybe you should bring out the magic card again," Jon whispered.

"Hmm, I don't think so."

"Excuse me. I'm Doctor Frankel. What are you people doing here?"

"We want to get my brother out. I think he's in 484. There's nothing wrong with him, but somehow he was picked up at the Port Authority and unlawfully incarcerated, so somebody had better do something before I call my lawyer and believe me, you do not want to meet that man under any circumstances—" Jon's voice got louder as he spoke.

"Hold it, sir. Are you threatening me?" the doctor, said, angry now himself.

"I'll do more than threaten you—"

At this the doctor pulled out his pager, but Eleanor yanked on Jon's arm, whispering, "Stop!"

"What?" Jon snapped.

Turning to the doctor, engulfing him in warmth, Eleanor said, "No, no, certainly not. He's concerned about his brother, that's all."

"What patient are you talking about?" The doctor glared at both of them.

Keeping her hand on Jon's arm to stop him from talking, she said, "Walter Neel. He's fine really, just a little slow, and he must have gotten upset at the bus station. This is his brother, who is fully prepared to sign him out and take charge of him. He'll be in good hands, and you'll have one less patient to deal with."

"Well, I can check on him. Wait over there please, if you're really willing to sign him out?" He indicated two green plastic chairs in the hallway.

"Absolutely," Jon said, visibly stunned at how fast Eleanor had managed to turn things around. "Good work," he said. They watched the doctor open four-eighty-four and go in.

"Doctors like to move people out quickly, if there's any humane way to do it."

He patted her on the back awkwardly. "I didn't think you had it in you, not that you're not competent, but I mean, the whole deal of— " He stopped talking abruptly.

"Why would you think that? I work in a hospital."

"I know that."

"Maybe if you trusted people more, you'd do better."

"Do better? I do very well."

"Right, except for the ad disaster and the brother and, let's see, what else? It's unbelievable how you've sucked me into your life this way. You need someone else to live it for you, I guess." Exhausted, irate, she barely knew what she was saying.

Jon turned on her, livid himself. "I didn't suck you in. You came to see me, you told me about Sasha, you planted yourself there, remember?"

"Your life is just such a mess that anyone who shows up gets to play a role. That must be it."

"No, no, I'm busy, that's all."

Even to himself, he sounded like an idiot. He wanted to amplify on his busyness, but the doctor returned, telling them to wait downstairs for his brother, who would be with them in about an hour.

Striding down the hall, Jon grasped Eleanor's hand, and she held onto his strong warmth, even while thinking she shouldn't. Who knew what one might encounter in Bellevue? The hallways and waiting rooms had an acrid, Lysol smell, nothing like New York Hospital, and it bothered her. Finally he said, "You might not want to wait. You've probably been here all night."

"Yes, I have been, but I will wait, definitely." She pulled her hand away as they walked more slowly now down the dingy corridor.

"This marriage idea must have fired him up to see me right away. He doesn't speak to our parents anymore, so they couldn't remind him I wasn't here," Jon said.

"Does he have an actual illness?"

"No, he's just slow. I remember one doctor told me he was an FLK, a funny looking kid. I guess it was funny to him, but never to us at home. A loss of oxygen to the brain at birth caused it. He takes medication that keeps him on an even keel, sometimes."

"It sounds horrible to call him an FLK."

Jon nodded distractedly and brushed his hair back. "Doctors need ways of coping too, apparently."

He fell silent now as they walked, and finally Eleanor said, "Susan is downstairs waiting."

"I've never met her."

Walter's girlfriend sat placidly sipping her soft drink, looking around, no longer agitated. Jon strode up and introduced himself. They all tried to have a real conversation, but by now it was past breakfast time, and they were sleepy and hungry. After considerably more than an hour, Walter appeared, carrying a large paper bag, looking unnerved and still confused but very happy to see them. He rushed to Jon and gave him a bear hug, then he grabbed Susan and said, "See, here she is."

Susan kept saying to Jon, "I can't believe you're here. Walter says you're never around."

"I have a difficult job," he replied. "Walter, do you know my friend Eleanor?" The younger Neel got very excited, while Susan chose this moment to embrace her again.

"Hi. Are you Jon's girlfriend? I hope so," Walter said.

"No, just a friend," she choked out the word. What was she doing here? This was someone else's drama, and she should get out of it.

"Let's have ice cream," Walter said, and so Eleanor found herself in Bellevue's cafeteria eating chocolate ice cream for breakfast. While they ate, Jon's younger brother giggled, apparently unfazed by recent events, and informed them of his plans. He and Susan wanted to get married right away and might just go up to Niagara Falls, but they were worried about his parents. Susan's were enthusiastic, not so the Neels, who had never returned Walter's call after he left them a message on their answering machine. "That's so mean, Jon, don't you think? They wouldn't call me."

"It certainly is," Jon said and put his arm around his shoulders.

Eleanor went over to the self-serve coffee bar, and while she was gone, Jon made Walter promise not to get married until after the holidays, when at least he could be present. "Things are just too busy now," he said. His pager vibrated in his pocket like crazy, and he was wondering who'd rammed himself into a buffalo now, but he couldn't answer it. He sat trying to reassure his brother that he would tell their parents, and they would come around. Jon gave his brother his pager number once again with the admonition that he must call before doing anything drastic, like coming back into the city. Thrilled to be reunited, Susan and Walter whispered together and laughed like children. Jon had arranged for a car service, and as they all waited in the downstairs lobby, he turned to Eleanor. "I left my shoot in the hands of the man who might be trying to do me in at work. Possibly he's the one who set up that Buffalo Grill disaster, remember it?"

"How could I forget?"

"I don't know if he's the culprit for sure, but he was the only agency person available to take over for me in Arizona. I had no choice. Anyway, I had to come get my brother."

"I was here." Suddenly she wanted him to know how seriously she took her promise to look after the poor man, but stopped herself from saying so.

"I've been having the weirdest thoughts of revenge; it's as if I'm obsessed, but I don't really know whom to try to get or how to do it. My boss keeps asking me to help the poor son of a bitch —his name is Guy Danziger—who also happens to be the president of LaGuardia and Knole. In my opinion, he's one jump away from hospitalization himself, though sending that guy to rehab would be like putting a wig on a werewolf. It's hopeless," Jon said.

"You have thoughts of revenge? Like what?"

"I could seriously damage him with his client, Synergene. One of their honchos is out in the desert with him right now."

"Synergene's a great company. They've been doing clinical trials on Oncreon 1 at New York Hospital," Eleanor said.

"My boss thinks they're going to save the world. We're shooting my commercial and his at the same time out in Tucson, both of which mysteriously involve buffalo. He obviously stole his ideas straight from me."

"He must be desperate." How desperate was she, she thought? What was she going to do to harm this very man?

Jon looked over at her. "Revenge is a strange thing. You can think of a hundred ways to hurt somebody, but then you don't want to become the kind of person who could actually do those things."

"I know what you mean." She was a hands-down failure at it herself. "My stepfather used to say, 'Be kind to your enemies. It weakens them.'"

"I don't know about that. Besides, every time I think of something to do to him, he does much worse to himself. He's biting the karmic wienie, that's all I can figure. He did evil in another life." Eleanor laughed, despite their parallel tracks in the universe.

When the livery car arrived, Walter kept exclaiming over its luxury and beauty, insisting that Eleanor come with them. "I'd love a ride. I'm already late in feeding my landlord's bird, and he gets very annoyed."

"I would like to have a bird," Walter said and asked her to describe the creature to him in great detail, even making a sketch as she spoke. He and Susan were to spend several hours with his brother, then get on another bus home. As for Jon, he planned to take the early afternoon flight back to Tucson, in plenty of time for his shoot the following day.

When they dropped Eleanor off at Gramercy Park in front of her apartment, Jon insisted on walking her to her door. The snow floated down once again, and she turned to shake his hand, but he leaned forward and kissed her on the cheek. Startled, she said, "It must be difficult, all this with your brother."

"It's changed my life. It makes it easy for me to take care of people and very easy to let them go. Does that make any sense?"

"I guess."

"I let go of Sasha too, way before—" his voice trailed off.

"You have to be prepared for the worst," she said, unaccountably, then trembled at the thought of Sasha's own preparations.

"True," he said and leaned forward once more to kiss her on the cheek. She would have pulled away, but he was holding her hand tightly. As he did so, she saw Walter lean out of the car window and yell, "Good-bye, beautiful lady. I will paint you."

No one had ever called her beautiful before.

twenty-eight

OPTIONS

The snow came down around New York City thicker and thicker, and Jon's flight was delayed until late in the afternoon. He sat in the bar gulping coffee and praying, literally praying, that somehow or other his plane would leave this town within a reasonable amount of time. Every moment that went by threatened a fifteen-year career, and just thinking about it made him giddy. He tried to watch a Knicks game on the monitor above the bar, in order to shut out visions of Jimmy, Juan Angel, Guy, and Serena in playful combination. When his flight was finally called, he thanked God that he was off to the land of sun and saguaro. Somewhere over Missouri, he roused himself out of a deep sleep and took a look at his cell phone record of calls from the shoot. For the first time in years, he simply ignored them and fell back asleep.

When the plane landed at eight o'clock in the evening, Jon got himself to the hotel, thinking the crew would be finished for the day, only to learn that they were still out in Sabino Canyon. First he called Jimmy, who wasn't in, and left him a message, then decided to take a cab out to the location because all the

shuttle buses were still at the site. Climbing up over the hill leading to where the tents were set up, Jon could see Leslie de Santis
and Juan Angel in intense conversation. The rest of the crew sat
in chairs or lounged, an unusual sight since it was well after sun-
set, and they couldn't possibly shoot anything else. There was
another person there, a tall woman with dark hair. Surveying the
landscape apparently, she wrapped her shoulders in a white
shawl. As he walked toward these people over the rocky terrain,
he had the uncomfortable feeling that they were staring his way,
registering his every move, and as he got closer he saw that the
woman was none other than Guy Danziger's wife. "Hello, everybody," Jon called out to them. "Marsia, what a surprise."

He shook her hand, and she gave him a slight smile. "I decided to come out and join you after all. Juan was so insistent."

"Right. Fantastic." Even to himself he sounded like an insin-
cere high school student.

Juan Angel walked heavily toward them over the dusty
ground and said, "Excuse us a moment, will you dear?" to Marsia,
pulling Jon out of earshot.

"Dear, *dear*? Juan, what is happening?"

"They're dropping like flies."

"Who? But listen, my first priority is Jimmy. Where is he?"

"Golfing, or he was earlier," Juan Angel said.

Before he could wrest any more explanations from the director, Leslie de Santis approached, covered in hat and jacket,
slathered in sunblock, even though it was now dark. "Jon, we
need you."

"Where is everyone? Shouldn't you be finished for the day?"
he said to her, as he watched Marsia wander off into the brush,
still gazing into the far distance.

"We are finished, as much as we can be. Serena and Guy have disappeared," Juan Angel said.

Leslie nodded her head up and down vigorously, "We can't find them anywhere."

"Did they oversee the shoot?" Jon asked.

"For a time, but then at about noon they simply left, gone, good-bye. I can't remember when I noticed, but at some point, they were just nowhere." Juan Angel seemed like a real human being in his perplexity. "There's some other problem, related, though, I think."

"Would that be Marsia?" Jon asked, trying for discretion around a client.

"They did leave right after she got here."

"You'd think Guy would be happy to see her," Leslie said.

Jon cleared his throat. "What was your other problem, Juan?"

"My shotgun is gone."

"Jesus," Jon said. "What were you doing with a shotgun?" He shouldn't have asked this question. Juan Angel thundered on about his rights as a director, his concern for rattlesnakes, the fact that in Arizona one could carry a gun to the supermarket, and even claimed that he needed to assert his authority as a director. "We're making a television commercial, not knocking over the Dodge City bank. Don't give me this horseshit about needing a gun."

From under her giant hat, Leslie literally wailed at the two men. "Don't fight, please. It's not helpful."

Juan Angel now turned on her the full force of his Latin machismo, "This is man's business. Don't interfere."

No fading flower, Leslie yelled back, "I'm a doctor. You can't speak to me that way."

"Without me you're dead, you're nothing, you won't have any commercial and you've already spent two million dollars, so shut the fuck up. *Qué chingada che!*" Juan Angel shouted.

"Quiet!" screamed Jon. "Everybody be quiet. First off, did you finish the Synergene shoot?"

"Yes," Juan Angel snarled. "We finished without Guy and Serena. I don't need them anyway, two pussies, though that producer-woman, Jesus, I should give her a good fuck just to keep her in line."

"Outrageous! Who'd want to have sex with you anyway?" Leslie stalked off toward the shuttle and pounded on the door, demanding to be taken back to the hotel.

Juan Angel seemed pleased with this latest dustup and said to Jon, "I'll give her cancer."

Jon ignored him. "I think we should consider our options."

"You're beginning to sound like them, Jon. I always thought you were different, but here you are, among the hacks and hustlers."

"Juan, let me tell you something," and he was about to set off on a diatribe that would send Juan Angel back to the hell he inhabited, but then thought better of it, what with his own day of shooting still not accomplished. "Never mind. We've got to find them."

"Why?" Juan Angel lit up a cigar, puffing great rings of black smoke Jon's way. "Perhaps they are in love?" he said, and started to laugh.

"How did they react to Marsia's arrival?"

"I tried to keep Guy out of the way. Maybe he passed out before he realized she was here, but that Serena, she went nuts. She should be taken out and beaten."

"Cut the violence, Juan. Save it for *fútbol*. I take it you'll look after Marsia for a while?" Juan Angel raised his formidable eyebrows at him. "Does she know that they disappeared together?" Jon said.

"I think so, yes. She's a smart woman," he said, flicking his cigar ash.

"Not that smart. Look who she's married to." Jon was tired of being polite.

Jon approached Marsia as she stood on the hill, still looking pensively into the dark. Was she scouting for Guy? "Such magnificent country," she said, turning to face him. She looked inexplicably radiant.

"Let's go back to the hotel and wait for everyone there," he said, not wanting to name any of the thousand thoughts that must be coursing through her mind. Had she come there to see Juan Angel or Guy? He had no idea and certainly wasn't going to ask. The director joined them, throwing his heavy jacket around her shoulders, while he and Jon walked her to the van. They could hear coyotes and strange scrabblings and scratchings in the desert as chill night enveloped them.

In the lobby of the hotel, as Jon tried to phone Jimmy again, Mr. Buffalo Grill himself walked in front of them, pulling his golf clubs behind him. "*Qué pasa*, gentlemen?" he said, ridiculously cheery.

"Marsia and I are going out for a drink," Juan Angel whispered to Jon and put his arm around Guy's wife, who didn't seem to object.

"Jimmy, how was your round?" Jon greeted the CEO, hoping their strange little playlet was a mystery to him.

"Fantastic, shot five over par. That's better than I've played in a long time." He patted Jon on the back and said heartily, "You came back. Hope all is well with your family."

"Fine. It was very important." He didn't elaborate.

Later, in the bar, while the two of them watched the many varieties of cactus lit up by red and green lights, Jimmy pointed out some strange goings on he'd noticed while on the shoot in the morning. "I was only there for a couple of hours, but those two, Serena and Guy, they seemed to be having some kind of fight. It looked serious."

"It probably was, from what I gather," Jon said, confident enough now in his client to tell him the truth.

"Thank God you're here," Jimmy said. "I would have fired you if you hadn't shown."

"I know." As soon as he could, Jon hied himself back to his room to try to find Guy. No luck with the phone, no response to a page, nothing. Next he tried Serena, still nothing. Maybe they were in danger. It could get freezing cold out there in the canyon at night, and at this time of year it might even snow. Were they prepared for December in the desert? Serena always seemed prepared for anything, but maybe she wasn't with Guy. Was she out there alone? Or had they finally killed each other? Perplexed, he called Claudia at home, even though it was after two in the morning in New York.

"Claudia, I'm sorry, this is an emergency. Serena and Guy have disappeared."

"Don't be ridiculous."

"They're gone. The crew hasn't seen them, Juan Angel hasn't seen them. I don't know if I should send out the police. They don't have a car, from what I can see, though I was away from the shoot myself for a while."

"You were away?" Now she sounded angry. "Your job was to stick with him."

"Just for a few hours."

"That's enough!" she screeched. "How the hell could you have left them alone?"

"It was a family emergency that I had to handle. But Jimmy's cool, there's no problem there."

"Except that there's no Guy or Serena. You've failed me, Jon, you really have. I was counting on you." Her voice became uncharacteristically shrill. "The whole agency could fall apart, don't you understand? None of us will have jobs."

"You mean we'll have to struggle along like regular people?"

"Don't joke at a moment like this," she thundered. "What time does your shoot start tomorrow?"

"There'll be two hours of prep at eight o'clock; then we'll probably actually roll at ten or ten thirty."

"Let Juan Angel do the prep, and you go find those two."

"I don't want Jimmy to think I'm not at the helm."

"You're right. You'll have to go out to the location at six o'clock, before everybody else, and find them."

"There's something else."

"Oh God, I can't take anymore."

"Marsia's here, and Juan appears overjoyed." There was silence on the line. "Claudia?"

"OK. We have to focus. Whatever happens, we need two brilliant commercials out of this. It doesn't matter who screws whom or when or where, just get that stuff on film and get out of there. You read me?" She hung up.

After four hours of fitful sleep, Jon got up before the sun, had coffee and a muffin, and borrowed a crew SUV to get himself out to Sabino Canyon. Logan Piersall was already there, and he immediately asked him if he'd seen Serena and Guy. He'd seen exactly what Jimmy had the day before, a protracted blowup between the two. "Do you have any idea where they might be now?" Jon said.

"There are outbuildings all over the place, down the wash, over by the corral. Why don't you check those? You know what, I'd better go with you. There may be scorpions or other critters."

"Good man," Jon said. In the icy morning air, he and the vet passed by a ranger bulletin board that had a posting tacked up. Its headline read "Problem Mountain Lions in Sabino Canyon!" Jon stopped and squinted at the safety advice, which included the stunning notion that you should always make eye contact with a six- to nine-foot-long cat. He doubted that Guy could even look himself in the eye, let alone coldcock an angry cougar. "Jesus," he muttered.

Logan registered the announcement along with him and said, "We'd better find them quickly. There are Gila monsters, javelina, bighorn sheep, even rattlesnakes out here."

"No shit!" The two of them tromped up and down the wash, opening the doors to old shacks full of dirty tools and rusted out pails, long since taken over by the desert. Finally, at the bottom of a rocky arroyo they spotted a slightly larger shed and approached it slowly.

"People might actually live in this thing," Logan whispered. "Farm workers or something like that."

"OK," Jon said. "I'll be careful." He knocked on the door. "Hello in there." Silence. He walked around to the back of the rickety structure but could still hear no sound. He peeked through one of the gaps in the two-by-fours. Nothing in his earthly existence prepared him for what he saw next. Guy was lashed to an old chair, tied up with bungee cords, five or six Band-Aids taped across his mouth. On the floor sat Serena, a shotgun and a box of buckshot on her lap, candy wrappers strewn around at her feet. They were both asleep. Jon lurched through the brush and almost fell, just as Logan came up behind him.

Serena shouted from within, "Who's there?"

"It's Jon Neel. What's going on?" He pulled Logan over to peer in along with him. Serena pulled herself up and stood behind Guy's chair, pressing the shotgun directly against his temple.

"Don't come in here," she said.

"Jesus," Logan said. "We should call the cops."

"No, no, we don't want any publicity, might affect the clients. Besides, if it comes to that, the two of us can take them," Jon said, still whispering.

"True, but that gun could go off at any minute."

"She'd never shoot her meal ticket. I'm going in."

"I'll be right behind you," muttered Logan.

Jon opened the door, stepping onto the rotted floorboards, and Serena instantly swung the gun toward him. "What the hell's going on here? Are you insane?" he said. He looked down at Guy, who was rolling his eyes frantically.

"Stand back, Jon. I don't have a problem with you. I'm just dealing with Guy Danziger here."

"You've been seeing too many movies, Serena. We don't kill people anymore. We talk, we hire lawyers, we go on television. Guns are for pussies. Pull those Band-Aids off his mouth." Fortunately he could feel Logan right behind him.

"No," she said. She racked the pump on the shotgun.

"Put it down, Serena. Whatever happens, you don't want to spend the rest of your life in prison. In fact, do they have the death penalty in this state? You'll be fried. Wouldn't you rather just go on making three hundred thousand dollars a year shooting commercials and driving out to the Hamptons on weekends?" Jon said and slowly leaned in to rip the Band-Aids off Guy's mouth.

Guy screamed, "Get me out of here! She's insane, a crazed insane bitch. She's a drug addict, a mental case, and she's trying to blackmail me."

Serena swung the shotgun back toward Guy, "Shut up, you fucking asshole."

"Shut up both of you, and put down that gun," Jon said. Serena backed away from Guy's chair.

"Put it down," Logan yelled, sounding like a sheriff.

"Not until I get what I want."

"What do you want?" Jon said.

"Don't ask her that. She's a lunatic."

"I want stock options."

"What?" Jon almost screamed with laughter. "We're out here in Bumblefuck just doing our jobs, and you want stock options?"

"I told you, she's insane," Guy moaned.

"From what I can see, both of you are in serious need of counseling," Logan said.

"Be quiet, dickhead. What are you doing here anyway?" Serena screeched.

"I'm trying to protect the animals," he said with a drawl.

"Fuck. Go wrangle a gopher. Anyway, I don't see why upping my retirement plan isn't a good idea, since this jerkface son of a bitch bastard has been promising me money for years. 'We'll up your compensation package, darling.' Yeah right. I haven't seen a dime."

"Stock options?" Staring at a woman with a shotgun, Jon somehow grasped the intensity of the request. "Why should you get paid anything extra for balling this guy and doing drugs?"

"As if you executives don't get paid for crap you shouldn't do. I wasted hours and hours of my life cavorting in a hotel room with this asshole, and what do I have to show for it?"

"Good times?" Jon said. Despite the situation, Logan laughed.

"You loved it, you ragged-out cunt." Guy could certainly finish a sentence now. Serena slapped the side of his face with the gun.

"Watch out, that thing might go off," Jon yelled.

"Want to know who fucked up your little commercial for Buffalo Grill? Tell him, Guy," Serena announced, glowing with rage.

"I didn't do it." Guy really looked scared now.

"You told me you wanted to confess to something right before I went back to New York. Is this it?" Jon said.

"No, no, I didn't say anything about confessing, did I? I don't remember what I said. I say a lot of things."

Serena shouted, "Tell him or I'll shoot you now."

"I didn't, Jon. She's crazy, she's trying to get you to believe that." This remark produced a guffaw from Serena. "She did it!" Guy yelled. "I wanted to tell you that she did it!"

"No, no, it was his idea."

"You fucking bitch! It was not!" Guy yelled, "I'm too hammered to have any ideas."

"Now wait a minute everybody," Logan said.

Serena smacked Guy again with the gun, and as she did, Jon lunged for it, grabbing the stock, turning the heavy firearm toward the ceiling. It went off with a tremendous bang, blasting a hole in the roof. Still he hung on to it, even though it threw him backwards onto the floor. As he lay there, he grabbed for the box of ammo. Serena ran out the front door, and Jon followed right behind her, clutching the gun, determined to reload. Suddenly, she stopped and turned to face him. "I did do it. I let myself into the Traffic records on the computer and created an alternate log, right before the time codes were to be delivered to the network. The Traffic guys never even noticed, since they'd already checked the numbers themselves. It was quite a feat."

"You actually wanted to destroy my career?" Jon said.

She grinned proudly, "Not destroy it, just mess with it a little."

"Why?"

"Because you're such a smartass, and because I wanted Guy to be head of the agency, not you."

"You pathetic weasel." Jon started chasing her, gun upraised. He shot it once, then lowered it to slide in another shell. "I'll shoot you in the ass, you bony bitch. Just keep going. Run right toward Albuquerque and don't come back to New York, ever!" He fired up into the sky one more time, even though his shoulder was killing him. "If you see a mountain lion, remember to make yourself big!" Exhausted, he sank down in the dirt and hugged the shotgun, which was hot and smelled of oil and lead. Above him thunderheads closed in, and it began to rain.

When Jon got back to the shed, Logan was using his Swiss Army knife to slash the knotted bungee cords and get Guy out of the chair. His head hung forward, and his body rolled to one side. As he checked the back of Guy's neck for wounds, Logan said, "She's not dead is she, or hit?"

Guy reared up and shouted, "Please tell me she's gone."

"Let's just say she's on the run at the moment," Jon said.

"I swear, I had nothing to do with fucking up your commercial." He looked on the verge of tears, as he slid down onto the floor.

"I sure hope you didn't."

"It was horrible, an awful thing to do. She's a witch."

"Guy, you're going to have to do something about your life. This can't go on. You're like a talking monkey strapped to a chair who'll say anything for a banana," Jon said.

"I know. I need a rest."

"There's an excellent hospital, halfway between here and Scottsdale. You should seriously consider signing yourself in," Logan said.

"No way. They kill you in rehab. All those sons of bitches saying how great it is to be sober. It isn't fucking great. It's repulsive."

"When were you last in one?" Logan asked.

"Who knows? Five or six years ago."

"They've changed. Besides, what choice do you have?" Jon said, as the two of them helped Guy stand up. The heavens had opened up again outside the hut, and the rain poured through the hole in the roof. Jon had the dreary thought that, on top of everything else, his shoot would be delayed. The two men each took an arm and dragged Guy to the crew SUV, piling him into the back seat, where he slumped, possibly asleep. Jon put the shotgun in the trunk. Blinding rain came down, thunder boomed in the distance, and lightning slashed across the road as they drove. Throughout this nasty journey, the vet said almost nothing, but when they came to the Sabino Canyon turn, he suggested to Jon, "The Oro Valley cutoff is just up ahead and will take you toward Smathers House, the rehab center at Gurney Hospital. It's about thirty minutes away."

"Good plan. It's only seven now. No one will show up at the location until eight," Jon said, and swung the truck onto the smaller road. Balls of mesquite rolled crazily across the pavement as the rain pounded down. He could barely see, but miles later he spotted the sign for Smathers House, where he turned in. They drove through an elaborate Spanish gate, then up a long driveway, stopping in front of an adobe entrance. The place looked like an old-style hacienda, even though housed next to a gleaming white, modern hospital. "Guy, get out of the car."

The president of LaGuardia and Knole lifted his head and said, "Where are we?"

"You get out here. I'm not taking you inside. You have to walk in that door yourself."

"What is this?"

"You really need to do this, Guy," Logan said, "It could change your life."

"Fuck that," Guy muttered.

"Get out of this car and go in," Jon said.

"You son of a bitch, this is just you punishing me. You think I wrecked your TV spot. You believed her," he said, wailing.

"It's not that. It's where you're headed in the future that worries me," Jon answered.

"You're jealous, you want my job. You're going to destroy me with Leslie and take away Synergene." He leaned forward against Jon's seat and began banging his head.

"I won't take Synergene, but only if you go in. If you don't, I swear I will take your job and that huge account with it. Believe me, I can do it."

"I'm a very important man in advertising. People depend on me. Besides, my wife is here, somewhere around anyway." Guy was in tears.

"They can't depend on you now because you're out of it all the time. Listen, you and I have been a couple of shits. I'm trying to fix my situation, but you're just wrecking everything around you. I'm taking one stab, but only one, to help you." Jon wiped his forehead with his jacket sleeve and turned to look at the bedraggled man in the seat behind him.

Guy finally raised his head. "I have no clothes, no nothing."

"Do you have your wallet?" Jon said. Guy nodded. "That's all you need." He finally got out of the car and walked slowly up the wooden steps, only pausing a moment to look back at the two men.

The storm had drenched the shoot location too and continued unabated. In honor of this unexpected weather delay, Juan Angel had initiated another impromptu soccer game. Many were aware that they could get hit by lightning during this frolic, but they rousted about in the mud nevertheless, to avoid their director's wrath. Under the tent sat Jimmy Goodlaw, waiting for Jon. "Jesus, I thought you'd abandoned me again," he said, as the younger man ran toward it for shelter.

"Of course not. Just a little business with Guy to attend to." Jimmy gave him a look but asked nothing. "Sorry about the rain. Usually Serena Rawlinson dances and howls and gets up perfect weather, but today she's out of commission."

"What? I thought she was your producer on this commercial too."

"She had a pressing job to do elsewhere. I'm sure we'll see her later. Her assistant can help." Jon promptly lined up the eager young woman accustomed to carrying Serena's coffee and getting her dry cleaning, to supervise the rest of the Buffalo Grill shoot. She filled in expertly right away, as if she'd been waiting a long time for this very moment. He spoke to Logan too about keeping the events they'd just seen a secret.

"No problem, Jon," he said. "I'm good at keeping secrets. Besides, I have to deal with the animals."

Juan Angel began motioning toward Jon to join the fun—seven guys on each side running and slipping in the mud, but Jimmy said, "When are we going to do some work? This is my money."

"It's raining. We may even have to postpone until tomorrow," Jon told him.

"I'm not paying for these shitheads to sit around in the hotel eating food definitely not from Buffalo Grill. Let's just film something."

"It's a typhoon. Get a grip. If the sun doesn't come out in a few hours, I'll rewrite the script, and we'll shoot anyway. How's that?" Jon felt manic with confidence now that he'd shot off a gun.

"My man," Jimmy said, slapping him on the back, and promptly insisted on joining the game as well.

Playing *fútbol* with Juan Angel was always a serious contact sport, and what with the thunder and lightning, this game took on particularly hellish aspects. The director played forward and put Jon on the opposite team as a midfielder, the position he'd held in college fortunately, while Jimmy was a fullback. Play was slapdash and ferocious, Juan Angel dominant, and since there was no ref, anything went. When the Argentinean piled in side-ways under him to kick the ball, Jon slid forward perfectly in position to headbutt it into the goal. He screamed and yelled and so did Jimmy, and then they high-fived each other, doing a little dance. Not appreciating this show of victorious cama-raderie, Juan Angel bellowed about how they had to prep the commercial and why were they wasting time playing stupid games? He stalked off, just in time for a climactic thunderclap and a slash of lightning that made even the most seasoned hands flop down on the ground.

When Jon and Jimmy finally managed to clean themselves up, they emerged from the tent into a sky filled with round, fluffy clouds and glorious sun. Jon ran to the SUV and recovered the gun, which he then presented to the mud-covered director. In spite of the recent goal-winning header, Juan Angel was pleased. "Let's shoot a commercial," Jon shouted, and they finally did.

twenty-nine

EXPLANATIONS

B y the end of the day, every person at that location was covered in mud and stray cactus needles, even the buffalo. Sitting in the tent though, as Leslie, Jon, and Jimmy watched the
playback on Juan Angel's monitor, they realized that their director had gotten the most wonderful footage. The hills looked
pink and inviting, the animals majestic in their movements,
whether running or just loping off into the distance. Leslie
brushed away a tear, and Jimmy was moved to slap Juan Angel
on the back. Now, as if nature had finished its required work for
the day, the sky covered over with clouds, and the rain came
down once again. Jon made for the crew shuttle, but Juan Angel
grabbed him and demanded he drive to the hotel with him in his
big Jeep Cherokee.

"What did you do with them?" Juan Angel said, as he started
up the truck.

"You mean the 'missing ones'?"

"I mean the *puta de mierda*, that's fucking bitch to you, and
the *drogadicto*."

For one moment Jon felt a pang of remorse for the poor

souls. "One disappeared, and the other, he's gone to a better place, as we say at Buffalo Grill."

"Better than what? He's not dead, is he?"

"Juan, I'm just not going to tell you. You'll have to trust that I did the right thing."

"The right thing? As if I care about the right thing."

"How's the little woman?" Juan Angel stared at him. "Mrs. Danziger?"

"Oh, the beautiful Marsia. She will join us for dinner tonight. It's good for me that he's gone. You probably want him out of the way too, so you can move to the top."

"I might want to be king, Juan, but never an assassin. You should think on that. Besides, he'll be back."

Later that evening, before the dinner that Juan Angel had planned as a farewell, Jon lay on his bed at the hotel, exhausted beyond what he had ever experienced. He hadn't slept in days. He hadn't had time to call Walter, though he'd checked messages and since there were none, hoped that all was well. Now, in his head, he had a list of explanations that must be made: to Leslie, but she too would be at dinner and perhaps he could speak to her there; to Marsia—should he call her right now?—and to his boss. He compromised and wrote Claudia an email. "After he finished his shoot, Guy decided to check himself into Smathers House at Gurney Hospital. He'll be there one month, but his junior team can finish the edit on the commercial. Serena seems to be AWOL at the moment, but I'm sure she'll resurface when she needs to." He knew this cryptic communiqué would send Claudia to the phones, but he had to tell her something.

The lavish dinner at a local Mexican eatery that night involved margaritas of pure agave tequila and tacos filled with filet mignon. Despite the fact that there was no Buffalo Grill food in sight, Jimmy radiated happiness, and Marsia was resplendent in a black velvet skirt and a black turtleneck, with a turquoise belt slung low over her hips. She never once approached Jon about her husband. Looking flushed and giddy, Leslie de Santis too was pleased from what she'd seen of the footage, and of course Juan Angel was never jollier than when making a display of his money—actually the agency's money—and tonight he flamed and flared as brightly as he could. Amid the tense hilarity, Jimmy muttered in Jon's ear, "Haven't we lost several of our people?"

"Not lost really. They've reassigned themselves," Jon said. From across the table, Logan Piersall stared at him, raising his eyebrows.

Leslie leaned in. "Where is Guy? I thought you said you'd found him, and he'd be here to celebrate."

"He's resting, Leslie, and sent his regrets. Anyway, we at the agency never celebrate until the spot is in the can. Juan Angel is partying though, indulging himself in a display of wealth. Think of it as a potlatch, you know, where the natives burn all their possessions to show how rich they are. In his own way, Guy is working on this commercial, don't worry." As he spoke, he thanked God for the various assistants who'd subbed for both Serena and Guy, one of them even redoing the Synergene storyboards. He wondered, though, when Leslie would learn the real story.

Dinner dragged on, the assembled guests consuming too many chips and tequila shooters. The only people having fun were Juan Angel and Marsia, who whispered together and laughed. The big Argentinean kept touching her, on the hand, on the arm, sometimes even on the neck. Jon disliked such public displays but figured that Guy's wife deserved at least a moment of happiness after the unending hell that must have been her marital life. Still, he had to wonder about her choices in men. Anxious to leave, he rushed through his prickly pear cactus crème brûlée, but Juan Angel rose from his chair and approached his side of the table. He dropped down on those powerful legs and said, "Come have a cigar with me. You too, animal doctor."

Outside, the three sat cowboy style on a railing, blowing their smelly black smoke into a clear night sky. The restaurant was in the old part of town, in an adobe building close to the university. A brown mutt waggled past them, looking over at the men, appearing to wait, and Logan reached down to pat him. Two pretty college students sauntered by, attached to the dog somehow, and they called out its name. He came running. Logan looked after them. "Animals are so much easier than people," he said.

"Those buffalo seem just stuck in their own block of fat and hair, and they hardly move. I don't call them easy," Juan Angel said. "You're amazing on a horse," he added.

"Animals are at peace, though," Jon said, almost choking on his cigar. It really was vile, and he felt overcome by the strange aura that existed around Juan Angel wherever he went. Was he human?

"They're at peace because they have no future and no past," Logan added.

"Bullshit. They only have the pain of the present, which they feel intensely because they have no hope," Juan Angel said.

"They have us," Logan said. "We're their hope."

"Aha, the man of hope. I'm pleased that there's one such here," Juan Angel said. "Jonathan Neel, of course, has no hope whatsoever."

"What are you talking about?" Jon said.

"You have no hope of being a better man than you are."

"You have a hell of a nerve talking to me that way considering all that you've done."

"It's not what I've done. It's what I've created. It's out there every day, all the time."

"Who do you think helped you create that? You didn't write it or think it up," Jon said.

"That's true. Don't upset yourself. You're sensitive, a feeling man, a thinking man. Better to be hard and impervious like me, a magnificent asshole. You react to everything in your world, like a sea creature. Better to be the shark."

"Sharks, buffalo, the worst these animals have done is to give us tawdry metaphors for our own bad actions," Logan said.

Back at the hotel, very late that night, Jon and the vet went for a nightcap in the bar. Sipping some cognac, by now beyond exhaustion and rationality, Logan speculated on what sort of relationship had led up to Guy's being lashed to a chair by his girlfriend. Jon tried to explain to him several of the more convoluted romances at LaGuardia and Knole, in the process mentioning that a very different sort of woman had come into his own life. He described Eleanor and how he had met her, via the death of his former girlfriend, Sasha Cole.

"I actually heard something about this already, from a friend of mine, Tony Lowe. I think you know him," Logan said.

"I sure do, *Blowing Smoke*. What a coincidence. He was a friend of Sasha's too."

"Coincidence doesn't have much to do with it."

* * *

Perhaps because of all the drinks, fatigue from the shoot, and genuine compassion for the man, Logan gave Jon to understand that Sasha had directed Eleanor his way. He did not mention the word *get*, but he said enough to make clear that this was no random act on Eleanor's part. "Your meeting with her was deliberate."

Later that night, Logan phoned Tony and sketched for him some of the more colorful events of the shoot, but he didn't tell him about his and Jon's conversation. "I don't know why your lady friend hates him so much. He's the most human of the bunch, by far, and you can tell her that's my read on his character. I got sucked into their calamitous doings. Somebody could have died! Anyway, he did a good deed today, actually took a guy to rehab."

"He needs to do good works, Logan, after all that he's done before. Remember, I know more than you do about this," Tony said.

"Right," Logan replied. "You always know more than I do," he said but wasn't buying it.

On the flight back to New York, Jon couldn't speak, lost somewhere between rage and humiliation, feeling like the last one to know about more or less everything. Fortunately, he didn't have to talk to Jimmy, who was worn out himself, asleep most of the way. Serena Rawlinson, where was she now? No matter how hateful he found her, it still pained him that she had conspired against him so successfully, which fact he would still have to verify with Seth. Then there was Eleanor. Why had Sasha wanted her to meet him? He was too exhausted to get his mind around this one and attached himself to the headphones, never taking them off. Christmas was a day away, he hadn't heard from his family at all, and nothing from Walter about the timing of the wedding either. One of Juan Angel's crew told him that the director and Marsia had gone up to his place in Sedona, a complication that would undoubtedly affect LaGuardia and Knole, but he had no idea how severely. Surely Serena would reappear, and he would have to deal with her somehow. What about Guy? Would he be able to stick it out in rehab, especially when he knew that other people were working on his commercial?

Over the snowy city they were delayed, circling for an hour. When the plane finally landed, it spun a mound of white around the wings like a whirlwind. Jon and his client got into separate cars, Jimmy waving jauntily, saying, "I'll see you in the editing rooms." He liked to watch every second of the finishing of a commercial to make sure he got his money's worth.

Jon's apartment looked the same, his cello sitting forlornly under the piano. The pile of mail was alarmingly high, but the housekeeper had been there, and everything was clean. He grabbed a can of tomato juice out of the fridge and sat looking at the snow out of his immense living room window. Eighty-Sixth Street was blanketed white, children and parents bundled up, sliding through the frozen piles. It felt good to be home, no matter what turmoil he might find within his own family or even at work. Eleanor, though, that was where he was stuck mentally. How deep that possible chasm? Instead of going through his mail, he pulled out his bow, tuned his cello, and played for almost an hour, pieces from the romantic repertoire, Dvorak, Schumann, Elgar. If he made a mistake, he didn't stop. Isn't that what his hero, Janos Starker, would do? Whenever he thought of someone to advise him in his deepest troubles, it was always Starker. "Sit tall," "Don't grip the bow," "Keep going." Starker never succumbed to romantic sentimentality. Showing up was the ultimate creative statement.

His phone messages revealed that, despite every promise they had made to him, Walter and Susan had gotten married in Erie, Pennsylvania. There were several irate messages from his father and mother, the gist of which was "Where the hell are you?" They had grudgingly given up on him for the holidays, and he wasn't sure if they even knew about the wedding. At the office the next day, Christmas day, he called Walter and learned that the ceremony had been "wonderful, Jon, just wonderful. We had cake and champagne and then, well, we couldn't go to Niagara Falls because it was snowing, so we went to the movies. Your friend Eleanor helped us with everything." Eleanor? Why was she there? He asked Walter but didn't get a satisfactory answer. She was just present and helping. "She's a friend of yours, isn't she?" Walter asked. "Besides, we needed her."

The day after Christmas the wedding was a subject too for Tony and Eleanor, who lunched at the trustees dining room of the Metropolitan Museum of Art. They sat at a table next to the floor-to-ceiling windows that afforded a view of the serpentine paths of Central Park. Bare limbs of the trees hung with ice and swayed slightly every time another flurry of snow fell upon them. "This is the most wonderful place," Eleanor said as she ate her frisée salad. "I had no idea it existed."

"It exists for you if you give the museum five hundred dollars, and now that I'm rolling in dough, I'm just giving it away. Want some?'

"Thank you, no. I'm still spending Sasha's money, and that's the most by way of gifts that I can handle. I'm too guilt-ridden to accept all this luxury."

"Why are you guilt-ridden?"

"No idea. I must have done something wrong in another life."

"Oh, darling, we've all done something mighty wrong. Let's just hope no one, especially not God, finds out about it." Tony was handsomely dressed and full of his good fortune. "So, Logan did indeed report back from the shoot."

"Tell me."

"First let's hear about this wedding. And why were you there at all?"

"It was Jon's brother. He's slow."

"From a brain injury?"

"Not sure, just way slowed down, but a very good painter."

"I should hook him up with Teddy Bonin. You know, you met him at Sasha's funeral. He's desperate for someone new to fill February at his gallery."

"He painted me, in fact. I haven't seen it yet, though. Suddenly he and Susan felt so alone, with no parents, fairly confused about all the legal stuff. They called me. I had to go, even though it took forever. Jon was just working away in Arizona, lost in his big world."

"Logan really liked him, said he was the best of the bunch. In fact, he called him a good man."

"Right, and the guy in the third circle of hell seems like a nice guy compared to the ones lower down."

"Do I detect true hatred in your voice? Before you seemed to think he was just misguided."

"I felt kind of sorry for him, but then it hit me: how was it that I, someone entirely unknown to the family as a whole, was the only one standing up for his brother? It was extraordinary, no matter what the circumstances that led to its happening."

"You should ask him about this, because the story doesn't seem quite right. Why don't you plan a little dinner and invite him?"

"I don't want to ruin my holidays. I'm going back to Ithaca to check up on my cat." As Eleanor gazed out the window, she saw her reflection and for a moment didn't even recognize herself. She dressed differently now, and she carried herself with a certain importance. Beneath the sleek coat, she wore a red sweater that showed off her breasts and around her neck curved a pencil-thin silver lariat. She paused, remembering that last dinner with Sasha, how unhappy she'd been with her own appearance.

Tony watched her too. "You look so New York today. Is the seduction on hold? Does he seem interested at all?"

"He did seem interested, I think, while we were at Bellevue."

"Bellevue? Jesus Christ, you pick the oddest places for dates. Explain please."

Eleanor told him the story of Walter's rescue and her role in it. "It's amazing. I can see it all. You seduced him by existing, by being your own true, beautiful self."

She started. "Oh, Tony, you're just trying to get me to do something more about the guy."

"Yes, that's my job. You'll have to hang tight now, if he puts the moves on you. Remember, 'seduce and abandon.' Logan really did think he was charming, in a heterosexual kind of way."

"I've got to get home, back into a saner environment for a few days."

On the front steps of the museum, Eleanor pulled out a round black hat with a fake fur border and tucked her sleek hair under it. "You look truly gamine and gorgeous," Tony said. "I'll see you after the holidays, and I expect you to have news. We need to find out about that bonus. Well, I don't, but you do."

At the office that day, Jon received several startling pictures on his computer. Susan worked at a day care center for the elderly, and when she received the snapshots from the wedding, someone helped her scan them. She sent two photos to him by email, one of which had Eleanor in the background holding a small clump of roses and lilies, smiling straight into the camera while the newlyweds beamed. The other email contained the image of a large oil painting that Walter had done of Eleanor. He had her sitting before a piano, looking out a picture window at the skyline of Manhattan. She turned slightly away from the viewer, black hair flowing down and, unaccountably, had on a Hawaiian shirt decorated with palm trees. Atop her head sat a beautiful yellow bird remarkably like Harry the sun conure, and above him flew a small musical note, as if he were singing. In this dreamlike image, Walter had captured a winsome, wistful woman, and it was a very good likeness. When he spotted a tiny sketch of Sasha from the *Leptra* series in the background, he realized that his brother had pictured Eleanor in Jon's very own New York apartment. Suddenly he knew that he must do something about her right away, though the holidays were never a promising time to do anything. First, however, he had to confirm all that he had learned in Arizona. He dialed up Seth, the only person who, like himself, almost never left the building. "Hey, what happened about the alternate traffic log on Buffalo Grill? Have you figured it out?"

"I've got the answer, but I didn't want to call and wreck your holidays. It was Serena Rawlinson."

"Yes, I knew that already. She actually told me, but I wanted absolute confirmation."

"She faked a log and sent it over to the network. It's a bummer. You can't really work with her after what she's done."

"You're right, but she may have taken care of the problem herself," Jon said, picturing scrawny Serena hotfooting it across the desert. As he tinkered with the robotic claw of Torquemundo, Jon mused on the multiple punishments being meted out to him. He should go home, reflect, take at least one day off before he had to get these commercials going. Instead, he printed out the emailed picture of Eleanor at the wedding and decided that as soon as he could decently do so after Christmas, he would call her and arrange to get together. When he reached her machine, which announced that she was in Ithaca, he realized he wanted to see her right away but resisted the impulse for as long as he could. Hours passed before he called her at home, and she sounded reluctant. He swayed her with his gratitude for her help at the hospital, though he said nothing about the wedding. He didn't want to overthink this mission.

The next day, after an endless journey in a rental car, he made his way to the address that Eleanor had given him and stood now before a two-story craftsman-style house. In the window was a fuzzy Santa and on the front door a wreath. Though the house wasn't large, it perched on top of a hill, and beyond the downward sloping front lawn he could see a small, frozen lake. It was altogether beautiful, something from a fantasy that, he thought ruefully, he might have invented for a commercial. When Eleanor's face appeared at the door, she seemed to grimace, at least to Jon's eye.

They sat in uneasy conversation for a minute or two before her big fireplace, the calico rubbing herself up against his calf. It was almost eight at night. "Would you like some wine?" Eleanor said, mystified at this hurried visit all the way up in Ithaca.

"Yes, some red would be good, if you have it."

Out in the kitchen she puttered long over the bottle and the glasses, glancing at her reflection in the window, running a hand through her hair. She had the eerie thought that now was the moment to seduce him. Could she do something like this? It seemed impossible. Contemplated from a moral vantage point, she thought Sasha was probably wrong to want someone else to do her bidding, wrong to feel that a man could be harmed by someone other than his beloved. She brought the wine glasses into the living room and sat down beside him on the couch. He took his and clinked hers in return, fixing her with those dark eyes. "Thank you so much for going to my brother's wedding."

"Oh my goodness, it was supposed to be a secret. How did you know?"

"Susan emailed me pictures and there you were, holding flowers. She sent Walter's portrait of you too."

"I'd really like to see the painting myself."

"It's beautiful," he said.

In the dim firelight, his remarkable features softened, he appeared less formidable to Eleanor, less difficult. "Walter called and said no one would be at his wedding, so would I come? It seemed horrible that they would be alone, and they were missing a few papers. But they both wanted to keep it secret from your parents—that's why they went to Erie. They couldn't seem to remember what they'd said to you about it at the hospital."

"There's a short-term memory problem with those two. My family still doesn't know."

Without thinking Jon rested his hand a moment on Eleanor's. "I really do owe you a lot." He wanted to talk to her about Sasha, about why he'd abandoned her and so badly, but didn't know how to begin.

"Walter is remarkable, in his way," Eleanor offered.

Jon stood now, carrying his wine over to the fireplace, while he surveyed Eleanor's family photos. "Remarkable now maybe, but having him in our family, it broke my mother and father, me too, practically destroyed us. I love him, but don't believe any sentimental stories about mentally disabled people. My parents thought it was their fault and felt wretchedly guilty." He fell into a pained silence, staring into the fire. "I think I should explain about Sasha." Eleanor stood now and moved closer to him. "In some respects, I barely knew her. Two years was a long time for me in a relationship, the longest one I've ever been in, but it was incredibly intense. She scared me, her neediness, her pain, which I guess I tried to ignore. We were so alike we would have gone up in flames." Jon flushed at the analogy. "I've wondered over and over again why I ended it the way I did, by just not calling. I couldn't bear a scene with her, that was it. She took life so hard, and it reminded me of my family. I couldn't stand it."

Eleanor touched him on the arm and murmured, "There was so much we didn't know about her. Oh," and now she broke down into tears, "How could she have died so horribly? It changes everything. I just reread the crash inquiry report in the paper. She was driving too fast, they think, and in the fog she ran straight into the rock band's bus, which was also speeding."

Jon looked intently at her, "She was a bad driver."

"Not bad, don't say bad. She was fast."

"Maybe, if you want to put it that way." He paused a moment and gazed at the snow coming down outside. "A friend of Tony Lowe, a veterinarian, said Sasha wanted me to meet you."

"What? Why did he tell you that?" she said sharply.

"I guess because he thought it might be important," Jon said.

"It's none of your business, it's a secret." She regretted these words instantly and could feel her face burn.

"What's so horrible about it? It's not that unusual, that a friend would recommend another friend."

"It wasn't quite like that."

Eleanor wanted to jump behind a door and hide. She was discovered, and he probably knew everything. Anyway, she'd done what Sasha wanted, and now she had to get him out of the house. She would no longer, in this lifetime, perform any other such acts of deception. "I don't want to tell you, I don't want to talk about it. Maybe you know anyway. It's late. You should probably go."

"I should. Still, I don't understand why we can't be friends, even if I was bad to Sasha, even if we did meet in this weird way."

"You don't understand anything," she said, filled with shame for all that she couldn't say.

Jon took the last sip of his wine and backed away. "All right then, that's what people have been telling me for years, and it must be true." He waited for her to speak and, as the silence deepened, he finally muttered, "Yes, I will go."

Eleanor stared at him, mute, blank with pain. "I don't even know why you came here."

"Neither do I, because obviously you don't want to know me." Agonized, enraged, how Jonathan Neel got out of that house he could hardly remember.

Later that night as she got ready for bed, Eleanor had recovered somewhat from her embarrassment and humiliation. It was over, done; she'd fulfilled her part of the bargain. It had cost her, though, and in ways she only now began to contemplate. Still, she had gotten to know a very different kind of man. He was warm, intense, driven, kind to his brother, comically self-absorbed, successful at his work, and not entirely without morals. Snuggling next to Coco, she saw that her path was clear. He wanted her, didn't he, at least wanted to see more of her? That desire had been obvious in his eyes. Now she could cut him off, coldly refuse to see him, in exact duplication of his behavior toward Sasha. Surely she would have no problem whatsoever in never meeting up with him again. Even to think of spending more time with him was evil, since her dead friend would come back from the grave and haunt her. But then as she slid down beneath the covers, her cat flinging a paw against the side of her face, she realized that Sasha haunted her already and had been doing so for a long, long time.

thirty

THE BONUS

A week and a half after Jon's journey north, Tony and Eleanor sat on a banquette at a trendy restaurant in Manhattan enjoying a plate of scallops piled high like a tower. "You've done it. Of course, I have to take credit for the hair and the makeup. And now good-bye! Poof, just like that, you disappear." Tony chortled, downing a margarita. "It's too delicious."

"It is, isn't it?" Eleanor said, resigned to this messy end of it all. "Listen, there's something important here that I need to talk to you about. Your friend Logan told him that Sasha wanted the two of us to meet. I don't know what else he said, but Jon didn't seem angry or anything, so he probably doesn't know the whole assignment."

"What? He swore to me he wouldn't divulge anything. But if he only said Sasha wanted to introduce you to him, that might not be so bad. Think of the guilt. Now you have him miserable in his huge apartment and his whole crowded, confused life. OK, I say we go get the bonus—or you do it. What better time of year?"

"I've only spent twenty-five thousand dollars, but the lawyer said I could have the rest whenever I thought the job was done."

"It's done! I can tell from your description of the evening.

He wants to get something going with you. Has he called?"

"Yes, three times. I haven't returned any of them. Maybe he's just calling because I told him not to, you know, someone who runs after any woman he can't have."

"Fine. Let him keep running."

"Should I do more? Really plunge the knife in, the way Sasha wanted me to?

"How dramatic. You're turning into a New Yorker. If you can, you should do it."

A little boy approached the table. "Mr. Lowe, could I have your autograph?"

"Of course. What's your name?"

"Max."

"Here you go, Max. Where's your mom?" Max pointed and Tony waved over to her. "You see, fame is great. I didn't tell you yet, but I'm going with the show to LA."

"You can't leave," Eleanor wailed. She felt dependent on him for all kinds of moral support.

"I'm not going for another two months. But there might be a film in Canada. That's how I live, sweetie. Here, there, and everywhere. It drives Logan crazy. Don't worry, you can call me on my cell. I think you should get the bonus, assuming it's not too big for you to carry, and then go back with me to El Dharam, where we read the tarot and began our quest." Outside Tony gave Eleanor a big kiss, but she felt as if she were losing her best friend.

Jonathan Neel had spent every one of the succeeding days in the same editing suite at Black Dog. He alternated work on both

Synergene and Buffalo Grill, moving sporadically between one Avid machine and another next door. Normally he didn't take calls while he was conferring with the editor, but since Eleanor hadn't been returning his messages, he left his cell phone on. Just as he worked on the buffalo charging through the arroyo, it rang. Juan Angel barked questions at him, apparently from close by. "I want to see the commercials now, Jon. I have to leave tomorrow, and I'm sure you need help." The imminent arrival of the Argentine director was never a happy thought, but this time he didn't know if he could cope.

On impulse Jon decided to try Eleanor at the hospital one more time. When he heard her soft voice at the other end of the line, he hesitated. "Ellie?" he finally said.

"Yes?" she answered.

"It's Jon. I've been trying to reach you for days."

"I know."

"Why haven't you called me back?"

"I didn't think it would be a good idea," she said, uncharacteristically acid.

"Why not? I mean, I'm really busy but kept calling you and got no response." He was becoming angry and had already forgotten why he thought it was so important for him to get himself into her good graces.

"Right. Your whole work scene is so important that it's tough even to make a call. Now you know how Sasha felt. You extinguished her, made her feel dead, and then she did die. Maybe you fooled Sasha, but you can't fool me. You've sold yourself to that wasted life of yours." Eleanor's voice rose as she felt her own wild anger.

"That's right. I'm responsible for everything awful that happened to her. She was a saint, and I'm evil. The commercials I've done, fifteen years of solid creative work for clients who make useful products, that's all garbage too. In fact, all the bad crap in my family is my fault. Thank God you figured that out before we could even go out and have a drink." At this, he hung up on her.

Before he had time to rethink what he'd just said and call her back, Juan Angel arrived, accompanied by a couple of flunkeys who were helping him pick up delivery on a Franz Kline painting. Never had the director's complaints about the wretched excesses of his life fallen on deafer ears. The problems of someone who owned a fleet of Ferraris, an art collection worthy of the doge, but couldn't get to as many LA Lakers games as he would like because he was busy making $50,000 a day seemed plain grotesque. Jon brushed back his hair and prepared to do battle.

Juan Angel sat down in the chair next to him, barely saying a word. "Put up Buffalo Grill," Jon said. The video editor's hands flew over the console, and before them ran what they had done so far. The Arizona sky glowed with warm, yellow light. The Santa Catalina mountains curved in pink and blue combination against the dry brown land. Down through the arroyo pounded the buffalo, and as they did, a voice intoned that long drawn out cry, "Buff-aa-ll-o Grii-ii-ll," only once. It was simple, nostalgic, magnificently photographed, and said entirely what it was supposed to. It captured the mystery and intrigue of the Old West.

The director didn't speak for a moment, then muttered, "It's good, fine. You'd better fix that last shot though. The buffalo were out of order. Put up Synergene."

"We've barely started working on it." About this one Jon felt grim. The commercial was a mess, and right at this moment, he didn't know how to fix it. A spate of fleeting images flashed be-

fore them. The buffalo ran down the hill, then staggered back
up, then back down, while the sky turned first dark and next
sunny.

"Do you have a plan for this or is your drunken partner going to fix it?"

"Guy isn't my partner, and he isn't drunk."

Juan Angel hooted and slapped his hand on the table, jig-
gling the console. "I like that, Jon. Deny the facts before you.
Perhaps that's the key to your success. You have a lot of work to
do. Want me to send one of my producers over?"

"No, I just want you to get out. We'll finish it somehow, and
I don't think for fifty-thousand fucking dollars a day I need to
stare at your face. Go home and deal with your art, better yet go
steal someone else's wife. Where is the beautiful Mrs. Danziger,
by the way?" Suddenly Juan Angel looked old, and Jon no longer
cared. The director rose without answering—was it to hit someone?—but then he and his henchmen left without a word.

The video editor grasped Jon's arm and said, "Finally someone spoke up. You're my hero."

On his way home that night, he braved the bitter cold of
New York in January on foot. It was horrible, didn't seem like a
new year at all. He walked once again past the pet store at
Eighty-Fifth and Lexington Avenue and observed new corgis, a
schnauzer, and a Maltese, all very cute. Maybe he should get a
dog? Walking across Eighty-Sixth Street, he looked into the
subway landing. There was the dying man, though he didn't
seem very dead. He had surrounded himself with old newspapers that he folded into small hats, handing them to people, festive in an odd sort of way. He wore a shirt, a thick woolen jacket,
and before him rested a paper coffee cup. Jon leaned down, fold-

ing into it a twenty-dollar bill. The man smiled. Ah well, he thought, it was a new year after all.

When Eleanor called Sasha's attorney, he said that he would rush the bonus over to her at the hospital. Brusque on the phone, he commented only that he was glad to be done with the whole business. It came to Eleanor in the form of a large white envelope, sealed with the red wax imprint of an S. How eighteenth century, how Sasha, she thought.

El Dharam no longer seemed the exotic locale it had when she first came to New York, and this time she walked confidently among the black-clad skinny young men and women, all of whom seemed to smoke. Where was Tony? She spied him lounging at the bar, surrounded by gaping people, laughing and drinking. He waved her over, and she stepped toward him confidently, even though she had on unnervingly high heels and a tight jersey dress, Sasha's watch fob dangling around her neck. The actor embraced her, whispering, "I don't see the tarot lady. Should we try to talk to her before we do anything?"

"I don't think we need to. I have the bonus with me, and after the last few phone conversations with Jon, I really deserve it."

"You certainly do. Damn, I thought it would be some huge thing."

"No, it's just an envelope."

"Quick, let's sit down and see what's inside." Tony hustled the maître d', and they were seated in a booth.

"No, I have to have something to drink first," Eleanor said.

"Have one of these pomegranate martinis. They're amazing."

When Eleanor showed Tony the envelope, he held it up near to the candle at their table and then toward the ceiling, but it was dim in the restaurant, and the paper was too thick to see through. She continued to sip her drink, propping the envelope up in front of them with an ashtray. It sat like that while they dined on saag paneer, chicken korma, and basmati rice. Finally when the dessert course came, carrots cooked in milk and flavored with ginger and lemon, which Tony and Eleanor ate with separate spoons out of the same bowl, she said, "Should we open it now?"

"I don't know. You've got me spooked. I was so ready earlier."

"I don't think the tarot lady is here." Eleanor looked around. "But I do remember that she said something about karmic uplifting, didn't she?"

"Exactly, that we would have a role in it, whatever that means. I'm going to open it," he said. He held the envelope up high again, then brought it down to the table and ripped apart the back seal. A white sheet of paper fell out, and on it was Sasha's distinctive bold handwriting. "Damn, I don't see any extra money in here, only kidding, just an extra hundred thou would be fine. It's a letter."

"I can see that. I need another martini."

Tony waved his hand dramatically at the waiter. They sipped their drinks a moment, and by then she had gotten up the courage to read Sasha's note out loud. "'Dearest Eleanor, Forgive me, please. I don't know how long after our dinner this will reach you, but it won't be that long.'" Eleanor looked at Tony wonderingly.

"She predicted her own death? It can't be," he said.

"'I'm very sick and have been for almost nine months. What

I thought was cured five years ago, an astrocytoma, has come back. It's grade four glioblastoma, a malignant brain tumor, and I've exhausted all possible treatments. The only things left to me are holistic and herbal remedies, and they won't do much. A few people were informed, my attorney, my mother.'" Eleanor's face had turned white. "This is incredible. Did you know about this?"

Tony shook his head. "Of course not."

"We had it wrong all the time. It wasn't the crash."

"You don't think she committed suicide, do you, by running into the tour bus?" he asked.

"I can't imagine that. According to the newspaper fog descended very quickly, and suddenly there was a pileup," Eleanor said and sipped her drink. "Poor Sasha, how she must have suffered, and all by herself." She continued reading, "'I've always admired you, Ellie, your intelligence, your independence, your goodness. You mean so much to me, and I moaned over my darkness and difficulties and felt better when I thought of you. You made me like myself because you liked me.'" Eleanor began to cry and covered her face with her napkin. "She admired me?" she wailed.

Tony took the letter gently from her hand. "Of course she did." He began to read, "'And so, did you *get* him? I'm certain that you did, but perhaps not in the way you thought. When Jon and I were together, I could see him becoming more and more unhappy, until I knew that nothing I did would ever be enough. I was angry when he turned on me, and yet over the weeks and months I had to think about him, I realized that there was someone in my world whom he could love, and that was you. It was a crazy thing to do, tell you to *get* him, to write this letter, to arrange for the money. People who are dying do crazy things. I hope I did right. Perhaps you aren't sure yet whether you love him or hate him? In this regard, how can we see the future? It's not for us to know. Sounds like a line from a bad show tune, doesn't it? You see, wherever I am, I can still joke. Wherever I am, I send you my love. Your Sasha.'"

Eleanor sobbed now into her martini, and Tony wiped his eyes with his napkin. "This is too horrible. She wants me to be in love with him. Did you know about all this? You must have."

"Nothing about the illness, absolutely nothing. She lost a little weight, that was all I noticed. There was one thing, though."

"What?"

"She was complaining about Jon one night over drinks and did say something I thought was weird at the time, that there was only one person she knew who would ever have been able to deal with him, and that was her friend Eleanor."

Eleanor had taken her napkin, dipped it into her water glass, and was now touching it to her neck. "Why didn't you tell me?"

"I couldn't. I didn't want to confuse you beyond what you were already going through. Besides, 'deal with' wasn't really the same as 'get,' so I was at a loss."

"She introduced us the only way she could, because if she'd told me that she thought I would like him, I would never have done anything about it, especially not after her death. And how on earth would I have encountered the world of advertising? Not in the stacks of the Schulman Library in Ithaca."

"True. You wouldn't have run into him at all." Tony gazed at her and frowned. "Do you totally hate him?" Eleanor didn't speak. "Uh oh, uh oh, tell Uncle Tony what's going on in that beautiful head."

"I'm not beautiful. Sasha was beautiful. If there's one thing my mother made clear to me, it was 'Don't count on your looks, sweetie.'"

"Isn't it amazing how the most beautiful people don't know that they are, as opposed to *moi*, that is?"

"Anyway, I just said hateful things to him on the phone. Regardless of how I feel, he'll never talk to me now."

Tony and Eleanor walked in silence for a long time after their amazing dinner, though the snow had frozen into three- and four-foot-high mounds. January had that blank, flattened feel that made Manhattan pleasant, in an after-the-party kind of way. The streets of Soho, usually packed, were almost empty. As they strolled, Tony took her arm, and they didn't speak, but when they passed by Dean and Deluca, the actor insisted they go in for a coffee "to cheer us up," he said. Unlike the deserted streets, the place teemed with people. "Look at all these New Yorkers wanting a five-dollar tomato. I love this town," he said with a sigh, as they sipped the foam off the tops of their cappuccinos. "What will you do now?"

"I have no idea."

"You have the apartment for another two months."

"I know, and I could stay at the job. They seem to like me."

"Everyone likes you," he said and put his arm around her. "I can see why poor Sasha trusted you so, but what are you going to do about Mr. Right?"

"He's not Mr. Right. That's ridiculous."

"But you do like him?"

"Tony, you're being difficult. We're never going to get together. I said the cruelest things to him."

Tony snaked a whipped cream covered pastry toward her

mouth. "You've seduced and abandoned him, for real. Now you can go get him. Do what Sasha really wanted you to do."

"It's too late. Besides, I'm not a go-get-him type, haven't you noticed?"

"But you've changed so much."

She reached down, fingering Sasha's necklace and said, "I have changed, haven't I?"

The next day she phoned Sasha's attorney in an attempt to get more details on her friend's illness. He couldn't provide much information. "All I know is that the diagnosis had been made for some time and that she seemed resigned, Miss Birch. She feared very much being debilitated and having everyone find out, had bought a small place in Vermont and was fully prepared to have a team of people look after her; not her friends though. She was too proud for that."

"It's incredible that she'd be killed in a car crash, isn't it? You don't think she committed suicide, do you?"

"There would have been much easier ways to do herself in, and she wouldn't have wanted to harm other people in the process. No, I think her death involved a strange intersection of fate, the way someone who's scheduled to board a plane that crashes and avoids it, ends up being hit by a car a year later. You hear about such things all the time. In any case, she didn't have to suffer through a lingering death. I always say that the thing you fear most is invariably the one thing you don't have to fear at all." Eleanor hung up, in a state of wonder and distress.

Exactly two and a half weeks after he walked into Smathers House, Guy Danziger appeared at the offices of LaGuardia and

Knole. The reaction to his return was muted because everyone from the mailroom boy on up knew where he'd been—and was still supposed to be. Despite all he'd been through, Guy looked spiffy in a short wool coat and a turtleneck sweater, his eyes clear, his hair combed. Though he hadn't stayed in rehab for the requisite term, he planned to go back as soon as the spot was finished; at least that's what he was telling people. He just couldn't bear to leave his Synergene commercial unattended or attended to by somebody else. It needed his touch. When he popped his head into Claudia's office, she rushed to him and gave him a big hug, overcome that he was back. "Oh, Guy, you look wonderful." She stood and surveyed him. "How do you feel?"

He sat down across from her. "I feel good, exhausted, but good. They really put me through it."

Suspiciously Claudia said, "Didn't you leave early?"

"I had to check on Synergene, but I promise I'll go back. Where is everybody?" He meant Janey and Serena but was afraid to say so.

Claudia came round to the front of her desk and crossed those formidable legs of hers. Today was a friendly two-bangle day. "Serena has taken a prolonged leave of absence. I believe she went to throw pots somewhere, Chiapas, that's right, Chiapas, Mexico. Lifting herself to a higher plane, no doubt."

Guy guffawed. "And Janey?"

"Janey moved over to Petzler/Bowman, the new agency in Brooklyn. Everyone thought it best, don't you agree? There were some legal issues with her, which we handled in house."

"Yes, yes, it's all wonderful." He was so grateful he found himself craving a glass of water, which she poured out for him from her carafe. She poured one for herself, and he toasted her. "Claudia, thank you. I don't know how you can forgive me, but if you can, please do."

"Oh, Guy, I forgave you long ago."

"I don't deserve all this kindness."

"No, you don't."

When he appeared at Black Dog, everyone was unnerved to see him, especially Jon, who suspected him of fleeing rehab. "I know what you're thinking," Guy said to him.

"I'll bet you do."

"I'm going back in a couple of days, after I help finish the Synergene spot, if you need my help, that is."

"Actually, we do." Jon eyed him closely. He seemed sober, if a little shaky.

"I swore that the commercial would bring Leslie to tears, and I don't want to let her down," he said.

The two men spent the next few hours in front of the Avid, cutting, pasting, and writing a voice-over that would somehow explain how buffalo and cancer were related. "Maximum ponderosity," Guy instructed Jon, who came up with a screed that leaned heavily on the metaphoric connection between the animal images and the miraculous activity of Oncreon 1. The effect was similar to what Jon called "BBC documentary-type wallpaper," beautiful images, haunting music, and narration that evoked the biblical world of miracles, created anew in the modern world through drugs. The commercial worked, and all the while Guy Danziger was finishing sentences like crazy.

thirty-one

ART

Several days later Jon received a phone call from the art dealer Teddy Bonin asking for samples of the latest artwork of Walter Neel. The request threw him into a frenzy of activity. Impressing upon Susan the importance of FedExing the slides, he heard Walter drop the phone, so excited he was incoherent. Jon too felt this was a wondrous event and asked Teddy several times how he knew of his brother's paintings. Uncharacteristically reticent, the dealer said only that several of his friends had seen a sampling of the younger Neel's pieces. "Where?" Jon said, realizing he wasn't quite sure how widely Walter circulated his slides. Perhaps he'd been searching for a gallery on his own.

"Oh, here and there. I can't remember. I have a lot of scouts you know, have to in this business. It's word-of-mouth."

Teddy had been admonished by Eleanor and Tony not to reveal the source of Walter's good fortune.

It all began with a fight between the actor and Logan Piersall. "Why in hell did you tell him?" Tony had screeched into the phone at his boyfriend.

"I didn't tell him everything, not the revenge part. I just indicated that there had been some sort of understanding about him between Sasha and your friend Eleanor. I don't know, it was the end of the shoot, and after three or four tequila shooters—"

"You were drunk," Tony said accusingly.

"I was not drunk. I was happy, especially that it was over. Anyway, he's a nice guy compared to the rest of those lunatics. Besides, he seemed so sad, but I didn't tell him the whole thing."

"This really is a mess now, Logan. Why'd you stick your nose in? Clearly, I'm going to have to start fixing. What with the show and the LA gig, I'm running out of time and ideas."

"You stuck my nose in, may I remind you. Besides, you like to fix things. That's your job. When are you coming out here?" Logan said, and arranged for him to visit Arizona on his way to Los Angeles.

Before the actor could devise any sort of plan regarding the Jon/Eleanor problem, however, she phoned him with one of her own. "I've got an idea, well really it's your idea, but maybe it could work, though it's a long shot. It'd be a way for me to do something for Walter Neel and possibly see Jon again."

"Lay it upon me because I've come up totally empty."

"Can't you meet with Teddy Bonin and somehow make him want to do a show of Walter's work? Sort of insinuate it into his mind? You said he didn't have anything going on right now at his gallery. I could attend the opening. Even if nothing ever happens further with Jon, I will have helped somehow or at least made some good come out of the whole mess."

"Brilliant. I'll invite him to lunch and threaten him with a knife if he doesn't do it."

Several days later, consuming a heavy meal of steak and mashed potatoes at Kathleen's Down Home in the West Village, Tony feigned only mild interest in the art dealer's whining about the bleak January to February period, nobody coming to the gallery, everybody tapped out after Christmas. Idly, he sipped his glass of wine and muttered, "It sounds bad, Teddy. You should find a hot new talent, someone completely unknown, maybe from someplace else. Besides, if you're not selling anything, what difference does it make?"

"You are so right. Anyway, I'm bored with all the artists in this town, corrupt little suckers. I need something fresh, work that no one has seen, but where?" In the middle of their second bottle of wine, Tony hit him with the idea of a show for Walter Neel, whom he represented as the most important new artist on the horizon. He described in great detail paintings that he had never seen and promised him slides almost instantaneously. "But this would be wonderful, the perfect antidote for such a dreary time. We could do it the last week of February. Could we get a show up that quickly, Tony? These artists are such children, and you need a lot of work for an exhibit. I usually plan them at least a year in advance."

"From what I know, the man is singularly untemperamental," Tony said, putting the spin on Walter's mental state that he and Eleanor had agreed to. "I'll contact his brother, an ad guy, and get him on the case. By the way, Sasha sort of knew the family, so there's a connection with our poor, lost friend."

This last bit of information guaranteed Teddy's interest, and when he saw the work in its entirety two days later, he called Tony and said, "They're quite wonderful, innocent and charming. I really would like to do this, but everybody's out of town, the weather's so hideous." Tony perceived that more pressure was needed, so he invited Teddy and Jon to lunch at the Carlyle hotel.

"I'll pay for all the hors d'oeuvres and drinks at the opening," Jon said. The art dealer squinted at him. "And the publicity. In fact, I'll get the one sheets done at LaGuardia."

"Don't be cheap, Teddy. This is a great idea," Tony said.

Teddy bought it. "It's a deal."

For the publicity posters, Walter insisted on using his very large portrait of Eleanor and also on the card announcing the event. Jon had to agree that it was a good piece to draw people in, typical of his newer work, a blend of Chagall's joyful romanticism with the hard-edged oomph of a Marvel comic book. There were fourteen paintings in all, but Jon requested that Walter include the small cartoon drawing of *Leptra* from his earlier series—Sasha—looking as intense as she had in life. Jon and Teddy spent the better part of a day first with the framer, then hanging the pictures. When they finished, Jon sank down on a bench in the center of the all-white gallery space and scanned the collection from one side to the other. Here was Walter's take on life, his brilliant color sense, his humor, his ability to light up the mind and world of his subjects. It showed a depth of feeling that lurked beneath that sometimes blank expression, and he identified with his brother's hidden reserves of emotion and strength. The paintings seemed way too good-hearted to appeal to the black T-shirt crowd in Chelsea; still, Teddy pressured Jon to price the works high, as the art dealer believed in emphasizing his confidence in the artist's future. Eleanor's portrait was marked at twenty thousand dollars.

Eleanor awaited the exhibition eagerly, but when she received the invitation just as she was about to head back to the city after two weeks in Ithaca, she was stunned. Surely her very own face, albeit a stylized likeness of it, adorned the front of a postcard. What could it mean? She had wanted stealth participation in the event. Immediately she called Tony, who told her not to worry, that now she was a New York player, her image spread across the town. "This is bad news, Tony. The invite seems to cry out, 'Eleanor did this, she's plotting again.'"

"Don't be crazy. No one would ever think that."

"Yes, but how did my picture get right on the cover?"

"The dealer must like it or think it's a very major piece."

"I wonder if Jon made Walter use it? No, that couldn't be."

"Who knows? Teddy probably chose it. Anyway, every kind of fame is fun, except the embezzlement kind. When are you coming back?"

"Tomorrow night. Listen, I had no idea our little plan would balloon into such a big thing. I just imagined a couple of pictures on the wall."

"This is New York, Ellie. Nothing's small here," Tony said.

Back in Gramercy Park, after a slow ride on the bus, Eleanor noticed yet another postcard invite. Maybe it was the dealer who wanted her there, or perhaps it was Tony ensuring her presence. Alarmed, excited, hungry to see her "own" painting, she could hardly tell which emotion gripped her more.

The assigned Saturday night came, but not before Tony and Eleanor together designed her entire ensemble, right down to the shoes. She wore a blue Armani suit of supple velvet. Around her neck she had tied a purple scarf, and between her breasts hung Sasha's necklace. On her small, elegant feet she wore a pair of Italian pumps. She had rethought her hair, this time swept back slightly behind her ears, for a sophisticated look. By now she knew exactly how to arrange for a livery car, and stopped to pick up Tony, who looked dashing himself, as usual. "Do we have a plan?" he said, snuggling next to her in the back of the Lincoln Town Car.

"We don't need any kind of plan, Tony. Despite my fancy outfit, nothing's going to happen except the exhibit."

"Maybe," he said. "I'm quite proud that we've pulled this all together so quickly. I don't know what will happen, but let's hope and pray for good things."

"*Prayer*, that's the operative word," she said.

On the drive down to the gallery, Eleanor didn't say much. It had been over a month since she'd seen Jon, but she didn't feel ready. He probably detested her now or had just plain written her off. Still, she was curious about the paintings and over time had grown accustomed to seeing her own face before her on a card. Deliberately, her dress was quite different from the one in the picture—no Hawaiian shirt for this gathering—so maybe nobody would notice her. "Let's stop for a drink first," she said. "I'm too nervous."

"We've got the car. We can go anywhere. Look, you succeeded at everything so far, especially making him miserable. Now we just have to see what develops."

"Why does it all feel so eerie?"

"Because of how it began, because of our friend Sasha. Maybe the two of you could talk about it. He doesn't know of her illness."

"It would be too peculiar, and I'm not good at tell-all situations."

Tony directed the driver to turn around, and they made their way to the Time Hotel on Forty-Ninth Street, where they ordered margaritas. In the minimalist atmosphere, all white and celadon and faded blues, the two of them seemed rapturously vivid, and they got more vivid as they drank, reliving all their plotting and planning, right down to her clothes. "I'm too nervous to see him anymore," Eleanor wailed. "Sasha made it sound as if I was supposed to harm him. That's how anyone would have interpreted it. Now it's turned into a cosmic fix-up."

"There is a perverse element to it, and, I hate to say it, but Sasha could be quite perverse in her own little way."

When the two of them arrived, the opening was already in full swing. An astonishing number of people filled up the gallery, mostly Jon's colleagues and acquaintances from business, but then Teddy had invited a sprinkling of second-line critics, along with selected collectors from his mailing list. The actor grasped Eleanor's hand and pulled her forward. She looked around nervously as Tony got pulled away and repeated to herself all the while Sasha's mantra for public functions, "You've just won the Nobel Prize in physics for your insights into wave oscillation theory. Soon you'll be in Stockholm. Smile." Even though she wanted to stop herself from looking for Jon, she couldn't. Finally she spotted Susan, who had positioned herself over the hors d'oeuvres and was passing them out to people. Eleanor headed toward her. "How are you?" she said, and Walter's new wife reached over to hug her.

"I'm so glad to see you. I don't know what I'm doing."

"You're doing very well. Do you need help?"

"No, no, go look at the pictures. I hope Walter sells something."

Eleanor scanned the paintings from the left side of the room to the right, and, of course, the first one she saw was *Leptra* in black leather with flaming cartoon eyes. How extraordinary the picture was, an immediately recognizable Sasha captured in her own dreams of glory and power. Yes, Walter would have understood her, even if he'd only seen her in Jon's photographs. She tried not to cry because it would ruin her mascara, but she felt tears welling up. Just as she went to wipe them with a napkin, a stocky man with a red face strode up to her and thrust out his hand. "I'm Jimmy Goodlaw, and I wanted to meet you."

"Why?" she said blankly.

"Because of your picture, of course." He took her arm and led her to the center of the room, where Walter's portrait of her rested on an enormous wooden easel. People circulated in front of it, gesturing, leaning forward to get a better look. The fanciful magic of it, the sparkling yellow and green colors, even the improbable bird had transfixed the crowd. Eleanor herself smiled at its extraordinary beauty and peered down at the title card pinned on the wall behind it, *Ellie At The Piano*, it read. It took only a moment for the onlookers to realize that the subject of the painting was standing right next to it, and shortly thereafter cameras flashed as several people tried to engage her in conversation all at once. Eleanor beamed, shook outstretched hands and said things that later she couldn't remember at all. Still trying to locate Jon, she surveyed the room, though now every time she did, someone tried to catch her eye. So this was fame; the whole world wanted to know you.

Slowly she backed away and headed for the hors d'oeuvres again, but suddenly wondered where the artist himself had disappeared to. She spotted a black curtain and peeked behind it to see a small office with a desk and computer, then dozens of paintings by Teddy's other artists resting on their sides on the floor and in racks up to the ceiling. Walter sat on top of a crate in the corner.

"What are you doing in here?" she said, "Not hiding, I hope."

"Too many people."

"It's wonderful, congratulations. I saw lots of small red dots."

"What does that mean?"

"It means that the painting was sold."

"Sold? Wow, does Susan know?"

"I think so. I'll just sit here and calm my nerves. I'm not good in big groups either," she said, "but I love the picture you did of me. Thank you so much. And the other one too, *Leptra* I think you called it. Did you know Sasha?"

Walter smiled happily. Outside, the noise swirled around them. "No, I saw her in Jon's photos. I don't think she's alive."

"No, sadly," Eleanor said, feeling herself near tears again.

"I didn't like that hospital."

"Nobody would. I'm so glad your brother got you out."

"He loves me," Walter said, smiling and looking down at his hands.

"Yes, he does." They sat in silence. "It's cozy here," she finally said and, at that moment, two older people leaned into their hideaway and greeted Walter.

"Are you avoiding us, boy?" the man said.

Walter jumped up, agitated. "Mom, Dad, oh, I didn't know if you'd come."

"Jon made sure that we did," Martha Neel said. Walter threw his arms around both his parents, while Eleanor slipped out behind them.

She stood uncertainly as people smiled at her until Guy

Danziger, late of Smathers House, chose this moment to lurch her way and greet the woman in the picture.

He had, of course, lapsed. Holed up in his empty townhouse ever since his return, he'd brought a flask to this event for security's sake, and vodka, his only true friend, had once again asserted itself in his life. The sight of his beautiful wife standing next to Juan Angel Peña was what tipped him over the edge this time; Marsia dressed in a tuxedo jacket and black pants, her luxuriant hair swept into a black velvet ribbon. Guy hadn't heard from or seen her since the shoot, but he knew that Juan Angel had done lots more than that, probably in Sedona, and now here they were, standing side by side.

Claudia Thompson, encased in green silk with one tiny gold bangle on her wrist, seemed to be avoiding him too, and thus he understood the urgency of resuscitating his career, which at this moment lay comatose on a slab. If the first two weeks of rehab had accomplished anything, it had been to convince Guy that he was the most loathsome piece of shit currently on the planet. Not having finished the course of treatment, he was stuck with this feeling and figured that he deserved every bad thing he was getting and therefore had earned the right to drink—drink and work, since clearly he would have to pay his soon-to-be ex-wife piles of money. She could just drive a truck up to the house, and into it he would have to dump millions of dollars.

"I'm Guy Danziger, and you must be the woman in the painting," he said to Eleanor.

"Yes, I am."

"How do you know him?" he asked.

"Who?"

"The artist."

"I'm a friend, and I know his brother, Jonathan Neel."

"Aha, Mr. Creative. 'Buff-aa-ll-o Grii-ii-ll,'" he whistled expertly, just as it sounded on television.

All of a sudden, Eleanor realized that this must be Jon's rival, the man whom he'd suspected of engineering the infinitely running commercial, at least the last time she heard talk of it. She felt moved to defend Jon, "Yes, he is creative. And I'm sure his new TV spot will be a huge success."

"Oh, la-de-da," Guy murmured, trying to twinkle. "Want to blow this joint and get high?" He smiled seductively. Maybe he should start to date, he thought.

"No," she blurted out, lurching away from him.

Feeling hot and fearful, Guy spotted the be-curtained back office and hied himself there to drink in private. He encountered Walter, though, who had retreated once again from the crowd. The two artists proceeded to discuss the merits of watercolor versus oil, while Guy kept pouring the younger man shots from his flask.

Eleanor scanned the overflowing gallery for Jon, but she couldn't spot him anywhere. She hated crowds and had just about decided to go outside, even though it was freezing, when Jimmy Goodlaw elbowed his way past several people and came up to her side. "Hello again. You like these little steaks?" She hadn't noticed the food but saw now that Buffalo Grill had apparently catered it all, everything made small for hors d'oeuvres. She smiled, couldn't resist, and said, "We must have come to a better place."

"You bet we have, my dear," Jimmy replied and kissed her on the cheek. She pulled back, startled. "I'm sorry, I feel I know you, from Jon Neel. You work at New York Hospital, right?

"Weill Cornell, yes."

"He's a deep one, he is, quite taken with you really."

Eleanor stared at the man, shocked and embarrassed, but then sighed, "Not anymore he isn't, I'm sure. I haven't even talked to him tonight. I don't know where he is."

"He's over there, next to the giant man of the Pampas, Juan Angel Peña, the director of our latest commercial." Jimmy pointed out the two tallest people in the room, standing in front of her painting apparently arguing with the dealer, who interjected a few words every moment or two. Juan Angel saw her, recognized her in an instant, and waved her over, but she didn't respond to the summons. Jon frowned at a woman beside him and bent down to talk to her. Thanking Jimmy for what he'd told her, she squeezed herself toward another corner of the room, still watching Jon. He was dressed in a handsome dark suit, with an open collar and no tie, his hair even longer than usual. As she'd seen him do several times, he pushed it back behind his ears when he got more agitated, which he appeared to be at this moment. What was he saying? She couldn't tell. She turned away and looked out the sole window in the place, fingering Sasha's necklace. So he'd been here all along and had made no effort even to greet her. The snow fell thick and white on the dirty pavement now, as she mused upon the man. After tonight she'd probably never see him again. This was his world, teeming, expanding all the time with money and people and urgent doings. She felt thousands of miles apart from it.

In the midst of her reflections, she heard flurries of movement behind her. She turned around to see Walter and Guy Danziger, arm in arm, angry expressions on their faces, lurching toward Juan Angel, who still conversed with Teddy Bonin. She could just make out Guy mouthing, "I'll bash his head in, I'll kill the bastard," into Walter's face. The younger man nodded and bobbed his head up and down, ready for some aggressive action.

"Want me to sock him?" she heard Walter say above the noise. Apparently they had decided to combat Juan Angel together and advanced now as a team. In an instant, Eleanor saw the movements and their meaning. She looked around in panic and finally spotted Jon, waving to him and motioning toward the hostile pair. He followed her eyes and saw what was coming. As if by silent agreement, the two of them intervened in concert. Eleanor went straight toward Guy, who was nearer to her, grasped him by the arm and yanked the older man backwards. Jon threw his arm around a tipsy, confused Walter, leading him away to Susan and out of danger.

Guy sputtered at Eleanor that he "deserved to die, the mean-ass son of a bitch," but as he burbled incoherently, Marsia came up from behind and put her arm around her husband, whispering into his ear, "Guy, get hold of yourself." She smiled slightly at Eleanor, pulling her husband toward the outside patio.

Flustered, upset, Eleanor was longing to speak to Jon alone, but perhaps she wouldn't even get a chance. Uneasily she watched as Juan Angel now bore down upon her, a man completely unaware of the threatened physical attacks against him. He didn't even bother introducing himself. "Jonathan Neel insists on snatching this painting away from me. I appeal to you, as the subject of it, don't you want to be in a major art collection? You could sit next to Franz Kline." The assembled group turned and gaped, as Jon suddenly appeared too, fixing her with a stare.

"You want to buy the painting?" she said to Jon, who came closer to her now.

"Of course I do. They always say to buy the biggest, most important piece in a show." He looked hard at Eleanor.

"Along with the small painting at the front of the gallery, of Sasha, of course," Eleanor said.

"Yes, along with that one," he said and smiled slightly.

In an instant it came to Eleanor that she, and she alone, must have both the paintings. "I could buy them myself, yes I definitely want them, but the price seems a little high."

An ecstatic Teddy Bonin said, "Juan Angel has already offered twenty-five thousand for just the one."

"And I stand by that," the director said, not wanting to lose, ever.

"I could pay twenty-two thousand, but only if you include the painting of *Leptra* over there."

"You're asking me to take less money for more art," the dealer said. "What kind of a deal is that?"

"Don't we have to ask the artist?" Jon said. "Besides, there's such a thing as truth in advertising. If you said originally that the big one was twenty, then that's it. You can't do a bait and switch."

"What the hell are you talking about, Neel? The painting is on the market, and it will fetch whatever the market will bear," Juan Angel barked above the crowd.

"Why don't we ask Walter? Isn't it up to him?" Eleanor said, nevertheless unsure whether it was his decision.

"It most certainly is not," Teddy said, but even he gave way to charity in the instance of this damaged young man. "Only this once he can decide, but it's no kind of precedent and will never happen again."

Recovered from his momentary attempt at assault, Walter appeared stupefied by the amounts of money discussed and so, when consulted by the dealer, couldn't speak. "You answer for me, Jon," he finally said.

"Eleanor must have her portrait and the one of *Leptra* too," Jon said, smiling at her.

Finally, after much protest, Teddy agreed to let her have both pictures for twenty-five thousand dollars. There, she had done it, spent every single cent of Sasha's money on herself. She didn't think it possible. Juan Angel was furious, but the dealer consoled him with a Jasper Johns drawing he parted with for a mere forty-eight thousand. After this heady transaction, Eleanor extricated herself from the group, all of them looking at her, and headed outside, even though it was freezing, and the snow fell in clumps. Chelsea was so strange when no one worked the warehouses, industrial yet abandoned, with pockets of partygoers looking at art. She shivered and put her arms around herself, but soon enough Jonathan Neel came up from behind and threw a heavy coat over her shoulders. They stood together in silence. Unnerved, Eleanor knew that she had to plunge ahead and say everything she felt because she would never get another chance. "I'm sorry I was so cruel the other day."

"Did you really mean all that? Have I wasted everything, my life, my talent?" He stumbled over the last words.

She turned around and faced the man, his warm, dark eyes upon her now so intensely. "No, no, I'm ashamed of what I said. I wanted to hurt you, and I pretended some things because of Sasha."

"What did she ask you to do to me?"

"She asked me to hurt you, for her sake, but she wanted me to care for you, for mine." Jon looked at her hard, and she felt herself blushing. "There's something you don't know," Eleanor said. "I only just found out about it myself. Sasha was very, very sick. She had a malignant brain tumor and had been fighting it for a long time, actually even before she met you. The disease went into remission but then came back, and there was nothing the doctors could do. All her thoughts, even before the crash, were of death. In a way, it was divine intervention because it was over so quickly."

Jon started and turned away, troubled, silent, staring at the snowflakes. Eleanor gently slid her arm through his, and together they observed Marsia helping her husband into his black Town Car. She slammed the door and hurried back inside the gallery.

"Looks as if she's finally leaving old Guy," Jon sighed. "You know, he didn't mess up my commercial after all. It was someone else."

"Oh, that's good. He seems so sad."

"I took your advice, or was it your stepfather's advice? About being kind to your enemies. Don't know if it helped, though." He turned and gazed back through the window at the gallery-goers. Marsia had taken up her place beside Juan Angel, who leaned in toward her, laughing, holding her hand. "Poor Sasha! I didn't even know her. I didn't understand her."

"None of us really did," Eleanor said, as she felt herself going blank and tearful. "Try not to despise me when you think back on this." Why wasn't he helping her? Why didn't he say something?

Jon searched her face and took Sasha's watch fob for a moment in his hand. "Look back on this? No, no, we'll think of the mystery of it all, how we couldn't comprehend the forces driving us on." He let the watch fall back against her.

Eleanor looked up at him wonderingly, as he enfolded her in his arms. "I thought it would be wrong for us to be together, but now I think it would be exactly right, and so would Sasha," she said.

"Someday you'll explain all this to me, won't you?"

"Of course."

Some months later, Eleanor got up the courage to tell Jon the specifics of Sasha's strange charge and how it was that she had tried to fulfill it. He was horrified and amazed and grateful that somehow his own bad acts had finally brought him to the woman he loved.

THE END

ACKNOWLEDGMENTS

As ever, profound thanks to:

My agent, Elizabeth Trupin-Pulli. She is a wonderful friend and a real inspiration.

My assistant, Jesse Holcomb, who just keeps on getting everything right.

Eileen Rooney, whose prophetic Irish sayings will stay with me always.

The inspired women at She Writes Press and SparkPoint Studio: Brooke Warner, Samantha Strom, and Crystal Patriarche, Jennifer Caven, Melinda Andrews, Mary Ann Smith, Julie Metz, Stacey Aaronson, and Leah Lococo. It is a pleasure and an honor to work with you.

ABOUT THE AUTHOR

Credit: Deborah Geffner

A. R. TAYLOR is an award-winning playwright, essayist, and fiction writer. Her debut novel, *Sex, Rain, and Cold Fusion*, won a Gold Medal for Best Regional Fiction at the Independent Publisher Book Awards 2015 and was a USA Best Book Awards finalist. In addition, it was named one of the 12 Most Cinematic Books of 2014 by *Kirkus Reviews*. Her second novel, *Jenna Takes the Fall*, was published by She Writes Press in 2020 and received the 2021 Readers' Favorite Bronze Medal in the Fiction–Intrigue genre. She's been published in the *Los Angeles Times*, the *Southwest Review*, *Pedantic Monthly*, *The Cynic* online magazine, the *Berkeley Insider*, *So It Goes*—the Kurt Vonnegut Memorial Library Magazine on Humor, *Red Rock Review*, and *Rosebud*.

In her past life, Taylor was head writer on two Emmy-winning series for public television. She has performed at the Gotham Comedy Club in New York, Tongue & Groove in Hollywood, and Lit Crawl LA. You can find her video blog, *Trailing Edge: Ideas Whose Time Has Come and Gone* at her website: www.lonecamel.com

SELECTED TITLES FROM SHE WRITES PRESS

She Writes Press is an independent publishing company
founded to serve women writers everywhere.
Visit us at www.shewritespress.com.

A Matter of Chance by Julie Maloney. $16.95, 978-1-63152-369-4. Guilt, hope, and persistence propel New York fashion editor Maddy Stewart in her search for her daughter, abducted from the Jersey Shore—a quest that takes her through Brooklyn's dangerous underworld and eventually to Bavaria, Germany.

Royal Entertainment by Marni Fechter. $16.95, 978-1-93831-452-0. After being fired from her job for blowing the whistle on her boss, social worker Melody Frank has to adapt to her new life as the assistant to an elite New York party planner.

Chuckerman Makes a Movie: A Novel by Francie Arenson Dickman. $16.95, 978-1-63152-485-1. New York City bachelor David Melman is a successful brander of celebrity fragrances. Laurel Sorenson, a leggy blonde, is a screenwriter on the brink of Hollywood success. When David, pushed by his bossy sister, agrees to take a screenwriting class taught by Laurel, an unlikely romance blooms—and that's just beginning of their troubles.

Unreasonable Doubts by Reyna Marder Gentin. $16.95, 978-1-63152-413-4. Approaching thirty and questioning both her career path and her future with her long-time boyfriend, jaded New York City Public Defender Liana Cohen gets a new client—magnetic, articulate, earnest Danny Shea. When she finds herself slipping beyond the professional with him, she is forced to confront fundamental questions about truth, faith, and love.